PENGUIN BOOKS

# FRAGMENTS FROM MY DIARY

Maxim Gorky is the pen-name of Alexei Maximovich Peshkov, who was born in 1868 in the city of Nizhny Novgorod, now renamed after him. After his father's death he spent his childhood with his mother and grandparents in an atmosphere of hostility. He was turned out of the house when his mother died and left to work in various jobs – in a bakery, in an icon-maker's shop, on barges – until his unsuccessful attempt at suicide. For three years he wandered in the south like a tramp before publishing his first story, *Makar Chudra*, in a Tiflis newspaper. After his return to Nizhny he worked on another newspaper in which many of his stories appeared; he quickly achieved fame, and soon afterwards his play *'The Lower Depths'* was a triumphant success at the Moscow Arts Theatre. By now active in the revolutionary movement he was arrested in 1905 by the Tsarist government but released following a petition signed by eminent statesmen and writers. While in America in 1906 he savagely attacked American capitalism, and wrote his best-selling novel, *Mother*. During the First World War he was associated with the Marxist Internationalist Group, and in 1917 he founded *New Life*, a daily devoted to left-wing socialism, but which outspokenly attacked Kerensky and Lenin's 'Communist hysteria'. In 1921 he went to Italy, where he wrote *My Universities*, the third part of his great autobiographical trilogy; the other parts are *My Childhood* and *Among the People*. He returned to Moscow in 1928, and from then on he was a champion of the Soviet cause. In 1936 he died – allegedly poisoned by his political enemies – and was given a hero's funeral in the Red Square.

# MAXIM GORKY

# FRAGMENTS FROM MY DIARY

*Translated by*
MOURA BUDBERG

PENGUIN BOOKS

Penguin Books Ltd, Harmondsworth, Middlesex, England
Penguin Books Inc., 7110 Ambassador Road, Baltimore, Maryland 21207, U.S.A.
Penguin Books Australia Ltd, Ringwood, Victoria, Australia
Penguin Books Canada Ltd, 41 Steelcase Road West, Markham, Ontario, Canada
Penguin Books (N.Z.) Ltd, 182–190 Wairau Road, Auckland 10, New Zealand

—

First published in Penguin Books 1940
Revised edition published in Allen Lane The Penguin Press 1972
Published in Penguin Books 1975
Translation copyright © Moura Budberg, 1940, 1972
Preface and new material copyright © Moura Budberg, 1972

—

Made and printed in Great Britain by
Hazell Watson & Viney Ltd, Aylesbury, Bucks
Set in Monotype Ehrhardt

# Contents

# CONTENTS

# Preface

THOUGH Gorky started collecting the *Fragments From My Diary* in 1922, he was working from notes he had put down at various times throughout his life and the book is, therefore, a work reflecting the growth of his talent and of his personality.

Everyone who had ever spent an hour in his company left him both richer and bolder than he had been before because he took away with him a particle of Gorky's dynamic quality, his intelligent and obsessive faith in work, goodness and knowledge, the three fundamental features of tomorrow's human society. He never taught anyone to imitate him; he used to say that all instruments, all voices were needed in the great orchestra that humanity would hear when it got the world it deserved. He had no patience with indifference; every human being aroused his curiosity, his sympathy, his attention, and the *Fragments* are the result of this. His life can be likened to a march to the stars, and one sees in the *Fragments* how passionately he tries to elevate all the 'little people' whom he came across.

'Truth is greater than compassion, and these stories are the stories of every simple Russian man,' he said.

Facing life, with all its 'leaden meannesses', did not prevent him from having an 'unconquerable hope' in man's victory over them. That is why however grim his descriptions there is no pessimism in them, but a keen interest in and a true love of humanity. 'When I was a child,' he says, 'I felt like a bee-hive, into which all simple folk would bring, like bees do, the honey of their knowledge and of their thoughts about life, generously enriching me, each in his own way. Often the honey wasn't very clean, but all knowledge is honey, all the same.'

Knowledge with him was a god. On the manuscripts of *In the World* one can read in the margin the titles of the innumerable books he read, or wanted to read, before he was fifteen. There was everything in that medley: classics, Russian and foreign, and queer, unusual books that unscrupulous booksellers would palm off on the inexperienced reader. Then came a series of French and English adventure novels, which he read because 'he felt he was participating in an extraordinary life, unlike the grey and sinister one he saw around him'. He thought then that 'life abroad, as these books seem to tell, is more interesting and easier than the one I know'. And elsewhere he wrote: 'All this chaos of books, though not preventing me from seeing reality as it is, not quenching my desire to understand real, live people, screened me with a transparent and at the same time impenetrable cloud from a lot of poisonous and filthy sides of life.'

The author's 'visual convincingness', as D. Mirsky called it, was equal to his musical one and therefore he brings into his dialogue numerous comparisons and epithets drawn from the rough vocabulary of the poor folk he is mainly describing. How can one translate, without a racy adaptation, such sentences as: 'Under a whipping one should relax like jelly. . . . The lifted faces of the men had an amusing likeness to dirty plates after a meal. . . . There sat the green old woman, like a rotting stake in an old hedge'?

His memory was inexhaustible and he never stopped telling his friends about the most unexpected meetings in far-away, desolate places in Russia with people of different classes of society – ship-loaders and rich merchants – and their odd way of life.

You will remember the story about Bugrov, a millionaire from the Volga. He was a simple man, with no European polish. He left 60 million roubles to his wife. Everyone, including the governor of the district, was afraid of him. At that time all sectarian activity was strictly forbidden. But Bugrov, under the very nose of the governor, had built a school for sectarians in Nijni-Novgorod itself.

Gorky's humanism was not the result of a theory; it was something that organically belonged to him as much as his smile, his way of walking. He loved everything vivid, strong, decorative, everything that improved life. When people mentioned his literary realism he would laugh and say, 'What sort of a realist am I? That's something that belongs to Tolstoy. I'm an incorrigible romantic. My grandmother instilled this into me and I've kept it forever.'

Gorky was a magnificent story-teller of the past. People stand out as if alive in his stories with their movements, words, their smiles and tears. In his memories all events acquire a character of history, of permanence. Artistic truth is more convincing than the empiric brand, the truth of a dry fact.

Tolstoy liked listening to Gorky's tales. He asked him once: 'Come on, tell me a story, you are so good at it. Tell me something about yourself as a child. I can't believe that you ever were a child. You seem to have been born an adult.'

Gorky's realism is not a photographic one, his task is not to give 'a snapshot' of reality; he organizes it in his mind and gives a picture of his own conception of life. Therefore there is no contradiction in his assessment of himself as a romantic. But his romanticism was in no way an idealisation of reality, it was an artist's rendering of it.

He was very particular about style. In his conversations and correspondence with young writers he showed his powers of observation and criticism: 'You have used the verb "to be" seven times on the same page. This is inadmissible!' He introduced Vsevolod Ivanov, later a distinguished Russian writer, into the young group that began to write during the war and revolution, although he had before not written a line, simply because he sent Gorky his first story, that began with the words: 'Palm trees do not grow in Siberia . . .'.

He could never lag behind the rhythm of life. He wanted to know everything, to participate in everything that was growing, expanding, changing, giving birth to something new. He wrote thousands of letters to children. He loved children, he loved people, their oddities and passions, the deep differences between them and the humane factors that united them. He loved trees. He was himself like a tall, knotty tree, which had grown in spite of all the inclemency of the weather. He believed vehemently, ecstatically in progress. When he spoke of a new discovery, a new experiment, he smiled like a child. This man, corroded through and through by a cruel life, counterposed the purity and integrity of his wise childishness to the pseudo-scepticism of both great and mediocre writers.

Born a poet, he became a teacher, not because he liked teaching but because he liked the future.

He used to say: 'Go on telling a man that he is a good man, and he will *be* good.' He accepted the responsibility of the risk in considering that praise is often more effective, and one might say educational, in the field of art than the most deserved and justified criticism. It is always hard to see the good in man, but he should always be approached with an optimistic hypothesis, even at the risk of being disappointed. This was a quality which Gorky possessed supremely.

He worshipped the Book. It was curious to see the fantastic miscellany he had on his bookshelves: Stevenson, Balzac, Flaubert, Edgar Poe, Baudelaire, Verlaine, Gibbon, then, suddenly, *Twenty-six Moscow fools, male and female, The history of Russian pubs*; Pushkin, Turgenev, Chekhov, Alfred de Musset, Théophile Gautier, Eckermann's *Conversations with Goethe*, the Bible, the Talmud, *The Religions of the East* by Maspereau, Stendhal, Mérimée, Shakespeare, Schiller, Thackeray, Jane Austen – and *Pansalvini – Prince of Darkness*!

'There are very few good things in the world. The best is art and the best and noblest thing about art is the art to invent something good,' he told me once just before starting on his trilogy.

It was interesting to watch the relationship between Chekhov and Gorky – the one with his sweet longing for a beautiful sunset, a painful dream about emerging from the everyday boredom, the soft and tender colour of his words, the other also longing to emerge, but how? His muscles tense, his voice challenging, with faith in tomorrow, not in 'two hundred years hence'.

Beggars in Arsamas, where he was deported, soon heard about his generosity and would come in crowds to test it. 'Gorky gave all he had in his pockets, then emptied his wife's, then turned to me,' says A. Tikhonov. He gave the money as casually as if it was matches to light a cigarette.

He loved music, also in a kind of haphazard way – Grieg, then Beethoven. His favourite among the works of Beethoven was the *Largo* and *Presto* in the piano sonata in G major. He would say that the grief in it was so intense that it ceased to be personal, it spoke for the whole world. He considered it an epic work, more like a symphony than a sonata.

His love for Beethoven was so great that he wrote to Romain Rolland in 1916 or 1917, asking him to write a biography of the composer for children of thirteen to eighteen. 'An objective book, describing the evolution of his soul, to inspire the young with love and faith in life; bring the heroic element into their lives. A man must learn that he is the creator and master of the world, that he carries a responsibility for all the disasters as well as the glory for all the good that there is on earth.'

More about his memory, for which there was nothing either unduly important or unimportant. When he told a story, it seemed sometimes to be about uninteresting details or people, about fleeting events, but in the end one got such a vivid picture of people's way of life, of a landscape, that you could not eradicate it from your memory. His almost childish naïveté was very endearing. When he listened to some particularly wild, unusual story his eyes would open wide and he would exclaim, 'It is impossible! You must be inventing it all, my dear friend. But it's true,' he would add slowly, 'one can expect anything from man. It isn't as if it were a wolf or a hyena.' He loved faking, telling something funny with a dead-serious look on his face. His grim appearance, quite incompatible with gay irony, made it an easy task for him.

It was interesting to watch him with children. He talked to them as with adults and they loved that. One day he said to a small girl of seven who would not part with her huge shabby doll: 'You call her Mashka. That is quite unsuitable. She is a respectable middle-aged woman. Been in service in a rich house for twelve years, collected her earnings and then married a porter, Nikanov Semionovich, an old soldier of Skobelev's times, and is now called Maria Fillipovna, not Mashka.' They both laughed. Another small incident: one July, after the revolution, he sat on a bench in a public garden outside his house in Petersburg. Children milled around. He was collecting small pieces of wood and branches, then lit a match and set fire to the little heap. A whiff of blue smoke rose swiftly in the darkling sky. The children gathered around in delight. A militiaman came up and said severely:

'Citizen, who allowed you to make bonfires in the garden?'

'Is it forbidden?'

'If everyone begins to take an interest in bonfires, the whole town might go up in flames. Come with me to the station, they'll explain it to you.'

'Please forgive us,' Gorky answered politely. 'We won't do it again. Come on children, let's put it out – nothing doing.'

'That's good,' the grumbling militiaman approved. 'Any disorder in a public place is open to prosecution. It's written there on the board.'

'Very sorry,' repeated Gorky, 'but we can't read, you see. . . . We must learn. Good-bye.'

He knew everything about birds, better than any ornithologist. One day at the seaside a peculiar bird raced through the reeds. Immediately Gorky told me its name, its antecedents, then picking up a stone delivered a lecture on mineralogy, the history of an extinct volcano . . .

One day he showed me a paper on which I could see his unusual square writing, almost like a pattern.

'A globe. Make a globe out of cardboard, cutting the pieces according to the layers of volcanic and neptunic elements, show the insertion of minerals: coal, iron, salt, naphtha, turf etc. Putting the globe together the child will learn automatically the structure of the soil.'

The man who as he dies thinks of the future is truly immortal.

After the revolution, like Peter the Piper Gorky played on his flute, and people, frightened and bewildered, began to peep out of their caves. Gorky had that privilege over them that his life had been entwined with the history of revolution and belonged to it. He was the biography of his century. He always believed that literature was a bridge between modern science and the people. He wanted to bring from science into literature precision, concentration, the ability of man struggling against the irrationalities of nature. From literature he wanted to carry into science poetry, idealism, the purity of language.

One day I wrote down merely some of the subjects of Gorky's stories:

1. The captain of a Volga steamship who used to maintain that cards were transparent for him and that that was why he never played cards.

2. A young merchant who was in love with the wife of the governor, who had a student as a lover. The merchant was desperately jealous and drank himself to death.

3. A Moscow merchant, a millionaire, who went to Istanbul only to have a look at a harem; after his hair-raising adventures in the sultan's harem he had the good luck to escape.

4. Chaliapin and two double agents. Chaliapin, completely ignorant of who they were, used to play rounders with them. And so on.

He had a passion for bonfires. At Sorrento he used to gather the branches of orange trees; near Moscow, branches of birches and poplars. This pyromania seemed to be a symbol. Maybe it reminded him of his youth, of his vagabond's life, roaming on high roads and through villages.

He could be incredibly gay, full of fun. One evening he spoke only about Chekhov and his life in Yalta. There had been a Tartar there who used to wink constantly with one eye. He kept visiting famous people and winking. Chekhov did not like him. One day he asked his mother: 'Mamma, why did the Tartar come?' 'He came to ask you about something, Antosha.' 'What was it?' 'How one catches whales.' 'Whales? Well, it's quite simple. You pick up a handful of herrings and throw them to the whale. The whale swallows all these salty fish and is thirsty. The water in the sea is also salty so he swims to the river to drink fresh water. As soon as he reaches the river people build up a dam so that he can't get back. And so the whale is caught.' Mother rushed round the town, searching for the Tartar to tell him how whales were caught.

He told another story: 'I was walking in Samara along the Volga banks late at night and suddenly I heard "Help, help, brother!" It was dark, the sky covered in clouds, great big barges standing on the river. Someone was spluttering in the black water between the bank and one of the barges. I got into the water, reached the drowning figure, snatched him by his hair and pulled him out onto the ground. He seized me by the scruff of my neck.

'"What right have you," he says, "to pull people by their hair?"

'I was not a little surprised. "But you were drowning," I said. "You were shouting for help."

'"You devil! How could I have been drowning when I was standing in the water which came up to my shoulders and also holding on to a rope? Are you blind or what?"

'"But you were shouting 'Help'."

'"What if I did? I can shout what I like. If I shout that you're a fool will you believe me? Come on, give me a rouble or I'll take you to the station. Come on!"

'I argued with him for a bit but saw that he was not as wrong as all that. I gave him all I had on me – thirty-five kopeks – and went home wiser than I had been before.'

He had a deep reverence for science. True, when he was younger he was of the opinion that art knows more about man than science does, but at the end of his life, dreaming of a biological philosophy, he admitted the all-importance of positive sciences.

I can go on like this for ever, and it is now time that you should read his book.

MOURA BUDBERG

# Gorky's Life

MAXIM GORKY (Alexei Peshkov) was born in 1868 in Nijni-Novgorod on the Volga, now re-named after him. His parents' was a love match, sharply criticized by his mother's father, who had risen from nowhere to a merchant's status and did not wish his daughter to marry a mere working man. The latter, however, was intelligent, and soon obtained an administrative post in a building company in Astrakhan. But in 1872 he died of cholera and his widow returned with her four-year-old son to the parental home. There little Maxim's terrifying life began. That layer of society had a truly bestial aspect at the time. The future writer grew up in an atmosphere of senseless cruelty and miserliness. The only human being in it was his grandmother, of whom he gave an epic image in his book *My Childhood*. She was his closest friend. Gorky was taught to read and write by his grandfather from religious books, and even that tyrant had to admit that his grandson had a 'horse's' memory. He then went at the age of eight to a technical school for two years, but 'owing to lack of means', as was stated in his identity papers, was unable to finish it. When his mother died Gorky was sent out to work, which he did willingly to bring money to his grandmother: he washed and scrubbed floors and cleaned silver, sawed wood and ran errands instead of learning a job. A year later he ran away from home, and was too ashamed to return and face his grandmother, to whom he had promised to 'have patience'. He lived on the Volga shores and soon got a job in the kitchens on one of the steamships. The head cook there became his first 'teacher'. He was a great reader and carried about with him a caseful of books of the strangest variety and devoured them all indiscriminately. This began Gorky on his crazy passion for culture.

After that, hard and humiliating jobs succeeded one another

– but there was one bright spot – a book. Finally he decided to go to Kazan and try for the university, but soon realized the futility of such a dream – life consisted of finding means for existence. This was the period of his life with the 'bare-footed' which provided subjects for many stories and caused some critics to consider Gorky an apologist of the 'bare-footed', which he was far from being. On the contrary, he considered the apathy of these men a tragedy, for his mind was given to activity, to attempt to create a better life. Gradually he was drawn into student intellectual circles with their revolutionary discussions. But earning a living had to go on and he got a permanent job in a large bakery, where he began to spread new ideas among his co-workers. When the Kazan police first raised a 'case' against Gorky, it was for his influence on the political convictions of these men. But he had no friends among them and felt all the stronger the confusion, the lack of coherence in his life. The result was an attempt at suicide in 1887; leaving a note that said, 'The person responsible for my action is the poet Heine, who invented toothache in the heart.' The bullet went through the lung and his condition was grave, but a surgical intervention put him on his feet again and a month later he was back in the bakery. But not for long. In the spring he went at the invitation of a serious and active revolutionary to work in a shop, in reality to promote revolutionary propaganda in a Volga village. The man had so earned himself the hostility of all the rich peasants, because he sold his wares cheaply, that he and Gorky were at one time nearly killed by them. Then began Gorky's wanderings in Russia and his writing.

In the winter he got jobs on the railway. He was due for military service, but pronounced unfit for it because of the damaged lung. By now he had only one ambition – to write, though his life was still full of complications and problems, among them also a 'first love' which ended disastrously, the object of it being a married woman who would not leave her husband. In despair he 'wandered away' again, this time to the Caucasus, and there was published in 1891 his first story, 'Makar Chudra'. After that things began to look brighter, and soon Gorky became a top journalist, first on a Samara paper, then in Nijni. The dream of 'a better life' never left him and this found its expression in his continued revolutionary activities. He was put under police surveillance on the grounds of the great popularity he had won among the 'poor'. He was first arrested in Tiflis in 1891 and incarcerated in the castle there. When liberated he wrote *Foma Gordeyev*, which had considerable success. But the police authorities remained suspicious and finally sent him into exile to Arsamas, and only after numerous appeals did his friends succeed in having him transferred to the Crimea. While there, he was elected to the Academy of Science, but at the Emperor's personal order the election was cancelled. As a result Chekhov asked for his name to be taken off the list of Academicians. Gorky meanwhile had written *The Lower Depths* and *The Philistines*, two plays that had great world-wide success. The authorities began to see how difficult it was to deal with a man of European reputation, but reaction after Bloody Sunday became so acute that he would have been arrested again had the revolutionaries not elected to send him to America to collect money for the revolution. He left in 1906. While in America he wrote *Mother*.

Return to Russia was made impossible and Gorky settled down in Capri, becoming a political émigré. Many of his works were forbidden in Russia and some, like the present one, describing the activities of the Secret Police, were only partially published. Only one third of *The Life of a Useless Man* saw the light of day. But he returned to Russia after the amnesty declared at the celebration of 300 years of the Romanoffs' reign, and in 1917, in spite of an ever-increasing tubercular condition, founded the daily *New Life* which, although he had warmly greeted the revolution, attacked all extremist parties. He went back to Italy in 1922, a lonely, torn, tired, sick man. But his life abroad gave birth to another creative period: *Stories of 1924, Fragments From My Diary, The Astamonov Affair, My Universities*, and finally his great, last work, *Klima Samgina*, the story of a mediocre member of the intelligentsia and of Russia seen through his eyes. He followed eagerly everything that was going on in Russia. Overcome with nostalgia for his homeland, he left for Russia in 1928. His work had remained unfinished and he had to return several times to Italy to continue it, life in Russia being too hectic and unendurable for his health. However, in 1933 he decided to remain there, feeling that he was needed by his people. In 1936 he succumbed to a new sharp development of his tuberculosis and died in Moscow on 18 July.

MOURA BUDBERG

## SOME OF GORKY'S MAJOR WORKS

'Makar Chudra', his first short story, published in 1891 in Tiflis, Georgia

*The Song of the Stormy Petrel*, his first volume of short stories, 1898

*Foma Gordeyev*, his first novel, 1899

*The Lower Depths*, his most important play, 1902

*Mother*, 1907

*The Life of a Useless Man*, 1911

His three-volume autobiography, *My Childhood, My Apprenticeship* and *My Universities*, published between 1913 and 1923

*Fragments From My Diary*, collected between 1922 and 1924, published in 1925

Gorky also wrote a vast number of stories, essays and articles. At the time of his death in 1936 he was working on an unfinished four-volume novel.

# A Sophisticated Traveller

To the west the clouds were sharply dyed with blue and orange. In the pearl-coloured sky above the shaggy block of pine-trees hung the transparent fragment of an almost expired moon. The pine-wood, extending from the marsh, reached the horizon and there huddled together in a dark heap, for the factory-chimney had lifted a threatening red finger at it. At noon a warm shower had sprinkled the earth, but during the afternoon, and till sunset, the soil had been drying under a hot, withering sun; now a stifling moistness filled the air. The marsh seemed to have swollen up, and its dreariness added to the pervading sense of oppression.

Sasha Vinokuroff, a medical assistant, walked like a bear on all fours along the hill sown with rye, adjusting his nets for quails, while I lay under a water-elder bush and thought aloud:

'It would be fine to start life again from the beginning, say fifteen years old.'

Here Sasha, continuing a conversation we had previously had, called out in a thick voice:

'The existing surroundings of life satisfy nobody.'

He rolled down the hill right to my bush, wiped the muddy palms of his hands on his boots, and began examining the quail-traps. Great wrinkles furrowed the forehead of his bald skull, his eyes seemed to have grown round like a fish's.

He is an interesting personality. He is the son of a barrister, but 'incapable of supporting the weight of knowledge imparted to him at school, and persecuted by the barbarism of his father' (as he says), he ran away from home, roamed about for two years – in prison and at the other customary halting-places of nameless tramps – then, 'exhausted to a state of unconsciousness even of the things of which one is always conscious', he returned to his father's house, was 'thrown like a dead mouse into an ant-heap'

– that is to say, enlisted in an infantry regiment, and entered the Army Medical School. Having served his time as a soldier, he sailed about for seven years on various training-ships.

'I have sampled the alcoholic drinks of all nations,' he said. 'Not because I am a drunkard by nature, but because one's nature must have some outlet. I drank such enormous quantities that even Englishmen came to watch me. They would stand and watch me as though fascinated, then shrug their shoulders and smile: of course it pleased them immensely: here was a really fine drinker at last! Here was someone for whom it was worth while brewing gin and whisky! One of them even said to me: "Say, have you ever tried bathing in whisky?"

'For all that, the English are a fine nation; it's only their language – which is far worse than Chinese . . .

'Without noticing how it came about, I found myself in Persia, married to the maid of an English merchant, a very nice girl, only she turned out to be a drunkard – though perhaps it was I who drove her to drink. Two years later she died of cholera, while I moved on to the most hideous town in the world – Baku. From there I came to this frog's hole. This is a town for you, if you like – the devil tear it to bits!'

'Sasha,' I said, 'tell me about your travels in China.'

'Travelling is a very simple matter; you simply go on board a ship and leave the rest to the captain. The captains are all drunkards, all of them swearers and bullies too – such is the law of nature. Give me a cigarette, will you?'

He lit a cigarette and inhaled a ringlet of smoke with one nostril:

'Very light tobacco this; *pour les dames*, as one might say.'

Vinokuroff is more than fifty, but he is still a strong, sturdy man. His wood-cut, soldierly face is lit by a pair of clear eyes that look at you calmly, with the look of a man who has seen a lot, who has lost the habit of being astonished at anything and is a stranger to all anxieties. He looks somehow across people, not straight at them, and treats them with a certain amount of condescension – a trifle forbearingly, as it were. He no longer practises medicine. 'I discovered that medicine is a blind,' he says.

In town he keeps a 'kephir establishment and sale of Bulgarian whey, delivered daily according to the recipe of M. Mechnikoff.'

'Tell me about yourself,' I insisted.

'Your insatiability astounds me. Where do you manage to store all this drivel of words? Well, what shall I tell you about?'

'What you have seen.'

'Oh, that! It would take about a year to tell you. I've seen all there is to see, all the drawbacks. Drawbacks? Well, what else would you call them? Your ship leaves harbour, you make the sign of the cross and say: "Now get on with it; carry me safely to the place you are bound for." And you sail day and night, day and night, and all around you there's nothing but empty sea and sky. Well, I am a quiet man; I like that. Then there's a whistle – that means we're there. But I don't want to stop. There's a drawback, to start with. It's as though you ran into a hedge when you were out for a country walk at night. Well, then begins the hysterical bustle of the impossible passengers on deck. Passengers are a type by themselves, the most idiotic type. A man on board ship acquires a funny childishness, apart from the fact that almost everybody is humiliatingly sea-sick. And at sea one notices, more acutely than one does on shore, what a non-entity man is. In this fact lies the moral which sea voyages teach us. To cut it short, I can safely assert that on the whole surface of the globe, land or water, there is nothing worse than passengers. For an idler life is just one long boredom. Well, at sea boredom is especially poisonous, and all passengers are by nature idle people. Out of sheer boredom they lose their personalities to such an extent that in spite of high titles, decorations, riches and other distinctions, they treat simple firemen as equals. Like dogs at the sight of oatmeal biscuits, they rush to the deck to enjoy the view of a foreign shore. Enjoy it by all means, but why bustle? But no – they begin to stamp their feet and disagree: "Oh, just look at that! Oh, just watch that!" As a matter of fact there's nothing to watch; everything is there just as usual: earth, buildings, people, all looking smaller than mice. And always at that particular moment some unfortunate accident occurs: at Alexandria, for instance, the confounded stewardess smashed an eight-ounce bottle of carbolic acid in my suitcase. The smell spread, of course, to all the first-class cabins, and the first officer danced round me like a madman, swearing so fiercely that one of the ladies was driven by his expletives into a state of nervous prostration and complained to the captain – by mistake, however, she complained of me. Or take this instance: a little girl got her finger squeezed in the surgery door, and her father, just because he was a diplomat, thought he was quite within his rights in prodding me in the stomach with his stick. And it's always like that – absurd and unexpected.

'Briefly, I've seen nothing particularly interesting anywhere on the whole of this globe; everywhere one is equally liable to be insulted by word or deed – in the Asiatic hemisphere more particularly than in the others, but that is all. Only two hemispheres did you say? That is a vulgar error: if you look at the matter from a strictly practical point of view and cut this globe of ours along the line of any latitude you choose, starting from the poles, you will get as many hemispheres as we have latitudes, and possibly more. Pass me a cigarette, please.'

Lighting it and closing his eyes, he muttered:

'One oughtn't really to smoke, quails don't like it.'

And he continued calmly, in a low voice:

'From time to time interesting events occur, but for the peace of one's soul it would be better if they didn't. For instance: In the Chinese sea – there is a sea of that name, although it differs in no way from the others – well, as we were slowly sailing in that self-same sea to Hong Kong, the look-out man noticed one night a peculiar light which flared up in the inky darkness. I, the second officer, the boatswain, and the steward were playing cards, when suddenly we heard a shout:

' "Fire at sea!"

'We jumped up to have a look, of course, leaving the game unfinished. When people have been long at sea every trivial incident excites their interest. They even go so far as to watch dolphins with enjoyment, although that uneatable fish resembles a pig more than anything else – thereby demonstrating the extreme foolishness of passengers.

'Well, to continue my story. I came out of the deck-house to have a look and all I saw was just an ordinary stuffy night, hot

use, the sky covered with black felt and just as
the sea. Pitch darkness, of course, and far away
, a small fire blazing like a flower and with one of its
ing ends stuck into the seas, and bristling like a hedgehog,
so to speak, only of course a very large hedgehog, about as big
as a lamb. There it was, spluttering and spreading and getting
bigger and bigger. Nothing particularly interesting in that –
besides, I was winning at cards.

'I've noticed that people usually have a kind of idolatrous
passion for fire . . . All high festivities, royal anniversaries,
birthdays, marriages and other little motives of human rejoicings
– excepting funerals – are accompanied by fireworks and illu-
minations. Divine services, too – but there one must also include
funerals. Small urchins amuse themselves by lighting wood-
piles even in summer time – for which they ought to be unmerci-
fully spanked, as these pranks are usually the cause of forest fires.
Fires appear to cause peculiar gratification to all men, and everybody rushes at them like moths. A poor man is pleased to see
a rich man's house burning; in fact every person endowed
with organs for seeing is attracted by fire – as indeed is well
known.

'All the passengers rushed up on deck, and while enjoying the
sight began to argue as to what it was that was burning. It was
obvious to the meanest intelligence that it could only be a ship
of some sort, for there are not many haystacks floating around on
the ocean; but what was clear to a deaf and dumb child was by
no means clear to them. It always strikes me as marvellous that
passengers cannot understand the simplest possible things. An
abundance of superfluous words cannot dispel the boredom of
life.

'Well, I listened meekly to the animated conversation of the
passengers watching the fire, and all of a sudden a woman
exclaimed:

' "Oh! there may be people on board it!"

'What perspicacity! Ships don't often go to sea without men
on board, but she had only just found that out!

'Then she cried again:

' "They must be saved!"

5

'This started a fresh argument: some opined tha[...]
put about at once, others, more business-like, point[...]
we ourselves were considerably overdue already withou[...]
out of our way to encounter this new obstacle. But the lady[...]
both vociferous and energetic – later on I learnt that she was
going from Kars to Japan, to join a sister who had married
someone in the Embassy in Tokyo, another reason for her
journey being tuberculosis of the lungs – well, I was saying, she
turned out to be a regular nuisance, demanded that the people
in the burning ship should be saved, and incited the passengers
to send a deputation to the captain, asking him to assist the
burning ship. Some of the passengers, however, objected very
strongly, saying that the ship might be a Chinese one and the
people on board it Chinese too. But that didn't alarm her at all.
Her hysterical outburst had such an effect on three others that
they went off to appeal to the captain, and although he told them
that to do what they asked would delay us still more, they
threatened him with the law, asserting that under maritime law
a ship is bound to go to the assistance of another in distress and
that if he didn't do so they would report the matter as soon as we
arrived at Hong Kong.

'In the end the squabblers won, and the captain put the ship
about and steered for the burning vessel. We paddled along the
shaggy sea, over the hillocks of waves, into the pitch darkness,
towards the fire. The crew, thoroughly annoyed, began un-
fastening the boat, and when we got closer we saw that it was a
good-for-nothing little Chinese two-masted junk that was
burning. Two little boats were rowing round it, filled with
people, all of them shouting and howling, while on the stern of
the burning ship stood a tall, slim man – just standing there
motionless. The fire was burning steadily, one could hardly see
the deck for flames; the masts looked like candles, and flames
were spurting out of the hold and lashing the sides of the ship;
but the man stood there like a sentinel on duty, quite motionless.
One could see him quite clearly.

'We took the men from one of the boats on board; the three
men who were in the other threw themselves into the water
from premature fright and were all drowned. The rescued men

told us that their captain was still on board the burning ship and that he intended to perish with his property. Our sailors shouted out to him, "Jump into the water, you devil; we'll pick you up." But he paid not the slightest attention, and we couldn't very well lasso him, could we? However, we had no time to tackle his obstinacy further, for the captain was whistling piercingly for the boat to return. Just as the fire reached the stern of the ship I distinctly saw the Asiatic spring up, as though spewed up by the fire, seize his head with his hands and dive into the flames as though into an abyss.

'But the essence of the incident does not lie in the behaviour of that Chinaman, for his race is perfectly indifferent as regards self, owing to the enormous number and crowded condition of the population. In fact things have got to such a pitch in China that in cases where the number of superfluous people is a hindrance, they cast lots, and those on whom the lot falls, kill themselves, quite honestly. Whenever a second girl is born in a family she is thrown into the river – they can't stand more than one girl in a house.

'But the essence of the incident, as I say, lies not in the behaviour of the Chinaman, but in that of the consumptive lady. She rushed up to the captain and screamed at him that he hadn't given any orders to put out the fire on the junk.

' "My dear lady," said he in a dignified tone, "I'm not a fire-engine."

' "But," she screamed, "a man has perished there!"

'The captain explained to her that this was not an unusual event in a fire, even on land, but she still kept harping on it.

' "Do you realize what it means; a man?"

'Everybody was smiling at her, but like a little lap-dog she dashed from one to othe other, babbling: "A man, a man!"

'The onlookers, beginning to get fed-up with her, walked away; she continued to ramp about the deck and at last burst out crying. A very eminent and dignified man – a lord, I think, I've forgotten his name – went up to her and tried to calm her.

' "Everything that could be done has been done," he assured her.

'But she shrugged him off insolently. Then I thought I'd try my hand, so I went up to her and said soothingly:

' "My dear lady – will you allow me to offer you some baldrian drops? . . ."

'But she just muttered, without looking at me:

' "Oh, idiots, what idiots! . . ."

'This rather offended me; I thought, however, that I'd try again. So I said as gently as I could:

' "My dear lady, this scandalous behaviour, shown up by the nobleness of your heart, has revolted me too."

'She turned to me, stuck her face close to mine, and screamed shrilly into my nose:

' "Go away, do you hear!"

'Of course I gallantly went away, leaving a glass with some baldrian drops in it behind. I stood aside and watched her. She blew her nose and sniffled. To me standing there, it seemed that there was something indecent in those tears shed over an unknown Chinaman. It was hardly possible that she was in the habit of weeping bitterly over everybody who perished under her eyes. In Singapore hundreds of natives were dying of hunger; yet not one of our passengers ever shed a tear over them. I grant they are not like Europeans, of course. Yet I have seen numberless cases of our own Russian men, sailors, workmen and others, being torn to pieces, smashed, bruised under my eyes, without this affecting the passengers in the slightest, unless one counts the natural anxiety and nervous perturbation that occur when one is unused to seeing blood flow freely. I thought and thought a lot about this incident of the woman, in fact I gave it more attention than it deserved, but I could find no solution to it.'

Vinokuroff tugged his whiskers, listened to some far-off sound, and muttered crossly:

'I suspect there was some foolishness in it.'

Night had fallen. Dull stars shone in the watery blue of the sky. The fragment of moon had disappeared. The low, emaciated pine that grew close to us had become dark and reminded me of a monk.

Sasha Vinokuroff proposed that we should go to the forester's

# Fires

## I

COMING, one dark February night, to the Osharsk* square, I saw a frisky fox-tail of fire peep out of a garret window and shake itself in the air, speckling the night with large fluttering sparks that fell to earth slowly and unwillingly. The beauty of the fire excited me. It was as though some red beast had sprung suddenly out of the moist, warm darkness into the window under the roof, had arched its back and was gnawing furiously at something; one could hear a dry crackling – as a bird's bones crack between one's teeth.

As I stood watching the sly artfulness of the fire I thought: 'Someone ought to go and knock at the windows, wake people up, and cry: "Fire!"' But I felt incapable of moving or shouting: I just stood, captivated, watching the quick growth of the flame: the hue of cock's feathers had begun to flash on the edge of the roof, the top branches of the trees in the garden became pink and golden, and the square began to light up.

'I must go and wake them up,' I said to myself, but – I stood watching in silence until I noticed the figure of a man in the middle of the square. He was leaning against the metal column of the fountain and could hardly be distinguished from it at the first glance.

I came up to him. It was Lukich, the night-watchman, a quiet, meek old man.

'Well – what are you thinking about? Why don't you blow your whistle and wake people up?'

Without taking his eyes away from the fire he answered in a sleepy – or was it a drunken? – voice:

'In a minute . . .'

I knew that he was a sober man, but I could discern a drunken gleam of ecstasy in his eyes, and his reply did not astonish me. He began murmuring in a low voice, swallowing his words:

* In Nizhni Novgorod.

hut and wait there until dawn, when the quails would be on the move. We rose to go. Walking heavily in the wet grass, he said slowly:

'When meat is very hot one does not notice whether it is salted.'

'You just watch how sly it is. Look what it's doing, look! It's eating it all up, guzzling it, the hefty brute! It's only a few minutes ago that it was just a bit of a flame next to the chimney, a bit no bigger than a chisel. And how it began to lash out and set to work on it! It's great fun, watching a fire, 'pon my word it is!'

He stuck a whistle into his mouth and, balancing himself with difficulty, made the deserted square resound with a shrill call, at the same time brandishing a rattle which crackled hurriedly. But all the time his eyes, unwaveringly, were directed upwards, towards the spot where the red and white snowflakes wheeled and danced over the roof, and the black, thick smoke gathered into a sumptuous head-dress. Lukich grinned at it and muttered into his beard:

'You old scoundrel, you! . . . Well – I suppose I must wake people up.'

We ran round the square, knocking at the doors and windows, shouting: 'Fire! Fi – ire!'

I felt that I was performing a duty: my heart was not in it. As for Lukich, after knocking at the windows he rushed back to the middle of the square and, with his head thrown back, screamed, 'Fi – ire!' with evident ecstasy in his voice.

Great is the attraction of the magic power of fire! I have often noticed that the most self-denying people yield to its fascination, and I am not free from its influence myself. It is always a delight to me to set fire to a wood-pile, and I am just as ready to sit for days watching the flames as I am to sit and listen to music.

2

It was during a fire at the Snetinski congress in Nizhni; the houses above the narrow cleft in the ravine were alight. The ravine, cutting across the clay hill, descends steeply from the upper part of the town to the lower one, towards the Volga. Owing to the situation of the place the fire brigade was unable to get near enough to the spot where the fire was raging; so the pumps and water-barrels remained on the slope below. Lumps of molten slag rolled across the edge of the ravine, and blazing beams tumbled down from above.

A dense crowd of onlookers stood on the opposite side of the slope. Although one could watch the fire very well from there, some twenty or thirty people climbed down to the bottom, where they were met with angry scoldings by the firemen; for the smouldering beams, as they fell down the hill, might easily have knocked them off their legs.

In order to watch the fire swallow up the ancient houses, the onlookers were obliged to throw their heads back. Their faces were quickly strewn with ashes and cinders; sparks pricked and stung their skin. This had no effect whatever upon them; they shouted and laughed, yelling when the beams came rolling down to their feet. They crawled on all fours along the steep slope to the side of the ravine that lay opposite the scene of the fire, then again, like black clods, they jumped down into the ravine.

This game seemed particularly to attract an imposing-looking gentleman in a smart coat with a panama hat on his head and well-blacked shoes on his feet. He had a round, well-groomed face with long whiskers, and carried a stick with a golden knob, which he held upside down and brandished like a mace. Dodging the beams that fell down from above, he shouted in a low bass voice:

'Hurrah!'

The onlookers cheered him; over his head the golden knob flashed as he twirled it; black stains left by smouldering sparks appeared on the brim of his hat, his neck-tie worked up like a black snake under his chin. But the man was unaware of all this. He was entirely unconscious of his surroundings; his aim was that of a small boy – to wait until the blazing beams almost touched his feet before he jumped aside.

In this he succeeded unerringly.

In spite of his height and corpulence he was most agile. Here comes a beam! – it will hit him . . . but no – a quick spring to one side, and the danger is past.

'Hurrah!'

He even jumped several times across the beam, and was rewarded for this by applause from the ladies among the audience on the top of the slope. There was a number of them up there, in all sorts of costumes, some with umbrellas open, to protect themselves from the crimson rain of sparks. I thought to myself that the man was surely in love and was showing off his fearlessness and agility to the lady of his heart.

'Hur – rah!' he cried. His panama hat had slipped to the back of his head, his face was purple and his necktie had twisted itself higher than ever.

With a loud shout, drowning even the greedy crackling of the fire, the firemen now tore out several beams with their gaffs at one stroke, and the smouldering beams, flashing with golden light, sauntering clumsily, rolled along the slope of the ravine, their progress becoming more and more rapid as they fell. At length, their ends whirling in the air, they rolled one over the other and struck the stones of the pavement with deep thuds.

'Hur – rah!' The man in the panama hat cried wildly, flourishing his stick. But as he jumped over one of the beams the end of the next one, rolling lazily, struck him across the legs. He threw up his hands and dived to the ground. Immediately the blazing end of a third huge firebrand ran into his side like the head of a serpent of fire. A sharp cry rang out from among the crowd of onlookers. The firemen quickly dragged him away by the feet and carried him to one side, while the panama hat remained on the pavement among the burning beams. It twisted a little from side to side with the heat, shrunk together, and then all of a sudden flared up gaily in an orange flame, the whole hat ablaze.

3

In the year 1896 there was a great fire in the Home of Industry* in Nizhni; the tow which was stored on the lower floor of the building caught fire. The fire spread very rapidly, and the iron stairs leading to the second floor soon became red-hot. The old women who lived there were all gathered at the top of the stairs, and all of them – more than twenty – were suffocated by the resinous smoke and burned to death.

* Workmen's home.

I came on the scene of the fire when it was nearly over. The roof had fallen in; through a huge brick casement with iron bars the fire was furiously bubbling and snorting, vomiting out a deep oily smoke. Through the red-hot iron bars of the windows the smoke broke out in heavy black tufts and, without rising very high above the blazing house, sank on to the roofs of the neighbouring houses and descended in a suffocating fog into the streets. At my side stood a man of bad reputation, Kapiton Sisoeff, the owner of many houses in the town, a thickly built man, healthy-looking, in spite of his fifty years and the drunken life he had led. In his clean-shaven face with high cheek-bones a pair of narrow, restless eyes were set in two deep, bony sockets. He was shabbily and carelessly dressed, whatever he wore seemed not to belong to him, and his whole person breathed something unpleasant, of which he seemed to be aware. It was his habit therefore to assume an aggressive attitude towards all folk, and to treat them with pointed impertinence.

He was watching the fire with the look of a man to whom life and all that it includes is merely a spectacle. He spoke cynically of the 'roasted old women', and said that it would be a good thing if all old women were burnt. But something was disturbing him, for he kept putting his hand into his coat pocket, pulling it out again, flourishing it in the air in a peculiar manner, then plunging it into his pocket again, and furtively looking round to see if anybody was watching him. Finally I noticed that he had a small paper parcel, carefully tied up with black tape, between his fingers. He bounced it several times on the palm of his hand, then suddenly, with a quick movement, flung it across the street into the fire.

'What's that that you've thrown?'

'Nothing of importance. Just a superstition I have, that's all,' he answered, winking at me, evidently very pleased with himself, and smiling broadly.

'What superstition?'

'Oh, I can't tell you that.'

About two weeks after this I met him at the house of Lawyer Venski, a *bon vivant* and a cynic, but a highly cultured man. Our host, having drunk steadily, fell asleep on the sofa, while I, recalling the incident at the fire, persuaded Sisoeff to tell me about his 'superstition'. Sipping his benedictine mixed with brandy – his favourite beverage, which turned his ears purple – he began to tell me about it in a bantering tone, but I soon noticed that his tone was forced.

'I threw my finger-nails, which I had clipped off, into the fire. Funny, isn't it? I've been collecting my nail-clippings ever since I was nineteen. I decided to keep them until there should be a fire somewhere – when I could wrap them up together with two or three copper pennies and throw them into the flames. What for? Well, I must tell you how all this nonsense began . . .

'When I was nineteen I was dogged by every kind of hard luck: I was in love with an unattainable woman, my shoes kept splitting, I had no money, and couldn't even pay for my studies at the university. Through these misfortunes I sank into a state of pessimism and decided to poison myself. I got some cyanide of potassium and went to the Strastnoi boulevard. I had a favourite bench there, behind the monastery, and there I sat down and said to myself: "Good-bye, Moscow, good-bye, life, curse you all!" All of a sudden I noticed that a fat old woman was sitting beside me, all in black, with her eyebrows grown together on the forehead – a horrible face! She opened her eyes wide at me and we sat looking at each other in an oppressive silence.

' "What do you want?" I asked presently.

' "Give me your left hand, my young man!" she said, in a harsh, commanding way.'

My companion glanced at our snoring host, looked round the room, peering intently into its dark corners, and continued now in a lower key, abandoning the artificial, bantering tone.

'I stretched my hand out to her and – on my word of honour – felt the weight of her piercing glance on my skin. She looked at my palm for a long time, then said:

' "You're doomed to live" – that's exactly what she said: doomed! – "You're doomed to live long and well, comfortably, lightly."

'I told her I did not believe nonsense of that sort – fortune-telling, magic, witchery; but she replied:

' "That is why you live so gloomily, that is why everything goes badly with you. You just have a try and believe . . ."

' "How can I?"

' "Well, here's an idea for you: cut your nails and throw the clippings into a stranger's fire; only – be sure it is in a stranger's!"

' "What do you mean – a stranger's fire?"

' "Dear me," she said, "is it so hard to understand? A wood-pile in the street on a frosty day – a house on fire – or else when you are sitting with some friends round their fireplace . . ."

'Was it because in my heart I was unwilling to die – after all, we all die only when we are forced to do so, even when we think it is of our own free will – or else because that woman inspired me with some faint hope. Anyhow, I put off my suicide for the time being. I came home, cut my nails, and wrapped the clippings up in a sheet of paper. "I'll try her witchery," I thought to myself.

'During the following week the house on the Bronnaia, opposite mine, caught fire. I tied a small weight to my parcel and flung it into the flames. "Well," I thought to myself, "it's done now – the sacrifice has been made! – let's see how the gods will answer it." I had a friend, a mathematician, who was extraordinarily good at billiards and could beat me as easily as falling off a log. I offered him a game, just to test the force of the witchery.

'He said contemptuously, "What handicap do you want?"

' "None – nothing!"

'We played and I won. You can imagine my feelings. I remember that my legs trembled so that I could hardly stand. I felt as though I had been sprinkled with holy water! "Jupiter!" said I to myself, "what about my unattainable lady now – what if I should win there too? That would be something more than a coincidence!" I went straight along to her – and succeeded with such marvellous ease that it frightened me and I couldn't sleep. Were they both coincidences?

'I lived between two fires – love, my first greedy love, and fear. I used to see the old hag at night: she would stand at some corner and glower at me from beneath her shaggy eyebrows. I told my beloved all about it and she, like all actresses, and bad ones especially, being very superstitious, got excited and begged me, "Do cut your nails and look out for fires!" So I clipped and kept my nail-parings, not forgetting for a moment that it was all rubbish and that the whole matter lay perhaps in the fact that when a man loses faith in himself he must look round and find some dark horror to have faith in.

'But this consideration did not appease my uneasiness. After I had collected a certain amount of nail-parings and thrown them into the fire again, behold another devilry: a bald little man carrying a despatch-box came to see me. "You had," says he, "a maiden aunt who has just died in Nizhni-Novgorod and you are her only heir." Never, never before had I heard of such an aunt, in fact I was almost as devoid of relations as I was of cash. There were, as a matter of fact, only two of them: my grandfather on my mother's side, who lived in an almshouse, and an uncle burdened with a large family, a prison inspector whom I had never seen in my life.

'I looked at the little bald man and said politely: "Possibly you are the Devil?" He got offended and answered that he was a lawyer and an old friend of my aunt's.

'"Perhaps it was the old woman who sent you?" I said.

'"Well, yes, of course," he answered; "of course she was an old woman – fifty-seven on her last birthday."

'I looked at him with something like hatred in my eyes, and warned him that I had no money to repay him for his efforts.

'"You'll pay me when you have taken possession of your aunt's capital," he said.

'He was a very nasty old man, very intrusive and pompous, and I could see that he despised me. He brought me here, and that is how I came to own these houses. For some reason I pictured to myself that I should inherit a small wooden house with three windows, five hundred roubles in cash and a cow, but it proved to be two houses, shops, stores, tenants and all the rest of it. Fine business! But somehow I don't feel at home with it all; my life is guided by a strange, mysterious will, and there's growing up in me a peculiar attitude towards His Highness the

Fire – the attitude of a savage towards a Being that possesses the power to bring both joy and destruction.

' "No," I said to myself, "confound it all – this won't do – I won't have it!"

'And so I began to turn my riches into smoke and ashes, fidget about restlessly like a dog on a chain, lead a fast life. And I still go on cutting my nails, collecting the chips and throwing them into "strangers' fires". I can't exactly tell you why I do this and whether I believe in this witchery; anyway, I can't forget the old woman, although I hope and suppose that she is dead long ago.'

An eerie curiosity overwhelmed me.

'What does it all mean? I left the university, I lead a disgracefully easy life and feel a kind of restless insolence that incites me to test in every possible way the patience of the police, my own physical power of endurance, and the benevolence of Fate. And I come out of every trouble without a scratch. But in spite of that I live in the certainty that presently someone will come and say, "Step this way, if you please." Who it will be and whither he will lead me I do not know – but I'm waiting for him! I started to read Swedenborg, Jacob Boehme, Dupreil – what rubbish! What perfect rubbish! Insulting the intellect, I call it! And I wake up at night and wait. For what? Just that. If one kind of devilry is possible, why should there not be some other kind, worse or better than the first? I do nothing whatever to encourage it, and I wonder why it is that I don't go mad. I am a rich bachelor, women like me, I'm disgustingly lucky at cards. Also there is not a swindler nor a scoundrel among my friends. They are all drunkards, it is true, but very decent fellows all the same. So I have lived up to fifty years of age, and at that age every man ought to go through a crisis of some sort – it's said to be the general penalty. Well; I'm waiting for the crisis.

'In Kiev, where I was once on business, I kicked up a row with some aristocratic Pole and he challenged me. "Ah, there it is, the crisis," I said to myself! On the eve of the duel there was a fire on the Podol;* some Jewish houses were burning. I rode to the scene of the fire, threw my nails into it, and mentally

* Lower part of Kiev.

wished that I might be killed tomorrow or severely wounded at least! But on the evening of the same day my Pole was out riding and his horse shied and threw him, and he broke his right arm and smashed his head. His second informed me of this, and I asked him how the accident happened.

' "An old woman threw herself under the horse's feet," he replied.

'An old woman? An old woman! The devil himself take her! Is that a coincidence again, confound it? For the first time in my life I was seized with hysteria and was sent off immediately to Saxony, to a sanatorium in the mountains. There I told the whole story to the professor.

' "Oh," the German said, "this is a very interesting case." And he gave it the name of an insect, in Latin. Then he made me take shower-baths, and run up and down the hills for two months; but nothing came of these experiments. I felt precisely the same, and longed for fires. Do you understand what I mean? I just longed for them. For "strangers' fires". And I went on collecting my nail-parings . . . To myself I said, "I know it's all nonsense, of course, all trash and superstition." But I went on collecting my nails . . .

'Soon after this I mortgaged my houses, for my money was coming to an end. "Well, what will happen next?" I asked myself. I took to travelling to Nuremberg, Augsburg and so on – how dreary it all is! One day, sitting in the hall of an hotel, I threw my nail-clippings into the grate. Next morning, while I was lying in bed, someone knocked at my door: a telegram to say that one of my three Governmental Shares had won fifty thousand roubles, another one thousand roubles! I remember sitting up in bed, looking round in fear, and swearing savagely. I was afraid – stupidly, shamelessly afraid, like a woman.

'Well, it would take too long to tell you all about this absurd business. Here I have been living with it for thirty-four years. I give you my word that I have tried to do everything I could to get ruined, to break my neck; but, as you see, I am flourishing. I've given up caring about it now, and I don't care what happens.'

Apparently, however, he did care very much, for his high

cheekbones flushed angrily and his face wore an expression of hatred, his sharp, narrow eyes shining wrathfully.

'Why, then, do you still go on throwing your nail-parings in the fire?' I asked.

'Well – how can I live without it? What else have I to wait for? This devilry must come to an end some day, mustn't it? Or perhaps it won't. Perhaps I'm never going to be given the chance to die, eh?'

He grinned fearfully and closed his eyes. Then, lighting a cigar and staring at its end, he said in a low voice:

'Chemistry is chemistry, of course, but still there is something hidden in fire beyond what we know, something that we cannot understand. And fire can hide so marvellously well, too, so cleverly. Nothing – no one – can hide like that. A small bit of pressed cotton, a few drops of sulphuric acid, a few grams of oxyhydrogen gas, and then . . .'

He smacked his tongue and was silent.

'It seems to me,' I said to him, 'that you have expressed it all very clearly yourself by saying: "When one loses faith in one's own strength, one has to seek faith in something outside oneself." Well – you have found it . . .'

He nodded his head in affirmation, but had evidently not understood or not heard my words, for a moment afterwards he asked, frowning:

'But it's all absurd, isn't it? What does he want my nails for, do you think?'

*

About two years later I was told that he had had a stroke in the street, and died on the spot.

## 4

Zolotnitzki the priest was sentenced to thirty years' imprisonment for heresy, and spent those thirty years in the prison of a monastery. If I am not mistaken it was in Suzdal, in strict solitary confinement, in a stone pit. During the languid course of eleven thousand days and nights, the only consolation of this captive of a Christ-loving Church, as well as his sole companion, was fire: the heretic was granted permission to light the stove of his cell unaided by others.

In the early years of this century Zolotnitzki was released, for not only had he forgotten all about his heresy, but his mind had ceased to work altogether; the light in it was practically extinguished. Dried to the bones by his rigorous imprisonment, he bore but a remote resemblance to the inhabitants of the earth's surface. He walked about with his head bent low, as though he were continually descending, sinking into a pit, looking for a place wherein to hide his weak, pitiful body. His dull eyes watered constantly, his head shook, and his incoherent speech was impossible to understand. The hairs of his beard, no longer grey but of a greenish, decomposed hue, stood out in sharp contrast with his pallid, withered face. He was half-witted and evidently lived in terror of all men, but, fearing them, tried to dissimulate his terror. When he was addressed by anyone, he lifted his dry little childish hand as though he expected to be struck a blow across the eyes and hoped to be able to protect them with his weak, trembling hand. He was very quiet, talked little and always in a whisper, in timid, rustling sounds.

He left prison a fire-worshipper, and grew animated only when he was allowed to light a wood-pile in the stove and sit in front of it, watching it. Seating himself on a low little stool, he lit the logs lovingly, making the sign of the cross over them, and murmured, shaking his head, all the words that still lived in his memory:

'Thou, who art . . . Eternal fire . . . Burning the sinners . . . Omnipresent . . .'

He pushed the burning logs gently with a small poker, swayed backwards and forwards as though about to poke his head into the fire, while the wind drew the thin green hairs of his beard inside the stove.

'Thy will be done . . . Thy image be blessed for ever and ever . . . And they fly . . . So they fly . . . From the image of the fire . . . Like smoke from the image of the fire . . . Thy name be praised . . . Unquenchable . . .'

He was surrounded by kind-hearted people who wondered

how men could torture a man so much, and how pertinacious is
the vital spark.

Zolotnitzki's horror was great when he first saw an electric
lamp, when the white, colourless light, imprisoned in the glass,
flared up before him mysteriously. Having stared at it for some
moments intently, the old man waved his hands in despair and
began muttering plaintively:

'What! the fire imprisoned too! . . . oh – oh! . . . What for?
The devil's not in it, is he? Oh – oh! Why have they done it?'

It took some time to comfort him. Tears streamed from his
dull, colourless eyes, he trembled all over, and, sighing sorrow-
fully, cried appealingly to the people round him:

'Oh, you slaves of God, why do you do it? Imprison a sunbeam! Oh, you sinful people, beware of the fire's wrath!'

He sobbed, lightly touching the shoulders of those who stood
close to him with his small, dry, trembling hand:

'Oh – let it go – set it free!'

## 5

As my chief, A. I. Lanin, entered his office, he said irritably:

'I've just been to the prison to see that new client of ours.
He seems a nice, quiet chap, yet the police swear he's guilty of
four arsons! The indictment's very strong, the evidence is
highly incriminating. The man himself is evidently sick with
fear and doesn't say a word. How the devil I'm going to defend
him I don't know.'

Later in the evening, working at his table, the chief, glancing
up at the ceiling, said crossly:

'I am sure the fellow is innocent . . .'

A. I. Lanin was an experienced and successful lawyer. He
could deliver the most convincing and beautifully-worded
speeches in court, and this was the first time I had ever seen
him agitated about the fate of a client.

Next day I went to court. Our case was the first on the list.
A young boy of about twenty, with a heavy mop of reddish,
curly hair, sat on the prisoner's bench. His face was very white,
and his grey-blue eyes were wide open. A faint, golden mous-

tache adorned his upper lip, and his mouth was very red. Whenever the president, V. V. Behr, or the prosecutor addressed a question to him he jumped to his feet and answered in a low voice.

'Louder!' said the judge.

He cleared his throat but continued to speak low. This irritated both the judges and the jury, while everybody else began to get bored. A butterfly flapping at a window-pane served to increase the general feeling of boredom.

'So you refuse to admit your guilt? The witness Priakhine, please!'

A long, one-eyed old man stepped up into the witness-box. He had a rigid, set face, and straight, grey hairs hung from his cheeks and chin. Questioned as to his profession, the old man replied in a dull voice, 'I live by charity'. Then, leaning his head on one side, he whined away:

'I was walking away from the town, very late it was, the sun had set long ago, and as I came up to the village I noticed a light in the darkness in front of me, and all of a sudden it flared up . . .'

The prisoner sat holding tightly to the edge of the dock, his mouth half-open, listening intently. His eyes had a strange look – his attention seemed to be concentrated not on the witness but on the wall opposite.

'I started to run, while it raged.'

'What raged?'

'The fire, the flames . . .'

The prisoner bent forward and all of a sudden asked loudly, with obvious contempt and scorn in his voice:

'When did all this happen?'

'You know very well when it happened,' the beggar answered, without looking at him.

The boy stood up and addressed the judges:

'He's lying: you can't see the place where the fire was from the road . . .'

The prosecutor, a sharp-nosed little lawyer, promptly shouted him down, hurling questions at him in a shrill voice. The prisoner relapsed into his lethargy again and replied unwillingly in a low tone. This disposed the jury still more against him. In the same unwilling, lazy manner he answered the questions put to him by his own lawyer.

'Continue your story, witness,' the president commanded.

'I was still running, when all of a sudden this man comes rushing at me, jumping over the fence.'

The young fellow smiled sarcastically, and muttered something, scraping his feet on the floor.

The beggar was soon relieved by a thick, fat peasant, who spoke quick, carefully-chosen words in a clear tenor voice:

'We've long had our suspicions about him, although he's a quiet chap to look at and not a smoker; but we noticed all the same that he likes to play about with fire ... I had come home by the last train – the sky was clouded – when suddenly near the corn-stacks in the field – whizz-z-z! – something goes off, just like a rocket.'

The prisoner jumped to his feet, shoved the warders aside and shouted indignantly:

'You lie, damn you! "Like a rocket," indeed! What do you know about it! As though a fire ever broke out like that! – whizz – flare-up! You are blind, all of you! At first little snails come out, little red snails that crawl up the sides of the stacks, then they swell up and join together – and only then the whole thing flares up! And you say – "all of a sudden!" ...'

His face had become crimson, he shook his head violently and his eyes flashed fire. He was very excited and spoke in a didactic manner, with great force. The judges, the jury, the audience – all sat in a dazed silence, listening. A. I. Lanin, rising from his seat, turned to him, watching him closely. The prisoner stretched his arms wider and wider apart, and raising them above his head continued excitedly:

'Yes, that's how it begins; then it gets to work, shaking like a mast in the wind. Once it's like that it's as swift as a bird; oh yes, you can't catch it then, you can't! At first they crawl like snails, but it's from them that the flames start – all the harm comes from them, those little red snails. It's them that you've got to get hold of – seize them – and into the well with them! It would be a good plan to make sieves, deep iron sieves like those one uses for flour, catch the snails in them, and throw them into the bogs, rivers, wells. There wouldn't be any fires then. You know the saying: "If you don't check the fire in time, you'll let it get loose."* These idiots all lie like blind men . . .'

The fire-catcher sank heavily back on his bench, shook out his mane of hair that had become dishevelled during his speech, blew his nose and sighed. The whole of our case fell to the ground for with his next few words he admitted to having committed five arsons, but added in explanation, with considerable concern in his voice:

'They're much too quick, those darned snails, there's no catching them.'

V. V. Behr pronounced the usual sentence in a dull voice: '. . . owing to the complete responsibility of the accused for his actions . . .'

Lanin appealed for the opinion of a medical expert. The judges, after a whispered conference, refused this; the prosecutor delivered a short speech, Lanin a long and very eloquent one, then the jury left the court and seven minutes later returned with their verdict:

'Guilty . . .'

Listening thoughtfully to the verdict, the condemned man replied indifferently to Lanin's suggestion of an appeal, as though the matter did not interest him at all.

'Well, if you like, of course, you can appeal.'

The warder whispered something to the young fellow, and he answered him loudly:

'Of course: I tell you they're all blind, every one of them.'

6

There was a great forest fire in the year 1893 or 1894 beyond the Volga, opposite Nizhni Novgorod; the flames spread over hundreds of acres. An acrid, opaline smoke hung over the town, and an orange-coloured sun hung in the smoke, a sun without rays, a weird, pitiful sun that gleamed unhealthily in the murky waters of the Volga, as though about to sink to the muddy bottom

* Russian proverb.

of the river. The meadows beyond the Volga acquired a brownish hue and the town itself seemed to be dyed with dull, mud-stained colours. In the smoky, suffocating mist all sounds were deadened; the bees deserted the gardens and even the in-domitable sparrows began to chirp in lower tones and fly in a less hurried manner.

It was depressing to watch the discoloured sun set behind the Volga and sink into the earth, and to know that there would be none of the usual splendours of sunset. At night one could see, above the black wall of the distant forest, a dragon of fire moving its notched spine and breathing black clouds into the sky, like some dragon of ancient myth.

The smoke filled the streets and penetrated into the rooms of the houses – the whole town became one vast smoking-room. Cursing and coughing, people came out at night on to the steep bank of the river, on to the 'Slope' and, watching the flames beyond, ate ices and drank lemonade and beer, telling each other that it was the peasants who had set fire to the trees. One day someone said gloomily:

'It is the first rehearsal of the play: "The agony of the earth".'

A priest whom I knew, gazing at the horizon with the red eyes of a drunkard, muttered: 'There's something apocalyptic about it – meanwhile, let's have a drink . . .'

All these jokes seemed to me to be out of place and irritated me intensely; in fact everything that was said in those blurred, suffocating days unveiled mercilessly the barrenness and bore-dom of every-day life.

An infantry officer, a dreamer, who was composing a 'Botany in Verse for Middle-aged Maidens,' proposed that I should accompany him to the scene of the fire: some soldiers of his company were working there. We rode to the place on a stuffy night, on two of the regimental horses; the ferry took us across the river to the village of Bor, and the well-fed horses, snorting angrily, cantered along the sandy road into the suffocating fog. Enfolding the peaceful fields in a deathly shroud, the fog thinned above our heads into wisps of muslin, through which the dull sunrise slowly broke. The nearer we came to the forest, the more blue the fog appeared, till it tore at our throats and made our eyes water. The orderly with us sneezed loudly, and the officer, wiping the lenses of his eye-glasses and coughing harshly, recited some of his verses, boldly making 'love' rhyme with 'rough'.

Three peasants with spades and axes stood aside to let us pass, and the infantry poet shouted out to them:

'Where is the detachment working?'

'Dunno . . .'

The orderly, taking a pull at the reins, asked them:

'Where are the soldiers?'

A peasant in a red shirt pointed with his axe to the left:

'Over there . . .'

In a few minutes we came to a grove where some men in white shirts were working amid a thicket of fir and pine trees. A subaltern came up to us and reported that all was well, only the Chuvasch* soldier had burnt himself a bit. Then he 'took the liberty to say that' in his opinion it was useless to carry on any longer.

'It's done its business over here, sir: the fire moves along on the top in a half-circle; it'll swallow up this bit over here, and as it's got nothing more to do farther on, it'll just die out by itself . . .'

Then, pointing with his lean hand to the right, he warned us:

'When you go over there, mind that turf-marsh – the dry one. The fire's crawling low down in that direction. The people are beginning to get anxious . . .'

The officer looked worried, too, evidently not knowing quite what orders to give; but at that moment a big bearded peasant emerged from the wood like a great bear, carrying a cudgel in his hand and wearing a tin-plate on his chest. He took off his hat, strewn with ashes, and gazed motionless at the officer with an intelligent look in his dark blue eyes.

'You're the bailiff, aren't you?'

'Yes, sir.'

'Well, how is it going on?'

'It's burning, sir.'

* Mongol population of Northern Russia.

'We must carry on the fight,' said the officer. 'The forest is enormously valuable . . . Yes . . . The forest, my dear fellow – it's not merely trees, but the home of human beings, like for instance, your village . . .'

'Ours is a poor village . . .'

On the ground at my feet millions of ants were crawling in dark rows, getting out of the way of a large beetle that was striding rapidly along the road. I went back to look at the place whence this ants'-heap was transplanting itself.

I became aware of a strange rustle in the air, as though some invisible being were walking beside me, trampling the grass and stirring the leaves. Even the branches of the trees trembled uneasily, incomprehensibly. Behind us walked the bailiff, telling us of his troubles.

'Here I am – walking about for three whole days . . . You're one of the authorities, aren't you? Ah – you've come to have a look . . . So that's all right . . . Come this way. I'll take you to a hillock not far from here where you can see everything beautifully.'

The sandy hillock was shaded by large pine-trees, their tops resembling chalices, but filled with an opaline muddiness. In front of the hill, in a valley, some emaciated fir-trees and slim, graceful birches were scattered here and there; silvery poplars trembled anxiously; farther on the trees clustered more and more closely together, and among them the fir-trees rose again, their bronze trunks covered with the greenish tint of lichen.

At the roots of the trees merry little flames ran along like squirrels, flourishing their red tails, while a low blue smoke crept over the ground. One could see well how the playful fire climbed on to the bark of the trunks, twined itself around them, hiding away somewhere; and then, behind it, the golden ants came crawling, while the green lichen became first grey, then black. Now the fire appeared again from somewhere and began to gnaw at the rusty grass and low shrubs, then hid again, and suddenly a whole crowd of quick red little beasts appeared, scurrying and bustling among the roots.

Leaning on his cudgel, the bailiff grumbled:

'Our men are there . . . God help them . . .'

We could see no one at that distance, but across the crackling and rustling and far-away drone we could hear the short strokes of the axe, the resounding sighs and heavy, scraping sound of falling trees. A field-mouse rolled from a bank to my feet, a white hare shone as it raced across the marsh.

There was no chirping, although the forests of the Volga are rich with singing birds; nor were there any bees, nor bumble-bees, nor wasps in that heavy atmosphere, that hot, blue, intoxicating fog. It was sad to watch the green leaves take on a deadly greyness or become covered with a red rust; often, without flaring up at all, the leaves of the poplars simply crumbled to the earth, like ashen butterflies, plaintively exposing the thin branches. But sometimes the leaves, dried by the heat, blazed up all at once and then scattered in hundreds of red and yellow moths. I could see the luxurious fir-trees, far away in the distance, rapidly lose their dark-green velvety brilliance and sprinkle broadcast a thick rain of ruddy golden sparks that reminded one of golden commas. Now they whirl up all together in the air with a light, cheerful crackling, strewing the whole pyramid of the fir-tree; then shoot up and disappear, leaving the tree quite black, only the ends of its naked branches glittering here and there with small yellow flowers. Now another fir-tree rapidly bursts into blossom and dies in the same way; then another, and another. There is a sharp crack, and a low-growing tree splits like a rotten egg, and reddish-yellow snakes twist about and crawl in every direction across the marsh, lifting their sharp heads and peering out of the grass, stinging the trunks of the trees on their way. The delicate leaves of the birch rapidly become yellow as the fire climbs swiftly along the white trunk; the resinous bark, the branches, smoulder with a blue smoke; thin jets of flame curl up with a wonderful beauty, whistling as they do so. And in that low whistle fragments of songs seemed to ring out – strange and deep songs.

One was imperatively drawn nearer and nearer the fire. The bailiff called out and unconsciously began descending the hill, brandishing his stick and exclaiming:

'By heaven, what a sight! Oh, my God, Thou createst wonders . . .'

The drone in the wood ceased suddenly, to be supplanted by the wail of an anguished wolf. 'Uh-uh-uh . . . !'

'They're running,' the bailiff said.

And he was right. To our left, far away between the trees, human figures appeared running. They appeared so rapidly that they seemed to have been thrown out of the wood. To the right, on the marsh, two soldiers emerged in high boots grey with ashes and in shirts without belts. They were leading a short little peasant, holding him under his arms like a drunken man. The peasant was snorting and spitting, his dishevelled beard and torn shirt spattered with blood, his nose and lips torn, while his staring eyes seemed to be deprived of sight. When they came nearer we saw that he was smiling with a plaintive, childish smile.

'Where are you taking him?' the bailiff asked sternly.

The Tartar soldier, grinning good-naturedly, answered:

'He was committing arson, – dragging the fire from one place to another.'

His companion added angrily:

'Yes, he was blowing up the fire, making it blaze. We saw him.'

'Making a blaze indeed! I was only lighting my pipe.'

'We'd been told to look out for you, and we saw you set fire to a branch and carry it along.'

'Set fire to it indeed! It was already burning and I just kicked it along.'

Here one of the soldiers gave the man a blow on the neck.

'Now – now – don't you strike him,' ordered the bailiff. 'That's one of our men . . . He is, I don't mind telling you, not quite right in his head.'

'Then why don't you keep him chained up?'

They began to argue angrily, while the flames danced on the marsh, meeting the peasants who came running out of the wood. About seven men, jumping heavily, came in our direction; they ran up to us, panting, coughing hoarsely and swearing, and fell on the sand at the foot of the hill:

'Precious nearly caught us!'

'What a lot of birds were burnt down there! . . .'

At the sight of these blackened, exhausted people, the soldiers calmed down, and releasing the man to whom they had been giving a thrashing, disappeared in the warm clouds of smoke. The smoke had become more blue and more acrid as time went on. The sparks still glittered on the marsh, ringing the trunks of the trees. The yellow leaves of the birches and elders withered and curled up; the lichen on the trunks of the fir-trees stirred uncannily and became a live thing, reminding one of a swarm of bees.

It grew very hot on the hill; it was difficult to breathe. The peasants, having rested a little, disappeared one by one into the thicket on the top of the hill.

The bailiff turned to the beaten man:

'You are always getting into a mess, Nikita,' he grumbled. 'Nothing ever teaches you anything, neither a fire, nor a church procession . . .'

The man remained silent, picking his front teeth with a dirty finger.

'They're quite right when they say you ought to be on a chain, they are.'

The man took his finger out of his mouth and rubbed it on the edge of his shirt. He moved his head from one side to the other, his motionless eyes scanned the marsh watching the jets of smoke. The whole marsh was smouldering, and blue and purple ringlets of smoke emerged here and there out of the black earth. And everywhere they were followed by flames that flared up suddenly in a pointed heap out of the turf, balanced themselves, shook, and disappeared again, leaving behind them a golden-red stain, from which thin red threads stretched out on all sides, joining presently into knots of new fires.

Suddenly right at the foot of the hill a juniper-tree flared up like a heap of cotton wool. The bailiff, brandishing his hat, stepped back.

'Look out!' he cried; 'we'd better be getting away from here . . .'

We turned, and made our way across the thickly carpeted ground, the bailiff muttering: 'What's the good of me walking about here? What can a man do against such flames? Meanwhile my own work's at a standstill. More than a thousand people, maybe, are wasting their time in the same way . . .'

We descended through the thicket into a valley at the bottom of which a stream glittered dully. Here the smoke lay thicker still, so that the stream itself seemed but a ringlet of smoke. A quail rose suddenly out of the grass and fell like a stone among the shrubs, a small snake crawled rapidly past us, and behind it, like a grey clod, a hedgehog was careering towards the stream.

'We'll catch 'em up,' said Nikita, and stooping his head he crashed like a bull through the shrubs.

'You look out what you're doing, and don't play the fool,' the bailiff shouted after him; then, looking furtively at me, he added: 'He's a bit wrong in his head – his house was burnt down three times, so he's just a bit . . . you know. The soldiers swear he started the fire, but he doesn't go as far as that. All the same, his brain's gone, and he's always out for trouble . . .'

Our eyes smarted with the smoke and kept watering; my nose tickled abominably, and it was hard to breathe. The bailiff sneezed loudly and looked round anxiously, brandishing his cudgel.

'Look at that: see where it's thrown itself!'

In front of us, along the juniper-bushes that fringed the valley, small spurts of fire were dancing with sparrow-like hops. They resembled a flock of bullfinches, their pointed wings glittering rapidly in the grass, their heads dipping and nodding without a sound.

'Nikita,' called the bailiff and listened. We could hear a dry, crackling sound, a warning hiss and a low whistle. Somewhere far away the drone of a crowd came to our ears.

'Blast that man!' shouted the bailiff. 'He's more trouble than the rest of the people put together. I hope they won't catch him. Flames go to his head like wine to a drunkard's. Wherever there's a fire he's the first to rush there like a madman. He'll come and open his eyes wide and stare dumbfounded, as though he were nailed to the ground. It never occurs to him to help – he just stands and grins. And if people shove him away from one side of a fire he'll run round to the other. He's just crazy about fire . . .'

Looking back, I saw that the flames, which were coming lower and lower, were hurrying along, as though trying to catch us up; and the water of the stream, now become crimson, flashed with golden rays.

'Niki – ita!'

Suddenly someone came running out of the forest in front of us. The bailiff stopped and wiped his streaming eyes as a young fellow with his chest bare and his shirt rolled round his head like a turban emerged from the trees.

'Where are you rushing to?'

Pointing backwards and panting, the young fellow replied:

'They're all running away from there . . . the fire's gone up to the top . . . don't go there . . . it came quite suddenly . . . Ough! . . . I didn't half get a fright!'

'Well, where's one to go now?' the bailiff muttered. 'Let's go straight on; what do you think? I don't know this part of the forest – it's no good us going over there. We should only get lost. The people have only one thought today – to hide from the men in command . . .'

His voice became more and more bitter.

'A fine life this is! Whether it's a drowned man, or a man found dead in the wood, or a murdered man found on the road, or a fire – they must needs put the blame on a peasant. Haven't the peasants got their own business to attend to? What's the good of it all? . . . Niki – ita! – blast you! . . .'

When we had gone a short distance through a young, sparsely planted pine-forest, we came out on to a meadow in which about fifty peasants were gathered. Some of the women had brought pails of 'kvas' and bread. Catching sight of the bailiff, the men called out:

'How much longer have we got to swallow this smoke? Our work's waiting at home . . .'

Bluish ringlets of smoke crawled about on the grass, and stroked the spades and the axes. A fine, grey rain of cinders, unseen in the opaline mist, fell on the heads of the men, who, like the grass, were ashen from it. The broad, stretched-out paws of the fir-trees seemed to be covered with foam. It was a sign that the fire was spreading along the top.

33

'Get away from here!' the bailiff commanded. 'Into the field, all of you!'

The men rose heavily and, grumbling at each other and at the women, went along the ride in the forest into a fathomless grey hole of smoke. I wandered with them from field to field until nightfall; at our side two policemen rode on their well-fed horses, driving the crowd stupidly from spot to spot. One of them, a little brisk dark-haired man, brandished his *nagaika**
and shouted:

'You hounds! There's no need for you to get excited; it's not your belongings that are burning . . .'

At night I lay on the dry, hot ground and watched the purple flames swell and balance in the sky over the forest as though bringing a sacrifice to propitiate the Wood-Goblin, incensed with thick smoke. Small, red animals jumped and crawled on the tops of the trees; bright, broad-winged birds whirled up into the smoky sky; and everywhere the fire played, full of magic and caprice. At night the forest acquired an indescribably weird, fairy-like aspect: its blue wall seemed to grow higher, and inside it, among the black trunks, the red hairy little beasts scampered wildly. They ran to the roots, and, clasping the trunks, crawled up like dexterous monkeys, struggled with one another, breaking the branches; hissed and roared and snarled; and the forest cracked as though a thousand dogs were gnawing bones.

The silhouette of the fire among the black trees changed like a kaleidoscope, and the dance of the flames was untiring and relentless. Here a large, red bear of fire rolls out on the meadow, jumping clumsily and turning somersaults; losing tufts of his flaming hair, he crawls along the trunk as though to gather honey, and, reaching the top of the tree, hugs its branches in the hairy embrace of his crimson paws, balances on them, strewing pink needles in a rain of golden sparks. Now he heaves himself lightly across to the next tree, while on the one which he has left numerous blue candles light up on the bare, black branches; purple mice rush up and down the boughs, and by their rapid movements one can see how capriciously the blue ringlets of

* Whip.

34

smoke dance; hundreds of fiery ants climb up and down the bark of the trunk.

At times the fire crept slowly out of the forest, like a cat on the look-out for a bird, and then, suddenly lifting its pointed muzzle into the air, watched as though choosing its prey. Or else another bear, a sparkling, fiery beast, would appear from the thicket and crawl on its stomach, throwing out huge paws and raking together the grass into its huge red mouth. Or else a crowd of little dwarfs in yellow caps would come running out of the wood, followed from afar in the smoke by a dark being, tall as a mast, who marched brandishing a red banner and whistling. In light hops, like a hare, a red clod hurries away from the forest, all covered with needles like a hedgehog, flourishing a red tail of smoke behind it. And fiery worms and golden ants crawl about the trunks; red beetles wheel with dazzling wings.

The air grows more and more stifling and acrid, the smoke thick and hot; the earth smoulders, one's eyes seemed scorched, eyelashes burnt, and one can feel the hairs of one's eyebrows move with the hot blast. It is impossible to stand the smoky air which tears one's lungs any longer, yet one feels strangely unwilling to go: when shall we have the chance again to watch such a magnificent feast of fire?

Out of the wood a huge serpent comes twisting itself crookedly and hides in the grass, nodding its pointed head; then suddenly it disappears as though diving into the earth. I gather my feet under me, expecting it to appear next moment at my side – for it is me that it is looking for. But I cannot move: the weird feeling of danger intoxicates me even more than the heat and the smoke.

# Arzamas Characters

I AM sitting on the outskirts of the town, on a bare hillock sparsely covered with turf. The graves around me are scarcely noticeable; they have been trampled by the hoofs of cattle and their mounds dispersed by the winds. I am sitting beside the wall of a small brick building that looks like a toy house covered with an iron roof; from a distance one might mistake it for a chapel, but a closer inspection shows it to be more like a dog-kennel. Behind the iron-studded door is preserved a collection of chains, whips, knouts, and other instruments of torture with which the people who are buried here were tortured. They have been left here as a memento for the town: a warning to those who rebel!

But the inhabitants have already forgotten who the people buried here were. Some say that they are Stenka Rasin's cossacks, others affirm that they are the Mordva and Chuvasch clans of Emelian Pugacheff. And it is only the eternally drunken old beggar Zatinshchikoff who still boasts:

'We stood up against both of 'em.'

From the arid, hillocky field the low grey houses of the town seem like heaps of refuse. They give one the impression of being pressed into the earth. Here and there their roofs are overgrown with thick dusty grass and weeds. The towers of ten churches and one fire-station stand erect among the blocks of grey rubbish; the white walls of the churches glitter in the sun, looking for all the world like clean patches on dirty rags.

Today is a holiday. The townsfolk attended church until midday, spent the time from twelve to two eating and drinking, and now they are resting. All is silent in the town; even the shouts of the children are stilled.

The day is oppressively hot. The iron-blue sky is pouring invisible molten lead on to the earth. There is something impenetrable and foreboding about the sky: the blinding white rays of the sun seem to have been spilt across the clouds and absorbed by them.

The pitiful, meagre and rusty grass on the graves is motionless and dry. The ground cracks and scales under the sun like dried fish. On the left of the hillocks beyond the river (invisible from where I sit), a mirage flickers over the barren fields; the broad tower of the village beyond the river trembles and disappears in it. A hundred years ago that village belonged to the celebrated Saltichikha, who made her name notorious by her refined cruelty to her slaves.

And the town looks as though it were covered with a blanket – in reality with a cloud of blurred, yellowish dust. Perhaps it is the breath of the people sleeping in it.

*

Strange people live in that town. The owner of the felt factory, a steadfast, intelligent man, has been reading Karamsin's *History of the Russian State* for four years, and has now reached the ninth volume.

'A great work,' he says, stroking the leather binding of the book with respect. 'A Tsar's book. One can see at once it was written by a master. On winter nights one's only got to start reading it and one forgets all one's troubles. It's as good as the fairy tales a nurse tells to a child. 'Tis a great consolation for a man, a book is. Especially if it's wisely written.'

One day, playing with his sumptuous beard, he said to me with an amiable little smile:

'Do you want to have a look at something curious? Opposite the back-yard of my house lives a doctor who is often visited by a lady – a strange lady, not from our town. I can watch them making love to each other from the dormer window in my attic; the curtain of their window is only half drawn down and through the top pane you can watch them enjoying themselves. I've gone so far as to buy a telescope from an old Tartar, and sometimes invite my friends for a lark . . . An interesting debauchery . . .'

The hairdresser, Baliassin, calls himself 'the city's barber'.

37

He is long and lanky, walks with his shoulders thrown back and his chest thrown forward. He has the head of an adder – small, with yellow eyes and a mildly suspicious glance. The town considers Baliassin to be a clever man and turns to him for treatment more readily than it does to the local doctor.

'Our inside's a simple one, while doctors are for the learned folk,' the inhabitants say.

The hairdresser bleeds them and applies poultices. Quite recently he operated upon a corn and the patient died from blood-poisoning. This inspired someone with the following joke:

'He's a very thorough surgeon: he was asked to cut off a corn and he cut the whole man off the earth . . .'

Baliassin is troubled by the thought of the insecurity of life.

'I think the scientists are all lying,' he says. 'Even the way of the sun is not known to them for certain. For instance, I sometimes watch the sun set and think: what if it didn't rise tomorrow? No sunrise – and there's an end of us all! It might get hitched up on something – a comet, for example – and then we should have to go on living in the dark. Or else it might just stop on the other side of the earth, and then we should have to put up with eternal darkness over here. I don't doubt that the sun knows what it's doing. If it ever got tired of us we should have to make forest fires and light huge wood-piles in order to be able to see what we were doing.'

He laughed, closing his eyes, and went on:

'A fine sky we should have then! There'd be stars in it, but neither sun nor moon. In the place of the moon there'd just be a small black ball staring at one – if it's true that the moon borrows its light from the sun. You'd be able to do just what you liked – nothing could be seen! Good business for thieves, but pretty unpleasant for everyone else, eh?'

One day, as he was cutting my hair, he said to me:

'People have got used to everything. Nothing frightens them nowadays, not even fires nor anything else. There are some places where they have earthquakes and floods – but we never have anything here. Not even cholera – although it's been raging everywhere else! And man needs something unusual, something

38

terrible to happen, to keep him up to the mark. Terror for the soul is like a Turkish bath for the body – most wholesome . . .'

\*

The one-eyed manager of the town baths, who is also a 'man milliner', making caps out of old trousers, is a man whom the whole town is afraid of. Nobody loves him. When they meet him in the street the townsfolk brush past him apprehensively and glare at him like a wolf. Occasionally, however, some 'tough' marches straight at him, as though about to butt him in the side. Then the hat-maker stands aside, letting the man pass, and in his turn follows the aggressor with a smile in his half-closed eyes.

'Why do they hate you so much?' I asked him one day.

'Because I'm merciless, that's why,' he answered boastfully. 'It's my habit to drag into court every man who doesn't deal straight with me.'

The whites of his eyes are intersected with a fine network of arteries, and a round, rusty-coloured pupil flashes proudly inside that net. The hat-maker is a thickset man with long arms and bandy legs. He resembles a spider.

'It's true people don't seem to take a fancy to me just because I know the law,' he went on, rolling a cigarette of cheap tobacco. 'If a strange sparrow flew into my orchard I'd say to it, "Just you step across to the court!" I had a law-suit with a man not long ago that went on for four months. It was all over a cock. The judge said to me: "You must have been born a man by mistake, for your nature's that of a gadfly!" Some of them have even beaten me for my mercilessness, but it isn't good for any man to beat me. It's like grasping a hot iron – one only gets one's hand burnt. As soon as they've finished it's my turn to start on them again . . .'

He whistled shrilly. He was, it is true, a pettifogger; the local judge had his hands full of the man's petitions and complaints. His relations with the police were, however, of the best; they said he was a fine hand at writing reports denouncing his fellow-townsmen, and that he kept a diary in which he noted down all the crimes committed by the townspeople.

'Why do you do it?' I asked him.

'Just because I respect my own rights,' he replied.

\*

The fat, bald lock-and-coppersmith Pushkareff is a free-thinker, an atheist. Pressing his strangely curved flabby lips, the colour of rain-worms, between his teeth, he talks in a hoarse bass voice:

'God is nothing but a lie. There's nothing above us, only blue air. And all our thoughts come from this blue air. We live and think in a blue way – that's where the riddle is buried. The essence of our lives – yours, mine – is very simple: we were – we are no more . . .'

He can read and write and he has read many novels. The one which he remembers best of all is entitled *The Bloody Hand*.

'There's a French bishop in it who revolted and besieged the town of La Rochelle. Fighting against him was Captain Lacousin – and what that doughnut didn't do, my word! It makes one's mouth water to read it. His sword was always ready and never failed: he'd just poke it out – and there was another dead 'un. Some soldier! . . .'

One day Pushkareff said to me:

'I was sitting like this one night, on a holiday, reading a book. Suddenly the local accountant – "statistician" he calls himself – comes to see me, saying:

' "I'd like to get to know you, chum."

' "Well – get along," I said. But I kept my back turned to him all the while. He began to twist this way and that; I pretended to be a fool – sat there and stared at the wall.

' "I've heard," says he, "that you don't believe in God?"

'Here I flared up at him: "What?" I said, "what are you getting at? Why, what are the churches there for, the priests, the monks? What if I report you to the police for trying to induce me to renounce the faith?"

'Then he got frightened and said, "Excuse me, I thought . . ."

' "That's just it," I retorted; "you think about what you've got no business to think. I've no use for those thoughts of yours."

'He rolled out of my house like a ball. Soon after this he committed suicide.

'I don't like them Zemstvo *folk – they're false people. They suck the peasants: that's how they live. There was no other way to get rid of these learned folk, so they gave them the Zemstvo. "Try counting," they were told! So they've gone on counting ever since! It's all the same to a man what work he has to do, so long as he gets well paid for it . . .'

*

The watchmaker Korzoff, nicknamed 'the pointer flea', a small, hairy little man with long arms, is a patriot and a lover of beauty.

'There's no stars anywhere like the Russian stars,' he says, watching the sky with his round eyes, flat as buttons. 'The Russian potato, too, is the finest in the world, so far as taste goes. Russian accordions, too – the best in the world. Russian locks as well. We can pull a long nose at America over lots of things we make.'

He writes verses, and when he is drunk he sings them himself. His poetry is meant to be absurd – at least, so it seems – but the song which he sings oftener than any other is this:

> A little blue birdie, a titmouse,
> Sings underneath my window;
> It will lay a little egg.
> The day after to-morrow
> I will steal that little egg,
> And carry it off to the owl's nest.
> I don't care what happens next
> To this daring head of mine.
> Oh, why must I dream every day
> That my skull is being pierced by an owl –
> The same night-birdie that
> Lives alone in the forest?

Korzoff sings this song to a dashing, cheerful tune. And his skull is faultlessly round and quite bald, save that a rusty-coloured fringe of curly hair hangs from one ear to the other at the back of his head. He loves going into raptures over the scenery, although the environs of the town are dreary and deserted, swollen with graves, intersected with ditches, and hideously depressing. But the watchmaker stands on the edge

* Local government.

of blurred waters that exhale a filthy smell from the poison pumped into them by the felt factory, and cries with lyrical enthusiasm:

'How glorious! What exquisite beauty, eh? Broad, wide, flat. You can go wherever you like. I love it madly, this beautiful country of ours.'

The courtyard of his house is dirty, overgrown with nettles and weeds, and littered up with old wood and iron. In the middle stands and rots an old sofa, tufts of horse-hair protruding from its seat. The rooms are dusty, not cosy – everything is pushed against the walls; an old piece of lead tubing is tied to the chain of the clock in place of the weight.

In a corner Korzoff's sick wife moans and grumbles, while in the yard her sister skips about silently; this sister is an old maid, yellow and thin, with protruding teeth; on her feet are a pair of men's slippers; the back of her skirt is hitched up to her knees and exhibits legs covered with blue, knotty veins.

Korzoff has invented a lock that can be loaded with three gun-cartridges and that fires when a key is put in it. It weighs twelve pounds and looks like an oblong box. I told Korzoff that I thought it ought to shoot into the sky, not at anyone who wanted to turn the key in it.

'No, it'll shoot you straight in the face!' the inventor assured me proudly.

He is liked as one likes queer fellows. Or perhaps the townsfolk appreciate the fact that he has very bad luck at cards and that every one can win money off him. He is fond of thrashing children – it is said that he thrashed his own son to death – but this does not prevent his friends from inviting him to all the executions of the youngsters whom they catch robbing their gardens and orchards – as a connoisseur.

*

Leisurely, his hands clasped behind his back, long, lanky Yakov Lessnikoff, with his long, narrow beard and his large, gloomy face, walks about the town. His hair is unkempt, he is shabbily dressed in a coat that resembles a monk's cassock; a student's cap adorns the grey, coarse curls on his head. His big, watery eyes seem to be making an effort to remain wide open, as though the man were fighting with sleepiness, for sleep he must not. He keeps yawning, and, looking over people's heads, he asks them with a far-away glance:

'Well, how are things going on?'

The answers, evidently, interest him but little; besides, they are all known to him:

'So-so. Not bad. We're getting on.'

He has the reputation of being very fond of women and a great debauchee. Korzoff proudly informed me that: 'He once lived even with a Spaniard, in the olden days. Well, now, of course, he doesn't scorn Mordovian women either.'

They say that Lessnikoff is the bastard of some important personage – a bishop or a general. He owns several acres of orchard land and pasture, but has given it all in trust to the villagers and lives in solitude in the flat of my neighbour, a clerk in the Treasury, a sick man.

One evening he was rolling about on the grass under the lime-tree in the garden, drinking iced beer and growling as he yawned. The clerk, a thin, sour yet amiable little man in spectacles, came up to him:

'Well, Yasha how goes it?'

'I'm bored,' said Lessnikoff. 'I'm wondering all the while what I can do to pass the time.'

'It's a bit late in the day for you to begin doing anything.'

'Ye-es. I suppose you're right . . .'

'You're a bit too old for it . . .'

'Ye-es . . .'

They remained silent for a while. Then Lessnikoff muttered slowly:

'It's very dull. Suppose one were to believe in God, for a change?'

The clerk approved:

'It's a good idea. You'd be able to go to church occasionally.'

And Lessnikoff, with a wailing yawn, concluded:

'Yes . . . that's it.'

*

Zimin, a shopkeeper and a churchwarden, a cunning peasant, said to me one day:

'People are suffering from their brains. It's brains that are the cause of all the trouble in the world. We've got no simplicity left – we've lost it all. Our heart's honest all right – but our brain's a swindler!'

\*

I sit gulping down the hot breeze, calling to mind the speeches, the movements, the faces of these men I have described, and all the time I am watching the town, enveloped in a hot, opaline mist. Why should this town exist at all – to say nothing of the people inhabiting it?

It was here that Leo Tolstoy experienced for the first time the horror of life, the 'Arzamas', the Mordovian horror; but can it be only for this that the town has existed ever since the time of Ivan the Terrible? I do not think there is any other country where people talk such a lot and think so incoherently and fruitlessly as they do in Russia, particularly in provincial Russia.

The thoughts of Arzamas are fortuitous and remind one of birds tortured by village urchins, which sometimes in fear fly into dark rooms in order to dash themselves to pieces against the impenetrable illusion of the window-panes, transparent as air itself. Sterile 'blue' thoughts they are.

I watch these townsfolk intently, and what strikes me about them first is that they live in a stupid way and, purely as a result of this, they live dirtily, dully, bitterly and criminally. They are gifted people – but only for anecdotes.

A splashing sound comes from the river – the boys of the town have gone to bathe. But there are not many of them in the town today – most of them have gone to the woods, the fields, the ravines, where it is cooler. A fine blue smoke rises from the gardens: the housewives have awakened from their afternoon naps and are putting on the kettles to boil for their tea.

The thin voice of a small girl rattles piercingly:

'Oh mammy, oh dear, don't beat me on the stomach . . .'
And the wail seems to sink into the earth.

The heat becomes more and more oppressive. The sun seems

to have come to a standstill, and the earth gasps with a dry, dusty sultriness. It is as though the sky had become still more molten – and this dull molten hue exasperates one, yet fills one with anxiety. Surely this sky is not the same as it is everywhere else? It must be a special sky, a local one, a flat, indurate sky, created by the heavy breathing of the people who live in this strange town.

The blue darkness beyond dies out taking on the colour of smoked glass, and, growing denser, comes nearer and nearer the town, like a transparent though impenetrable wall. Like black dots, flies flash past in disorder, and again one is reminded of the impenetrability of glass. And the hot, heavy silence grows thicker and heavier all the time.

In the silence the half-sleepy, languid voice of a woman rings out like a song:

'Taissia – dressing?'

And a voice which sounds kin to it, only in a somewhat lower key, answers languorously:

'Dressing – yes.'

A silence. Then again:

'Taissia – are you putting on your blue dress?'

'Ye-es . . . the blue one . . .'

# Peculiar Tramps

THE following notice from Vladivostok appeared in the review entitled *The Doctor*:

We regret to report the death of Dr A. P. Riuminski, who lived here for many years as a tramp. During his illness the unfortunate man was taken to the town hospital, where, however, he was refused admission because of an old debt which he had never settled. He was therefore brought to the police-station to die. After his death the tramps arranged to give him an impressive funeral, and one of them delivered the following farewell address: 'You lived among us,' he said, 'deserted and forgotten by your own kin. . . . Together we sinned and together we suffered. Now, we have come here to bear you to your grave – the resting-place for which we all long.' . . .

It so happened that I had twice met the man, the first time in 1891 near Maikop on the Laba, and again ten years later in Yalta. On the high road, over the Laba, a group of Rostoff tramps were breaking road-metal. I came across them at night, when their day's work was ended and they were getting ready to have some tea. A fat tramp with a long grey beard was busy boiling the kettle over a small wood-fire; three of his comrades were resting among the shrubs at the side of the road, while on a heap of stones sat a man dressed in a light cotton summer suit, and wearing a wide-brimmed straw hat and white shoes. He was holding a cigarette between his fingers, and as he slashed the grey, thin smoke of the tobacco with a cane, he talked to those around him, without troubling to glance in their direction.

'Well, what's the trouble?' he asked of a young man near by.

The dull red reflections of the sunset trembled on the blue waters of the Laba. A heat haze rose from the rust-coloured, shaven steppe; huge stacks of straw glimmered like heaps of brocade behind the river; on the misty horizon the purple hill

46

rose to meet the sky, and somewhere far away a threshing-machine was droning patiently.

A young man, whose swollen face showed that he was suffering from dropsy, answered sulkily. 'Don't you try to throw dust in my eyes, sir,' he said. 'I'm a medical man myself.'

'Is that so?'

'Yes. So there you are.'

'Is that so?' repeated the other, brandishing his cane and slashing at the smoke. Then he glanced at me in a curious way. 'And who are you, young man?' he asked.

'Just a young man,' I answered, and the tramps smiled in approval.

The other's protruding eyes were strangely brilliant. They smiled in a mocking way, and seemed somehow to cling to my face. That dry, devouring glance gave me an unpleasant tickling sensation which I can recall today. He had a fine, well-groomed, clean-shaven face. Clearly he had not lost his pride. When one of the tramps, lazily rolling over, brushed against him, the man started and quickly moved his legs out of the way, and with his slim, white hand raised his cane in the air in warning.

On his fingers he wore the 'stone of misfortune' set in a golden ring, and in the rainbow-tinted colour of it there was something akin to the proud gleam in his eyes. In a lazy but aggravating, provoking baritone he kept asking people who they were, and when they answered him unwillingly, sullenly, he was in no way abashed, but shifted his piercing glance from one face to another and continued his questions.

'And what will happen,' he asked, 'if everybody begins to live as irresponsibly as you do?'

'What do I care about it?' the medical man murmured angrily, and the bearded man at the fire joined in with a hoarse whisper. 'And you,' he asked, 'what about yourself?' adding triumphantly, 'There, you see!'

Quite suddenly, and with marvellous rapidity, the southern night swept down upon the steppe; a thick sprinkling of stars flared up; the waters of the river beyond trembled like black velvet, and golden sparks flashed here and there. In the solemn and mournful silence the bitter smell of tobacco seemed for some reason to become more perceptible. The men brought out bread and bacon from their wallets and began to eat, while the gentleman, tapping his shoes with his cane, kept up his fire of questions:

'Well,' he enquired 'and what will happen if one breaks every link with life?'

'Nothing will happen,' replied the grey-haired man sullenly.

From somewhere beyond the river came the dreary creaking of a cart and the whistling of a siskin. The fire was dying out, little crimson sparks flew into the darkness, and the charred pieces of smouldering wood slipped noiselessly apart.

'Arkadi Petrovich!' The clear voice of a woman came from afar.

The man with the ring rose at once, flicked the dust off his knees with his cane, and with a friendly gesture disappeared along the shore of the river into the darkness. The others watched him go off in silence.

'Who is that man?' I asked, and they all began to answer me.

'The devil alone knows.' 'He's living here in the cossacks' villa, we hear.' 'Says he's a doctor.'

They spoke loudly on purpose, as though they wished the man to hear what they were saying about him. The thin, red-haired little vagabond with the ulcerated face stretched himself out on the ground, face upwards. 'You can't reach a star by spitting at it,' he murmured.

'We'd better try to find our way to Turkey, my boys,' grumbled the medical student sulkily. 'The Turks are a fine people. I'm fed up with life over here.'

*

One day, many years later, failing to find Dmitri Narkissovich Mamin-Sibiriak in the town park of Yalta, our usual place of meeting, I went to call on him at his boarding-house. As I entered his room I came face to face with a pair of protruding eyes, whose brilliant gleam instantly recalled to me that night on the Laba, the tramps and the doctor in the light summer suit.

'Let me introduce you,' said Dmitri Narkissovich, motioning

48

to his guest with his short, plump hand. 'Here's a poisonous specimen for you!'

The guest raised his head and lowered it again, leaning his chin on the edge of the table, so that he looked as though he had been decapitated. He sat in a crouching attitude, his chair pushed as far away as possible from the table, and his hands hidden under the cloth. From both sides of a bald head shocks of greyish hair stuck out in a provoking way, like horns, disclosing two small ears. The lobes of his ears had a very definite contour and seemed to be swollen. His chin was clean-shaven, but a grey moustache protruded from under his nose, giving him a martial appearance. He wore a blue shirt. His collar, torn and unbuttoned, exposed to view portions of an unwashed neck and a muscular right shoulder. He sat as though he was about to spring across the table. His bare legs, shod in Tartar slippers, peeped out from under his chair. He watched me with curiosity and spoke in a lazy baritone which I recognized.

'There is a fungus,' he said, 'called in Latin *Merulius lacrimans* – the weeping one – which has the wonderful power of drawing moisture out of the atmosphere. A tree, attacked by it, decays with amazing rapidity; and if one beam in a newly-built house becomes infected by it, the whole begins to rot.'

Raising his head, the doctor began slowly to sip his beer. His protruding Adam's apple, which, like his cheeks, was covered with a dark, thick down, moved about as he swallowed his drink. Mamin, already rather drunk, listened to him very attentively, rolling his huge eyes round, and puffing away at a little pipe, which he held close to his Armenian nose. He shook his head from time to time and sniffed, his thick round body sinking lower and lower into his garden chair.

'The fellow's lying the whole time,' he said, as his guest began to drink.

The latter emptied his glass, filled it again, and, passing his tongue over his moustache, wet from the foam, continued to talk.

'Well,' he went on, 'what I wanted to say is that Russian literature is very much like that fungus. It draws out of life its dampness, its filth, its abomination, and unavoidably infects

49

with its gangrene every healthy body that comes into contact with it.'

'Well, what do you say to that?' asked Mamin, jogging me with his elbow.

'Literature is just as unwholesome and gangrenous as that creeping fungus,' insisted his guest, quite unmoved.

Mamin began to abuse the wicked critic violently. Seizing an empty bottle, he struck it against the table, and fearing that he should aim a blow at the bald head of his guest, I suggested that he should take a walk with me; whereupon his visitor rose and gave an unceremonious and, as I thought, artificial yawn.

'I'm going for a walk,' he said with a smile, and went away with the light, rapid step of a trained pedestrian.

Dmitri Narkissovich told me that the man had fastened on to him down at the harbour, after attracting his attention by his wild talk. For two days the man had been irritating him, uttering every sort of slander against literature.

'I can't shake him off,' he said; 'the man's like a leech, and I haven't the heart to send him away. After all, he's a cultured sort of scoundrel. His name is Doctor Arkadi Riuminski, or Riumin, most likely derived from "riumka".* He's a clever devil, as wicked as sin! Drinks like a camel and never gets drunk! I sat drinking with him all day yesterday. He told me he had come here to see his wife, so he says, who is a celebrated actress . . .' Mamin mentioned a name that was famous at that time. 'She is actually here at present, but I'm positive that the fellow's lying!'

Rolling his eyes fiercely, he began chaffing me.

'There's material for you,' he jeered. 'Here's your hero. What a splendid fellow! The biggest liar in the world! Failures are always liars! Pessimism itself is a lie, because it is the philosophy of the unsuccessful . . .'

Two days later, as I was wandering among the Darssan hills late at night, I met the doctor again. He was sitting on the ground, his legs wide apart. In front of him stood a bottle of wine and on a sheet of paper lay some sandwiches, cucumbers and sausages. I stopped and raised my hat. Lifting his head with

* Wine-glass.

a jerk, he looked at me and greeted me with a gesture and a sharp exclamation.

'Ah, it's you, is it! Would you care to keep me company? Come and sit down!'

I obeyed, and he handed me the bottle, measuring me with one of his tenacious glances.

'You must drink out of the bottle,' he said; 'there's no glass. It is very strange, but I feel as though I had met you some time when I was a child.'

'Not when you were a child.'

'No, of course not. I must be about twenty years older than you are. But I include in my childhood all the years of my life before I was thirty, all the time that I lived what is called a cultured life.'

His fine baritone rang out gaily, and the words rolled lightly from his tongue. His thick linen military shirt, his wide Turkish trousers and the shoes on his feet showed that he was earning a decent living. I reminded him where I had first seen him; and he listened to me attentively, picking his teeth with a stem of grass.

'Is that so?' he exclaimed in his familiar way. 'What are you doing now? You're a man of letters? Really? What is your name? Never heard it before. It's not surprising, for I neither know nor want to know anything of modern literature. You heard my opinion of it the other day, at Sibiriak's. By the way, isn't he wonderfully like a crab? Literature – the Russian brand particularly – is a gangrene, poisonous to most people and a mania as far as you writers are concerned.'

In this tone, but quite good-humouredly and with evident pleasure, he continued to talk for a long time. As for me, I listened to him patiently, without interrupting him.

'You don't contradict me?' he said.

'No.'

'Then you agree?'

'No, of course not.'

'Ah, then you don't think me worth contradicting. Is that it?'

'No, not that either. But I place the dignity of literature too high to wrangle with you about it.'

'Oh, so that's your reason, is it? That's fine . . .'

Throwing back his head and closing his eyes, he first sipped at the bottle and then emptied it, smacking his lips.

'That is fine,' he repeated. 'There speaks a good church-goer. Only when the smithy is the church of the blacksmith, the ship the church of the sailor, the laboratory the church of the chemist, will a man be able to live without hindering others by his wickedness, his whims and his habits. To live well is to live like a blind man, seeing nothing and desiring nothing except what you want to see and desire. That is very nearly happiness, a snug corner in which a man can hide himself, just a small dark lumber-room. Have you read Chateaubriand's *Letters from my Grave*? He says in them "Happiness is a desert island, inhabited merely by the creatures of my imagination."'

He spoke like a man just freed from solitary confinement, as though trying to make sure that he had not forgotten the use of words.

From the town, near by, came the sound of a piano and of horses' hoofs striking against the pavement of the quay; a black emptiness brooded over the town; and, far away, the lights of a steamer, crawling through the night like a golden beetle, spoke of the unfathomable sea. The man was staring into space, and his eyes reminded me of the opal that had flashed so beautifully in his ring that night on the bank of the Laba.

'Happiness – that is when a man has successfully discovered his own self and is satisfied with the discovery,' he continued in a low voice.

The light of his cigarette, flaring up, illuminated the thin, straight nose, the bristling moustache, the dark chin.

'Love of self comes naturally to a pig, to a dog, to any animal – it is an instinct. A man must love only what he has created for himself.'

'And what do you love?' I asked him.

'The morrow,' he answered quickly – 'my own morrow, and that alone. I have the good fortune never to know what it will be like. For you it is different: you know that on waking up in the morning you will begin writing or doing something else which you are obliged to do; that later you will meet that fat crab,

Mamin, or your other friends. Besides, you have to think about clothes. I, on the other hand, don't know what I shall want to eat tomorrow, or what I shall do, or with what people I shall allow myself to talk. Probably you think that you are listening to a drunkard, a debauchee, an outcast? If you do, you are wrong. I hate alcohol, drink only very good wine, and beer very seldom. It is not I who have been rejected, it is I who have rejected others.'

Such was the enthusiasm with which he spoke that I could not doubt his sincerity.

When I asked him to tell me why he had rejected the normal life of an educated man, he slapped me on the knee. 'You are looking for "copy",' he exclaimed with a laugh. Then, quite willingly and a little boastfully, hanging on his words with admiration, he began to tell me the story of his life, a story which surely was as truthful as are most autobiographies.

'I started my accountable life,' he began, 'with a mistake: I was infatuated with the natural sciences, biology, physiology, all the sciences which deal with man. Naturally this infatuation drove me to take the medical course at the University. In the very first year of my studies, when I was dissecting a corpse, I began to ponder on the inferiority of man. I felt that some cruel irony was directed against myself, and I began to experience a disgust towards men in general and towards myself in particular as a being whose duty it was to become a corpse.

'I ought to have given up the filthy business, but I was obstinate and wanted to conquer myself. Have you ever tried to conquer yourself? It is quite as impossible as it is to cut off your head and replace it by the head of your neighbour; the impossibility of doing this does not lie merely in the fact that your neighbour is hardly likely to consent to such an exchange.'

He was pleased with his joke and laughed over it with relish. Then, closing his eyes, he drew in the fresh, salty breeze with a deep breath.

'What a wonderful smell comes from the sea! . . . Well, to go on with my story: I pondered as to where the soul was and what it was like, also where and what was reason; and soon – very soon – it became clear to me that reason was a half-blind dog belonging to the devil, and that it depended upon the condition of the body; that the world was particularly abominable when I had toothache, or headache, or a bad liver. All reflection is a matter of function, only the imagination is independent. This was well understood by a certain English bishop, but for Heaven's sake don't think that I am an idealist or indeed any other kind of "ist". I struggle fiercely with every kind of philosophy, although – although I understand, of course, that philosophy is an incurable disease of the brain.

'To put it plainly: I am a man who refuses to take all this nonsense seriously – to deceive others as well as himself – this nonsense called culture, all the outward and inner shams and tinsel that draw men deeper and deeper into the chaotic uselessness of labour. But you, most probably, are an admirer of all culture? I don't want to offend you.'

'Go on. You won't offend me. I want to find out what kind of a man you are.'

'Do you, really? Well, then . . .'

In about a hundred cleverly chosen words this man destroyed all culture and shattered it to pieces. He did it with a gay ferocity, the ferocity of a school-boy who tears up his books after having ended his studies. He seemed to have shrunk in the fresh night air. As he sat there, slim and supple, in a crouching attitude, his hands in the sleeves of his shirt, he looked little more than an adolescent youth. Below, far away in the mist, a straggling cluster of sparks hung in the sky, floating towards the north, to be lost in the darkness and moisture of the night. In the windows of the houses yellow gleams trembled and disappeared, as though the houses were being thrown one by one into the blackness of the sea.

'I was handsome in those days, and clever,' he went on. 'My conversation was amusing and women loved me. When I was thirty years old I married one of them, an actress, married her out of obstinacy. She loved me less than the others did. At that time I had already begun to feel that all those theatres, concerts, talks about literature, weighing of pros and cons on questions of politics – that all that was not for me. After I had seen some twenty, thirty, or perhaps even a hundred people tortured for an unknown reason and exterminated by the most painful diseases – Tchaikovsky, Ostrovsky, Dostoyevsky and their like – I was reminded of a cold-blooded, disgusting old woman called Bukina, a sick-nurse in one of the hospitals who had a mean habit of consoling the sick and the dying by telling them with relish of the horrors of Hell.

'In cultured surroundings I felt myself something like a counter-jumper in a ladies' hat-shop; to me personally none of the articles were of any use; nevertheless I had to bother myself with them, even handle and praise them, just as a matter of form. Life is war, and you cannot use formality as a fig-leaf with which to hide the beast, the animal in a man.

'I have a good figure and never liked wearing braces, since my trousers kept up all right without them. But my wife insisted on my wearing them, because everyone else did! And – can't you picture this for yourself? – on these questions of braces, neckties, and so on my wife and I used to quarrel tragically! I think she often made scenes for purely professional reasons, just for the sake of practice. She would say to me, "Oh, Arkadi, Nihilism is *quite* out of fashion." She is not a stupid woman and she has frequently been called a gifted actress.'

The doctor laughed – not a very happy laugh, it seemed to me. Then, fidgeting about on the ground, he said, 'I think it is going to rain, confound it!'

He took a Crimean felt hat out of his trouser-pocket and pulled it tightly over his bald head. 'The rest of the story,' he continued, 'is too long to tell; besides, it would be boring to go on with it. The moral of it is simple: If I am doomed to die, I have the right to live as I like. The laws of men are quite useless to me if I, too, must submit to the elementary law of general extinction.

'When you met me there, in Kuban, I had just begun to understand this. But, of course, the idea came *post factum*, as the Romans used to say; and they were the best people in this world, for all sentimentality, all humanity and the like were organically and positively distasteful to them. Ideas always come after facts; they are provoked by our bad habit of trying to explain, of trying to justify ourselves. Why, I do not know. Yes, to put it plainly, I got out of it all because I wanted to do so, and the explanations came afterwards.

'The number of obligations, responsibilities and other farcical matters in our lives makes it hideous. I want no more farces, I said to myself, so I made a farewell bow to culture.

'About ten years have passed since that day. I have lived them in a very interesting way, quite independently, and hope to live ten more in the same fashion. Well, now, thank you for your company, and good-bye until we meet in a better world!'

'In which do you mean?'

'Oh, here, on earth, of course, but in the world in which *I* live. I hope you will drink yourself into a state that will bring you on the right road – away from all that rubbish!'

He descended the hill rapidly in the direction of Mordvinoff Park. Very soon after his departure there came a shower of rain that fell in glass beads, and made the grass rustle under it . . .

I spent two days looking for the man in cafés, in the market, in night lodgings, at the harbour – but failed to find him. I wanted to hear his arguments again.

Mamin-Sibiriak wrote a story about his meeting with the doctor-tramp and his wife, the celebrated actress. I do not remember what the story was called. But he represented the tramp as an unfortunate, miserable little drunkard who does not in the least resemble the man whom Doctor Riuminski had taken pains one day to lay bare before me.

*

Men of this type, men who, according to their own words, deliberately get away from the 'normal' conditions of life, must be rather numerous in Russia. Here is another notice from the *Novoye Vremya* about a man evidently of the same kind as Doctor Riuminski:

### A PECULIAR TRAMP

A peculiar kind of tramp, a certain G., a man about fifty years of age, was arrested during a police raid, reported the *Varshavsky Courier*. His papers were all in perfect order, but he was unable to name his residence. Further inquiry disclosed the fact that he was a man of wealth, with a craving for strange experiences. He had been deeply interested in the way of life of the homeless tramp, and on the death of his wife had placed his daughter in a boarding-school while he himself became a professional tramp, finding shelter at night in the stoves of brick-kilns and similar places. Only in winter, during the great frosts, did he return to Warsaw and await the coming of spring in an hotel. When caught by the police with a crowd of tramps, G. promised to try to alter his mode of life, although he added, 'I cannot answer for it.' . . .

After 1890 I used to collect all newspaper notices of this kind that I came across. I had got together about thirty of them when in 1905 the parcel in which they were kept was taken away from me during a perquisition and later on was mislaid in the Petersburg Police Station.

I have come across many such people in the course of my life. The tramp who remains impressed most vividly on my memory is 'Bashka', a man I came to know during the construction of the Beslan–Petrovsk railway. Meeting him in a narrow mountain-rift, among a bustling crowd of workmen, he immediately attracted my attention. He was sitting on the edge of the ravine exposed to the sun, in the midst of a litter of stones dislodged by dynamite. At his feet a motley and noisy crowd of men were boring, blasting and carrying the heavy stones about. Taking him to be the 'boss', I made my way to his side and asked whether there was any work for me to do? In a thin, piercing voice he replied:

'I'm not an idiot – I don't work.'

It was not the first time that I had heard such words, and they did not surprise me.

'Then what are you doing here?' I asked.

'As you see, I sit and smoke,' he answered, showing his teeth as he smiled.

In his wide coat and melon hat with a torn brim he reminded me of a bat. His small, upright ears seemed to be listening to some imperceptible sound. He had a large, frog-like mouth; when he smiled the lower lip sank flabbily, disclosing a thick line of small teeth, which made his smile peculiarly cruel. His eyes were wonderful; the pupils, dark and round like those of a night-bird, gleamed in the narrow golden circles formed by the whites of his eyes. His face was as hairless as a priest's, and the nostrils of his long, thin nose were hideously compressed. In his fingers, thin as a musician's, he held a cigarette. This he stuck into his mouth with a quick gesture, inhaling the smoke and coughing hoarsely.

'It is not good for you to smoke,' I said.

He replied, very quickly; 'And for you to speak – one can see at once that you're a fool . . .'

'Thank you!'

'Glad to oblige.'

After a short silence, during which he watched me stealthily, he spoke in a softer tone:

'Go away, there's no work for you here.'

In the sky, across the ravine, the wind was at work, anxiously gathering the clouds together like a flock of sheep. On the side exposed to the sun the rust-coloured shrubs of autumn trembled violently, shaking down their dead leaves. From afar came the sound of blasting; the reverberations thundered among the mountains, and mingled with the crunching of cart-wheels and the regular pounding of the hammers as they drove the steel 'needles' into the ore and drilled the deep holes for the charges.

'You want food, I suppose?' the little hunchback asked me. 'They're going to ring the bell for dinner in a minute. What crowds of people like you are roaming about the world! . . .' he grumbled, turning away to spit.

A piercing whistle sounded. It was as though a metallic chord had slashed the air in the ravine, deafening every other sound.

'Off with you,' said the hunchback. With his arms and legs he propelled himself rapidly over the stones, catching at the branches with the dexterity of a monkey, and rolled noiselessly down the slope, in an ugly, huddled mass.

The men dined outside in the open, sitting round the kettles, on stones and wheel-barrows, and eating a hot and salt porridge of millet with lamb. There were six people besides myself at our kettle. The hunchback behaved like a man in authority; having tasted the gruel, he wrinkled up his nose, lifted the spoon threateningly in the direction of an old man in a woman's straw hat, and shouted angrily: 'Too much salt again, you idiot!'

The other five men growled fiercely, and a big black peasant put in: 'He ought to get a thrashing!'

'Can *you* make gruel?' asked the hunchback, turning to me. 'Really? You're not lying? Let's give him a try,' he suggested, and the rest agreed with him at once.

After dinner the hunchback disappeared in the direction of the camp, while the old cook, a red-faced, good-natured fellow, showed me where the bacon, the grain, the bread and the salt were stored. In a whisper he warned me: 'Don't make any mistake about him. Although he's a cripple, he's a gentleman all right, and a landowner too. He's been a big man in his time, he has. He's got a head on his shoulders, *I* can tell you! He's like a regular master with us! Keeps the accounts and all that. Strict? I should think he was! He's a rare bird, he is!'

An hour later work roared and rumbled once again in the ravine and the men rushed about. I began to wash the kettles and spoons in the brook, built up a wood-pile, hung a kettle with water over it, and started peeling the potatoes.

'You've been a cook before, eh?' rang out the piercing voice of the hunchback. He came up stealthily and stood behind me, watching attentively how I managed my knife. As he stood there his likeness to a bat was still more accentuated.

'Not served in the police, have you?' he asked, and immediately answered his own question: 'No, you're too young for that.'

Flapping the wings of his cloak like a vampire, he jumped from one stone to another, rapidly climbing the hill. When he reached the top he sat down and puffed heavily at his cigarette.

My cooking was approved, the workmen praised me and then scattered about the ravine. Three of them started playing cards, and five or six went to bathe in the cold hill-stream. Somewhere among the stones and shrubs several voices struck up a Cossack song. There were twenty-three men in that gang, counting myself and the hunchback. They all addressed him familiarly, but with respect and even, I thought, with a certain awe.

He sat down in silence on a stone near the fire, shifting the coals with a long stick, and slowly about ten men gathered round him. A black-haired peasant stretched himself out at his feet like a huge dog, and a slim, colourless youth murmured something in an imploring voice.

'Shut up, you!' said the hunchback. 'Don't make that noise . . .'

The hunchback then began talking, without looking at anyone. His voice rang out loudly and confidently: 'I tell you there are fates, semi-fates and lots . . .'

I glanced up at him in amazement and noticing this he looked sternly at me: 'Well?' he asked.

All stared at me, as though expecting something. Their glance was hostile. After a short silence, however, the hunchback went on, wrapping himself up tightly in his cloak.

'Lots –' he said. 'They are like guardian-angels, only that they're assigned to a man by Satan.'

'And – the soul?' someone asked in a low voice.

'The soul is a bird, which Satan tries to catch – that's what it is!'

He went on telling them rubbish, and a sinister sort of rubbish it was. He had evidently read Potebnia's article 'On Fate and the Creatures Akin to It', but the serious side of that scientific essay had become confused in his mind with fairy-tales and gloomy fantasies. Very soon, too, he dropped the simplicity out of his speech and began speaking in a refined, literary style.

'From the first days of its existence,' he said, 'humanity has been surrounded by mysterious powers, which it does not understand, which it is unable to conquer. The ancient Greek ...'

His piercing, tensely ringing voice, the extraordinary combination of words and probably also his weird outward appearance – all these made an extraordinary impression on the men. They listened in silence, watching the face of the master as worshippers adore an image. The bird-like eyes of the hunchback glittered fiercely, his flabby lips moved and seemed to swell, to become heavier and thicker. And it seemed to me that in his dismal fancies there lay something in which he himself believed and which he feared. His face, bathed in the crimson reflections of the fire, became darker and gloomier as he talked.

Grey, motionless clouds seemed to hang over the ravine in

the twilight; the flames of the wood-fire grew thicker and more crimson; the rocks appeared to expand, making the rift in the mountain appear narrower. At my back the stream crawled and splashed, and something rustled as though a hedgehog were making its way through dry leaves.

When it became quite dark, the workmen, cautiously looking round, disappeared one by one in the direction of the camp. Someone whispered, 'That's what comes of science!' And still lower came the answer: 'It's the work of the devil . . .'

The hunchback remained by the fire, poking the brands with his stick. When the end of it was alight he raised it, holding it up in the air like a torch, and watched with his owl's eyes the yellow feathers of the flames as they broke away and flew into space. Then he waved the stick in the air so that a crimson halo encircled him. The battered hat he was wearing made his head look like an iron weight which had been forced into his broad, crooked shoulders . . .

For two days, I watched him, trying to make up my mind what kind of a man he was. He, too, was watching me carefully and suspiciously, never addressing me if he could help doing it, and answering my questions coarsely and gruffly. After supper, sitting beside the fire, he would tell terrifying stories to the men.

'The body of a man is built like a pumice, or a sponge, or bread – that is to say, it is porous. And blood flows in all the pores. Blood is a fluid in which swim millions of grains of dust unseen to the eye, but those grains are alive, like midgets, only smaller.' And raising his voice almost to a shriek, he added: 'It's in those grains of dust that the devils live!'

I could see that his stories frightened the men. I wanted to argue with him, but when I put questions to him he never answered them, and his hearers, nudging me with their elbows and legs, growled: 'Shut up! . . .'

When a splinter of stone injured the face or leg of one of the workmen, the hunchback, with mysterious whispers, would dress the wound. When one of the youths got a swollen face from toothache, the hunchback climbed up the hill, gathered some roots and grasses, boiled them in the tea-kettle, made a poultice out of the hot brownish gruel and, after thrice making the sign of the cross over the youth, muttered something strange about the Alatir stone and the Alleluia that sat on it.

'Now you're all right,' he said to the youth.

I never saw him smile, although he might well have derived amusement from the people round him. His face usually wore a pout of suspicion and his ears were perpetually pricked. In the morning he would climb to the sunny side of the ravine and sit there among the rocks, like a blackbird, smoking and watching the people bustling about below. Sometimes someone would call out to him, 'Bashka!' He would then roll down the slope, working his way over the loose boulders with a speed and agility which always amazed me. He would settle the quarrels which flared up and would argue with the paymaster in a thin little voice which was never drowned by the rumble of the work. The quartermaster, a fat man with the wooden face of a soldier, would listen to him with great respect.

'Who is that man?' I once asked him as he was lighting his pipe at the fire. He looked cautiously round him before he answered.

'The devil alone knows,' he said. 'A wizard or something of the sort. A kind of were-wolf . . .'

Nevertheless, I at last succeeded in having a talk with the hunchback. One day, after he had delivered his usual lecture on devils and microbes, on illnesses and crimes, and was sitting by the fire when the others had gone, I had my chance.

'Why do you tell the men all this?' I asked.

He glared at me, wrinkling up his nose until it looked more pointed than ever, and tried to poke the burning stick into my leg, but I drew it away and showed him my fist.

'They will give you a thrashing tomorrow,' he declared with assurance.

'What for?'

'You see, they'll give you a thrashing!'

His queer eyes flashed angrily, and his flabby lip sank lower, baring the teeth, as he growled: 'You . . . confound you! . . .'

'But seriously,' I said. 'You don't believe in all this nonsense, do you?'

He remained silent for a long time, shuffling the brands with his stick, which he brandished over his head so that the crimson nimbus again swirled and gleamed around him.

'In devils, do you mean?' he asked unexpectedly. 'Why shouldn't I believe in devils?' His voice sounded almost caressing, but it rang false and he gave me a wicked glance.

'He will most certainly order them to beat me,' I thought to myself.

He went on, however, in the same caressing voice and asked me who I was, where I had studied, and whither I was going. Almost unconsciously his manner changed. I thought I detected in his words the superiority, the condescension of a *grand seigneur*, the strange indifference of the exalted towards the humble. When I asked him again if he believed in devils he smiled.

'Well,' he replied, 'you believe in something or other, don't you? In God? In miracles?' And he added, with a twinkle in his eye: 'Perhaps you even believe in progress?'

The fire sent a flush to his yellow cheeks, and over his upper lip flashed the silvery needles of his thin, close-cropped moustache.

'You are a theorist,' he continued. 'You sow the seeds of "the eternal, the wise and the kind"* among the people, don't you?' Then, shaking his head, 'You fool,' he said. 'As soon as I saw you I sized you up. I know your tricks . . .'

But as he said this he looked round suspiciously and a strange restlessness seemed to take hold of him.

In the golden glow of the burning logs purple tongues danced about and blue flowers blossomed. A luminous vault hung in the darkness over the fire. We sat under a shining dome, enclosed and oppressed by the surrounding blackness. The heavy silence of an autumn night pervaded the atmosphere, and in the failing light the broken fragments of rock might have been wisps of mist, frozen into solidity.

'Throw some more wood on the fire.'

I threw a handful of branches on to the embers. Thick smoke filled the vault above us, while the surrounding space became darker and narrower. Crackling yellow serpents began to crawl

* From a poem by Nekrassoff.

63

through the branches, curling and intertwining and, with a sudden violent blaze, dispersed the frontiers of the night. At the same moment the voice of the hunchback rang out. His first words were nearly inaudible and disappeared into space without reaching me; for he spoke very low, as though he were falling asleep.

'Yes, yes, it is no joke . . . They are just as real as men, cockroaches, microbes. Devils can be of different shapes and sizes . . .'

'Are you serious?'

He did not answer, but merely shook his head, as though beating his forehead against something unseen, soundless, but concrete. Watching the fire he continued in a low voice:

'There are, for instance, purple devils; they are shapeless, like molluscs; they move slowly like snails, and are transparent. When there is a lot of them together their gelatinous substance reminds one of a cloud. There are millions and millions of them. Their task is to propagate boredom. They give out a sour perfume from which the soul grows dismal and weary. All the desires of men are hostile to them, all desires . . .'

Is he joking? I thought to myself. But if he was, he was joking wonderfully well, like the most subtle of artists. His eyes were gleaming weirdly and his bony face grew more pointed. He shuffled the logs with the end of his stick and broke up the embers with light strokes, transforming them into sheaves of sparks.

'Dutch devils are little ochre-coloured beings, round and shiny like balls. Their heads are all shrivelled up like grains of pepper, their paws are long and thin like threads, their fingers are joined together with a membrane, and every finger ends in a crimson hook. They inspire men with strange desires; under their influence a man can say, "You fool!" to a statesman, he can violate his own daughter, light a cigarette in church. Yes, yes! Those are the devils of unfounded insanity . . .

'Checkered devils are a chaos of crooked lines; they move in the air spasmodically and freely, forming strange shapes and combinations, which they immediately destroy. They are wearying to the human eye, a kind of mirage. Their aim is to cross the ways of man wherever he may want to go ... wherever he should go ...

'The cloth devils by their shape remind one of iron nails with splintered ends. They wear black hats, their faces are green and from them emanates a cloudy, phosphorescent light. They move in bounds, like knights on a chess-board. In the brain of a man they light the blue fires of madness. They are the friends of drunkards.'

The hunchback kept lowering his voice and spoke as though he were repeating a lesson. Listening to him with avidity, I wondered if this was the babble of a charlatan or the delirium of a madman?

'Very terrible are the devils of chiming bells. They have wings – they are the only winged beings in the whole legion of devils. They draw people to debauchery. They flutter about like sparrows and, piercing a man through, burn and scald him with desire. Probably they live on the tops of the church towers, for they persecute a man most fiercely during the chiming of bells.

'But most terrible of all are the devils of moonlit nights. They are like soap-bubbles, on which one and the same face keeps appearing and disappearing without interruption; it is blue and transparent and sad, and has marks of interrogation instead of eyebrows and round eyes without pupils. They move only in vertical lines, up and down, up and down, and penetrate a man with the thought of his eternal solitude. They whisper ceaselessly to him. On earth, he says to himself, among other people I live merely in the presentiment of solitude. Perfect solitude will come for me after death, when my spirit shall fly away into fathomless space and there, chained motionless to one spot, seeing nothing in front except emptiness, I shall be doomed eternally to look into myself, remembering the most futile details of my life on earth. Just that one memory for ages and ages: to live in remembrance of the sad folly of the past. And silence. And emptiness ...'

He held the stick motionless among the logs, and the pointed flames slowly crawled along it towards his hand. When the heat reached his hand the hunchback started, brandished the stick, shook off the sparks and rubbed the smouldering edge of the stick on a stone. It was smoking thickly. Then he began again to crumble the embers with the smouldering stick and to break them to pieces, tossing the sparks into the air. And he remained very silent.

A minute passed, then two, three. It was all very weird.

'You seriously believe . . .' I asked him at length.

He did not let me finish my sentence but screamed in a shrill voice, 'Go away!' And he threatened me with the smouldering stick. 'They will give you a thrashing tomorrow,' he said, 'you will see.'

I did not want his threat to come true, but I was inclined to think that it would. So when the hunchback had retired to sleep in the camp I left the place on my way to Vladicaucasus.

# The Sorceress

On the earthen bench outside the ancient hut old Mokeeff was sitting, a little, dried-up old man. He had taken off his shirt and was warming his time-worn body in the bright rays of a June sun, while he mended a dragnet with his knotted fingers. Under the old man's skin the collar-bones protruded pitifully, and his ribs heaved wearily. The day was glorious; the sun was doing his duty bravely; the lime-tree was in flower and gave out a delicious perfume; faint music floated in the warm air; it was the humming of the bees which, during the mowing, seem to work with unusual vigour and pertinacity.

'A stranger passing by one day told me,' Mokeeff grunts hoarsely to himself, 'that man's life is a blessing – and not the master's life only, but every peasant's life – a blessing and an honour. And out here when we say a man's a "regular blessing", we mean he's a bit wild, uncouth, wicked, if you like. We all have our own way of doing things.'

He had been practising the art of oratory for half an hour, and his hoarse droning was in harmony with the low murmur of bees, the chirping of sparrows, the songs of unseen larks. The chink of sickles and the swishing of scythes came from the river-bank, but not all these sounds together could disturb the peaceful stillness of the blue, far-distant sky, so pure and so fresh. Everything around was at once simple and marvellous, as so often it is in Russia.

'The Princes Golitzin? Why, there's bound to be princes, of course – you couldn't get away from that. You may swear about it as much as you like, but they remain princes all the same. I'm always telling the villagers to leave them alone. Don't measure your strength, I say, against princes; nothing will come of it. But it was Ivanikha who set the villagers on. Good-day, Ivanikha!'

A thick-set, sturdy woman in a dark *sarafan*,* with a blue kerchief on an unusually big head, came up noiselessly and stood by our side. She carried a stick in one hand and in the other a strong limebast basket, filled with fragrant thyme and herbs. Lifting her heavy head with an effort, the woman answered in a dull, angry voice: 'Good-day, you old chatterbox!'

Her dark, coarse, masculine face with its high cheekbones was adorned with grey whiskers and covered by a fine net of small wrinkles. Her cheeks were flabby and hung like a dog's. She had the dull eyes of a cow, and the little red veins on her eyeballs gave her a sullen, gloomy look. The fingers of her left hand moved incessantly, and I could hear the dry rustle of the skin. Pointing her stick at me, she said: 'Who's that?'

Mokeeff began a long explanation, saying that I had come from the solicitor's to investigate the case of the Prince Golitzin and the villagers, and that there would be a meeting on Sunday. The old woman, not waiting for him to finish, bent her head down and touched my knee with her stick.

'Come over and see me.'

'Where to?'

'They'll tell you. In an hour's time.'

She moved away, walking with a lightness incompatible with her age and her clumsy, ponderous body.

With that pride with which old villagers speak of something unusual and at the same time their very own, Mokeeff told me that Ivanikha was known throughout the whole district as a sorceress.

'Don't get the idea that she's a witch, though. No; her power comes from God. One day she was taken to Penza to cure a girl who couldn't walk. Well – she came and without any delay she just sent the girl off to get married! What do you think of that? The girl stood up and marched away, without a hitch. Then Ivanikha turned to the girl's parents and said to them: "You fools, what d'you get children for, when you don't know how to manage them?" They were rich merchants, those parents were. Yes, yes, she can cure everyone – beast, man, goose, hen – all alike. One day she was called to Nizhni, where there was a small boy lying in a trance. He'd been like that for two weeks,

* Russian peasant costume.

68

almost ready to be buried. Well – she just stuck a pin into him and the boy leapt up to the ceiling. That cured his trance. She got twenty-five roubles and a woollen dress for that.

'She's a great power in our village. She's respected and obeyed at all our gatherings, and even the local policeman is afraid of her. Once she pulled out three teeth for him, and each root was an inch long and had a hook at the end. No one could pull 'em out – but there's nothing she can't do. She's a fearless creature and the mistress of all secrets. She's only got to look at you and ask, all of a sudden, what you are thinking about; and you can't help yourself, you just fling your soul wide open, like a door, for her to see what's in it.'

Mokeeff had begun to speak proudly, even boastfully, but little by little he lowered his hoarse old voice; his manner changed and a fear crept into his tone. His knotted fingers, entangled in the drag-net, stopped working and rested wearily on the pointed knees.

I learnt that Ivanikha was the daughter of an unchristened Mordovian, a hunter of bears and a sorcerer, who was killed during the Mordovian movement of the forties. 'Her father was a friend of Kuzka himself, the Mordovian God . . .'

On her father's death, Ivanikha was left an orphan. She was christened on reaching maidenhood and soon after that married a forester, with whom she lived for three years in a childless marriage. In the spring of the fourth year the forester was killed by a bear, and after his death Ivanikha was allowed to remain in the little hut and began to hunt bears herself. The forests of Sergach were famed for the number of bears they sheltered, and until the seventies of the nineteenth century the Sergach peasants were regarded as the best bear-hunters and trainers in all Russia. Ivanikha used to strike down the bear in Mordovian fashion: she would bind her right arm in splints and tie a strap round it up to the shoulder, holding a knife in her right fist, and a short pole-axe, like a hacking-knife, in her left one. When the beast rushed at her with open jaws she would strike it across the paws with the hacking-knife and, thrusting the knife into the jaws, rip open the bear's throat.

'Only the Mordovians kill bears in that way. You need to be

very strong to do it. The seventeenth, however, broke one of her ribs, while the thirty-something twisted her neck a bit – you must have noticed the way she moves her head about – that's the reason for it. She didn't reach her fortieth, though; forty is the fateful number for the hunter,* and she got scared. Very few men escape from the fortieth bear alive. When he gets to the fortieth, the hunter knows just how much longer he's got to live. About twenty years ago I had a sort of Hindoo living in my house. He was a famous hunter who had come from the city, and he used all kinds of double-barrelled guns, terrible knives and bear-spears when he went out. His fortieth bear, however, didn't worry about all these weapons a bit, and just tore off the man's ears and beard, together with his chin.

'Why a Hindoo? Because he was just born that way, I suppose. He was a count by title, but born in India. There are many people like that behind the Caspian; they've all got bluish hair and are drunkards, every one of them. Persians? No, they are different. They are our captives in a way; they've got to obey us, like Tartars, Chuvashes and Mordva. But as for the Hindoos – they're a free nation, the people of an independent Tsar. They're supposed to have a golden tooth in their mouths to distinguish them from the others. Grand folk they are, and talk in a deep voice. As to the number of young girls that Hindoo of mine succeeded in damaging over here in the winter and in the spring – I bet you it was at least five. They took him away and put him in a hospital afterwards. They're not allowed to live without beards, these folk; it's considered to be a disgrace. They're like us in that, but in all other points they're a people with their own customs. What was his name, by the way? Ah – yes! Fedor Karlich! A jolly good master, he was.'

Mokeeff spoke jerkily, as though he were riding downhill on a winding road; probably he would have continued until late at night, but as I had already been with him for about an hour, and remembered Ivanikha's invitation, I asked him to show me the house where she lived.

'Over there, do you see it? The neat little *izba* on the slope ... People of that calling always live out of the way ...'

* A pun: *sorok* = forty, *srok* = limit.

When I came up to the clean hut belonging to Ivanikha, a cart of freshly-mown grass was standing in the open gate; the axle of the cart had caught against the jamb and a flaxen-haired youngster was trying hard to rein back the bay horse; but all his efforts were unsuccessful. Ivanikha stood in the porch, washing her hands in an earthen basin and scolding angrily.

'Unharness it. Unharness it, I tell you.'

The lad said nothing, but went on beating the horse's muzzle, hissing as he did so. The old woman came down the steps, rapidly unharnessed the horse and lifted up the shafts. Then she bent down, planting her iron legs squarely, pushed the cart some way outside the gate, turned round swiftly, yoked herself into the shafts, and easily bowled the cart into the yard.

'You stubborn little fool!' she cried.

'That's only because you're so strong,' the lad retorted in an injured tone, leading the horse towards the shed.

'Strong indeed! I'll soon be seventy! What's the use of you, you good-for-nothing!'

Catching sight of me, she measured me with a searching glance and then said invitingly, 'Come inside the hut.'

The evening sun was staring intently into the open window of the *izba*, fluffy little kittens were playing on the cleanly-washed floor, and the scent of dry hay permeated the house. In the corner a shining kettle was snorting and giving off steam; bottles, glass jars and tin sardine boxes glistened on the shelves by the stove. Under the sloping shelf of the stove hung trusses of various herbs. St John's wort, primrose, sea-cole, an ugly grass which grows in marshes, the roots of holy thistle, hemlock, and some twigs tied up in bunches.

Holding a saucer on her outspread palm, as is the custom of merchants, Ivanikha asked me:

'What do they say in the town? Will the peasants get some land? They had better look out, the peasants are getting angry. Just you tell that to the Golitzins. Ask them what they are thinking about. Here have they been shamelessly bringing law-suits against people for nine years – and no good comes of it for anyone. Fooling the peasants, that's what they are doing! They're supposed to have set them free, but what does this freedom of

71

theirs amount to? The peasants are just hanging over the land, jostling midgets. That's all their freedom has done for them.'

There was a strangely sinister look in her dark face with its flabby cheeks. Her bloodshot eyes peeped into the saucer, the wet moustache on her upper lip twitched. I noticed that she had a hairy mole on her neck, under her left ear. She munched a piece of sugar in silence, smacking her lips, and there was almost nothing about her except her protruding bosom to remind one that she was a woman.

I tried tactfully to wheedle out of her how she had killed her bears. But she answered reluctantly, and seemed to be intentionally making her voice sound hoarse and grumpy.

'Yes, I was strong. There were only two men in the whole district who could bring me down. Except my own man. I'd have got the better of him too, all right, but then – he was my husband, so I couldn't. I did fight him once for a joke, but not in earnest. I didn't dare to. The men here are of a strong, forest race.'

She grew hot and beads of perspiration appeared on her face. She took the shawl off her head and revealed thick grey streaks among the coarse mane of hair. She wiped her wrinkled face with a handkerchief and tied it round her injured neck. Her hands were capacious, like scoops, and her fingers moved restlessly, as though she were sorting or disentangling a skein of yarn. It was unpleasant to watch her. Altogether Ivanikha gave the impression of a supernatural, inhuman creature.

I asked her about the fortieth bear.

'The bear serves God. Keremet* drives a team of bears down the sky, carrying the sun with him. The sun is large – like a good-sized pond. It's heavy, and it's all made of pure gold. God needs people, too. The bee serves the man: man serves God. Keremet said to Man: Kill the bears while I suffer you to do so. When you've killed so many, the sun will rise – remember that! Then I will send a strong one against you, and he will kill you. The man agreed. He was worried about his cattle, his honey, his oats. The bear does a lot of damage.'

Scratching her scalp with the end of the knife, she spat on her palm and, smoothing down the dishevelled hair with her

* Mordovian God.

saliva, shot a dull, scrutinous glance at me. Her nose was broad and the nostrils were, like a camel's, turned inside out.

'You who are young ought to know this. For every man there is a woman who is like his fortieth bear. You may love three, you may love nine and it will be all right; but if this particular one appears in your path, whether she be the fourth or the seventh – your end has come. She'll cast a charm on you, and bind you, and you'll see no light in the world except her. Thereafter you'll live like a blind man. That's the fateful woman, whom Keremet sends as a punishment. God needs children. He needs men. And when it's mere play – no children – He is angry. He has no use for that . . .'

'Do you go to church?' I asked.

She seemed astonished at the question and answered sullenly: 'We do. Why shouldn't we? We've got a fine church, built by the Princes. And a nice, clever priest. The bees like him. We live calmly here and peacefully, blissfully. There are woods all round . . .'

The kittens scrambled on to her knees; she gathered two of them in her great paw and lifted the little animals to her face and asked them: 'Well – what d'you want?' And pouring some milk into her own saucer, which stood on the table, she pushed it towards them. A simple peasant would not have done that. 'Drink this. Where's the third? The little brother?'

The little brother was gnawing at my boot, so I lifted him up and placed him on the table.

'They're clever beasts, these are. They trust no one,' said Ivanikha. 'And their memory's marvellous. If you beat one of them he'll remember it in five years' time, when you have forgotten all about it. But people's memories are weak: they don't remember those who thrash them . . .'

It had grown late and the cows had been brought in from the fields. The peasants were walking up the street, their sickles glittering past the windows and reflecting the crimson light of the setting sun. The women, passing by, peered into the houses.

'Well – I've got to go outside for a bit,' said Ivanikha. 'Why did you stop at Mokeeff's? They're unlucky folk there. Next time, come and stay here. I like people to stop at my house.'

Accompanying me to the gate, she shouted out to a woman passing by: 'Maria – did you bind up your leg?'

'Oh, Mother Ivanikha, I'd no time to do it!'

'Fool! Well – let it be, I'll do it myself . . .'

After supper Mokeeff invited me to go to the river and help him fasten the nets. On our way there he told me that some ten years ago Ivanikha used to instruct young fellows how to treat their wives.

'She used to take five pennies for it, or a pound of cracknels; she likes cracknels with aniseed. At first they used to laugh at her for doing it, but afterwards they got used to it. As for her, she would scold them, call them fools. That's always her first word: fools. "You look after your cows," she would cry, "you look after your horses, and don't worry about the girls." I suppose she was right there. The boys are regular young bears. They get married and don't know how to treat girls. A boy will spoil his wife from the very first, and then thrash her because she's not sweet or wistful any more . . .'

The moon was shining and a strong, damp fragrance of new-mown hay hung in the air. Stumbling against the bare root of a tree, the old man swore and called God to his help almost in the same breath. Then, limping on, he changed quickly to another topic:

'She's feared, is Ivanikha. And respected too. She's a tough customer, my boy, I can tell you . . .'

He paused for a while and then added: 'And very useful, as well. They wanted to throw her out of her hut, out of the forest. A man with brass buttons came from the town to see that it was done properly and kept telling her to leave. Never before, said he, had it been known to custom or to Law that a woman should be a forester. Never, never before! People warned him. It was true, they said, that she was a woman, but the wood-demon himself could not be more terrible. He wouldn't believe it. Well – what d'you think she did? She wrapped up her arm in leather, took a knife and all the rest of her equipment, and went for him as though he were a real bear. She gave him a rare fright. "Confound you," he said. "You ought to be sent off to Siberia, you she-devil." So she stayed in the forest until later, when she left it of her own accord. Her place was taken by old Jakov, who was eaten by the wolves his very first winter as he lay drunk in the woods ... Our country's a fine one, a peaceful one,' he concluded unexpectedly, but with perfect conviction.

Gently and stealthily the night was creeping from the woods, covering the meadows and fields with warm shadows. A stillness sank over the blue, lazy little river, while round the moon the stars flashed, like bees round a flower ...

About three months later, when I was on my holiday, my road again brought me to Berezianka. I stopped with Ivanikha, and assembling the villagers told them of the progress which their case had made since my last visit. Sitting with the old woman and drinking tea on the autumn night, I listened to her tales. She spoke to me of all the events of the summer: of the fire which had luckily destroyed only three shacks, of those who had been sick, and those who had been thrashed, of the people who had got poisoned with mushrooms, of the little girl who had been frightened in the wood and lost her reason. 'Now she sits in a dark corner by the stove and sings away, day and night: "Mummie, darling, let's run away, oh, let's!"'

Then, her fingers still moving, she asked, sternly: 'Nothing decided yet about the land over there, eh?'

When I answered, 'Not yet,' she glanced at me distrustfully. 'Don't you try to hide things from me,' she said. 'Take care; the peasants are getting sore about the land.'

Behind the windows the wind was shaking the trees and droning in the chimney, the rain was lashing at the panes, the country was smothered, wrapped in the gloom of a Russian October, a gloom which for dreariness can only be compared with a hopeless, deadly disease. I wanted to ask the sorceress to tell me more about Keremet, to explain the kind of God he is. So when she had finished her tea, washed and put away the plates, and sat down at the table to knit a stocking, I began very cautiously to ask her about him.

Her fat lips pursed in an unpleasant scowl; moving her fingers rapidly and flashing the steel of the needles, she answered unwillingly, her camel's nostrils contracting and her dark nose narrowing to a point.

'I'm no priest,' she said. 'I stand in no relation to God.'

'But is Keremet a good god?'

'God isn't a horse. You can't judge him by his teeth . . . You won't have a chance to get a look at them . . .'

For a long time she kept answering in the same constrained and angry manner, but at last I succeeded in touching her to the quick by some remark I made. Inflating her nostrils, baring her greenish, sheep-like teeth, her fingers working still more rapidly with the needles, she began to grumble in an irritated voice.

'What are you hammering away at like a cooper? God? You can't offer a man to God, as you offer a girl to an old man. You can't drag a man towards God against his own will. Such a marriage would be no good. There would be no truth in it.'

I noticed with amazement that she did not shape her sentences in a purely Russian style, although she spoke pungently and very fluently. With a brusque gesture, she pulled back the shawl on her head. Her forehead appeared to be higher, while the eyes that now stared expressively at me from under the shaggy eyebrows were smaller and clearer. At the same time her crumpled face had shrunk and hardened.

'Your God loves faith, but Keremet loves truth,' she continued. 'Truth is greater than faith. Keremet knows that if God and man are friends, there will be truth. A man's soul is his soul, which he won't pass on to the devil. Your God, Christ, wants nothing, only faith. Keremet wants the man, because he knows that the union of God and man means truth. God by Himself is untruth. Keremet is bountiful. The beasts, the fishes, the bees – he gives them all to man. He gives them land. He's a shepherd of men. Not the shepherd who is a priest, but the shepherd who is God. With you it is the priest. Christ says, "Have faith"; Keremet says, "Live in truth. If you do, you'll be my friend." You won't buy truth for money. Priests are fond of money. They've set Keremet and God against one another like dogs. They fight and snarl – your God at us, our God at you.'

She stopped knitting, threw down the wool and the needles, and, smacking her lips, went on gloomily and dully:

'The Mordva have ceased to be a people – they don't know

in whom to believe. You, too – you're not a people any longer. Keremet is angry with you, and therefore he entangles your lives. Both Gods are doing that: ours to you, yours to us. They're both evil-minded. God fattens on man, and man has become evil-minded and bitter too.'

The eyes of the old woman grew clearer and sparkled with harsh disapproval. She became less and less like a Russian. Something authoritative rang in her voice. Slowly inclining her neck, she seemed about to butt her head into me, a prospect so unpleasant that I straightened myself in my chair. Words, sounding strange and foreign to me, Mordovian words, appeared more and more frequently in her speech. My movement, however, apparently sobered her somewhat, for she seized the stocking from the table, and the needles started flashing rapidly again.

After a pause she continued in a lower key: 'God is an unkind man, but the priest is the most unkind of all. People should be divided honestly, some to this God, others to the other. Then the gods would live in peace and accord, each with his flock. Good masters bear no grudge. You say, "God loves truth, but isn't in a hurry to admit it."* Why is He not in a hurry? If you know the answer, give it at once. Keremet knows that truth is better than faith. He used to say so, but when they began to track him he desisted. He was offended. "Live without me," he said. This is bad for us, but it is good for the devil.'

Some villagers, drenched with the rain, looked in to see me; snorting and wiping their wet beards with the palms of their hands, they sat down on the bench and began a careful discussion about the town and the land, trying to sound me as to whether there were any signs of life becoming easier. They got nothing out of me, however.

When they had gone, Ivanikha, sighing heavily, begged me: 'Don't tell them in the town what the peasants are saying. Don't tell the Governor, please don't . . .'

She lay down to sleep by the stove, and I on the shelf, in the stifling aroma of dried hay.

In the middle of the night I was awakened by the wail of the

* Russian proverb.

wind in the chimney and a heavy, spluttering whisper. Glancing down from the shelf, I saw Ivanikha on her knees praying. She seemed just a shapeless heap, a something grey and uncouth, something resembling a stone. Her dull voice bubbled curiously; it sounded like water boiling fiercely, or a throat being gargled. Gradually, out of that effervescence emerged strangely connected words.

'O Christ, how wrong! . . . What a shame! Christ . . . Elijah is angry, you are angry. Keremet too. You are strong and many people follow you. You should be kind. Who will be kind to the people if God is unkind? O Christ! you must listen to me! You must! I know a lot. Your women are tormented, your men are tormented. Why? It's wrong . . .'

Without making the sign of the cross she flung her hands about, now stretching them out to the dark shapes of the ikons, now pressing them to her hips or beating her chest. And all the time she was whispering dully or reproaching fiercely, choking over her words:

'Your priests offend Keremet, O Christ! How dare they? Is Keremet then worse than you? How wrong, how wrong, O Christ! God offending God – what will people think? O Christ, you are a bad God, a jealous God, an unkind God, not a human God at all. It's hard for the people to keep loyal to you. Make your purpose clear to us. Why did Ivan die so young? And Mishka – quite a child, bright little Mishka? Why? Gusseff's cow perished – for what object? Aren't you sorry for your own even if you have no pity for others? How sad, how sad! Whom are you serving, Christ? What people are you serving? Here am I, a woman, serving people, helping both yours and the Tartars and the Chuvashes. They are all alike to me. But what about you? Your priests say that you are there for us all, and you don't even love your own. No, you don't! Shame, oh, shame, Christ; this is not the way to act. I'm telling the truth. Shame to you! Look at your people. They are good people, but how do they live? Eh, Christ? Don't you know? God does well when He listens to people, just as people do well when they listen to God. Listen to me. I'm saying nothing that's wrong. I'm telling the truth. You should open your eyes and see. God

78

ought to know the truth better. I know the truth better than you, before you, O Christ! . . .'

Thus she blamed Christ for a long time, her smothered voice droning weirdly, the foaming words, bubbling in her throat, sounding now plaintive, now bitter and fierce.

The rain lashed the thatch of the roof with sharp whips, the wind squealed piercingly, inhumanly, trying to deafen the heart's complaint of a human being.

At dawn, I left the village and carried away with me the memory of one of the finest conversations of man with God, perhaps the very finest, which I had heard in all my life.

# Makoff and the Spider

OLD Ermolai Makoff, a dealer in antiques, was a tall man, thin and straight as a post. He walked the earth like a soldier on parade, watching everything with his huge bull's eyes, in the dull grey-blue shine of which there was nevertheless something sullen. I thought him very unintelligent – and what convinced me of this still more was a wilful and capricious trait in his nature: for instance, he would come and offer one an ink-stand belonging to the clerk, or a ladle borrowed from the tapster, or an ancient coin, bargain obstinately about its price, and then, all of a sudden, say in a sepulchral voice, 'No, I won't sell it.'

'Why not?'

'I don't want to.'

'Why, then, did you waste a whole hour in bargaining?'

He would slip the object silently into the fathomless pocket of his overcoat, sigh deeply and go, without saying good-bye, pretending to be profoundly offended.

But in a day or so – sometimes in an hour – he would re-appear unexpectedly and place the object on the table. 'Take it,' he would say.

'Why did you not let me have it last time?'

'I did not want to.'

He was not avaricious as far as money was concerned, but though he distributed a lot to the poor, he took not the slightest care of himself; he walked about in winter and summer in the same old, padded overcoat, warm, crumpled cap and worn-out shoes. He had no home, but went about from one estate to another, from Nizhni to Murom, from Murom to Suzdal, Rostoff, Jaroslav and back again to Nizhni, where he usually stopped in the filthy lodgings of Bubnoff, the abode of canary-sellers, sharpers, detectives and other folk in search of happiness. They hunted for it, wallowing on badly-damaged sofas, in clouds of tobacco smoke.

Amid this human refuse Makoff was paid the greatest attention, as a man always on the spot and a good story-teller. His stories were always of the homes of the nobles falling to pieces, of the breaking up of great estates. He would enlarge on this theme with a sullen fierceness, underlining persistently and in deep colours the thoughtlessness of the landowners.

'They just roll balls about,' he would say. 'They like rolling balls about with wooden hammers – that's a game of some kind they've got. And they've become just like those balls themselves – rolling aimlessly here and there on the earth.'

Once on a misty autumn night I met Makoff on board a ship on the way to Kazan. The ship, with its paddle-wheels scarcely moving, was crawling blindly and cautiously down the stream. Its lights faded away and dissolved in the grey waters and the grey fog, while the siren lowed dully and continually and anguish clutched the heart, as in a troublesome dream.

Makoff sat in the stern, alone, as though hiding from someone. We began to talk, and this is what he told me.

'For twenty-three years,' he said, 'I have lived in an everlasting fear from which I can find no escape. And this fear, my dear sir, is a peculiar one: it is that a strange soul has settled in my body.

'I was thirty years old when I began to have relations with a woman who was no other than a witch. Her husband – my friend – was a kind man, but he was ill and on the point of death. I was asleep on the night when he died, and that cursed woman conjured my soul away and enclosed his soul in my body. She did this for her own profit, for her husband was more affectionate towards the miserable creature than I was. Well, he died, and I noticed at once that I was not the same man. I can say openly that I never loved that woman; I had merely been playing the fool with her – and now I found that my soul was drawn to her. How could that be? She was repulsive to me – yet I could not get away from her.

'All my fine qualities vanished like smoke; I was seized with a vague sadness, and became very meek with her. Her face blazed with fire, but everything else round me seemed to have become grey, as though strewn with ashes.

81

'She played with me and at night she dragged me into sin. At last I understood that she had changed my soul, that I was living with another man's soul. But mine, my own, the one God gave me – where was it? I was terrified . . .'

The weird note of the siren sounded, but its muffled bellowing was lost in the fog. The ship, as though caught in the mist, slipped along, and the water, dark and thick like resin, splashed and rumbled underneath. The old man, leaning with his back to the stern, stamped his feet, which were shod in heavy boots, groped strangely with his hands in the air and went on talking in a low voice.

'I was so terrified,' he said, 'that one day I went up to the garret, made a loop and tied it to the rafters. Unluckily the washerwoman saw me and they got me out of the loop in time. From that day I have had an extraordinary inexplicable creature continually at my side: a six-footed spider that walks on its hind legs, as large as a small goat, bearded and horned, with the breasts of a woman, and three eyes – two in the head and the third between the breasts – looking down and watching my footsteps. Wherever I go it follows me incessantly, an ugly, hairy beast, with six feet, like a shadow of the moon. No one can see it except me – here he is – only you can't see him. Here he is now!'

Stretching his hand out to the left, Makoff stroked the air about eighteen inches above the deck, and then, wiping his palm on his knee, murmured, 'He's quite wet.'

'Well, so you have lived with the spider for twenty years?' I asked.

'Twenty-three. Maybe you think I'm mad? Here he is, my guard; look at him, crouching; see him?'

'Why have you never consulted a doctor about it?'

'Why should I consult them, my dear sir? How can doctors help in such a case? It isn't as though it were an abcess, which they could open with a knife; you can't drive it away with a lotion or stick it up with plaster. The doctor couldn't see the spider, could he?'

'Does the spider talk to you?'

Makoff looked up at me in amazement.

'Are you joking?' he asked. 'How can a spider talk? It was sent to keep me in fear, to remind me that I can't dispose of a stranger's soul, can't kill it. Don't forget that the soul I've got now is not my own – it's as though I had stolen it.

'About ten years ago I made up my mind to drown myself. I threw myself into the water from a barge, but he, the spider, fastened his claws into me and to the gunwale, so that I merely hung overboard. I pretended that it was an accident; but the sailors said afterwards that my overcoat had caught on something and kept me back . . . Here it is – the overcoat that kept me back.' Makoff stroked and caressed the moist air again.

I remained silent, not knowing what to say to a man who lived side by side with a strange being created by his own imagination, and yet was not completely mad.

'I've wanted to speak to you of this thing for a long time,' he muttered in low tones. 'You talk so boldly of everything, that I trust in you. Tell me, please, tell me, what do you think about it? Does the spider come from God or from the devil?'

'I do not know.'

'Maybe you'll think it over . . . I suppose it's from God, it is He who is guarding the strange soul in me. He didn't set an angel to that job, for I'm not worth one. But a spider – that was clever of Him. And such a terrible spider, too. It took me a long time to get used to it.'

Taking off his cap, Makoff made the sign of the cross and began to murmur in a low and inspired voice: 'Great and kind art Thou, Almighty, Lord and Father of Reason, Shepherd of our souls.'

Some weeks later, on a moonlit night, I met Makoff in a deserted street of Nijni. He was walking along the pavement, pressing close to the wall, as though making way for someone to pass.

'Well, is the spider alive?' I asked.

The old man smiled, and, stooping down, stroked the air with his hand.

'Here he is . . . ,' he muttered softly.

Three years after, in 1905, I heard that Makoff had been robbed and killed somewhere near Balakha.

# Bodriagin the Grave-digger

WHEN I presented the shaggy, one-eyed grave-digger Bodriagin with the concertina which he had coveted for a long time, he pressed his right hand tightly to his heart and, electrified with joy, closed his solitary, gentle, and at times uncanny, eye.

'Oh-h-h . . .' he said.

Then, stifling his emotion, he shook his bald head and murmured in a single breath:

'Anyhow, Alexei Maximich, you may be sure I'll take good care of you when you're dead.'

He used to take his concertina with him even when he was digging graves, and when he was weary of working would lovingly and softly play a polka on it. It was the only tune he could play. Sometimes he called it 'Trang-blang' (with a French twang) and sometimes 'Darn-blarn'.

One day he began to play it when the priest was officiating at a funeral close to him. When he had finished, the priest called him up and abused him.

'You insult the dead, you swine,' he said.

Bodriagin came to me and complained.

'Well, I'll admit I was wrong,' he said, 'but all the same, how does he know that the dead were offended?'

He was convinced that there was no such place as hell. According to him, after the death of their bodies, the souls of the righteous flew to a 'holy paradise', while the souls of the sinners remained in their bodies and lived on in their graves until their bodies were eaten up by worms. 'After that,' he said, 'the earth breathes the soul out to the wind, and the wind scatters it about in intangible dust.'

When the body of the little six-year-old girl Nikolaeva, whom I had loved so much, had been deposited in the earth and the people had left the cemetery, Kostia Bodriagin, as he levelled the hillock of clay with his spade, tried to console me.

'Don't you fret, my friend,' he said. 'Perhaps in that other world they speak another, a better, a more cheerful language than ours. Or maybe they don't use any words at all, but just play on the violin.'

His love of music had a quaint and sometimes a dangerous side. It would make him oblivious of everything else. At the sound of a military band, a street-organ or a piano, he would prick up his ears and crane his neck in the direction from which the sound came. With his hands folded behind his back, he would stand motionless, his dark eye wide open, straining, as though he could hear with it. This often happened when he was in the street, and twice he was knocked down by horses and many times struck by cabmen, as he stood there enthralled, deaf to the cries of warning and heedless of danger.

'When I hear music,' he explained, 'it's as though I had dived to the bottom of the river.'

He had an *affaire* with the churchyard beggar Sorokina, a drunken old woman fifteen years older than himself – and he was over forty.

'What do you do it for?' I asked.

'Well – who is there to comfort her? ' he replied. 'There's no one except me. And I – I love to comfort the inconsolable. I've no sorrow of my own – so – well – I help to lighten the sorrow of others . . .'

We stood talking under a birch-tree, and were drenched by a sudden June shower. Kostia was thrilled with delight by the rain falling on his bald, angular skull. 'I like to be able to dry people's tears . . .' he muttered.

He was evidently suffering from cancer of the stomach, for he smelt like a corpse, could eat nothing, and had attacks of vomiting; but in spite of all that he went on working steadily, walked gaily about the graveyard, and died while playing cards with the other grave-digger.

# The Hangman

GRESHNER, the Chief of the Nizhni Secret Police, was a poet. His verses were published in certain conservative reviews and also, I think, in the *Niva* and *Rodina*.

I can remember several lines from them:

> From the stoves the longing crawls,
> It also crawls from every door,
> But, although it maims our soul,
> Life is gayer when it's there . . .
> I feel so lonely without my longing.
> Without men and beasts the world would be sobbing . . .

He once wrote some erotic verse in a lady's album, beginning:

> Against a pillar, before the front door,
> A boy of three stands leaning;
> His face is so familiar to me,
> The devil take it! – it is myself!

Some obscene allegories and comparisons followed.

Greshner was killed by a nineteen-year-old youth, Alexander Nikiforov, the son of a well-known Tolstoyan and translator, Leo Nikiforov. Tragedy pursued the father, for he had four sons and they all perished one after the other. The eldest, a social democrat, exhausted by prison and exile, died of heart-disease; another was burnt alive, having poured petroleum over his body; the third poisoned himself; and the youngest, Sasha, was hanged for killing Greshner. He killed him in broad day-light, in the street, almost at the very doors of the office of the Secret Police. Greshner was walking along arm in arm with a lady. Sasha overtook him and cried: 'Hi, policeman!' And as Greshner turned round at the cry, Nikiforov fired at his face and chest.

Sasha was immediately seized and sentenced to death, but

not one of the criminals from the Nijni prisons would undertake the abominable task of hangman. At length the chief of the police, Poiret, once cook to the governor Baranoff, a braggart and a drunkard – he called himself the brother of the famous caricaturist Caran d'Ache – bribed the bird-catcher Grishka Merkuloff to hang Sasha for twenty-five roubles.

Grishka, too, was fond of alcohol; he was thirty-five years old, long, lanky and sinewy; grew little tufts of dark hair on his horse-like jaw, and from under his prickly brows his sleepy eyes peered dreamily. After he had hanged Nikiforov he bought a red scarf, wrapped it round his long neck with its huge Adam's apple, stopped drinking vodka and developed a loud and imposing cough.

'What are you so proud about, Grishka?' asked his friends.

'I'm engaged,' he would answer, 'on a secret job for the Government!'

But when one day he let out by mistake that he had hanged a man, his friends denounced him and even gave him a thrashing. After that he sent a petition to the chief of the Secret Police, Kevdin, asking to be allowed to wear a red coat and trousers with red stripes.

'So that,' he explained, 'civilians may know who I am and not dare to touch me with their unclean hands – since I am an official hangman.'

Kevdin used him to hang several other murderers. Finally Grishka went to Moscow, hanged someone there and returned profoundly convinced of his own importance. But on arrival at Nizhni he went to see Dr Smirnoff, an oculist and a member of the 'black hundred',* and complained of having an 'air-bubble' in his breast which tended to lift him up to the sky.

'Its power is so strong that I have to make quite an effort to stay on the ground and am forced to grab at something or other, so as to prevent myself from jumping and making people laugh at me. It first happened after I had hanged a certain scoundrel – something started to beat in my breast and began to swell inside me. And now it has grown to such a pitch that I can't sleep. I'm drawn up to the ceiling at night and don't know what

* The extremely conservative, ultra-nationalist party.

to do about it. I take all the clothes I can and put them on me, and I even fill my pockets and sleeves with bricks, to make them heavier. But it's no use. I've tried putting a table on my chest and stomach, tying my feet to the bed – but I'm drawn up all the same. For goodness' sake cut me open and let the air out; otherwise I shall soon be unable to remain on the earth at all.'

The doctor advised him to go to a nerve specialist, but Grishka angrily refused. 'It all comes from my chest,' he said, 'not from my head . . .'

A short time afterwards he fell from a roof and broke his spine and fractured his skull. As he lay dying he repeatedly asked Dr Nifont Dolgopoloff: 'Will there be a band at my funeral?'

A few minutes before he died, he murmured with a sigh: 'There now, I'm going up . . .'

# Looking for the Causes of Luck

AT the Sestrorietzk baths lived an attendant, Stepan Prokhoroff, a fine, strong old man of sixty or thereabouts. His eyes,
which protruded like a doll's, had a strange look as they watched
the world about him; although there was something in them a
little too bright and hard, they held a gentle, even a benign
smile. It was as if he found in everyone something that deserved
compassion.

He treated humanity as though he considered himself the
wisest of men. He moved about with cautious footsteps and
spoke in a low voice, as though all the people around were
asleep and he did not wish to awaken them. He was a steady and
unrelenting worker, and readily undertook the jobs of others.
Whenever one of the officials of the baths asked him to do
something for him, Prokhoroff, who was usually a man of few
words, would at once agree. 'All right, old fellow,' he would
say, 'all right. I'll do it, don't you bother about it.'

And he always did other people's work without ill-feel-
ing or boasting, as though he were distributing alms to the
sluggards.

He did not mix with people as a rule, but lived alone. I
hardly ever saw him in friendly conversation with his companions
either in his hours of work or of leisure. The others had no
definite views about him, but I believe they did not think him
very clever. When I asked them what kind of man Prokhoroff
was, they would answer, 'Oh, there's nothing extraordinary
about him . . .' But once the hotel-servant added as an after-
thought, 'He's a proud fellow, a preening chap.'

One evening I invited Prokhoroff to come and have tea with
me in my room, which was as big as a barn and steam-heated,
with two great Venetian windows looking out over the park.
(Every night at nine o'clock the steam-pipes would hiss and

mutter, as though someone were asking me in a monotonous whisper: 'Is fish a good dish?')

The old man came, very smartly dressed, in a new pink cotton shirt, a grey suit, and new felt shoes. He had brushed his broad, pepper-coloured beard very carefully and oiled his grey hair with some thick unguent that had a strong, bitter smell. Solemnly he sipped his tea and talked to me.

'You have been good enough,' he said, 'to observe with perfect justice that I am a kind man. But I must admit that I was born and lived half my life as heedless of others as is everybody else. I became kind only after I had lost my faith in God.

'This happened to me after I had had a career of uninterrupted success. Fortune favoured me from the day of my birth. My father, a locksmith in Mzensk, used to say, "Stepanka was born for luck," because in the year of my birth his business was so prosperous that he was able to open a workshop of his own.

'In games, too, I was lucky, while learning was mere child's play to me. I never had illnesses or troubles of any kind. When I had finished my schooling, I immediately got an appointment in an estate office with some good, kind people. My employer loved me and his wife used to say to me, "You have great capacity, Stepan; you must take care of it." That was true: I had such unusual gifts that I kept wondering to myself where they came from. I even went so far as to give medical treatment to horses, without having any idea of the cause of their ailments. By kindness and without using a stick I could teach a dog to walk on its hind legs.

'As regards women – I was lucky there, too: any woman I glanced at would come to me, without fail.

'At twenty-six I was head-clerk and – there is no doubt at all – I might easily have become manager of the estate. Mr Markevich, like yourself a writer of books, used to go into raptures. "Prokhoroff," he would cry, "is a real Russian, a second Pursam." I don't know who Pursam was, but Mr Markevich was generally a very severe critic of people and his praise was no jest. I was extremely proud of myself and all went well with me. I had put away a small sum of money, intending to get married – for I had already discovered a pleasant and suitable young lady –

when suddenly, almost imperceptibly, I felt that a mortal danger had attacked me. The most curious of questions burnt me like fire: why was it that I was lucky in everything? Why should I be favoured like this? Such questions flashed persistently in my brain and kept me awake at night.

'Sometimes, when I was as weary as a plough-horse from a day's work, I would lie down and think, with eyes wide open. Why do I have so much luck? Of course I have capacity; I am a pious man, modest and sober, not stupid. Nevertheless, I see all around me people who are much better in every way than I am, and fortune doesn't smile on them. That is quite certain.

'So I thought and thought how God could allow this to be. Here was I, living as happily as a fly in a pot of honey, and where was the man who could harm me? The idea stuck persistently in my mind. I felt that some secret lay behind my success in life, that some charm was working within me. But to what end? Again and again I would ask God what His purpose might be, whither He was leading me.

'But God was silent . . . He said not a word in reply.

'Then I made up my mind. What will happen, I thought, if I do something dishonest? So I took four hundred and twenty roubles out of the safe, knowing that one is severely punished for the theft of any amount over three hundred roubles. Well, I took it. Of course the loss was noticed immediately. The manager, Filipp Karlovich, a very kind man, asked me what had happened to the money, for I had stolen it in such a way that no one but myself could be suspected. I saw that Filipp Karlovich was troubled and embarrassed. Well, said I to myself, what's the use of tormenting the good man? So I told him I had stolen the money. He wouldn't believe me; he said I was joking. However, in the end he had no choice but to believe; so he reported my statement to my employer's wife, who was amazed and alarmed. "What's the matter with you, Stepan?" said she. "You can have me arrested if you like," I answered. She blushed and got angry, pulling nervously at the fringe of her blouse. "I'm not going to have you arrested," she said, "but your behaviour is so impudent that you must confess." So I confessed and left their house, went to Moscow and returned the money by post, without mentioning my name.'

'Why did you do it?' I asked the old man. 'Did you want to suffer?'

He lifted his thick, shaggy brows in amazement and smiled in his beard. But the smile faded away as he passed his hand over his curly hair.

'Well, no, of course not. Why should I want to suffer? I like a peaceful life. No, it was simply that my curiosity over-powered me. I longed to discover the secret of my luck. Perhaps a certain caution urged me on – a desire to test how solid my fortune might be. Of course, I was young, playing, perhaps, a kind of game with myself. Although, as a matter of fact, what I did was not play to me – that is, not merely playing. My life had been so unusual. I had lived in love and comfort, like a little lap-dog. People round me frowned and complained, while I seemed to have been condemned by God to lead a quiet life until the end of my days. Everyone else had trials and troubles to encounter, while I had nothing of the sort. It was as though I didn't deserve the usual, human things. That is what it was, I think . . .

'Well, I lay in my room in the hotel in Moscow and said to myself that any other man would have been handed over to the police for a mere rouble – and I had got nothing for stealing four hundred! At that I laughed, for here was a piece of bad luck at last!

' "No," I thought to myself, "you wait a bit, Stepan." I watched the people in the hotel – it was a dirty hole and they were mostly sharpers, actors and unfortunate women. One of them pretended that he was a cook, but turned out to be a professional thief. I began talking to him. "How do you get on?" I asked. "So – so," he said; "there are ups and downs in the business." When we got better acquainted he was more communicative. "I have a fine thing in view," he admitted, "but I must have some good tools for it – expensive ones – and I have no money." "Ah," I thought, "here it is, at last." "Is it an attempt on someone's life?" I asked him. He seemed to resent my question. "Heaven forbid," he said. "I value my own head much too much!"

'Well, I gave him the money for the tools, on condition that he'd take me along with him. He made a wry face and shied at the idea, but finally agreed. I did not like his enterprise at all. We went to a house and pretended we had come to pay a call and not found the people at home. The door was opened by a nice-looking girl – evidently a friend of his. He at once tied up her hands and feet with great dexterity and began to rummage in a cupboard, whistling as he did so. All so simple, wasn't it? We went out as we had come in, without any trouble. Very soon afterwards the man disappeared from Moscow and I went on living by myself.

'So that's the way of it, I thought to myself. Luck again! It was all very funny and at the same time very infuriating.

'Feeling extremely bitter with myself and God, who, after all, is supposed to see all that I am doing, I went to the theatre one night; and as I sat in the balcony, I saw the nice-looking girl whom we'd tied up, in the next seat but one from me, watching the stage and wiping her eyes with a handkerchief.

'Between the acts I went up to her. "I think we know each other," I said. As she didn't seem inclined to talk, I reminded her of a thing or two.

' "Sh," she said. "Shut up, will you?"

' "What are you crying about?" I asked.

' "It's the prince I'm so sorry for," she said. (There was a prince being ill-treated on the stage.) After the play she went to a bar with me and from the bar I took her to my room and we began to live together as lovers.

'She thought me a regular thief and used to ask if I had any new jobs in hand.

' "No, none," I would answer.

' "Very well, I'll introduce you to some people." She did, and in spite of being thieves they turned out to be very good fellows, all of them. There was one of them in particular, Kostia Bashmakoff, a wonderful child of nature, a perfect innocent, with such a bright, cheerful disposition. We soon became great friends.

'One day I confided to him that, after all, that kind of life wasn't really what I wanted and that I had become a thief merely out of curiosity.

'"Same here," said he. "It's just high spirits that sent me to this job. There are such a lot of fine things in the world and it is so good to be alive! Sometimes I want to cry out in the street: 'Look here, boys, lay hold of me, I'm a thief!'"

'A queer fellow he was. One day he jumped from a train when it was going at full speed and broke his arm; afterwards he got consumption and went to the steppes to drink kumiss.*

'I hung about with those boys – there were three of them – for fourteen months. We robbed flats and thieved in the trains, and I was always expecting something wonderful and terrible to happen the next day. But all our stunts went off quite smoothly.

'One day the head of our gang, Mikhail Petrovich Borokhoff, a very respectable man with plenty of brains, called us together. "We've had luck," he said, "ever since the day that Stepan joined us." Those words brought me back to my senses. I came back to my old thoughts, which had been banished for a time by the exciting life I had been leading. I began to wonder: What am I to do now? Shall I commit a murder?

'This thought worked its way into my mind like a splinter. I could not get rid of it; it just stuck inside me and poisoned me. I would sit at night on my bed, let my arms hang between my knees and think: "What about it, God? You don't care how I live. Here I am, preparing to kill a man, a being like myself. It will be quite easy."

'But God made no answer.'

The old man sighed deeply and began spreading some jam on his bread.

'You are a proud man,' I said.

Again lifting his heavy, shaggy brows, he looked at me intently. His doll-like eyes seemed to become vacant, yet an ugly light shone in them.

'No; why should I be proud?' he answered, carefully arranging his beard so that it should not get sticky with jam. 'To my mind a man has nothing to be proud about.'

And carefully putting small pieces of bread into his hairy

* Mare's milk.

94

mouth, he went on as before, in a low voice, as though he were speaking of a stranger whom he did not care much about.

'Ye-es,' he said, 'so God remained silent. And very soon a tempting opportunity came. We got into a country house at night and were at work, when suddenly from somewhere in the darkness I heard a sleepy little voice. "Uncle, is that you?" it cried. My friend jumped out on to the balcony, but I looked round and noticed a door, and behind it – someone moving about. I opened it a little and saw there, in a corner, a boy of twelve lying in bed and scratching his head – such long hair he had. And again he asked: "Uncle – is that you?" I watched him and felt my hands and feet trembling, my heart beating wildly. Here was my chance!

'I said to myself, "Now, Stepan, now – get on with it." But I got myself in hand in time. No, I thought to myself, I won't try that, indeed I won't! Perhaps, God, this is the sin to which you've been tempting me during all these years of fortune and success? The murder of an innocent being! That's the pit you were drawing me into – to which my path was leading me. No, no, no!

'The idea angered me so intensely that I hardly know how I left the place and found my way back to the woods. A little later I was sitting underneath a tree, and at my side my friend was smoking a cigarette and swearing softly to himself. A little drizzling rain was falling on us, the woods rustled loudly, and before my eyes I could see, in the darkness, that sleepy little fellow, quite helpless, quite in my power. Another moment – and the boy would have been no more. Ugh! . . .

'The thought struck me with such stunning force that I began to feel like the helpless boy myself. There you are, I said to myself, sitting quietly, not knowing what I may not do in a minute, just as I do not know what you may do. All of a sudden – all sorts of queer ideas come like that, don't they? – all of a sudden, you'll go for me or I'll go for you. How tempting such mutual helplessness is! And besides – who directs our actions?

'In the morning I returned to town and went straight to the judge, Mr Sviatukhine.

'"Please arrest me, sir," I said to him. "I am a thief." He

95

proved to be a very good fellow, quiet and thin, only rather stupid, of course.

' "Why are you owning up?" he asked. "Have you quarrelled with your companions. Couldn't you agree about the booty?"

' "I had no accomplices," I said. "I worked alone." Very foolishly I told him the whole story of my life, just as I am telling it to you now, told him what a cruel game God had played with me.'

'But why God, Stepan Ilich,' I interrupted, 'and not the Devil?'

With calm assurance the old man explained.

'There is no Devil,' he said. 'The Devil is the invention of a cunning mind – people have created him to justify their own meanness; also for the benefit of God, so that He need carry no blame. There exist only God – and man – nothing else. All who have been likened to the Devil – Judas, Cain, the Tsar, Ivan the Terrible – they are all merely human inventions, made up so that the accumulated bestiality and sins of the multitude may be laid on one person. Believe me, it is so. Yes, we poor devils of sinners get entangled in our sins, and then we try to discover someone who is worse than we are – a Devil, in short. We are bad, we feel, but not very bad; there are worse folk than ourselves . . .

'But I was telling you about the judge. He had some pictures hanging on the walls and the room was tastefully and comfortably furnished. He had a kind face, though that means very little, since rotten wares are often sold under a good signboard. However, while I was telling him my story, above us, on the top floor, someone was strumming on the piano. The noise jarred on me. There, God, I thought to myself, see what a mess you've made of everything!

'I spoke for a long time, and the judge listened to me as an old woman listens to a priest in church. But he did not understand.

' "Of course, I shall have to arrest you," he said; "and you'll have to go to trial. But I can guarantee that you'll be acquitted if you tell the jury all that you have told me here. In front of you," he added, "I see not a prison, but a monastery."

'I felt hurt. "You haven't understood a thing," I told him, "and I don't wish to say another word."

'Well, he sent me to the police-station, and there the detectives took hold of me. "We know," said they, "that the thefts to which you have confessed have not been carried out by you alone. Tell us, where are your accomplices? Then – come and work with us."

'I refused to do either, of course – so they began thrashing me. They gave me nothing to eat. They left me to starve. Here I suffered a bit, it is true.

'Then came the trial. I did not like it and refused to say a word. The jury got angry and sent me off to prison. There I lay, among people who were little better than worms or beasts.

'Ha, I thought again, what a rotten mess you are making of it all, God! What a rotten mess! This thought kept coming back to me. It did not seem to me to matter what a man might do, since his life is ordered for him by God alone.

'I can't say much good of that prison. When I got out I looked about me, here and there, roamed a bit about the world, worked in an iron foundry – but gave that up very soon. It was too hot. Also, I am not very fond of iron or any other kind of metal – all the troubles of life come from them, all the troubles, the filth and the rust. Without metals a man would live more simply and more easily.

'I undertook all kinds of jobs, down to cleaning out lavatories; something drew me, I'll admit, to the dirtiest kinds of work. Then I decided to try my luck as a bath-attendant. For seventeen years now I have been washing people and trying not to upset them. What's the good of upsetting people? Nothing comes of it, if you look at it in the right way. I live without God. I pity people because they are so forsaken – and altogether I find life rather dull . . .'

# A Strange Murderer

ABOUT two months before his death Judge L. N. Sviatukhine said to me one day:

'Of all the murderers that have come before me during the last thirteen years, one only, the packhorse-driver Merkuloff, ever awoke in me a feeling of terror before man and for man. The ordinary murderer is a hopelessly dull and obtuse creature, half man, half beast, incapable of realizing the significance of his crime; or else a sly little dirty fellow, a squealing fox caught in a trap; or else again an unsuccessful, hysterical monomaniac, desperate and bitter. But when Merkuloff stood in front of me in the dock I instantly scented something weird and unusual about him.'

Sviatukhine half closed his eyes, recalling the picture to his memory:

'A large, broad-shouldered peasant of about forty-five, a thin, good-looking face, such a face as one usually sees on holy images. A long, grey beard, curly hair also grey, bald on the temples, and in the middle of the forehead, like a horn, a provocative, cossack forelock. From the deep orbits, quite out of keeping with that forelock, a pair of clever grey eyes glanced shrewdly at me, soft and full of pity.'

Breathing a heavy, putrid breath – the judge was dying of cancer of the stomach – Sviatukhine nervously wrinkled up his earthen-coloured, exhausted face.

'What startled me particularly was this expression of pity in his eyes – where could it have come from? And I confess that my official indifference disappeared, giving way to an anxious curiosity, a new and unpleasant experience for me.

'He answered my questions in the dull voice of a man who is not used to or does not like talking much – his answers were short and precise – it was clear that he intended to make a frank confession. I said something to him which I would never have said to any other man in the same circumstances:

' "You've got a fine face, Merkuloff; you do not look like a murderer."

'At this he pulled up the chair in the dock, as though he were a guest there rather than a prisoner, sat down firmly on it, pressed his palms to his knees, and began to talk in a curiously melodious voice, as though he were playing on a reed-pipe. Perhaps that is not a very good simile, for a reed-pipe has also a dull note in it.

' "You think, sir, that if I have committed this murder it means that I am a beast? No – I am not one – and since you appear to be interested in me, I will tell you my story."

'And he told it me, calmly, consecutively, as murderers usually do not do, without attempting to justify himself or to awaken compassion.'

The judge spoke very slowly and indistinctly, his parched lips, covered with a kind of grey scale, moved with difficulty and he moistened them with his dark tongue, closing his eyes.

'I will try to recall his own words. There was a particular significance in them. They were words that amazed and shattered one. That compassionate glance of his, directed at me, crushed me, too. You understand? It was not plaintive but compassionate. He felt sorry for me, although I was in quite good health at that time.

'He committed his first murder in the following circumstances: He was carting some sacks of sugar from the harbour one autumn night when he noticed that a man was walking behind the cart and had made a rent in the sack and was filling his pockets with the sugar. Merkuloff got down, rushed at him, gave him a blow on the temple, and the man fell down.

' "Well," said Merkuloff, "I gave him another kick and began fixing the torn sack, while all the time he lay under my feet, his face turned upwards, his eyes and mouth wide open. I felt frightened, so I knelt down and took his head in my hands, but it rolled from one side to the other, as heavy as lead, while his eyes seemed to wink at me and his nose bled all over my hands. I jumped up, crying: 'My God, I've killed him!' "

'Merkuloff then went off to the police-station, whence he was sent to prison.

'"Sitting in prison," he said, "and watching the criminals around me, I seemed to be looking at everything through a fog – I just couldn't take things in. I felt terrified, could not sleep or eat, but kept thinking: 'How is it, how can it be? A man was walking along the road, I struck him – and – no more man. What does it mean? The soul – where is it? It isn't as though he were a sheep or a calf – he could do this and that and believed in God, no doubt; also, although his nature might have been different, he was just the same kind of being as I am. And I – don't you see? – crossed his life, killed him as though he were a beast, no more. If it's like that, why, then it might happen to me too any day: I might get a blow – and it's all up with me!' So terrified was I by such thoughts, sir, that I seemed to hear the very hairs on my head growing."

'While telling his story, Merkuloff looked me straight in the face, but although his light eyes were motionless, I seemed to see the twinkle of dark fear in his grey pupils. He had folded his hands together, placed them between his knees, and was pressing them hard. For this unpremeditated crime he got a very mild punishment: his preliminary confinement was discounted and he was sent off to a monastery for penitence.

'"Over there," Merkuloff continued, "they appointed a little old monk to look after me. He was to teach me how to live. He was such a gentle little man, who spoke of God in the finest way possible. A very fine character, he was; and like a father to me, always addressing me as: 'My son, my son.' Listening to him, I could not help asking myself sometimes: 'Why, O God, is man so defenceless?' Then I would say to the monk, 'Take yourself, Father Paul; you love God and He, most probably, loves you, too – yet I have merely to strike a blow at you and you'll die like a fly. Where then shall the gentle soul go? And the matter doesn't lie in your soul – it lies in my evil thought: I can kill you at any moment. And as a matter of fact my thought is not even an evil one. I can kill you very gently, very softly – allow you to say a prayer first, then kill you. How do you explain that?' – But he couldn't, he only kept saying: 'It's the

Devil who rouses the beast in you. He's always goading you.'
I told him that it made no difference to me who was goading
me; all I wanted him to teach me was how to avoid being goaded.
'I'm not a beast,' I told him, 'there's nothing of the beast in
me; it is only my soul that is frightened for itself.'

' " 'Pray,' he said to me; 'pray until you are exhausted.' I
did so, I got thin doing so, my temples went grey, although
I was only twenty-eight at the time. But prayer could not still
my fear; even during prayer I went on thinking: 'Dear God,
why is it? Here I can cause the death of any man at any moment,
and any man can kill me at any moment he wants to! I can
go to sleep and someone can draw a knife across my throat, or
bring down a brick or a log on my head. Or any heavy weight.
There are so many ways of doing it!' . . . These thoughts pre-
vented me from sleeping, terrified me. At first I used to sleep
with the novices, and as soon as one of them stirred, I'd jump up
and shout out: 'Who's fiddling about? Keep quiet, you hounds!'
Everybody was afraid of me and I was afraid of everybody.
They complained about me and I was sent off to the stables.
There I grew quieter, with the horses – they're only soulless
beasts. But all the same I only closed one eye when I slept. I was
frightened."

'After his penitence was over Merkuloff got another job as a
driver, and lived in the market gardens outside the town, in a
sober, detached way.

' "I lived like a man in a dream," he told me. "Just kept silent
and avoided people. The other drivers used to ask me: 'Why
are you living so gloomily, Vassili? Are you preparing to take
the cowl?' What should I want to take the cowl for? There are
men in cloisters as well as outside them – and wherever there are
men there is fear. I looked at people and thought: 'God help
you! Uncertain are your lives and you have no protection against
me, just as I have none against you!' Just think, sir, how hard
it was for me to live with such a weight on my heart." '

Sviatukhine sighed and adjusted the small black silk cap on
his bald skull that shone like an old, bleached bone.

'At that moment, at those very words, Merkuloff smiled; and
that unexpected, uncalled-for smile twisted and distorted his

well-cut face so acutely that I was instantly convinced that the man was a fiend. Most probably he killed all his victims with precisely that smile. I experienced a most uncanny feeling. He continued with something like **v**exation in his voice:

' "So I went on walking about like a hen with an egg, the egg being rotten and I knowing it. The moment is bound to come when the egg inside me will burst, and what will happen to me then? I don't know – I daren't guess what it will be – but I can guess that it will be something terrible."

'I asked him whether he had ever thought of committing suicide. He was silent for a moment, his eyebrows moved, and he answered: "I can't remember – no – I don't think I ever have." ... Then he turned to me, wonderingly, with a look of inquiry in his eyes, and said, I think quite sincerely: "How is it I never thought of that? That's a curious thing . . ."

'He struck his knee with the palm of his hand, glanced vaguely at a corner of the court, and muttered pettishly:

' "Yes, yes, but don't you see, I didn't want to give my soul a free hand. I was so tormented in my heart with curiosity regarding other people and in the shameful cowardice of that soul of mine. I forgot about myself. As to my soul, it was just musing: what if I kill this fellow – what will happen then?"

'Two years later Merkuloff killed the half-witted girl Matrosh-ka, the daughter of a gardener. He told me about her murder in a somewhat hazy manner, as though he himself hardly understood the motives of the crime. One could gather from his words that Matroshka was slightly crazy.

' "She used to have a kind of fits which blotted out her reason: she'd throw down her work of digging flower-beds or weeding and walk along smiling, with her mouth open, as though some-body unseen were beckoning to her to come. She'd knock against trees, hedges and walls, attempting to pass through them. One day she stepped on an upturned rake and hurt her foot; blood was flowing from the wound in a stream, but she still walked along, feeling no pain – didn't even wince. She was an ugly girl, very fat, and inclined to debauchery, owing to her silliness. She used to accost the peasants, and they, of course, took advantage of her silliness. She pestered me, too, with her attentions, but I had other things to think about. What fascinated me in her was the fact that nothing affected her: whether she fell into a ditch or down from a roof, she came up safe and sound. Anyone else would have sprained their foot or broken a bone, but nothing happened to her. She was all bruised and scratched, of course, but was as tough as could be. She seemed to live in absolute security.

' "I killed her in public, on a Sunday. I was sitting on a bench at the gate and she began to be amiable to me in a nasty manner – so I just struck her with a faggot. She rolled down and never moved. I glanced at her – she was dead. I sat down on the ground beside her and burst out crying: 'God, oh God, what is the matter with me? Why this weakness, this helplessness?' "

'He spoke jerkily, as though in a delirium, for some time harping on the helplessness of men, and all the time a sullen fear shone in his eyes. His dry, ascetic face darkened as he said, hissing through his teeth:

' "Just you think, sir; here, at this very minute, I can strike you down dead! Just think of that! Who can forbid me to do it? What's to stop me? Nothing at all – nothing . . ."

'He was punished for the murder of that girl by three years of prison – the mildness of the punishment being due, he explained, to the skill of his advocate – whom he did not hesitate to vilify: "A young one, with dishevelled hair, a bawler. He kept on saying to the jury: 'Who could possibly say a bad word against this man? Not one of the witnesses has been able to. Moreover it is admitted that the dead woman was half-witted and debauched.' Oh, those lawyers! It's all tomfoolery, waste of time. I'll be defended from myself *before* the crime if you like, but once I've committed it I don't want anyone to help me. You can hold me while I stand still, but once I have started running you can't catch me! If I run I will go on running until I fall down with exhaustion. But prison – tomfoolery, an idle man's job, too.

' "I came out from prison dazed – unable to understand anything. People walked past, drove past, worked, built houses, and all the time I kept thinking: 'I can kill any man I choose and any man can kill me. Very terrible, this is.' And it seemed as though my arms were growing, growing, becoming a stranger's arms. I started drinking, but I couldn't keep it up, it made me sick. As soon as I had had a drop too much I began to cry – hid in a dark corner and cried: 'I am not a man but a maniac, there's no life for me.' I drank – and didn't get drunk, and was worse than a drunkard when sober. I began to growl, growled at everyone, frightened people away, and was terrified of them. I kept thinking all the time: 'Either he'll go for me, or I'll go for him.'

' "And so I went on walking about, like a fly on a window-pane: the glass might break at any moment and I'd fall through, falling God knows where.

' "My boss, Ivan Kirilich, I killed for the same reason – curiosity. He was a cheerful, kind-hearted man, and wonderfully brave. When his neighbour's house was on fire he acted like an immortal hero – crawled right inside the flames to fetch out the old nurse, then back again for the nurse's trunk, just because she was crying for it. A happy man was Ivan Kirilich, God rest his soul. It is true that I tortured him a bit. The others I killed at once, but I tortured Ivan – I wanted to see whether he would be frightened or not. Well, he had a weak constitution and was strangled very rapidly. People came running up at his cries, and wanted to beat and tie me up. But I said to them: 'You'd better tie up my soul, not my hands, you fools!' "

'Merkuloff finished his story, wiped the perspiration from his face, and said, rather breathlessly:

' "You must punish me severely, your Honour, punish me with death, or else – what is the good of it all? I can't live with people, even in jail. I've got a crime against my soul. I'm fed up with it and am afraid that I'll want to begin testing it again – and then more people will have to suffer for it ... You must put me away, sir, you must ..." '

Blinking with his dying eyes, the judge continued:

'He put himself away of his own accord – strangled himself in his cell, in a rather peculiar way – with the chains he was manacled with – the devil knows how! I didn't see it myself, but I was told about it by the governor of the prison. The latter said it needed great will-power to kill oneself in such a painful and unhandy manner. That's what he said: "unhandy".'

Then, closing his eyes, Sviatukhine murmured:

'It was probably I who inspired Merkuloff with the idea of suicide ... Ye-es ... There, my dear friend, there's a simple Russian peasant for you, but all the same ... Ye-es ... What do you think of it?'

# A Student's Plea

THE last words in court of the Moscow student Mankoff, who had murdered his wife, were as follows:

'She is dead, she is a martyr, perhaps by now she is a holy being, in paradise; whereas I remain here below to carry, for the rest of my life, the heavy cross of crime and repentance. Why punish me, when I have already punished myself! I can still eat nice little apples and eggs, just as I did before, but they no longer possess their former sweet flavour. Nothing gives me any joy now – why then punish me?'

# The Food of the Soul

COMING to pay a call on A. A. J., I found he was not at home.

'He's run off somewhere,' his landlady told me. She was a pleasant-looking old dame in horn spectacles, with a hairy mole on the left cheek. Urging me to sit down and take a rest, she said, smiling gently:

'It strikes me that all you young men of today live at a break-neck pace, as though someone had fired you out of a gun. In olden times people lived more slowly, they even walked differently. And their shoes did not wear out so quickly – not because the leather was any stronger, but because they walked more slowly and carefully.

'Now, for instance, before Jarovitsky lived here this room was occupied by a teacher of calligraphy, named Alexei Alexeivich, his family name being Kusmin. He was a wonderfully quiet man – it is strange to recall how quiet he was. He used to wake up in the morning, clean his shoes, brush his trousers and coat, then wash and dress, and all as quietly as if he thought that all the people in the town were asleep and he was afraid of waking them up. He prayed, too, and always used to recite the Lent repentance prayer. After that he would drink a glass of tea, eat an egg with a piece of bread and butter, then go to the University, come back, have his dinner, rest for a while, and then start painting pictures or making frames. These pictures here are all his handiwork.'

The walls of the small room were abundantly adorned with pencil drawings in home-made frames of black wood; the pictures represented weeping willows and birches growing over graves, over ponds, by the side of half-demolished water-mills, weeping willows and birches everywhere. Only on one rather small picture was there anything different – a carefully drawn narrow path that climbed a hill, the path intertwined with the huge root of a tree which looked like a serpent, the top of the tree being broken off and a quantity of dry branches showing.

Fondly examining the grey, timid pictures the old dame continued lovingly:

'He used to go out in the dusk of the evenings and preferred doing so when the weather was cloudy and rainy. That is how he caught cold. I used to say to him: "Why do you always choose such weather to go out in?"

' "Because on days like these," says he, "there are not so many people in the streets. I am a timid man and do not care about meeting people. Often too," he would add, "people make me think badly of them – and I try to avoid doing that."

'He would put on his cap and cloak, take an umbrella, and walk quietly along the hedgerows. If anyone came in his way he would step aside, letting them pass. He used to walk very lightly, as though he were not walking on earth at all. A pathetic man he was, small and slim, fair-haired, with a slightly hooked nose, his face clean-shaven and so young-looking, although he was nearly forty.

'He always coughed into his handkerchief so as not to make a noise. Sometimes I used to look at him admiringly and think: if only all people were like that!

'One day I asked him: "Aren't you dull, living alone like this?"

' "No," he replied, "not at all dull – I live with my soul, and the soul does not know boredom – boredom is an affliction of the flesh." He always answered like that – wisely, like an old man.

' "Is it possible," I would say, "that womenfolk do not interest you either and that you never give a thought to family life?"

' "No," he said, "I have no inclination that way. A family necessitates a lot of worries, and my health does not permit it, either."

'So he lived for about three years as my lodger, like a quiet little mouse, then went away to undergo a mare's milk* cure and died over there in the steppes. I waited for someone to come and claim his property, but probably he had no relations or friends,

* Kumiss.

for no one ever came and all his belongings have remained here ever since – a little underwear, those pictures, and a copybook with notes.'

I asked her to show me the copybook, and she willingly went to a chest of drawers and fetched from it a fat book bound in black calico. On a piece of pasteboard gummed to the binding was written in Gothic letters:

FOOD OF THE SOUL
NOTES FOR MEMORY
A.A. KMIN
YEAR FROM J.C.
1889 JANUARY 3.

On the first leaf was a vignette, very finely drawn with a pen: in a frame of oak and maple leaves, a stump of a tree, and on it a serpent coiled up, its head in the air and its mouth open, showing its fangs. And, evidently by way of an epitaph, the following words, carefully written in a fine round handwriting:

*It soon transpired that there were many Christians, – this is usually the case when one begins to investigate a crime.*
*From a letter of Plinius to the Emperor Trajan.*

Farther on one abruptly came face to face with a large and somewhat formal piece of handwriting, ornamented with curls and flourishes:

*I am considerably cleverer than the Corinthian Apollo,* not to mention that he was a drunkard.*

On almost every page there were drawings and vignettes, very often the fat face of a woman with a snub nose and a pair of Kalmuk eyes. There were not many notes, they rarely occupied more than a page or two, usually only a few lines, but always carefully written out. Never a blot or a mistake – there was an air of finality about the whole thing – everything seemed to have been inscribed after a rough draft had been made first of all.

* The pseudonym of a Russian writer.

Feeling more and more interested, I put the copybook in my pocket and carried it home with me.

Here are some of the things that I found in that black copybook:

*So-called art feeds chiefly on the representations and descriptions of different kinds of crimes, and I have noticed that the meaner the crime the more greedily is the book read and the more praised is the description of that crime. All things considered, the interest of art is an interest for criminality. The unwholesome effect of art on the young is obvious from this.*

*A carp ought to be stuffed with carrots, but no one ever thinks of doing that.*

*Prince Vladimir of Galich went to serve the King of Hungary and served him for four years. After that, returning to Galich, he devoted his time to building churches.*

*Every crime demands an innate talent for it – particularly manslaughter.*

*Ap. of Cor. wrote some nasty little verses, poking fun at me. However, I write them down here in complete indifference to his spite:*

> *The soul should be more nearly all elastic;*
> *That is, more supple, aye, more like a tool;*
> *One must indulge in spiritual gymnastic;*
> *That is, to put it simply, play the fool.*

*A successful, that is an unpunished, murder should be committed unexpectedly.*

These most curious thoughts had been inscribed by the quiet little man in different handwritings – rhomboidal, Gothic, English, Slavonic, and others – clearly displaying his skill. But everything that concerned murder was written in the same fine, round hand in which he had written the extract from Pliny's letter to Trajan. I should hazard the guess that this was his own individual handwriting.

Traced in beautiful scrolls was the following:

*To think is the duty of every educated person.*

In ornate Slavonic letters:

*I will never permit myself to forget any insults.*

While in his fine round handwriting he had written:

*The quality of unexpectedness does not, however, preclude a careful preliminary study of the life of the intended victim. Particularly important points are: the time and place of strolls: the hours at which the individual returns from lectures: the time he returns from his club at night.*

Two pages were filled with detailed and dull descriptions of a boating party on the Volga, then in a sloping hand was written:

*Pol. Petr. has the bad habit of scratching the underside of her left knee with her finger. She likes sitting crosslegged – that is what produces the itch under the knee – it stops the blood-circulation, probably. He does not notice that, the fool. He is altogether stupid. And she has an unpleasant habit of continually saying: 'You don't mean it?' – somehow on her lip it sounds mocking. Poline – that is Pelageia, Pelagia, a rather vulgar, peasant name.*

Then again in the round handwriting:

*How to leave the town and come back unexpectedly: take a cab – it is very silly to say 'take a cab' – one ought to say 'hire a cab' – on the way home jump off, under pretext of pains in the stomach, run to the place, kill, and drive on.*

Farther on was the face of a Kalmuk woman and a hideously short-legged little man, with a small face and marks of interrogation in place of eyes, and a heavy beard.

Then, in the ornate writing of a clerk:

*He began calling on, that is paying visits to, that old witch, the poetess Missovsky. All the local revolutionaries gather at her house.*

Again in the round hand:

*Suddenness of action is a guarantee of success. Hire an old cabman, if possible with poor eyesight. Jump off, and press your hands to your stomach to indicate pains. Walk down the side-street where he is and go straight towards him, but without recognising him. This will make him confused. Pass him and turn suddenly, and strike a blow at the correct spot.* (Here follows the abbreviated Latin name of a muscle.) *Return rapidly to the cabman, buttoning up your clothes, and make some coarse joke. As soon as you get home, send for some chlorodyne for pains in the stomach. In case everything is discovered behave with curiosity and light-heartedness. Assist at the funeral, of course.*

There were no more notes on this subject, the last one being ended by a vignette: a grave without a cross: over it a dead broken tree; and all round it long thick grass; while in the sky hung the tearful Kalmuk's face of a moon.

Farther on there were four more notes:

*A silly sentence in a German review: a professor asks his bride: 'Adele — why do you "repetition" everything I say?'*

*To-day, at sunset, a starling sang wonderfully in the garden; it sang as though it were the last time that it would ever sing.*

*To meet a man does not always imply danger; still, one ought to be more careful in the choice of one's acquaintances. I will never again get to know red-haired people . . .*

*Only he knows what toothache means who has had it, and then only while the tooth is actually aching. When it is over, a man forgets how tormenting it can be. It would be an admirable thing if the whole population of the earth could have toothache for at least several hours a month, all at the same time. That alone would teach people to understand one another . . .*

Thus ends the book of the quiet little teacher of calligraphy, entitled by him: *The Food of the Soul.* He appears to have kept this diary for nine years and four months.

# The Ruined Author

ONE night, in a dirty little public-house, in the smoky atmosphere of half-drunken, happy-go-lucky people a man, still young but badly battered by life, said to me:

'My life was ruined by Malashin, the telegraph clerk.'

He bent his head, crowned by a crumpled jockey cap, glanced under the table, moved his crippled leg with his hands, and gave a deep sigh:

'Yes, Malashin the telegraph clerk did it. Our priest used to call him the "nonsensical-faced youth," and the girls called him "Malasha". He was a small, slim youngster, rosy-cheeked, brown-eyed, dark-browed, with the hands of a woman – as pretty as a picture. Always merry, affectionate with everybody, he was a good deal petted, I might even say loved, in our little town, where the three thousand five hundred inhabitants leisurely carried on the everyday tasks that fall to the lot of human beings.

'When I was twenty years old I was filled with the boredom of life, numbed with it to the very soul; the quiet bustle of humanity got on my nerves, frightened me even. I could not understand the sense that lay behind it all, and I watched the goings-on around me with something akin to dismay. Once, on the spur of the moment in a gust of inspiration, I wrote a story, which I called "How People Live", and sent the manuscript to the *Niva*. A week, a month, two months went by, and at last I abandoned all hope of hearing from the editor. "He who grasps too much, holds little," I said to myself.

'Then, about three months later, I met Malashin: "I've got a post-card for you," says he, and he handed me a post-card on which was written:

' "Your tale does not awaken any particular interest in the reader, and cannot therefore be considered successful; but

113

apparently you have a certain gift for writing. Please send us some more."

'You can imagine how delighted I was with this. Malashin pleasantly informed me that the card had been in his pocket for three days. "I took it with me," he said, "intending to pass it on to you but kept forgetting it. I see you write and want to become another Count Tolstoy!"

'We laughed and parted at this. But that evening as I was going home the deacon, sitting at his window, called out to me, "Hullo, you writer! I'll give you what for!" and shook his fist at me. In my joy I misinterpreted the deacon's gesture. I knew him to be rather an odd fellow. In his youth he had aspired to sing in the opera, but he never got nearer the footlights than the third row of the chorus. Nor could he get on with his operatic career in his own country, owing to an inclination for exaggerated freedom of action. He was given to drink, and when in a state of intoxication he used to crack walnuts with his forehead for a bet; once he cracked a whole pound of them at a time, so that the skin of his forehead was all cut and bruised. In his pocket he used to carry a tin box in which he kept frogs in the summer and mice in the winter. At an opportune moment he would throw the little beasts down ladies' necks. These jokes used to be forgiven him on account of his merry nature and for his knowledge of the habits of fishes – he was a perfect fisherman. He did not eat fish himself, being afraid that a bone might choke him, but he distributed his catch among his acquaintances and thus increased the circle of his friends.

'So, you see, I went on my way rejoicing over my news. At that time I was a modest youth of a thoughtful nature, though doubtless rather uncouth in appearance . . .'

He took his thin, faded moustache between his lips, closed his dull eyes, and with a trembling hand began to fill himself a glass of vodka. At twenty he surely must have been a clumsy, lanky fellow; his shaggy grey locks must have been red, his dull eyes light-blue, and his face thickly freckled. Now his flabby cheeks were covered with a fine network of red veins, his purple drunkard's nose sadly overhung the scanty moustache. The vodka failed to rouse him, and he spoke with an effort, as though in a dream:

'I considered myself a beau, a man of some distinction. Very much so, in fact! Gifted, I was told I was! My soul sang like a lark. I began to write feverishly, spending entire nights in writing; the words flowed from my pen in a stream. Oh, the happiness of it! I began to notice, however, that the townspeople watched me with peculiar attention whenever and wherever I appeared. Ah, I thought to myself, jealous!...

'One day Malashin invited me to go and have tea at the exciseman's, who had a daughter, a very smart young girl. They had asked a number of young people there as well. Everybody who knew me came up to me and said, "You write, don't you? Will you have some sugar in your tea?"

'Ha, I thought to myself, they are offering me sugar now! I stirred the sugar in my cup with the spoon, tasted it, and wondered what was the matter with it, for it tasted salty – quite bitter, in fact. I drank it down all the same, so bashful was I. And then suddenly they all burst out laughing, and Malashin, straightening his face, said to me:

' "What's the matter? Surely a writer ought to be able to judge between good and bad, and you can't even distinguish salt from sugar! How's that?"

'I became greatly confused and my feeling of self-importance sank rapidly. "This is a joke, of course," I said.

'They laughed still louder at that. Then they all began urging me to recite some verses – I had attempted to write poetry too, and Malashin knew of this.

' "Poets always recite their verses in society, so you must do it too."

'Here the heavy-faced son of a major interrupted protestingly: "Good verses can only be written by army men."

'The young ladies started to argue with him about this, and in the uproar I disappeared unseen.

'From that evening onwards the whole town took to tracking me as though I were a strange animal. On the first Sunday after, I met the deacon carrying his fishing-rods, trampling along like an elephant.

' "Hold on," he cried; "so you write, do you, you idiot? I've been here training for the opera for three years," he continued, "and I'm no match for you. Who are you, after all? You're no more than a fly. Flies like you merely stain the mirror of literature, you skunk!" And he abused me so roundly that I felt considerably hurt. Why does he do it? I wondered.

'A short time after this, my aunt – I am an orphan and used to live with my aunt – came to me and said: "What is all this that they're saying about you – that you write? You'd better leave that alone; it's time you got married." I tried to explain to her that there was nothing wrong in writing, that even Counts and Princes did it, and that it was altogether a clean profession, a noble one. She wouldn't listen to me and began to cry, saying, "Good heavens! What blackguard ever taught you to do it?"

'And Malashin, meeting me in the street next day, shouted out to me, "Good morning, Count Tolstoy, Junior!" He composed a silly song about me, and the youngsters of the town used to break out into it as soon as they caught sight of me in the street.

> 'All the birdies, the canaries,
>     Sadly sing away,
> But they don't get any pennies
>     For their singing, I daresay.'

'Confound it all, I said to myself, I seem to have got into a fine mess with this writing! I didn't dare to show myself in the street at last – they all teased me so! The deacon was particularly furious and ready to give me a thrashing at any time. "I've been three years at it," he would growl; "you blighter, and you . . ."

'Sometimes at night I used to sit by the river and wonder why they all did it, what it was all for. There was a solitary nook across the river – a small islet and a grove of trees; I would crawl away there and, watching the stream, would feel as though the dark waters, filtered through the town, were rushing across my soul, leaving in it a bitter and soiled after-taste.

'I had a girl friend, an embroideress, whom I courted with the most honourable intentions, and I believed that my suit was favourably received. But she, too, began to grow quarrelsome and asked me with distrust, "Is it true that you have written something in the papers about us, about the town?"

' "Who told you that?"

'She declined to answer at first, but finally she owned up and said: "Malashin has got your manuscript. He reads it to everyone, and everybody is making fun of you, saying that you have gone over to Count Tolstoy. Why did you give this writing of yours to Malashin?"

'The earth swayed under me. Ugh! I thought to myself, this is a fine business – there was a lot about the excisemen and the deacon in that story, and I don't suppose they'll relish it particularly! That's why the deacon . . . Of course I had never given my treasure to Malashin; he had simply stolen it from the mail. Here my beloved added to my bitterness by saying:

' "My friends are all making fun of me because I go about with you . . . I really don't know what I'm to do . . ."

'Confound them all! I thought. But I went to Malashin.

' "Give me back my manuscript, please," I said.

' "What do you want it for," said he, coolly, "when it's already been refused?" I couldn't make him give it to me. I liked the man. As a matter of fact, I have noticed that just as useless articles are generally more treasured than useful ones, so evil-intentioned people are often more agreeable than others. A dray-horse is never so dear to one's heart as a race-horse, although men don't live by races, but by hard toil.

'The Christmas holidays came soon after this. Malashin invited me to a fancy-dress dance. I dressed up as a devil, and they stuck goat's horns into my fur cap and tied a mask on my face. Well, we danced and fooled about and all that; and at last, bathed in perspiration, I noticed that my face was smarting painfully. I decided to go home, but on the way three jokers caught me up and shouted, "The devil! down with him!"

'I started to run, but they caught me up and began pummelling me – not badly, but my face smarted so that I could have screamed with pain. I got to bed somehow, and in the morning I crawled to the mirror, and behold! my face was purple all over, my nose was swollen, my eyes hardly visible under the lids, and all watery. Well, I thought to myself, a fine sight they've made of me! They had smeared the mask inside with some acid liquid, and in the heat it began to eat through my skin. I had to go to the doctor and undergo a treatment for five whole weeks. I thought my eyes would burst and split. However, I got better in time.

'Then I decided that there was no more living for me in that town. So I went away, quietly. And now I have roamed about for thirteen years.'

He yawned and closed his eyes wearily. He seemed to be a man in the fifties.

'What do you live on?' I asked.

'I'm a groom. I've got a job in a racing-stable. And I give tips about the horses to a reporter I know.'

Then, smiling with a slow, kindly smile, he continued:

'What noble animals horses are, to be sure! There's nothing you can compare with them! But, worse luck, one of them made a mess of my leg some time ago . . .'

He sighed and added, as though reciting a line of poetry:

'The one I loved best . . .'

# The Shepherd Discusses Learning

TIMOTHY BORZOFF, the shepherd of the village of Vishenki, is a man out of the usual run: a bit of a wizard, a 'prophet,' a 'vet,' but knowing, too, how to treat human beings – a 'judge of family matters' and, as he calls himself, 'master in works of straw' – that is, he is clever at making boxes, hand-bags, cigarette-cases and picture-frames out of straw, ornamenting them with coloured paper and foil.

The more important villagers speak of him with pride: 'He's a brainy fellow, he is. He's a kind of a statesman here!'

The young stand in awe of him and call him 'Uncle Tim'. The whole village respects him for his brains, his sense of justice, his sober life and his wealth. At all meetings he is the boss, although always the last to say his word, after having carefully listened to all the other speakers.

When he was still a shepherd's boy a bull gored him in the side, and in his youth his ribs were broken by some recruits. Owing to this, Borzoff sways his strong body curiously from side to side when he walks, as though he wanted to lie down on his right side, press his ear to the earth, and listen to some sound in it.

He is about sixty, but is still a thick-set, broad-chested, iron-faced man; his large, white teeth are all in good condition; red locks push through among the grey mane of hair, which gives one the impression that his hair is turning red instead of grey. It is so thick and abundant that he never wears a hat in winter-time, even during the great frosts. To his flock and his helpers his voice rings out powerfully and loudly, but in conversation he speaks slowly and in an intentionally low tone, in order to make people listen the more carefully.

But the main point is that he is a philosopher. He often goes into the town to sell his articles of straw; he has seen a lot and thinks deeply about everything.

From dawn till sunset he sits in the field, on a hillock or in the shade of a solitary birch-tree or on the outskirts of the forest, shouting his orders sternly and menacingly to the shepherd-boys, his deft fingers incessantly braiding the straw, of which a sheaf lies at his side.

'Why is it that people live in such disunity?' he asks aloud, and then answers himself: 'It all comes from learning. People became dis-united on the day when some of them discovered that cursed education, books and laws and rules of all kinds, were necessary for them. That's what it comes to. You give your orders to me, but I can't make out what you mean, for I'm not educated. For instance: you're a doctor of animals, a "vet," as we call 'em; I, too, know my way about with animals; but we don't understand one another, and the fault of it lies with books. Yes – yes.'

I listened to him and looked at his double-tinted, red-grey beard, his large monkey's nose entangled in it, and through it flashing cunningly a pair of green toad's eyes which protruded like an owl's. No mouth was visible. When Borzoff speaks one is sensible only of something moving inside the beard, and occasionally a cold white row of teeth gleams between the hairs.

'You stand there in front of me and talk like a foreigner or a Hun. So does the police inspector, or any other official. If he uses bad language, well, that, of course, I can understand; but as soon as anyone begins to talk to me in a learned manner, a pit grows between us, right there! Here I am, on this side of it, and he's on the other, and neither of us can hear what the other is saying. Or else it's the priest: d'you think anyone ever understands what he yells about in church? It is all very fine in church, just like a dream, but as for understanding anything about it, not me! It's the same with the teachers: they gather the little kids together and teach them drivel, for years! It's a good thing the kids forget their learning when they grow up, or the peasants too would stop understanding one another. So I always say, the greatest evil that comes to folk comes from books.'

I tried to convince him of the opposite, but was quite unsuccessful. Half-closing, hiding his cunning little eyes, he listened to me in silence, sticking his chin out so much that his whiskers protruded in a hairy lump. His face took on an expression of stupidity, and shaking his stubborn head, he said pityingly:

'Heaven help me! What are we to do! I don't understand! Can't make out your words, let alone your thoughts. You listen what grand words they are, just listen! You say "instruct" – and I heard the word "insect," and I begin to think that you're a spider and are twining your web around me, as though I were a fly.

'Then you say again that we all ought to learn to read. But that's just rubbish; there wouldn't be books enough for every-one! Not only that but there wouldn't be enough food. Man, what are you thinking about! Lord, where that learning can lead a man to! My word!'

I saw, of course, that he was mocking me, but I was obstinate, too, and wanted to get the better of 'Uncle Tim.' He was pleased that I took his chaff good-naturedly, and began to speak more willingly and freely. But after one of his stories I sprang away from him like a ball hit with a stick.

He was sitting one evening after sunset on the bench by the gate in front of his hut. Frogs were croaking in the greasy waters of the pond, mosquitoes buzzed in the air above us. Borzoff was sorting stems of straw which he took from a sheaf beside him, and all the time he was lecturing me with a kind of lazy philo-sophy:

'Very well, let's come to an agreement of some kind; we both admit that we need a good man over us. But what must he be like in order to be good? Let's put it like this: he must not rob his neighbours, he must be generous to the poor, and work hard – then he'll be one of the very best. He must know all the rules: don't guzzle everything yourself, leave a bit for the dogs; don't touch what doesn't belong to you, and look after those things that do. "Dress warmly, then rely on God."* That's all he need know. It doesn't need much learning. And all our empire de-pends on such a man, master of all the tribes.

'This man who has charge of the earth has to feed the whole world, and every kind of people comes rushing at him; Huns and Frenchies and Turks – all come bothering him. You know

* A popular Russian proverb.

yourself how many times they've tried to master him – armed themselves to the teeth and gone straight for Moscow, the blighters. And he just sat quietly and waited. Yes. But when they all came up, the twelve nations – or was it more? – he stood up and – bang! And all the warriors just scattered like dust. Nothing left of 'em. They were – but they ain't any more. And with the years these bold blighters grew fewer and fewer and we grew more and more, so that now one doesn't know where to put 'em all. Yes, yes.

'But according to you it seems that a good man's a miserable creature and well-nigh half-witted. What's his job? No one can find anything to suit him. What good does he do? He shouts himself hoarse, yelling things which he's got no business to yell, and is sent to prison for it. That's how one pictures the good man, according to your ideas.

'I've known such fellows, I know ever such a lot of ne'er-do-wells and drivellers of all sorts. Even his Honour the police inspector has told me many times: "You know a lot, Borzoff, you've got a mighty clever head!" I took my hat off to him for those words, of course, but I thought to myself, "The man's a fool." He's got a wife who has been paralysed for seven years, and he just sits beside her like a well-fed hound over a bit of carrion. He died the same year she did – they said it was from sorrow. People used to say about him: "He's a good man." But the only good thing about him was his horse. I bled it once. A gelding, it was. A fine, strong beast, first class in every way.

'The funniest chap I ever came across among those "good 'uns" was the son of our lady of the manor, Olga Nikolaevna Dubrovina. She was a rum 'un: her husband left her and went and hid abroad. A sharp-nosed lady, she was; very high-spirited. She wore spectacles hanging on a black thread which was tied to her ear. "I'm a doctor," she used to say. And she did doctor some people, it's true. During a fire she got her leg broken, and that made her a bit quieter.

'Her son, Mitia, was a pal of mine; we used to play together when we were kids. When he grew up he went off somewhere to study, and I didn't see him for some years. Then, suddenly, just as though he'd popped out of the marsh, he came back again. I was already a shepherd at the time, and was sitting on the skirts of the forest, carving pipes, when he came running up. "Don't you know me?" he asks. He'd grown long and thin and bald, and wore spectacles, too, like his mother. He'd got a stick with a muslin bag on it in his hand, and a tin box strapped across his shoulder; with his thin little legs he looked exactly like a clown. He was catching moths and butterflies and beetles, and gathering grasses, like a blooming wizard. He kept talking to me about old times, when we were boys. "D'you remember, d'you remember?" he kept saying. I could see one thing very clearly: Mitia had learnt to be a fool most successfully. I felt ashamed of him. I was already married by then.

' "What are you doing with yourself, Dmitri Pavlovich?" I asked him.

' "I'm writing books," he said, "on insects and their lives."

' "So – so?" I said; "it's a pleasant occupation, there's no doubt about that."

'I used to watch him carefully, and I soon found out that he was as generous as a drunken man – thriftless to the limit. The villagers began to beg him to help them, first one then another. I did, too. I wheedled a straw hat out of him, a fine straw hat it was; it was through that that I learnt to make all kinds of rubbish out of straw. Of course I used to take money from him too, we being pals. And one day he gave me a knife, a beauty.

'He had the mind of a mouse, for he'd learnt and studied till he'd lost all his reason. He used to say: "The mosquito carries fever; beware of the mosquito!" I didn't laugh, of course, and pretended to believe what he said. So I asked him: "How's that?" Then he'd begin to unroll his spool. My God! He'd let out about a thousand words, and in all of them there'd be no more sense than in a bird's beak. Or else he'd start talking of the peasants: how hard it was for them! When he got on to that tack there was nothing you couldn't ask him for: "If it's as hard as you say, why can't you help me a bit?" Then he'd give you a hundred roubles. He was as soft-hearted as a woman. I watched him and thought to myself: "You may see farther than I do, but there's no doubt you're making a mess of your life. What is it you want? You're well shod, well dressed, well fed, your land's mortgaged, you've got money, what more do you want, you idiot, you darned blighter?" I used to get quite angry with him.

'He went on collecting small insects, sniffed at everything in his way, and I sent him into the very worst places in the marshes after bugs. There were some very deep pits there among the hillocks – one had to be continually on the look-out for them. Sometimes, if a shepherd boy's star-gazing, a calf or a sheep will lose its way in the marsh, and then you can say good-bye to it for ever. It's simply sucked into the ground. He, too, of course, promptly fell into one of those pits, stuck there and yelled.'

The shepherd frowned at the recollection, passed his finger through his beard, and continued in a lower key:

'One day he got in up to the neck; they dragged him out and he took his clothes off and hung them on the bushes to dry. Then I said to one of my boys: "Nikolka, run down and hide his trousers!" The boy was glad of a lark and ran off and did what he was told. It was getting near sunset. I ordered the flock to be driven home, and Mitia had to run home without any trousers on – it was a holiday, too, with girls and women wandering about – they didn't half laugh! But it had a nasty ending for me. Nikolka gave the show away and told everyone that it was my idea; the news reached Mitia and he came rushing up to me, jabbering like a windmill. He talked such a lot that his face got all red and the tears ran down his cheeks.

' "I've done this and that for you," he said, "and this is how you reward me, eh?"'

'That was the end of our friendship; he wouldn't listen to me, and soon afterwards he fell ill. He died in the town in spring. Consumption, they said . . .

'Well – there was a fine example of a "good man"; but what good was there in him? What could you do with him? What use was he? He was like a splinter in the finger. And I've seen a mighty fine number of such men among the gents. The old saying is not without truth: "Among gents, who's not a hound is a beast."* A calf, yes, yes.

'We had a teacher once, Peter Alexandrov. Well, he studied himself into such a state that he began teaching the youngsters

* Russian proverb.

that all sorrow came from the Tsar. I don't know in what way the Tsar had offended him. So Fedka Savin, the present village elder, did the right thing – he sent word to the police. Fedka got a golden seven-and-a-half-rouble piece for it, and the teacher was dragged off to gaol by the policemen at night. That was the end of him and his learning.

'So I say again: the learned are muddled folk of an excitable nature. No good comes of them, not a scrap of good, but a lot of drivel. Take you, for instance: you're a healthy fellow, simple in your manner of dealing with people, you seem to understand the kind of folk we are. But all the same there's something danger-ous about you, and I can't make you out. What is it you want? I, here, want a pouch for my tobacco, a leather one. Well, I daresay that if I were to ask you for one you'd go and buy one and give it to me. But that's only because your money's cheap. All the kind-ness of you learned folk is simply due to the fact that money comes easily to you. But what is it you want? I bet you don't know yourself. As for me, everything's clear to me, clear as candle-light. It's like this: I go along the straight highway, while you roam about in the lanes.'

The shepherd closed his eyes, flung his head back till his hairy Adam's apple protruded grotesquely, and emitted strange, bellowing sounds from his beard: he was laughing. Then, rubbing his eye with one finger, he continued:

'Now, you said some time ago, quite incorrectly, that the earth turns round. I've heard that said before, too. But it only turns round because your head turns round with all the books you read. And you go shouting, "Ha, the earth turns round! ha, the earth turns round!" Just a silly lie, I call it. The earth daren't turn round, men wouldn't stand it.'

His eyes flashed victoriously and he glanced at the red circle of the moon, then stared at its distorted reflection in the greasy waters of the pond.

'You don't know, for instance, what the weather will be like tomorrow, do you? I do: it'll be dirty weather. How do I know that? I shan't tell you; you don't know anything about it.'

He rolled a cigarette and added in a bragging tone:

'A shepherd always smells the weather.'

That evening I began to feel a kind of hostility towards Borzoff; I had no longer any desire to meet him, and indeed I lost sight of him for several months. Then suddenly I heard – I cannot remember from whom – that the shepherd had two orphan nephews who were both being educated at his expense, one at the Kazan Veterinary School, the other at the College in Vladimir. Happening to meet Borzoff again in a home goods shop I tackled him about it.

'Look here, Uncle Tim, why did you lie to me like that? Why did you deny that there was any good in learning while all the time you were having your nephews educated?'

He half-closed his toad's eyes and shaking his beard, answered:

'We-ell, why should I always tell you the truth? One frequently gets licked for telling the truth.'

He laughed a wizard's laugh, swaying on his feet, then said, very low through his laughter, winking one eye at me:

'The nephews are my own blood and kin, while you're just a stranger, like a passing beggar. So I act and say what's likely to profit me, just as every man does who's got any sense. My own folk must learn, but strangers shouldn't; see? Well – there you are.'

He put his heavy paw on my shoulder and added condescendingly:

'It is said that "every one is a brother to another against his own will."* Well, that's why I care only for my own people. Don't you think I'd like to see them become gents? We're gents too, all of us, of course; only at present we're at the bottom of the ladder. Now, come and have a smoke, you blessed young ass.'

We sat and smoked. I said peevishly:

'You fooled me very cleverly, Uncle Tim. You are a fine actor.'

He did not like that, and growled in reply:

'Muddled words again. Queer chap you are, 'pon my word! There's a good old Russian word for it – "clown." All the habits of you learned folk come from monkeys . . .'

* Russian proverb.

# Dora

IN the Sanatorium there were eight people suffering from consumption. Of all patients consumptives are usually the most capricious: for their temperature has but to rise a fraction of a degree, and they are rendered almost irresponsible through fear, anger or dejection.

The bacillus of tuberculosis possesses an ironical power: at the same time that it is killing a human being, it is awakening his thirst for life. This is betrayed by a heightened eroticism which usually is characteristic of consumption, also by the staunch, supreme faith in recovery, shared by the most incurable of patients. It was the pathologist Strumpel, I think, who called this condition 'the hope of the phthysical.'

Eight consumptive patients, living in one of the boarding houses in the Crimea, were all nursed and looked after by a maid named Dora, a woman of unknown antecedents. At times she would say that she was an Estonian, at other times she would say that her country was Karelia. Her manner of speech, however, was that of a person coming from Tauride. At one moment she spoke with a Tartar accent, and at another with an Armenian one. She was very large and stout, but light-footed, her movements quick and dexterous. There was a certain equine good nature about her face; her red lips were set in a kind, greasy smile, and her big eyes, of a strange mauve colour, were impregnated with the oil of that smile. When she became thoughtful, those rather lack-lustre eyes of hers clouded over and their glance grew leaden. She was illiterate and stupid, particularly stupid whenever she wanted to be very cunning. The invalids therefore called her, not too wittily, 'Dura,'* thus playing on her name. But the girl took no offence at this, and continued to smile. Towards the invalids she was as tolerant as a mother towards

* 'Dunce' in Russian.

her children. And when the consumptive males clawed with clammy, livid hands at her, she calmly pushed aside the pitiful, moist hands of the doomed wretches with her big red paws and said, 'No pawing – it's bad for you.'

Many people made love to her insistently: shopkeepers, undertakers, and once a stern, vigorous fisherman, a widower. They were attracted by her rough beauty, her physical strength, her tireless energy, her easy-going nature. Everyone wanted to win for himself this peaceful, humble creature as a partner for life; but her attitude towards men resembled that of a free, wealthy individual, who knows quite well when and how to invest his capital. She refused offers of marriage with the same unintelligent but soothing smile with which she listened to the endless whims of the invalids and pushed away their intrusive caresses.

She suffered from the heat even on those days when the wind was in the north, or a dense fog wrapped the little house on the top of the hill with a clouded rawness, when the invalids, muffling themselves up in thick plaids and warm coats, grumbled at the weather. At night, after putting everyone to sleep, Dora would wrap a black kerchief, with a red rose embroidered in one of the corners, round her head, come out on the terrace and there, kneeling down and looking up into the sky, she would pray, sighing, under my window:

'Oh, Holy Mother of God . . . Christ, Our Lord! Thou, St Nicholas, God's humble servant! . . .'

I could detect no tendency towards poetry in Dora. She did not care for flowers, holding that they only filled the rooms with dust and litter. One night, when a priest's wife, dying of tuberculosis of the intestines, went into ecstasies over the splendour of the sky and of the stars, Dora roughly swept away her enthusiasm. 'The sky,' said she, 'is like an omelette . . .'

One day the ninth patient arrived. With a great effort, panting for breath, he climbed the stairs leading to the terrace, and holding on to the top of the balustrade said to Dora: 'See what a fine fellow I am, eh?'

This was said with a mixture of plaintiveness and gaiety. Smiling, he glanced at the great big girl, at the fullness of her rounded breasts.

'Ha! what a healthy creature you are!' he rattled, rapidly gulping down draughts of air. 'Well, you'll help me to get well again, won't you?'

'Why, certainly,' Dora retorted with her Armenian accent.

He had the face of an owl, round cat's eyes, a nose curving down at the end, a little black moustache – a mocking, cruel face.

From that day Dora changed as if by magic, very much to our discomfort. She began to ignore our wishes, hurried over our rooms and cleaned them negligently, only grunted angrily in answer to our complaints and reproaches, while a light as of intoxication shone in her horse-like eyes. She seemed suddenly to have become deaf and blind and often turned her head with concern towards the terrace, where the little student Filipoff, who resembled an owl, lay coughing and panting for breath. She hurried to him at every free moment in the day, hid in his room after sunset, and there was no way of luring her forth from it.

As for him – he was dying. Dying in an unusual way, between laughter and mockery, trying all the time to whistle the tune of some musical comedy, an exercise which was usually interrupted by fits of coughing. There was an affectation about him; he was something of a dare-devil, cynical, but the mask was at least worn very cleverly.

'What do you think of all these little absurdities, my dear colleague?' he used to ask me, with a wink of his cat's eyes. 'How do you like it all? Day, night, birth, love, knowledge, death, eh? Funny, isn't it? *N'est-ce pas?* as the French say. Particularly funny for a man twenty-six years of age – by this I mean myself . . . Dora!'

I would then hear the rattling of spoons or the rumbling of furniture, and Dora would appear, waiting in silence, with eyes wide-open, for this man to command her.

'My good old elephant, bring me some grapes, quick!' he would order her and turning to me observe, 'A very ignorant and stupid woman.'

He hated all the patients and scoffed mercilessly at their little eccentricities. He was not liked, either. As for myself, he and I became friends because he loved literature and this brought us very close together.

'Literature is the best of all man's inventions,' he would say, passing his livid tongue over his lips. 'And the farther it is from life, the better . . .'

It seemed to me that he was dying less of consumption than of a heavy blow dealt to his soul.

He died on the sixty-ninth day after he had entered the boarding-house, muttering deliriously in his death agony, 'Phima . . . all my life . . . I loved you . . . alone . . . for ever, Phima . . . darling . . .'

I was sitting at the foot of the bed, and Dora was standing by Filipoff's side, sniffing and stroking his dry hairs with her huge paw.

She held a parcel squeezed under her arm.

'What is he saying?' she asked, drawing herself up anxiously. 'Who is that "Fima"?'

'Apparently a girl, a woman, whom he loved and loves still.'

'He? This – Fima?' Dora asked loudly in amazement. 'No – no, it's me he loves. He loved me, as soon as he came here . . .'

But listening again to the ravings of the student, she raised her pale eyebrows, wiped her wet face with her apron, and throwing the parcel on to my knees said, 'This is his shroud: stockings, a shirt, slippers.' And she left the room noiselessly.

Twenty minutes later the student Filipoff stopped raving. He looked very earnestly at the black square of the window on the white wall and sighed. Apparently he wanted to say something, but choked over the words. Then his small body, exhausted to the very bones, straightened itself out in eternal peace.

I went to look for Dora. She was standing on the terrace glancing down to where the sky and the sea, the one indistinguishable from the other and both equally dark, were joined. She turned her fat face to me, and I was amazed to see how stern it was.

'He is dead. Go and lay him out, Dora.'

'I won't.'

Dora began to scrape her feet on the ground as though obliterating spittle.

'I won't,' she repeated. 'I don't want to have anything to do with a man like that! Just think, what a man! He said he loved me, while all the time . . .'

'Yes, but didn't you see that he was dying!'

'Well, what of that? Of course I saw it. I'm not blind, am I? I even bought a shroud for him with my last pennies. I saw it immediately, the moment he came, and I said to myself: Poor boy! . . . Dying indeed! Everybody dies. But why play false? "I have never loved a girl," he said. Well, here you are, here's a girl for you. . . . Die as much as you like, but don't play false . . .'

She spoke in a low voice and seemed to be thinking of something else. Then, suddenly, she uttered a sob – such a painful sob, as though she had gulped down a cup filled to the brim with hot liquid and had burnt herself cruelly with it.

'Come, Dora! . . .'

'Go and dress him yourself, if you're as kind-hearted as all that! As for me – no, no. I won't. What was to him – a pastime?'

'I don't know how to dress the dead . . .'

'What do I care? I'm a stranger to him, am I not?'

'But he is dead, after all!'

'Well, and what then? Don't try to persuade me. I don't want to set my eyes on a man like him . . . Shouldn't play false . . .'

To the end she refused to go and dress him, remaining alone on the terrace.

While I was arraying the student Filipoff in his shroud I suddenly heard a low, heart-rending wail. I jumped out on to the terrace.

At times it is given to human beings to shed peculiar, fierce, scalding tears: it was with such tears that Dora was crying. Kneeling down on the floor, striking her head against the railing, sobbing and wailing, she was uttering these words in a high-pitched squeal:

'O my outrageous darling, my little monster, my dearest, my unforgettable kiddie . . .'

# Man's Behaviour when Alone

TODAY while I was watching a fair little lady in cream-coloured stockings, with the immature features of a child, who stood on the Troitzki bridge, holding to the balustrade with her grey-gloved hands as though preparing to jump into the Neva, I saw her stick out a sharp, pink little tongue at the moon.

The old man in the moon, the sly fox of the skies, was stealthily making his way through a cloud of dirty smoke. He was very large and his cheeks were crimson, as though he had had too much to drink. The young lady was teasing him very earnestly and even revengefully – so it seemed to me at least.

She recalled to my mind the memory of certain 'peculiarities' which had puzzled me for a long time. Whenever I watch how a man behaves when he is alone, I always conclude that he is 'insane' – I can find no other word for it.

I first noticed this when I was still a boy: a clown named Rondale, an Englishman, who was walking along the dark and deserted passages of a circus, took off his top hat to a mirror and bowed respectfully to his own reflection. There was no one in the passage but himself. I was sitting on a cistern over his head and so was invisible to him, and had thrust out my head just at the moment when he made his respectful bow. This action of the clown plunged me into dark and unpleasant speculations. He was a clown, and what is more, an Englishman, whose profession – or art – lay in his eccentricity.

Then I noticed how A. Chekhov, sitting in his garden, tried unsuccessfully to catch a sunbeam with his hat and to place both on his head. I could see that his failure annoyed the sunbeam-hunter; his face grew redder and redder, and he ended by slapping his hat on his knee, putting it on his head with a quick movement and impatiently pushing his dog away. Then, half-closing his eyes and looking stealthily at the sky, he stalked towards the house. Seeing me in the porch, he smiled and said:

'Good-morning. Have you read Balmont's verses, "The sun smells of grass"? Silly, isn't it? In Russia it smells of Kazan soap, and here – of Tartar sweat.'

It was Chekhov, too, who tried conscientiously to poke a thick red pencil into the neck of a small medicine bottle, thereby breaking a certain law of physics. He persisted with the quiet obstinacy of a scientist making an experiment.

Leo Tolstoy once said to a lizard in a low whisper: 'Are you happy, eh?'

The lizard was warming itself on a stone among the shrubs that grew on the road to Dulber, while he stood watching it, his hands thrust inside his leather belt. Then, cautiously looking round, the great man confided to the lizard: 'As for me – I'm not!'

Professor Tikhvinsky, the chemist, sitting in my dining-room, addressed his own reflection in the copper tea-tray: 'Well, old boy, how is life?'

The image made no reply; so Tikhvinsky sighed deeply and began carefully rubbing it off with his palm, puckering his brows and twitching his nose, which resembled the trunk of an embryo elephant.

I was told that someone once found N. S. Leskoff occupying himself by sitting at the table and lifting a tuft of cotton-wool into the air, then letting it fall into a china bowl and stooping over it, listening, evidently expecting that the wool would produce a sound as it fell on the china.

The priest F. Vladimirsky once placed a boot in front of him, and said to it impressively: 'Now then – go!' Then, 'Ah, you can't?' Then, with dignity and conviction, he added: 'You see! You can't go anywhere without me!'

'What are you doing, Father?' I asked, entering the room at this moment.

He looked at me attentively and explained: 'It's this boot. It's all worn down at the heel. Nowadays they make such poor boots!'

I have often noticed how people laugh and cry when they are by themselves. A writer, a perfectly sober man who rarely indulged in drink, used to cry when he was alone, and whistle the old hurdy-gurdy tune, 'As I come out alone on the road!' He whistled badly, like a woman, and his lips trembled: tears rolled slowly out of his eyes, and hid in his dark whiskers and beard. Once he cried in the room of an hotel, standing with his back to the window, spreading out his arms and going through the movements of swimming; but this was not for the sake of exercise, for the movements were slow and neither powerful nor rhythmical.

This, however, is not so queer: laughter and tears are the expressions of sane and natural states of mind: they do not puzzle one. Neither do the solitary nocturnal prayers of people in the fields, in the woods, in the plains, and on the sea. Masturbators always give the impression of being crazy – this, too, is natural, almost always distasteful, but sometimes funny, too. And very weird. A medical student – a rather unpleasant young woman, conceited, a boaster, who had read Nietzsche and been driven insane by him, pretended in a coarse and naïve way to be an atheist, but masturbated in front of Kramskoi's picture of Christ in the desert. – Come on, – she moaned softly and languorously – My dearest, my misery, come on, come on! Then she married a rich merchant, bore him two sons and ran away with a wrestler.

My neighbour in Kniagi Dvor, a landowner in the Voronezh district, came into my room one night by mistake, half-undressed, but perfectly sober. I lay still in bed, having already put out the light. The room was filled with moonlight and through a hole in the hangings I could see his dry face with its curious smile. He was carrying on a low dialogue with himself:

'Who's there?'

'It is I.'

'This is not your room.'

'Oh, I beg your pardon!'

'Please . . .'

He stopped speaking, looked round the room, admired his whiskers in the mirror, and began singing softly:

> 'I got in the wrong place, place . . .
> How did I do this, this, this?'

After this, instead of leaving the room, he took up a book, placed it face downwards on the table, and looking out on the street, said loudly, as though reproaching somebody:

'It's as light as day now – and in the daytime it was dark and horrid. A fine arrangement, eh? . . .'

Then he went out on tip-toe, balancing himself with his arms outstretched, and closed the door carefully and noiselessly behind him.

To see a child trying to remove a picture from the page of a book with his fingers is not very unusual; but to see a scientist, a professor, trying to do it and turning round and listening as though afraid of being caught in the act, is strange indeed.

The professor in question evidently was convinced that the printed drawing could be removed from the paper and hidden in the pocket of his waistcoat. Once or twice he thought he had succeeded. He took up something from the page and, lifting it between two fingers like a coin, tried to slip it into his pocket; but then, looking at his fingers, he frowned, held the picture up to the light, and again started to rub the printed impression persistently. Finally, seeing that this had no result, he threw the book aside and strode out of the room, stamping angrily. I examined the book very carefully. It was a technical work in German, illustrated with reproductions of different electric motors and their parts. There was not a single picture that was glued to the page, and it is obvious that anything printed cannot be removed from a page and slipped into the pocket! Probably the professor knew this too, although he was not a technician, but a professor of humanitarian sciences.

Women often talk to themselves while playing a game of patience or when they are busy at their toilet, but one day for five whole minutes I watched a well-educated woman eating sweets in solitude and addressing each of the candies, which she held up in the air with a small pair of pincers:

'Ah, I'll eat you up!' Then she would eat it up and ask, 'One wondered whom?'

'Well, didn't I?'

Then, again: 'I'll eat you up!'

'Didn't I?'

She was sitting at the time in an arm-chair at the window, at five o'clock on a summer's evening, and from the street the muffled noise of the big town filled the room. The face of the woman was serious, her greyish eyes were fixed earnestly on the box of sweets in her lap . . .

In the corridor of a theatre I once saw a pretty, dark-haired woman, who had arrived late for the performance, arranging her hair in front of a mirror and remarking to someone in a stern and rather loud voice:

'And still – one has to die?'

There was no one in the corridor except me, who had also been late in coming, but she did not notice me, and even if she had I hope she would not have thought of putting such an unseemly question to me!

Yes, many people exhibit 'peculiarities' of this nature when they are alone. Here is another instance:

Alexander Blok, standing on the staircase of a public library, was writing something in pencil on the margin of a book, when suddenly, pressing close to the balustrade, he respectfully made way for someone to pass by. I was watching him closely, but saw no one pass him . . . I was standing on the landing at the top of the staircase, and when Blok's eyes, which wore a smiling expression, in following the *someone* who had passed him, met my gaze – probably one of amazement – he dropped the pencil, stooped to pick it up, and asked:

'Am I late?'

# On Leo Tolstoy

ONE hot day he overtook me on the low road. He was riding in the direction of Livadia, mounted on a quiet little Tartar horse. Grey and shaggy, in a light, white, mushroom-shaped felt hat, he looked very much like a gnome.

Holding back his horse, he hailed me, and I walked along by his side, telling him, among other things, that I had just had a letter from V. G. Korolenko. Tolstoy shook his beard angrily.

'Does he believe in God?' he asked.

'I do not know.'

'That means you do not know the chief thing about him. He is a believer, but he is afraid to admit it in front of atheists.'

He spoke in a grumbling and peevish voice, peering angrily at me through half-closed eyelids. It was clear that he was in no mood to talk to me, but when I showed an inclination to go he stopped me.

'Where are you off to?' he inquired, 'I am not going too fast, am I?'

And he began to grumble again:

'Your Andreieff is also afraid of atheists, but he, too, believes in God – and God keeps him in awe of Him.'

When we came to the edge of the estate belonging to the Grand Duke A. M. Romanoff, we met three Romanoffs who were standing talking on the road, very close to each other. One was the master of Ai-Todor, another was George, and the third, I think, was Piotr Nikolaevich – all of them strong masterful men. The road was blocked by a one-horse vehicle, and a saddled horse was standing a little to one side. Leo Nikolaevich (Tolstoy) could not pass between them. He stared sternly and expectantly at the Romanoffs, but they had turned aside before he came up. At length the saddled horse pranced nervously and stepped aside, allowing Tolstoy's horse to pass.

After riding on in silence for some minutes he exclaimed: 'They recognized me, the fools.' And added, a few moments later: 'That horse knew that it must make way for Tolstoy!'

\*

'Take care of yourself first – and you will have plenty of care left for other people.'

\*

'What do we mean when we say we "know"? I know, of course, that I am Tolstoy, the writer, that I have a wife and children, grey hair, an ugly face and a beard – all that is written down in my passport. But of the soul the passport says not a word, and of the soul I know this: that it wants to be near to God.

'But what is God? God is that of which my soul is an atom. That is all. He who has learnt to meditate finds it hard to believe; yet it is only through faith that one can live in God. So Tertullian wrote: "Thought is evil." '

\*

In spite of the monotony of his preaching, what infinite variety is to be found in this almost legendary man! In the park, today, when he was talking with the Mullah of Haspra, he behaved like a trusting, simple-minded little peasant, for whom the time has arrived when he must collect thoughts for his last days. Small of stature and shrivelled up, he appeared, beside the broad, corpulent Tartar, like a little old man whose soul had just awakened to the sense of something that lay buried within it, and who feared the questions which that awakening might bring.

He lifted his shaggy eyebrows in amazement, blinking shyly with his piercing little eyes, and extinguishing the intolerably penetrating fire which burnt within them. His all-seeing eye was riveted upon the broad face of the Mullah, the pupil losing that sharpness which so confused people.

To the Mullah he put childish questions on the meaning of life, on the soul and on God, substituting the verses of the Bible and the Prophets for the verses of the Koran with incredible agility. Altogether he was acting with the marvellous skill of

138

which only a man who is at once a great artist and a great sage is capable.

Again, a few days ago, when he was talking about music to Taneev and Suler, he went into raptures over it, like a child. One could see that he was admiring his own enthusiasm, or, to be more precise, his capacity for enthusiasm. He held that Schopenhauer had written more wisely and profoundly about music than anyone else; told us, in parenthesis, a comic anecdote about Fet, and described music as 'the dumb prayer of the soul.'

'Why dumb?' asked Suler.

'Because it uses no words. There is more soul in a sound than there is in a thought. A thought is like a purse – it contains pennies, mere trifles, while a sound remains unsoiled – pure through and through.'

With evident delight and in charming, simple words, he expressed his ideas, choosing – this was unusual with him – the finest and the most tender he could think of. And unexpectedly smiling into his beard, he murmured softly, caressingly:

'All musicians are stupid people, and the more gifted the musician, the more shallow he is. It is curious that they should all be so pious . . .'

\*

To Chekhov, at the telephone, he once said:

'It is such a good day for me to-day; my soul is so full of gladness that I want you too to be joyful. You particularly. You are a very fine man, a very fine man.'

\*

When you speak to Tolstoy of things which he can put to no use, he listens with indifference and incredulity. In fact he does not ask – he merely inquires. Like a collector of valuable curios, he only collects things which are in keeping with the rest of his collection.

\*

One day he was sorting his letters:

'They all make a great fuss about me,' he said, 'writing and so on. But in the end, when I die, in a year or so, people will say: "Tolstoy? Ah, that is the count who tried to make boots; and then something curious happened to him. Is that the fellow you mean?"'

*

Several times I noticed on his face, in his look, the cunning and contented smile of a man who unexpectedly discovers something which he has hidden away. He hides it and then forgets about it. Where can it be? He spends long days of secret anguish pondering incessantly: 'Where, oh, where did I put that thing that I want so much?' He is terrified lest the people round him should notice his anguish, should get to know of his loss and worry him about it or injure him in any way. Then he suddenly remembers and finds it. Delighted at his success and no longer afraid to show his feelings to others, he watches those about him with a cunning glance, as much as to say: 'You can't hurt me now!'

But as to what he has found and where he found it – that remains a secret.

One never tires of speculating about him, but it is trying to meet him often. Personally I should find it impossible to live in the same house with him, not to mention in the same room. His surroundings become like a desert where everything is scorched by the sun and the sun itself is smouldering away, threatening a black and eternal night.

# Alexander Blok

IT seems to me at times that the Russian mind is sick with the fear of its own self; in its attempt to stand outside all reason it resents reason and is afraid of it.

That wise and crafty serpent V. V. Rosanoff laments bitterly in *Uedinenno**: 'Oh, what a sad experience is mine! Why did I want to know everything? Now I shall not be able to die in peace, as I hoped to do.'

In Leo Tolstoy's *Diary of My Youth* from 1851, occurs this stern pronouncement: 'Consciousness is the greatest moral evil which can take hold of a man.'

The same thing has been said by Dostoevsky: '. . . To be too acutely conscious is a failing, a real, a thorough failing; too much consciousness – I should even say every kind of consciousness – is a failing. I maintain that this is so.'

The realist, A. F. Pisemsky, exclaimed in his letter to Melnikoff-Perchersky, 'Confound this habit of thinking, this mange of the soul!'

L. Andreev has remarked, 'Reason has in itself something of the spy, of the *agent provocateur*.' And he also made the following surmise: 'It is very probable that reason is the old witch Conscience in disguise.'

One can collect a good number of such aphorisms from Russian writers, and they all bear witness to a lack of confidence in the power of reason. This is characteristic of the people of a country in which, more than in any other, life is built on principles which lack all reason. It is curious to note that even P. F. Nikolaeff, the author of *Active Progress*, a man to whom such a line of thought ought not to have come naturally, wrote in 1906: 'Knowledge augments requirements, requirements breed discontent, a discontented man is miserable and unhappy – there-

* Solitaria.

fore socially valuable and personally attractive.' A perfectly incomprehensible and somewhat Buddhist thought!

Montaigne, too, lamented: 'Why do we arm ourselves with futile knowledge? How sweet and comfortable is the pillow of the chosen – ignorance and simplicity of the heart!' He explained the longevity of primeval peoples by their ignorance of all science and religion – ignoring the fact that they possessed them all in the germ. The Epicurean Montaigne lived in the period of religious wars. He was full of bright, gay wisdom and considered that cannibalism was less repulsive than the tortures of the Inquisition. Three hundred years later L. Tolstoy said of him: 'Montaigne is common and vulgar.'

Tolstoy's mind was religious in its shape as well as in its essence. I do not think that dogmatism attracted him, and it is hardly probable that the process of thought itself caused him the same delight as it undoubtedly did such philosophers as, for instance, Schopenhauer, who used to contemplate with tenderness the development of his own thoughts. In my opinion Leo Tolstoy considered all thought, all reflection, as a kind of cursed duty, and I think he always remembered the words of Tertullian, words which express the despair of a fanatic, stung by doubt: 'Thought is evil.'

Maybe the sources of fear inspired by the mind and the hatred of it are buried for all dogmatists in the Book of Enoch:

Azazel taught man to make knives and swords . . . he initiated them into different arts . . . explained the ways of the stars and of the moon. And then came the time of great godlessness and corruption on earth, and the ways of men became tortuous . . .

*

I recalled all this after an unexpected conversation I had yesterday with Alexander Blok. I left the office of the 'Universal Literature' in his company and he asked me what I thought of his book, *The Decline of Humanism*. A few days ago he had delivered something like a lecture on that question in the form of a short article. The article seemed to me to be somewhat incomplete, but full of tragic forebodings. Blok, while reading it, reminded me of a child in a fairy tale, lost in the woods: a child sensing the approach of monsters out of the darkness and murmuring incoherent exorcisms in the hope that they will frighten the monsters away. His fingers trembled as he turned the leaves of the manuscript. I could not understand whether the decline of humanism was causing him sorrow or joy. His talent is not so supple in prose as it is in verse, but he is undoubtedly a man of a deep and destructive mind – in a word, a man of the 'decadent' period. It seemed to me that Blok himself was not perfectly clear as to what he believed in; words, like lichen on a stone, do not penetrate into the depths of the thoughts which are causing his destruction, as well as what he calls the destruction of humanism. Some of his thoughts seemed to me not to have been pondered over carefully enough. For instance:

'It is impossible and unnecessary to try to civilize the masses.'
'Inventions take the place of discoveries.'

The eleventh and twelfth centuries are so enormously rich in inventions precisely because they embrace the period of the most numerous and the greatest discoveries of science. And to speak of the impossibility and uselessness of civilization for the Russian people is evidently 'Scythian,' and I can only understand it as a concession to the organic lack of 'state' instinct in the Russian masses. But why need Blok be a 'Scythe'?*

I told him all this as tactfully and gently as I could. It is very difficult to talk to him – he gives me the impression that he despises everybody to whom his world appears in any way weird and incomprehensible – and certainly it appears as such to me. Lately I have been sitting twice a week at his side at the editor's meetings in the 'Universal Literature' and have often argued with him on the imperfections of translations from the point of view of the spirit of the Russian language. This kind of work does not bring people together. As it is with nearly all the men on the managing committee, his attitude towards his work is an indifferent and formal one. He said he was glad to note that I was freeing myself from the 'habit, dear to the intelligentsia, of solving the problems of social existence.'

* The Russian 'Eurasian' movement, which places Russia at the point midway between Europe and Asia.

'I have always felt that this is not your real self,' he said. 'Already in *Little Town Okurov* one can see that you are worried by "childish questions" – the most deep and terrible of all.'

He is mistaken, but I did not protest, I let him think what he liked.

'Why do you not write on these questions?' he inquired insistently.

I told him that the questions on the purpose of life, death and love were strictly intimate, personal matters, concerning only myself. I do not care to drag them out into the street, and if ever I do it involuntarily, it is always artlessly and without any skill. 'To speak of oneself is a subtle art – I do not possess it.'

We entered the Summer Gardens and sat down on a bench. Blok's eyes shone with what seemed to me very like an insane light. By their gleam, by the trembling of his cold, tormented face, I could see that he was possessed with a hungry desire to speak, to ask questions. Trying to rub out a sun-ray on the gravel path with the sole of his boot, he said reproachfully:

'You are hiding your real self. You conceal your thoughts on the spirit, on truth. Why do you do it?'

And before I had time to answer he began to speak of the Russian intelligentsia with hackneyed words of condemnation – words which are especially out of place now, after the revolution.

I told him that to my mind the negative attitude towards the intelligentsia is one that is bred by the intelligentsia itself. It could not have been born among the peasants, who knew the educated people only as represented by the self-denying district doctor or the exalted village teacher; neither among the workmen, who owe all their political education to that same intelligentsia. This attitude is an erroneous and unwholesome one, in addition to which it kills the self-respect of the intelligentsia, kills their esteem for their own historic works of culture.

For ever and ever it has played, and will continue to play, the part of the packhorse of history. Owing to its indefatigable work it has lifted the proletariat to the heights of a revolution, unparalleled in the vastness and depth of the problems which it has placed before us for immediate solution.

I do not think that he was listening to me, for he was sullenly staring at the ground under his feet, and as soon as I stopped he began again to speak of the hesitation which the intelligentsia has displayed in adopting the principles of bolshevism. Among other things he remarked very justly:

'Having invoked the spirit of destruction from the darkness, it is not honest for the intelligentsia to say: this was not done by us, but by those people over there. Bolshevism is the unavoidable result of the work of the intelligentsia in various pulpits, in editors' offices, and in their "underground" teachings.'

A nice-looking young woman who happened to pass by at that moment bowed her head to him in affectionate greeting; he answered drily, almost contemptuously – and she went on, smiling a little confusedly. Glancing after her small footsteps as she walked hesitatingly away, Blok asked me:

'What do you think of eternity, of the likelihood of eternity?'

He asked in a determined way and his eyes scanned my face unflinchingly. I replied that perhaps Lamennais was right; if we admit that the amount of matter in the universe is limited, it is to be presumed that its combinations are repeated in infinite variety in the infinity of time. This point of view makes it possible that in some millions of years, on a foggy spring afternoon in Petrograd, Blok and Gorki shall again be sitting on a bench in the Summer Gardens, talking of eternity.

'You are not serious, are you?' said he.

His persistence both astonished and annoyed me, although I felt that he was not asking out of sheer curiosity, but was being driven by a desire to crush and extinguish some heavy thought that troubled him.

'I have no reason to consider Lamennais' point of view on that question less convincing than all the other ones,' I replied.

'But you, personally, what do you think of it?' He stamped his foot impatiently. Until that night he had always seemed to me so composed, so unwilling to talk.

'Personally, I prefer to imagine man as a machine, which transmutes in itself the so-called "dead matter" into a psychical energy and will, in some far-away future, and transforms the whole world into a purely psychical one.'

'I do not understand – this is pan-psychism, isn't it?'

'No. For at that time nothing will exist except thought. Everything will disappear, being transmuted into pure thought, which alone will exist, incarnating the entire mind of humanity from the first flashes of it until the moment of its last explosion.'

'I do not understand,' Blok repeated, shaking his head.

I proposed that he should picture to himself the world in an uninterrupted process of dissociation of matter. Matter, dissolving, continually gives off such species of energy as light, electricity, electro-magnetic waves, Hertzian waves, etc. To these are added, of course, all signs of radio-activity. Thought is the result of the dissociation of the atoms of the brain; the brain is composed of the elements of 'dead' unorganic matter. In the brain-substance of man this matter is uninterruptedly transformed into psychical matter. I myself believe that at some future time all matter absorbed by man shall be transmuted by him and by his brain into a sole energy – a psychical one. This energy shall discover harmony in itself and shall sink into self-contemplation – in a meditation over all the infinitely varied creative possibilities concealed in it.

'What a dismal phantasy!' said Blok, smiling sarcastically. 'It is pleasant to know that the law of preservation of matter contradicts it.'

'As for me, I am pleased to remember that the laws issuing from laboratories do not always coincide with the laws of the universe, unknown to us. I am convinced that if we could weigh our planet from time to time, we should see that its weight was gradually diminishing.'

'All this is very dreary,' Blok said, shaking his head. 'It is all – simpler; the thing is that we have become too clever to believe in God and not strong enough to believe in our own selves. As a support for life and faith – there is only God and myself. Humanity? But can one have any faith in the wisdom of humanity after this war and on the eve of other still more cruel ones? No, this picture of yours . . . it is a terrible one! . . . But I still think that you are not serious.'

He sighed. 'If only we could entirely stop thinking, were it only for ten years! If we could extinguish this treacherous, misty little light that draws us deeper and deeper into the night of the world, and listen to the harmony of the universe with our hearts! The brain, the brain ... It is not an organ to be relied upon – it is monstrously large, monstrously developed. It is a swelling, like a goitre.'

He remained silent for some minutes, his lips pressed together, then he said in a low voice: 'To stop every movement, to make time "mark time"!'

'It would, if all the different types of motion were given the same speed.'

Blok looked at me out of the corner of his eye, raising his eyebrows. Then he began speaking quickly, incoherently, in such a delirious manner that I was unable to follow him. It was a strange impression – as though he were tearing worn rags off his body. Then he suddenly got up, stretched out his hand to me, and walked away to catch a tram. At the first glance his gait appears to be a firm one, but on looking more intently one notices that he walks without any assurance, shifting his balance from one foot to the other. And however well he may be dressed one always wants to see him dressed differently from other people. Gumiliov, even in the fur coat of a Samoyed or a Lapp, would seem to be dressed like everybody else. Blok requires an unusual attire.

\*

Just as I had written down this conversation with Blok, W—, a sailor from the Baltic Fleet, came to beg me to lend him 'an interesting book' to read. He loves science dearly, expects it to solve all the riddles of life, and speaks of it always with rapture and faith. Today he announced the astonishing news:

'D'you know, they say that a learned American has invented a machine, a wonderfully simple one, just a telescope, a wheel and a handle. You turn the handle and you can see everything: analysis, trigonometry, criticism, in fact the whole meaning of the world's history. The machine shows you all this – and whistles as well!'

What I like best about that machine is the fact that it whistles.

# Blok and The Strumpet

ONE day, in the Pekar restaurant, I was talking to a young woman from the Nevsky.

'This book of yours,' she said, 'is written by the famous Blok, isn't it? I knew him too, although it's true I met him only once.

'Late one autumn night, through the damp fog – you know how damp it is – the clock on the Duma was pointing to midnight. I was beginning to feel very tired and had decided to go home. Suddenly, at the corner of the Italianskaya a very smartly dressed man came up and invited me to go with him. He was extremely handsome and had such a proud face that I took him to be a foreigner.

'We went on foot – it was not very far – to Karavannaia 10 – where you get rooms by the hour. As we walked along I talked to him, but he made no reply to any of my remarks, which I thought was both unusual and unpleasant . . . It's beastly when they're rude . . .

'We arrived and I asked for some tea. The waiter didn't come, so my companion went out into the hall to call him, and I, you see, being so tired and cold, went to sleep straight away, curled up on the sofa. Then, suddenly, I woke up and found him sitting opposite me with his head in his hands, leaning on the table with his elbows and watching me with such stern eyes – awful eyes they were.

'But I wasn't a bit frightened, I felt rather ashamed of myself for going to sleep. I thought: "Heavens, he must be a musician, his hair is so curly."

' "Forgive me," I said: "I was so cold and tired." I'll get undressed at once."

'But he only smiled politely and said: "Don't worry." Then he came and sat beside me on the sofa, took me on his lap and stroked my hair: "Go to sleep again for a while," he said. And

148

do you know, I actually went to sleep again! There's fine behaviour for you! I knew it was stupid of me, but I simply couldn't help it.

'He rocked me gently to and fro, and I felt so cosy with him. I just opened my eyes and smiled at him and he smiled back. So I slept on until he shook me very gently by the arm.

' "Well, good-bye," he said; "I'm afraid I must go now." He got up and put twenty-five roubles on the table.

' "Look here," I said, "what's that for?"

'I felt rather confused, and asked him to forgive me – it was all so funny and unusual. But he only laughed gently, pressed my hand and – actually kissed it. Then he went off and the waiter came up.

' "Do you know who he is?" he said. "He's Blok, the poet – look here." And he showed me a photograph in a paper.

'It was quite true, it was he, all right. "Heavens," I thought, "how stupidly I behaved!" '

As she spoke her aggressive little tilted face puckered with regret; and in her eyes, mischievous, but pathetic as a homeless puppy's, I could see the reflection of sorrow. I gave her all the money I had with me, and from that hour felt very close to Blok.

I like his proud face and his head – the head of a Renaissance Florentine.

# Chekhov

FOR five days now my temperature has been above normal, but the idea of staying in bed is hateful to me.

A fine grey rain is sprinkling the earth with a fine wet dust. I can hear the guns rumbling at Fort Iko – they are being attacked by the enemy. The long tongue of the searchlight licks the clouds at night; it is a disturbing sight, for it does not allow one to forget this devil's invention – war.

I have been reading Chekhov. If he had not died ten years ago the war would certainly have killed him, having first poisoned him with hatred towards mankind. I remembered his funeral.

The coffin of the writer so 'dearly loved' by Moscow was brought in a green freight car labelled in huge letters on the side: FOR OYSTERS. A part of the great crowd that had assembled at the station to meet the writer followed the coffin of General Keller, which had been brought from Manchuria at the same time, and was profoundly astonished to find that Chekhov was being buried with full military honours. When the mistake was discovered, certain cheerful spirits began to giggle and crack jokes. Chekhov's coffin was followed by only about a hundred people, not more. I recall particularly two lawyers, both in new shoes and speckled neck-ties. Walking behind them I could hear one of them, V. A. Maklakoff, discoursing on the sagacity of dogs; the other – a man unknown to me – boasted of the comforts of his country home and the beauty of its surroundings. A lady in a lilac dress, carrying a lace-fringed umbrella, was trying to convince an old gentleman in large spectacles of the merits of the deceased. 'Ah! he was wonderfully charming, and *so* witty . . .' The old gentleman coughed incredulously. The day was a hot and dusty one. At the head of the procession a big, stout policeman rode majestically on a fat white horse. It all

seemed cruelly common and vulgar, and quite incompatible
with the memory of a great and subtle artist.

\*

In a letter to old A. S. Suvorin,\* Chekhov wrote:

There is nothing more tiresome and unpoetical, so to speak, than
the prosaic struggle for existence which takes all the joy out of life
and drives one to apathy.

Those words express an intensely Russian vein of thought,
which, to my mind, was not characteristic of A. P. Chekhov. In
Russia, where there is such an abundance of everything but
where people lack the love of work for itself, the majority thinks
in that way. The Russian admires energy, but finds it hard to
believe in it. A writer with an active mind like Jack London, for
instance, is impossible in Russia. Although his books are very
popular there, I do not find that they inspire the Russian with a
desire to act; they merely excite his imagination.

But Chekhov is not intensely Russian from that point of view.
With him this 'struggle for life' began in early youth, with the
drudgery, the sordidness of everyday life, the cares and worries
necessary to obtain a loaf of bread – and not for himself alone;
for a very large loaf of bread was needed in his family. To those
joyless cares he had given up all the strength of his youth, and we
can only marvel how it was that he managed to retain his sense
of humour. He saw life merely as a colourless aspiration for
satiety and peace; the great dramas and tragedies of it were
hidden for him under a thick layer of every-day matters. And it
was only after he had to some extent freed himself from the care
of seeing all the mouths round him properly fed that he was able
to throw a long-sighted glance at the essence of those dramas.

I have never known a man feel the importance of work as the
foundation of all culture, so deeply, and for such varied reasons,
as did Chekhov. This feeling expressed itself in all the trifles of
his life; in his habits, in his choice of things, and in that noble
love for man's works which, knowing no desire of collecting

\* Editor of the *Novoje Vremja*.

them, never tires of admiring them as the product of man's creative spirit. He loved to build, plant gardens, ornament the earth; he felt the poetry of labour. With what touching care did he watch the growth of the fruit-trees and ornamental shrubs which he had planted in his garden. Full of plans for the building of his house in Autka, he used to say:

'If every man did all he could on the piece of earth belonging to him, how beautiful would this world be!'

I had started to write a play called *Vasska Busslaev*,* and one day I read to him Vasska's boastful monologue:

Ha, were I only endowed with more strength and power
I'd breathe a hot breath – and make the snows melt!
I'd go round the earth and plough it through and through!
I'd walk for years and years and build town after town,
Put up churches without number, and grow gardens without end;
I'd adorn the earth – as though it were a maiden fair;
Clasp it in my arms – as though it were my bride;
Lift it to my heart, and carry it to God:
Just look, my God, at this earth down here,
Look how finely Vasska has adorned it!
You just threw it like a stone into the sky,
While I have made a precious diamond out of it!
Just look, my God, and rejoice with me!
Look how bright it flashes in the sun's rays!
I'd have given it to you, Lord, as a fine gift –
Only – no – it would not do – I am too fond of it myself!

Chekhov liked this monologue very much, and, coughing excitedly, he said to me and Dr A. H. Alexin, who was present:

'That's very fine indeed! Very true, and very human! In this lies the essence of all philosophy. Man has made the earth habitable – therefore he must also make it comfortable for himself.'

He shook his head in obstinate affirmation and repeated:
'He will!'

He asked me to read Vasska's boastful speech over again. I did so, and he listened attentively to the end, then he remarked:

* A hero of the Novgorod epos.

'The two last lines are unnecessary – they are impertinent. There is no necessity for that . . .'

*

Of his own literary works he spoke very little and very unwillingly; I should like to add with a certain chastity, and with the same caution as he used when speaking of Leo Tolstoy. Very rarely, when in a cheerful mood, he would tell us, laughingly, of a new idea he had had – usually a humorous one.

'You know, I am going to write about a schoolteacher; she will be an atheist, adore Darwin, be convinced of the necessity of fighting with the superstitions and prejudices of the people – but this will not prevent her from boiling a black cat in the bath-house at midnight in order to obtain from it a certain bone which is popularly supposed to be a potent love-charm.'

His plays he described as very 'gay' ones, and I think he honestly believed that the plays he wrote were 'gay'. Probably it was due to his influence that Savva Mozozov* used to persist in saying: 'Chekhov's plays ought to be staged as lyric comedies.'

But in general he followed literature with a serious attention that was particularly touching with regard to 'beginners.' With marvellous patience he would read carefully through numerous manuscripts by B. Lazarevsky, N. Oligez, and many others.

'We need more writers,' he used to say. 'Literature is still a novelty in our country, even for the elect. In Norway there is one writer to every two hundred and twenty-six men of the whole population, while in Russia there is only one to a million . . .'

*

His illness at times made him hypochondriacal, almost mis-anthropic. On such days he was capricious in his judgements and morose in his attitude towards all people. One day, lying on a couch, coughing and playing with a thermometer, he said:

'To live in order that we may die is not very pleasant; but to live knowing that we shall die before our time is up is profoundly stupid . . .'

* A great Muscovite merchant – both a revolutionary and a patron of the arts.

153

Another time, sitting at an open window and watching the far-away horizon of the sea, he murmured angrily, all of a sudden:

'We have got accustomed to living in hopes of fine weather, good crops, a pleasant love-affair, of becoming rich or getting an appointment as chief of police, but I have never come across people who live in the hope of growing more clever. We think "things will be better under a new Tsar, and still better in two hundred years" – but no one troubles himself about improving things tomorrow. Altogether life gets more and more complicated every day and just moves along of its own accord, while people become more and more stupid every day and more and more of them just potter about on the outskirts of life.'

He remained deep in thought for some minutes, then puckering his eyebrows he added:

'Like crippled beggars during a church procession.'

He was a doctor – and illness for a doctor is always harder to bear than for a patient; the patient only *feels*, while the doctor, in addition to feeling, *knows* the processes by which his organism is being destroyed. In such cases we may consider knowledge as causing the approach of death.

*

When he laughed, his eyes were very fine: tender, caressing and soft as a woman's. And his laugh, which was an almost silent one, was such an unusual kind of laugh. One could see that he delighted in it, revelled in it; I never met anyone who could laugh in – if I may say so – such a 'spiritual' way. Coarse anecdotes never provoked even a smile.

Laughing in his delightful manner one day he said to me:

'Do you know why Tolstoy's attitude towards you is so changeable? He is jealous, he thinks Sulerjitzky likes you better than he does him. Yes, it is so. He said to me yesterday: "I cannot treat Gorki with sincerity – I do not know why it is so – but I cannot. It is even unpleasant to me to know that Suler lives with him. It is bad for Suler. Gorki is an unkind man. He reminds me of a theological student who has been forced against his will to take the hood and has thereby become embittered towards everybody. He has the soul of a spy, he has come into the land of Canaan, where he feels himself a stranger, watches everything that goes on around him, notices everybody and reports to a god of his own. And his god is a monster, something like a satyr or a water-sprite such as you find in the tales of peasant women." '

Chekhov laughed till tears came while telling me this, and, wiping his eyes, he continued:

'I said to him: "Gorki is a very kind man!" But he insisted: "No, no, I know all about him! He has the nose of a duck – only unhappy and unkind men have a nose like that. Women, too, don't love him; and women are like dogs, they can scent a good man. Suler – that's another matter – he possesses the truly precious capacity of loving people disinterestedly. He is a genius in that line! To know how to love – means to know everything." '

Chekhov paused for a moment and then went on:

'Yes, the old man is jealous . . . What a wonderful old fellow he is! . . .'

*

He always spoke of Tolstoy with a peculiar, hardly perceptible yet tender and anxious smile in his eyes, lowering his voice as though speaking of something mysterious and fairylike, that demanded soft, cautious words. He often complained that there was no Eckermann* at Tolstoy's side, no one who could write down conscientiously all the sharp, sudden and often contradictory thoughts of the old wizard.

'You ought to do it,' he said to Sulerjitzky. 'Tolstoy is so fond of you, he talks to you so well and tells you such a lot . . .'

Concerning Suler, Chekhov once said to me: 'He is a wise child . . .' Which was very true.

*

One day Tolstoy was speaking with rapture about some tale of Chekhov's, I think it was *Dushenka*. 'It is like lace,' he said, 'made by a chaste young girl; there were such lace-makers in olden times; they used to depict all their lives, all their dreams of happiness, in the lace design. They dreamt in designs of

* Goethe's diarist.

all that was dear to them, wove all their pure, uncertain love into their lace.'

Tolstoy spoke with great agitation, his eyes full of tears. It happened that that very day Chekhov's temperature had gone up and he was sitting there with a high flush on his cheeks, his head bowed, carefully wiping the glasses of his spectacles. He was silent for a long time, then he sighed deeply and said in a low, bashful voice:

'There are many misprints in it . . .'

*

A lot could be written about Chekhov, but it would have to be done in a fine and subtle way which I do not possess. It would be well to write about him in the same manner as he himself wrote *The Steppe*, a tale with a peculiar atmosphere, so light and so pensively sad in a Russian way. A tale – just for oneself. It does one good to recall the memory of such a man, it brings renewed energy into one's life, a clear definite meaning.

Man is the axle of the world, in spite of his sins and defects. We all hunger for the love of our fellow men, and when one is hungry even an under-baked loaf is sweet.

# Some Views on the War

HE was a Muscovite cabman with a wooden, flat-eyed face and a horse which was a cross between a camel and a sheep. He wore a tattered, crumpled hat and a blue overcoat, torn under the arms; through a rent in his high felt boots I could catch glimpses of a dirty piece of stocking. It almost seemed as though the man had dressed himself in those rags on purpose, to show off. 'Just see what a poor man I am,' he might have been saying. He would sit sideways on the box of his cab, making the sign of the Cross in front of every church that he happened to pass; and as he sat he would talk lazily of how expensive living had become, not complaining, but just rambling on about it in a slightly hoarse voice.

Once I asked him what he thought of the war.

'Why should we think 'bout it at all?' he replied. 'It's the Tsar who's fighting – so it's his job to do the thinking.'

'Do you read the papers?'

'No – we're not reading folk. At times we chance to hear bits of news in a bar-room: advanced – retreated – and so on. But what's the good of the Press? There's a fellow in our village who lies a lot – he's called "The Newspaper".'

He scratched himself under the arm with his whip and asked: 'Is the German beating us?'

'Yes,' I told him.

'And who's got more men, the Germans or ourselves?'

'We have,' I answered.

Flicking his whip over the hairy flanks of his horse, he retorted with philosophic calm; 'Well, there – you see: butter doesn't sink in water.'*

*

A hairdresser was shaving a green uniformed customs official.

* A Russian proverb.

157

'There is no doubt whatever,' he remarked with great assurance, 'that the Germans will give us a licking; they've always done it.'

The man protested: 'No, we've had our turn, too, at beating them. For instance, during the reign of the Empress Elisabeth we even occupied Berlin.'

'Never heard that before!' said the hairdresser. 'I'm a soldier myself – but I've never heard *that* before.' And he added, as though he saw through the story, 'Perhaps it had been invented to cheer us up, to buck up our morale.'

Only last year this same hairdresser told me that he knelt in front of the Winter Palace and sang 'Bozhe Tsaria Khrani,'* his face bathed in tears. 'My whole soul was singing,' he said. 'It was a glorious hour . . .'

\*

In the garden in front of the Narodni Dom† a heterogeneous group of people was listening to the bold words of a little soldier. He had a bandage round his head and his bright eyes shone with inspiration. He spoke in a high-pitched voice, and clutched at the people standing next to him, in his anxiety to impress his audience.

'As a matter of fact,' he said, 'we are, of course, the stronger, but in every other respect we can't hold a candle to them. The German fights with calculation, he uses his soldiers carefully, whereas we – slap bang! – all the gruel's thrown into the pot at once . . .'

A huge, sturdy peasant in a torn overcoat here remarked in a weighty, business-like way: 'We've got more people than we know what to do with. Thank God we go to work differently from the Germans. Our whole object is to reduce the number of people in this country, so that those who survive can have more room.'

He yawned luxuriously as he said this. I tried to detect some irony in his words, but his face might have been carved out of stone, and his eyes were calm and sleepy.

A grey, crumpled-up little man chimed in. 'That's right,' he

* The Russian National Anthem.   † The Popular Theatre.

said. 'That's what the war is for – either to seize a foreign land or to diminish the number of people in our own.'

The soldier went on: 'Besides, a mistake has been made already in giving Poland to the Poles. They're all over the place. Some have gone over to the Huns, others to us, and now they are all mixed up. They're not anxious to go on killing each other.'

'Oh – if they were made to,' asserted the big peasant with calm conviction, 'they'd kill each other all right! If only there was someone to keep them at it, they'd go on killing! People like fighting.'

*

On the whole I find that the man in the street speaks of this abominable, desecrating slaughter as though it were something to which he is a complete stranger, something that he is watching as a spectator; sometimes he speaks of it with a certain amount of ill-will, though I cannot make out against whom this ill-will is directed. Criticism of the authorities has not perceptibly increased, not does opposition to them seem to be growing. What is noticeable is the rise of a disgusting, common anarchism. Opposed to it are the opinions of the workmen; fully aware how incomparably better developed are their understanding of the tragedy, their instinct of statesmanship, their humanity, even. This is apparent even among the unorganised workers, not to mention the regular party men like P. A. Skorokhodov.

Not very long ago, for instance, the latter was heard to remark:

'As a class we shall gain from a military defeat – which is, of course, the chief thing. But in spite of that, one's soul revolts at the idea. One can't help feeling ashamed of fighting and of being sorry for the people who fight. I simply can't tell you how sorry. Just think: all the healthiest people are getting killed over there, the people who should be starting their work tomorrow. The Revolution will want all the healthiest. Will there be enough of us?'

He fully understands the importance of culture.

'It is stupid,' he remarked, 'to say that culture is a *bourgeois* invention and therefore bad for us. Culture belongs to us; it is our lawful property, our inheritance. We'll find out for ourselves what is superfluous in it and cast aside whatever is not wanted. But first we've got to count the cost. No one but ourselves has any right to decide that. The other day I listened for an hour and a half to a young friend of mine who was abolishing culture at the Sampsonievsky factory, and I kept thinking to myself: This man's trying to convince me that a felt shoe is better than a boot. Fine teaching, to be sure! Fellows like that ought to have their ears pulled for them, that's the only remedy!'

# Substitutes for Monkeys

PROFESSOR Z., the bacteriologist, once told me the following story.

'One day, talking to General B., I happened to mention that I was anxious to obtain some monkeys for my experiments. The General immediately said, quite seriously:

' "What about Jews – wouldn't they do? I've got some Jews here, spies that are going to be hanged anyway – you're quite welcome to them if they are any use to you."

'And without waiting for an answer he sent his orderly to find out how many spies were awaiting execution.

'I tried to explain to His Excellency that men would not be suitable for my experiments, but he was quite unable to understand me, and opening his eyes very wide he said:

' "Yes, but men are cleverer than monkeys, aren't they? If you inoculate a man with poison he will be able to tell you what he feels, whereas a monkey won't."

'Just then the orderly came in and reported that there was not a single Jew among the men arrested for spying – only Rumanians and gypsies.

' "What a pity!" said the General. "I suppose gypsies won't do either? . . . What a pity . . .!" '

# Anti-Semitism

THINKING about the Jews makes one feel humiliated and debased. Although personally I do not believe that in the whole course of my life I have ever in any way injured a single person of that amazingly steadfast and persevering nation, nevertheless every time I meet a Jew I am reminded of my racial relationship with the fanatic sect of anti-Semites and of my responsibility for the insane actions of my fellow-countrymen.

I have read, thoroughly and attentively, a number of books which try to justify anti-Semitism. It is a hard and even repugnant duty to read books written with a definitely ugly and immoral design: to brand a nation, a whole nation. A remarkable task indeed! And I have never found anything in those books but a moral ignorance, an angry squeal, a wild beast's bellowing, and a grudging, envious grinding of teeth. Thus armed, there is nothing to prevent one from proving that Slavs, and all the other nations as well are also incurably depraved. And is not this the reason for the violent hatred of the Jews, that they, of all races of mixed blood, are the ones who have preserved comparatively the greatest purity of outward life as well as of the spirit? Is there not more perhaps of the 'Man' in the Jew than there is in the anti-Semite?

The composers and narrators of Jewish 'anecdotes' contribute largely to the disgraceful task of spreading anti-Semitism among the masses. It is curious that Jews are frequently to be found among them. It is possible that some of them wish to show how fine is the sad humour of their nation and through this to rouse some sympathy for their people among their enemies. It may also be that other anecdotists, in ridiculing the Jew, would like to convince the fools round them that he is not awe-inspiring. Of course there are also a certain number of downright degenerates and scoundrels among them.

'The brotherhood of nations', 'happiness for humanity'!

And, thus preaching, the nations spit into each other's faces with relish.

*

These anecdotists seem to have been particularly numerous in the eighties, and one of the most celebrated of them was Veinberg-Pushkine, who was said to be the brother of P. I. Veinberg, the 'Heine of Tambov,' a perfect translator of Heinrich Heine. This Veinberg-Pushkine even published one or two books of very stupid 'Jewish Anecdotes' or 'Scenes from the Lives of Jews.' I enjoyed his tales. He was an expert story-teller, and I often used to go to hear him in the Panaev theatre in Kazan, when he was appearing on the music-hall stage. I was a baker at that time.

One day I went there with the little student Greissmann, a very pleasant fellow, who later on committed suicide. I was highly amused by Veinberg's jokes, when suddenly I heard a rattling noise at my side, like the sound a man makes when he is seized by the throat and is being throttled. I looked round. Greissmann's face lit up by the moon and by the red light of the lanterns on the stage, had a horrible unnatural look, greyish-green, and terribly drawn; he was trembling violently; even his teeth seemed to be shaking; his mouth was half open, his eyes moist and very blood-shot. He grunted in a peculiar manner, hissing between his teeth.

'Skunks–s–s – oh, skunks–s – '

Then, straightening his arm, he raised his puny fist in the air, as slowly as though it had been an eighty-pound weight.

I stopped laughing. Greissmann turned rapidly and strode out of the hall, his head bowed, butting his way through the audience. I also got up and left, not following him, but taking another direction. For a long time I walked about the streets, the distorted face of the tortured man continually before me, and I felt very plainly that I had been gaily participating in his torture.

Of course I am aware that people of all races are constantly behaving in an ugly way towards each other, exercising their ingenuity to display every conceivable kind of baseness, but of all such animosities I consider anti-Semitism the most abominable of all.

# Rebellious Thoughts

THE Palace of Justice was in flames. The roof had already fallen in, the fire crackled between the walls, and red and yellow wisps like wool were creeping out of the windows, throwing a sheaf of paper-ashes into the black sky of the night. No one made any attempt to extinguish the fire.

About thirty people were admiring the fury of the flames. Like blackbirds, they perched on the ancient, treasured cannons of the gun-factory or sat on the tails of the guns. The guns themselves, stretched out in a line in the direction of the Duma, had an absurd and inquisitive look about them. The Duma itself resembled a kettle brimming over, and to it the arrested generals and Ministers were being carried in motor-cars or driven on foot, while about it people were hurrying to and fro in dark, endless crowds.

A young voice rang out clearly.

'Comrades! Who's dropped a loaf of bread here?'

Between the gun-carriages a tall, stooping man in a shaggy sheepskin hat was walking about like a sentinel. His face was hidden by the high collar of his sheepskin overcoat. He stopped and asked in a dull voice: 'Well – it means that all justice is to be abolished, doesn't it? Punishments all done away with, is that it?'

No one answered him. The night was cold, the bent figures of the onlookers were motionless, as, fascinated, they watched the huge wood-pile flaming between the stone walls. The fire illuminated a crowd of grey faces and reflected their unseeing eyes. The men clustered about the guns looked crumpled and shabby, wonderfully superfluous on this night when Russia is plunging along a new, still harder and more heroic road.

'I say, what about the criminals? No more prosecutions, eh?'

Somebody answered in a low, mocking voice: 'No fear, they won't forget you, they'll prosecute you all right!'

The weird conversation continued lazily.

'They'll go on prosecuting all right.'

'Who set fire to this?'

'The jail-birds, of course. Thieves.'

'Well, it's to their advantage, I suppose?'

'Such as that one, over there . . .'

The man in the shaggy hat called out fiercely and loudly: 'I'm no criminal, no thief, but the guard of this Palace. There's no one but me here – no one but me.'

He spat on the ground at his feet, carefully shuffled with his heavy leather, rubber-soled boots on the pavement, and then continued:

'I'm doubtful about all this. Even if they mean to pardon all the criminals, I'd have thought it would be too early for this sort of thing. They ought to abolish crime before they destroy justice. It's nonsense to burn papers and houses. It's the criminals who should first be abolished, or else it'll begin all over again – the writing, the papers, the judgements and the prison-building. I say it's the evil itself that should be put an end to at once . . . All the old machinery . . .'

He shook his head and added, 'I'll just go and tell them how to do it . . .'

He turned swiftly and walked along the Spalernaia, towards the Duma. The people around followed him with a vague, mocking murmur. Somebody laughed and then started coughing with sharp, barking sounds. This man, inspired not by reason but by his instinct, was the first to proclaim the motto: 'Everything should be done away with.'

Now summer has come and the speeches on this subject ring out more and more firmly and frequently. Yesterday after a meeting in the Narodni Dom a bearded soldier held forth in front of a crowd of fifty people, stammering enthusiastically and gulping down his words:

'What is it they're all jabbering about? It's the same old thing they're starting all over again, the same thing that's ruining us now. No, boys, let's tell them: "Here you are. Eat, drink and talk as much as you please among yourselves – but let us people alone. We'll manage for ourselves. We – don't you see? – have decided to clean away all this filth of yours over here, and we're going to tear up all these old roots and stubs." Yes, we'll do it! Isn't that so?'

And the crowd echoed in chorus. 'Quite right; that's the stuff.'

'Well – that's settled then. They've got to be told, straight away: "Stand aside, gentlemen – don't come interfering with us. Eat and drink as much as you like, but don't you come bothering us!" They tell us: "Go ahead again, go on making war." No – no, no more of that, boys! We've gone ahead and marched and fought and died enough already, haven't we? Eh?'

Again the crowd agreed, almost as one man.

'Right!'

Louder and louder swells the clamour for a social revolution. It comes now from the people themselves. A desire for action, for independence, has been born among the masses, a desire that ought to be a stimulant to organize them, to cure them of their political blindness. Leaders are no longer trusted. Recently in the Cirque Moderne a young lad, evidently a chauffeur, made a clever pun on the Russian words '*vozhdi*' (leaders) and '*vozzhi*' (reins). A crowd of about two hundred people greeted his sallies with laughter and applause.

Every day life acquires a more earnest, a sterner character – everywhere the tension is growing – growing.

# The Gardener

## February 1917

MOTOR-CARS, splashing mud against the walls and smothering passers-by, tear rumbling and hooting down the street. They are crowded to overflowing with soldiers and sailors, and bristle with the steel quills of bayonets, like huge hedgehogs running amok. Every now and then there is the crack of a rifle. Revolution! The Russian nation is scurrying about, bewildered with its newly-acquired freedom; it is trying to grasp it, but finds it somewhat elusive.

In the Alexander Park a gardener is engrossed in his solitary work; a thick-set man in the fifties. Clumsily and quietly he sweeps away last year's fallen leaves and the litter from paths and flower-beds, and brushes off the freshly fallen snow. He takes not the slightest interest in the bustle that is going on around him, and remains deaf to the screeching of klaxons, the shouts and songs and shots. He does not even see the red flags. I watched him to see if he would look up presently and notice the people running about, the motor-lorries glittering with bayonets. But he bent down over his work and went on with it as stubbornly as a mole. Apparently he is as blind as one also.

## March 1917

Along the streets, along the paths in the park, in the direction of the Narodni Dom, hundreds, thousands of soldiers in grey are moving slowly, some of them dragging machine-guns behind them like small iron pigs tied to a string. This is one of the innumerable machine-gun regiments that has just arrived from Oranienbaum. They say that there are more than ten thousand men in it. They do not know what to do with themselves, and ever since they arrived this morning they have been wandering about the town, looking for lodgings. The passers-by step aside when they meet them, for these men are war-weary, hungry and fierce. Some of them, I noticed, had squatted down by a large, round flower-bed and had scattered their rifles and haversacks over it.

Presently, not hurrying himself in the least, the gardener came up with his broom. He surveyed them angrily:

'What sort of a camping ground do you think you've got here? This is a flower-bed – flowers are going to grow here. You know what flowers are, don't you? Are you all blind? This is the children's playground. Come off it, I say. D'you hear me?'

And the fierce, armed men meekly crawled away from the flower-bed.

### 6 July 1917

Soldiers in steel helmets, just recalled from the front, are surrounding the Peter and Paul Fortress. They are marching leisurely along the pavements and through the park, dragging their machine-guns behind them, their rifles carelessly dangling from their shoulders. Occasionally one of them calls out good-naturedly to a passer-by:

'Hurry up; there's going to be some shooting!'

The inhabitants are all agog to see the battle and are following the soldiers silently, with fox-like movements, dodging from tree to tree and straining their necks, looking eagerly ahead.

In the Alexander Park flowers are growing at the sides of the paths; the gardener is busying himself among them. He has a clean apron on and carries a spade in his hand. As he walks along he scolds both onlookers and soldiers as though they were a flock of sheep.

'Where are you walking, there? Is that grass made for you to trample on? Isn't there enough room for you on the path?'

A bearded, iron-headed peasant in soldier's uniform, his rifle under his arm, says to the gardener:

'You look out yourself, old boy, or we'll shoot you straight away.'

'Oh, will you? You just try! Fine shot, you are. . . .'

'Don't you know there's a war on? There's going to be some fighting.'

'Oh, is there? Well, get on with your fighting, and I'll get on with my job.' 'I'm with you there. Have you got a fag?' Pulling out his pouch from his pocket the gardener grumbled: 'Trampling about where you're not allowed to . . .'

'It's war.'

'What's that got to do with me? Fighting's all very well for them that likes it, and you've got plenty of others to help you; but I'm all alone in this job. You'd better clean that rifle of yours a bit; it's all rusty . . .'

There is a whistle and the soldier, unable to light the cigarette in his lips, puts it hastily in his pocket and runs off between the trees.

The gardener spits after him in disgust and shouts angrily:

'What the devil are you running over the grass for? Isn't there any other road you can go by?'

*Autumn, 1917*

The gardener walks leisurely along the path, a ladder on his shoulder and a pair of shears in his hand. Every now and then he stops to cut off the dead branches by the side of the path. He has grown thinner – seems almost shrivelled; his clothes hang on him like a sail on a mast on a windless day. The shears snip angrily and creakily as he cuts down the barren wood.

Watching him, I could not help thinking that neither an earthquake nor a flood would prevent him from going on with his work. And if the trumpets of the archangels announcing the day of judgement were not shining brilliantly enough, I am quite certain that he would scold the archangels in precisely the same voice as he scolded the soldier.

'You'd better clean those trumpets of yours a bit, they're all dirty . . .'

# A Bit of Law

ON a wet morning in March 1917 a small man of about forty, neatly dressed in a tightly buttoned jacket, worn, but well-brushed, came to see me. He sat down on a chair, wiped his face with his handkerchief, and, panting for breath, said somewhat reproachfully:

'There's no denying that you live mighty high up – it's hard for a free people to climb up to the fifth storey.'

His hands were small and dark, like a bird's claws; his glassy eyes were stern, and something obstinate and suspicious gleamed in them. From his bony yellow face a pointed, yellow nose stood out like the beak of a rook. Sniffing cautiously, he examined the book-shelves, looked at me, and asked:

'I suppose there's no mistake – you really are Mr Peshek-honov, aren't you?'

'No, my name is Peshkov.'

'And that's not quite the same thing, I suppose?'

'Not quite.'

He sighed, and, scrutinizing me once more, agreed.

'You're not alike, either – the other one's got a little beard. I see I've landed in a misunderstanding.' Then he shook his head sadly: 'Everything's so confused nowadays . . .'

I told him he would probably find Peshekhonov on the Kamennoostrovsky, in the Elite cinema, where the commissariat of the Petrogradskaia Storona was being organized.

'May I ask what your business with him is?' I inquired.

The little man blew his nose abstractedly and loudly, then, taking up a book from the table, he glanced at its edges and at last replied: 'In accordance with my duty as a free citizen, I want to offer him a bit of law to stick on the walls.'

Scenting something unusual I inquired what sort of law he had in mind.

'I've got it here,' he said; and thrusting his hand into his breast-pocket, he produced a sheet of paper folded in four, and handed it to me. On it was inscribed the following, in large, carefully written letters:

### IMPERATIVE REGULATIONS:

The present regulations aim at strictly safeguarding freedom, owing to the state of general rioting; therefore:

### URGENT:

Parograf I. Arrest all persons who discuss events and freedom skoptically, and who continue to live according to their old custom, like gents.

Parograf II. Particularly: Anna Pogosova, named Varnashka, the wife of Jacob Fedorev, manager of a pleasure-house in Novaia Derevna.

Parograf III. and Notice: The above-named Varnashka sniffs fiercely at his Excellency, the Citizen Peshekhonov, on account of his wearing civil clothes and no sign of authority, also for his lawful refusal to allow her to take possession of barrels which do not belong to her, although they be empty.

Parograf IV. and Notice Continued: She likewise disapproves of his beard and altogether of his appearance. Also she said freedom is like an innocent girl – it costs dear and not everyone is allowed to grab at it.

Parograf V. Therefore: to arrest her first of all, regardless of remonstrations.

Right. Legislator

*Jacob Fedorov.*

Having perused the law I begged the 'legislator' to allow me to take a copy of his work. Half closing his eyes he inquired:

'For what purpose?'

'Only as a memento.'

He carefully folded up the sheet, saying, 'You can tear one off the wall, where they'll soon be stuck up.'

But I insisted on him allowing me to take a copy. Finally, after hesitating for some time, he gracefully handed the paper back to me. While I wrote he continued to sniffle and examine the titles of the books on the table. Then he sighed, shook his head, and muttered:

'Lots of these books will have to be forbidden now. Another bit of law's wanted. No doubt about that.'

Having finished my copy I said to him. 'So, in your opinion, everybody ought to be arrested who – '

'Who talks scoptically.'

'You mean "sceptically," don't you?'

He corrected me sternly: 'Pardon me. It comes from *skoptzi** – so it's "scoptically." You can't hide the true meaning by distorting a word. Skoptzi are people who do not count me as a member of humanity.'

Seeing that talking to him was no easy matter, I asked what his profession was.

'Why, this!'

And he brandished the law in the air.

'And before you started this work of legislation, what did you do?'

He rose from his chair, buttoned up his coat and said:

'I just thought.'

Then, straightening himself out, he muttered suspiciously:

'So this means that Mr Peshekhonov is not one and the same man as Mr Gorki the writer?'

'No, he is not.'

'That's rather difficult to understand,' he said, half-closing his eyes and making an effort to grasp the meaning. 'It's as though there were two persons – and apparently there are three. But if you count them as three, then you get two. Isn't a transgression of the law of arithmetic forbidden by the authorities?'

'Up to now, there are no authorities . . .'

'Ye-es. So-so. Also, from the point of view of passports, one mayn't have two passports, may one? Isn't that the law?'

Shaking his head disapprovingly he went to the door, stumbled over something, and, turning round, said to me:

'I beg your pardon – I landed in a misunderstanding. I'm nearly suffocated with thoughts – otherwise my head's quite clear, so everyone says. But, you know, in times like these . . .'

Outside the door, while trying to slip on his goloshes, I heard him mutter:

'Bismarck himself couldn't have made head or tail of this . . . Are there two of them, or are there three? . . .'

* A Russian sect practising castration.

# Snapshots of The Revolution

*1919*

IN the spring of this year, during the first warm days, weird, fantastic people crawled out on the streets of Petrograd. Where and how had they lived hitherto? Doubtless in some slum, in old, solitary, crumbling houses, hidden away from life, insulted and rejected by the world. One dominant thought cropped up in my mind every time I saw them: they have forgotten something and are trying to recall it, silently crawling about the town in search of it.

They were dressed in worn-out, tattered clothes, they were dirty and evidently very hungry, but they did not look like beggars and did not ask for alms. Very silently, very carefully they walked along, watching the ordinary passers-by with suspicion and curiosity. As they stopped before the shop-windows, they examined the things exhibited in them with the eyes of folk who are trying to discover – or remember – what use one made of all those things. Motor-cars terrified them, as they terrified country men and women twenty years ago.

\*

A tall, dark-faced old man with sunken eyes, a crooked nose and a greenish beard, politely lifting a crumpled hat with a hole in the brim, and pointing his long finger at a disappearing motor-car, asks a passer-by:

'Electricity? Ah! . . . Thank you.'

He walks on with his chest stuck out, his head held high, never stepping aside to let another man pass, and glancing at the people he meets with a repulsive look in his half-closed eyes. He is bare-footed, and as he touches the stones of the pavement with the soles of his feet he clenches his toes, as though testing the stability of the stones. An idle young loafer briskly accosts him:

'Who are you, daddy?'

'A man, most probably.'

'Russian?'

'All my life.'

'In the army?'

'Perhaps.'

Then, scrutinizing the youth, he asks in his turn:

'Making revolution?'

'Done it already!'

'Ah . . .'

The old man turns away and begins inspecting the shop-window of a second-hand bookseller, his beard tightly clasped in his left hand. The youth, still loafing round, asks him something again; but the old man, without glancing at him, only says in a low, quiet tone:

'Go away.'

\*

In Simeonevski street, pressed against the church gate, stands a woman of about forty. Her yellow face is swollen so that one can hardly see her eyes, her mouth is half-open, as though she were gasping for breath. Her bare feet are pushed into huge shoes, the tops of which are covered with a thick layer of dry mud. She is wrapped in a light, cotton, man's dressing-gown, her hands are folded across her breast, and her head is crowned by a straw hat with crumpled leaves and one cherry – there was a whole bunch of cherries there once, but only one has survived; the rest are just stems and broken fragments that glitter like glass.

Puckering her thick, beautifully curved eyebrows, she watches intently the people squeezing into the tramcars, jumping from the platforms and scattering as they alight. The woman's lips twitch, as though she were counting the people. Or perhaps she is expecting someone and is practising the words that she must say when they meet. Between the red, narrow clefts of her swollen eyes gleams an unkind, stern and cutting look. With disgust she brushes aside the street urchins who are selling cigarettes, several times she has even pushed them aside with a quick gesture of elbow or hip.

Someone asks her in a low voice: 'Maybe you need some help?'

She measures the intruder with an angry glance and answers, equally low: 'What makes you think so?'

'Pardon me . . .'

A neat little old woman in a lace cap is standing at her side, selling pastries made of hemp or clay. The strange woman addresses her:

'Are you – a lady?'

'I am of the shopkeeping class.'

'Ah . . . How many inhabitants are there in this town?'

'I don't know. A good many.'

'Yes, it is terrible how many . . .'

'You are a stranger in this town?'

'I? No. I come from here . . .'

She sways, and, nodding to the old woman, moves towards the circus, dragging along the heavy shoes that keep falling off her bare, dirty feet . . .

Now she is sitting on a bench in the garden behind the circus; at her side, leaning on a stick, is a big, ponderous old woman who breathes heavily; she has a stone-cut face, wears round, black spectacles, and is dressed in the remnants of a fur-coat, in rags of silk and grey fur.

Passing by, I can hear the hoarse voice and the sharp, cutting words:

'The last decent man in this town died nineteen years ago . . .'

And the old woman screams, as if she were deaf:

'The Palace of Justice has been burnt down. I went to look, the walls alone remain. All burnt down. God's punishment! . . .'

The woman in the enormous shoes leans over and says loudly in her ear:

'All my people are in prison. All.'

It seemed to me that she was laughing.

*

A small, very hairy man with the face of a monkey and a squashed nose is walking along, almost running, with quick, short steps. The dark-blue pupils of his eyes are anxiously dilated; the white of the eye surrounds them with a fine, opaline circle. The nankin cloak apparently does not belong to him; the edge of it is turned up unevenly, hanging like a fringe, as though a dog had been worrying it. On his feet he wears felt shoes that are worn down at the heels, and he has no hat; a grey shaggy mane stands upright on his head, a thick, strongly peppered beard grows disorderly from under his eyes, his cheek-bones, his ears. He is scuttering about and muttering something anxiously, brandishing his hands frequently, and interlacing his fingers tightly.

On the square near the Narodni Dom he addresses the soldiers:

'You must understand – it is you most of all who must understand this: a man is happy only when he recollects the fact that the life of a man is brief, and he has reconciled himself to it . . .'

He speaks very low, in a little thin voice, although from his appearance one would have expected him to growl. He shifts from one foot to the other; one of his hands is pressed to his heart, and with his other hand he gesticulates from the wrist as though conducting an orchestra; his hands are hairy, too, dark clusters growing on his fingers between the joints. In front of him, on the bench, three soldiers are chewing sunflower seeds, spitting the husks at the stomach and feet of the speaker; a fourth soldier, with a crimson hole in his cheek, is smoking and trying to blow smoke-rings on to the orator's nose.

'I maintain that it is useless to rouse in us, the people, the hope of a better life; it is inhuman and criminal, it is like roasting people over a slow fire . . .'

The soldier spits on his cigarette-end, throws it up in the air with a flick of his fingers, and, stretching out his legs, asks:

'Who's hired you?'

'What? Me?'

'Yes, you. Who hired you?'

'What do you mean by hired?'

'I mean what I say. Hired by the *bourgeoisle*, or by the Jews?' The man, confused, stops speaking, while one of the three soldiers lazily advises the last speaker:

'Give him a kick in the belly.'

'He's not got any belly to speak of,' replies the other . . .

The little man stands back, shoves his hands into his pockets, then pulls them out again, pressing them tightly together:

'I speak on my own behalf. I am not hired. I, too, have thought and read, have believed. But now I know: a man is a man only for a short while, everything must come to an end, and he . . .'

Here the soldier with the hole in his cheek shouts fiercely:

'Get out!'

The little man turns and runs, raising clouds of dust with his felt boots, while the soldier remarks to his companions:

'He thought he was giving us a fright, the skunk. As though we didn't understand him. We – understand everything, don't we?'

On the evening of the same day the little man was sitting on on the bench at the Troitzki bridge:

'Try to understand,' he urged his companions on the bench. 'All things considered, the man of the majority, the simple-minded man, whom we look upon as a fool – he is the true builder of life. The majority of people are fools . . .'

He was listened to by a pock-marked, bandy-legged sailor, broad and heavy, a militiaman, a fat woman in a blue dress, three grey-haired men, evidently workmen, and a Jewish youth clad in black leather. The youth was excited; he kept asking in a sneaking manner:

'Maybe the proletariat is a fool, too?'

'I am speaking of the people who want very little – merely that they should be allowed to live in the way they want.'

'The *bourgeois*, you mean, eh?'

'Wait a bit, *tovarisch*!'* the sailor said thickly; 'let him speak . . .'

The orator gave a nod in the direction of the sailor: 'Thank you.'

'Don't mention it.'

'A man is a fool only from the theoretic point of view, for he himself is quite satisfied with the amount of brain with which nature has endowed him, and well knows how to make use of it.'

* Comrade.

'Right,' said the sailor. 'Go ahead.'

'He is a man only for a short time and he knows it, but he is in no way disturbed by the knowledge that some day he will have to lie down in his grave ...'

'We've all got to die; you're right again!' the sailor repeated, winking at the leather-clad youth, and smiling broadly, as though he would proclaim to the world his conviction of his own immortality.

The monkey-faced orator continued lecturing in a low voice, as though imploring his listeners to believe him:

'Man does not want an agitated life full of hopes, he is satisfied with a slow running, peaceful existence under the stars in the night ... I say that to rouse unrealizable hopes in people who are here only for a short while is to confuse them. What can communism give them?'

'Ah!' said the sailor, resting his palms on his knees. Then he bent forward and rose to his feet: 'Now, you come along with me!'

'Where to?' asked the hairy little man, starting back.

'That's my business. *Tovarisch*, I command you to follow me ...'

'Oh, let him be,' said the youth scornfully, waving his hand contemptuously.

'Follow me, *if* you please!' the sailor repeated lower, but his pock-marked face grew darker and his eyes blinked sternly.

'I'm not afraid,' said the orator, shrugging his shoulders.

The woman, making the sign of the cross, turned away; the militiaman also departed, feeling the bolt of his rifle with his finger; while the other three rose to their feet so mechanically and simultaneously that they might have possessed only one will between them. The sailor and the leather-clad youth led their prisoner towards the Peter and Paul Fortress, but two passers-by, who came up with them on the bridge, persuaded them to release the philosopher.

'No – no,' the sailor protested, 'this poodle's got to be shown what a short time a man's got to live!'

'I'm not afraid,' the poodle repeated in a low voice, looking

SNAPSHOTS OF THE REVOLUTION

at the water under his feet. 'Only I am amazed to see how little you understand.'

He turned round suddenly and walked back towards the square.

'Look out, he's going!' the sailor said; 'the blighter's off. Hi! where are you off to?'

'Let him be, *tovarisch*, you can see he's not all there.'

The sailor whistled after the hairy little man and then laughed: 'Confound him! He's gone off and made no noise about it. A brave poodle . . . he *must* be dotty!'

\*

A sharp-eyed little old man, in a rusty melon-hat and a long cloth coat with fur collar, is skipping to and fro among the crowd assembled around the Narodni Dom. He stops in front of every group and, holding his head on one side and poking the end of his ebony-handled stick into the ground, listens intently to what people are saying. He has a rosy face, as round as a ball, and the round, flickering eyes of a night-bird; under his hawk's nose his grey, bristling moustache stands upright, and on his chin grows a goat's cluster of light-yellow hair, which he twirls with a quick movement of the three fingers of his left hand, poking it into his mouth, chewing it with his lips, and blowing it out again – 'P-ph!'

He edges his shoulders through the pressing crowd of people as though hiding among them, and then suddenly his challenging, arresting voice rings out:

'I am well aware which classes it is that are specially harmful to us . . . We must destroy them, smash them to pieces, grind their bones to dust . . .'

He is always listened to with great attention by soldiers, workmen, servants, and women of pleasure, who watch him open-mouthed, as though sucking in the stimulating words. While speaking he holds his stick straight across his chest and runs his fingers rapidly along it as though he were playing on a fiddle.

'No. 1, clerks and officials of all kinds. You know yourselves what a plague and nuisance they are to us – who are more unjust, more unmerciful, than officials? Law Court officials, Prison officials, Inland Revenue officials, Customs officials, Tax officials – they're everywhere. And what conjurers too! Aye – and, like conjurers, they've got whole boxes of tricks! They are in the first division, so we must destroy all officials.'

At this a red-haired girl, apparently a servant, asks angrily:

'Who're you, yourself, I'd like to know? I'll be blowed if you're not an official, too!'

He hurriedly denies this, in rather a pettish tone:

'Never have I done anything against the poor people, never! I'm a fortune-teller, a diviner: I know what the future has in store for all of us . . .'

Here several of his listeners shout to him to give an exhibition of his knowledge.

'No – it's a secret matter – you can't do it in public . . .'

And to the question, 'What's going to happen to us?' he answers, casting his eyes to the ground:

'It'll turn out badly if, now that you have undertaken this thing, you do not make an end of it at once – very bad it'll be. Bad teeth must be drawn out by the roots. All the officials must be mowed down. Also the learned people, the intelligentsia – for trying to blind our reason, giving us a penny for every shilling. Yes! We're learned now, so they've got to listen to us; we'll put the laws on them! And they got up a "pure-water" campaign and had notices stuck all over the place with: "Do not drink unboiled water!" Ha – ha – ha!'

It was difficult to make out whether he was laughing or sighing, for the 'ha – ha – ha' came curiously from his rounded mouth.

Then, making a face, he asks, triumphantly:

'Well? And do we drink that unboiled water, or do we not, eh?'

The audience, vastly amused, roars out:

'We do.'

'And we're still alive, aren't we?'

'SURE!'

'There you are, then. That's what their laws come to! See? Down with them all! . . .'

Whereupon, convinced that he has accomplished his task, he whisks out of the crowd and walks away, brandishing his stick. But coming to another group, he addresses the crowd again:

'There are two classes that are a particular plague to us . . .'

There is no doubt that he, too, has emerged from some dark corner to which life had driven him, remaining for years in solitude, crouching, accumulating anger and revenge.

*

Apparently there are not a few people who busy themselves with rousing animosity against the intelligentsia, and I think they are mostly to be found among the domestic-servant class – house-porters, butlers, cooks, and so on. After one of the meetings in the Cirque Moderne a fat, red-faced woman was telling the soldiers 'how the masters live.' Her story was witty and amusing, but she employed such language that three out of every ten of her words could not have been put down on paper. The soldiers laughed uproariously and spat with gusto as they listened to the alleged doings of a doctor who was a specialist in women's diseases, of the behaviour of a Jewish lady-dentist, and the way in which an actor trained his female pupils.

'All this rabble ought to be thrashed,' said a dark soldier, wearing a handkerchief tied round his neck, sternly – 'thrashed to the last man.'

In another group a limping man of forty, hairless as a eunuch, was shouting:

'I've spent my life in the stables, among the manure and the horses, while they live in beautiful flats, and lie on soft couches playing with lap-dogs. No more of that, I say! It's my turn to play with lap-dogs now; and as for them, they can go and work in the stables, eh?'

A young, one-eyed woman, her face all burnt by vitriol, spoke terribly, mercilessly:

'Look into the Bible – are there any masters in the Bible? Of course there aren't any there. There are kings, judges, and prophets – but no masters. God himself ordered the destruction of the tribes in which there were masters, and destroyed them head by head, with the women and children and even the slaves. Because even the slaves become infected with the masters' opinions and cease to be human beings, yes!'

'Go and hang yourself, woman,' someone in the crowd shouted to her. But, pressing her round bosom in her hands, she went on screaming sharply: 'I've been a lady's maid for eleven years, and I've seen things . . .'

Certainly she had seen things which were unknown to Octave Mirabeau when he wrote his *Diary of a Lady's Maid* – and her audience listened to her revelations without laughing, gloomily and in silence. Only when she had gone her way, red and perspiring with the excitement, did a snub-nosed little soldier, watching her disappear, remark:

'It's not for nothing that that girl got her face spoiled . . .'

Truly the injured man becomes terrible when he realizes his right to avenge and acquires the freedom of vengeance. It would not be unprofitable if our social reformers of today were to consider men in this category as worthy of first place in their list of 'classes to be destroyed'.

# The Monarchist

IN the eighties of the last century a sharp-eyed youngster used to roam about the streets of Nizhni-Novgorod with a box tied round his chest calling out, not loudly but half-inquiringly and in a peculiarly intrusive way:

'Little crosses to wear on the breast, books for writing the names of the dead in, hair-pins and pins.'

Meeting him very often, I noticed presently that he was inclined to be impudent: he would single out one of the passers-by and follow him relentlessly, walk alongside of him and repeat in his persistent way:

'Little crosses to wear on the heart, booklets for writing the names of the dead in . . .'

The passer-by would try to shake him off angrily, sometimes swearing at him, but the young tradesman would stare up at his face, and, smiling ingratiatingly at his victim, would offer him more crosses. It seemed to me that the lad was looking for trouble, that he wanted to be knocked down and beaten, but for some unknown reason I came to the conclusion that his heart was not in his trade and that his real business lay in something far more interesting and perhaps more dangerous.

I was considerably disappointed therefore when the youth set up a stall in the church-wall enclosure on the much-frequented Rozhdestvensskaia street, where he began selling calendars and 'leaflets.'* In a short time his stall developed into a shop bearing the inscription:

V. I. BREEFF: BOOKSELLER.

Shortly after this there appeared in Nizhni a little rose-coloured book entitled *Life of the Hermit Feodor Kusmich*. On the

* A small popular edition of the classics.

183

cover of this book there was a gaudy representation of a very tall, bald old man with a huge beard, while at the foot was printed: V. I. BREEFF: PUBLISHER.

I learnt that the book had been written in the following way: In a public-house called 'The Rook' a pilgrim had been telling the legend of the mysterious Siberian hermit. Breeff immediately commissioned the tramp Terentiev, a former school-teacher, to write the life of the old man 'for a sov.' It appeared that Terentiev had read or heard something about Feodor Kusmich before, and he succeeded in writing a 'life' of considerable interest. It spread in thousands of copies all along the Volga and the Oka, and Breeff made a good thing out of it.

When the first volume of my stories appeared on sale Breeff came to see me, dressed modestly but imposingly in a rough dark blue suit, a heavy silver watch in his waistcoat pocket, a rolled-gold chain across his chest, and new, creaking boots. He gave off a strong smell of boot-blacking and perfumed soap, a broad smile shone on his face, and he spoke in a hushed voice like a man inspired:

'Allow me to expound the dream of my heart! In order to glorify the name of this ancient town of ours, and desiring to render every possible assistance to the history of our State, I am planning to publish pocket editions of all our illustrious countrymen, such as Kosma Minin, the patriarch Nikon, the archpriest Avvakum, Kulibin, Mili Balakizev, Mr Boborikin, of Dobroliuboff of course, also of Melnikoff-Pechersky and of all the other geniuses of our Nizhni-Novgorod land. Will you contribute your literary assistance to this task?'

He spoke, as I have said, in a hushed voice, as though imparting a secret of immense importance. His language was fluent and his words were carefully chosen, but all the time he was trembling all over, fidgeting with his feet, and brandishing a spotted handkerchief in his hand. Suddenly plunging his hands into his pockets, he tinkled something, like the jingling of brass on a horse's harness, and then rubbed his face with his hands like a Mahomedan at prayer. He gave one the impression that he was smitten with a skin disease and that his whole body was itching unbearably.

There was something shaggy about his appearance, something funny and rather jolly – such a true Russian alertness, ready for every trial. His high-cheek-boned face was ornamented on the chin by an irresolute tuft of colourless hair which grew timidly into his Adam's apple. His moustache stuck straight out like the whiskers on an ear of wheat, as did his eyebrows. Looking at Breeff I thought to myself, 'You're the kind of man people call "hedgehog-head".' His eyes were most unusual – round, devoid of lashes, and of a greenish colour. They shone with inspiration, emitting little rays rather like the dust of sparks. It looked as if they were going to flare up and that the black hollows alone would remain in their place.

When I refused him my 'literary assistance' he blew his nose shrilly, sighed, and then continued, his inspiration unflagging:

'Then allow me to make you another proposition, a much easier one.'

He rose to his feet and, as though reciting poetry, announced in two breaths:

'The interest of your unusual life and its new beginning is nothing but a financial proposition! And if you will agree to write your auto-history for fifty roubles, upon my word I'm your publisher!'

I likewise refused to write my auto-history, but this did not prevent Breeff from publishing subsequently a silly book which purported to be my 'life.' The publishers threatened him with a lawsuit if he did not stop issuing it.

'Believe me, as a countryman of your own,' Breeff tried to justify himself, 'it isn't due to rapacity that I resolved to trespass on your modesty – what is money, after all? – but only to a burst of patriotic feeling.'

In 1905 I was told that V. I. Breeff had been elected president of the Nizhni-Novgorod section of the 'Union of the Russian People'* and was energetically fighting all revolution and consolidating autocracy. Then – I think it was in 1910 – Breeff sent me a letter to Capri in which he extolled the kindness and generosity of the Emperor Nicolas II and urged me to repent of my sins and beg for permission to return to Russia. The letter was

* An ultra-conservative organization.

written in a very amusing style and did not in any way annoy me.
I even answered Breeff, telling him that I did not consider myself
an *émigré*, and that I could return to Russia whenever I cared to
do so without asking anybody's permission. To this I added my
opinion of autocracy in general.* In 1914, on my return to
Russia, I heard that Breeff had left Nizhni.

In 1917, on a bustling, busy day in May, I was called to the
telephone. An agitated voice addressed me:

'Breeff speaking – Vassili Ivanovich Breeff, do you remember
me? The Nizhni-Novgorod dreamer?'

An hour later he was twisting about on a chair in front of me,
spluttering a torrent of words in every direction, – just as shaggy
in appearance and just as amusing as he had been twenty years
before. Only his bristling hairs had grown softer and lost some of
their sprightliness: he had shaved the irresolute beard and dishevelled moustache; his eyebrows alone still reminded me of a
young hedgehog. But his greenish eyes still gleamed with a fresh
lively fire, still emitted their spark-like rays. He was dressed in a
thick smoke-coloured material, a diamond sparkled in his neck-
tie, and a large ruby glinted from a ring on his left hand. Otherwise he was the same restless, excited individual who had
seemed to me to be suffering from a variety of scabies.

Throwing his hands about and gesticulating freely, he plunged
them suddenly into his trouser pockets, then into his waistcoat
pockets, and pulled out fragments of ore from various mines he
had visited. 'Gold-bearing quartz!' he explained as he rolled
his samples on the table; 'tungsten, ye-es! Lithographic stone
of the finest quality! An unknown stone, no one knows what it
really is! It's all mine, all belongs to me, yes, yes! I've pegged out
my claims! And now I've come to you, as a countryman of mine,
to ask you to help me realize it all, as you are on good terms with
the new rulers of our fates.'

My refusal to assist him in the matter in no way discouraged
him; he was merely slightly amazed and said:

'This is the fourth time that you've refused to do what I asked
you . . .'

* This answer of mine was published by someone in the English
*Manchester Guardian* under the title 'A Letter to a Monarchist'.

'But I don't know anything about such matters!'

He shrugged his shoulders: 'What's there to understand about gold? All you've got to do is simply to extract it, and then our lives will be lined with it.' He half closed his eyes and, shaking his head, continued in a lyrical strain:

'If you only knew what supernatural riches are buried in Siberia! It's not a land, it's the udder of a cow that never runs dry! Upon my word it is! It just begs you to come and milk it! And there's no one to do it. We don't know how to. There's only one lot of expert milkers over there, and that's the English on the Lena . . .'

I asked him how long he had been living in Siberia.

'Three years, just three years. As soon as this absurd war began I went there. I'm just burning to tell you what an extraordinary life I've had, for I am sure that you, a Nizhni man, would be delighted to hear the story of the successes of a fellow-countryman. Who else but you ought to know the wonderful story of a Russian man's life? You, apart from being a countryman are, so to speak, a lawful registrar of the flights of a Russian soul, and your fate is to build up literary memorials to us, the people of the ancient town to which all Russia is indebted for having been saved from a premature extermination three hundred years ago . . .'

As he was going away he said:

'I hear that you, too, have been offered a post in the Government. Is that so? No? What a pity! We Nizhni folk would have been flattered to have had our own man among the Ministers.'

He looked at me scrutinizingly and added:

'Even if it were only for public instruction.'

*

The next evening Breeff, sitting in my room, agitated, perspiring, his flaxen hair bristling, and gesticulating as though he were kneading dough, said to me:

'The crisis in my life began during the insulting years of the Japanese war. Until that time I had existed merely on my love for our beautiful town. I never dreamt of politics – my dreams were of a different sort: I dreamt them even when I was awake.

My ambition was to work hard, become rich, and build a house in Nizhni, the most beautiful house imaginable – so beautiful that not only Nizhni but even strangers would marvel at it. They should even come from Paris and London to gaze at Breeff's house! It should be illustrated in all the papers: people would write, "Even in the provincial towns of Russia there are houses such as we never see in our own country!"'

From the street below came a heavy rumble; the horns of motor-cars hooted loudly; bearded soldiers marched past in an endless grey torrent; a sinister whisper seemed to pervade the land; one could hear vaguely suppressed screams and cries – it was the Russian empire shaking and crumbling to pieces.

'I'm not a fool, and I know the measure of my strength. But if I, Vassiutka Breeff, a flea in this huge Russian land, could feel so keenly the indignity of this disgrace – that a foreign nation should defeat our great empire, the mother of our men of genius – if in my miserable little heart this indignity is so unbearably bitter, what then must it be to other Russians, greater and cleverer than I am?

'From that time onwards the intelligentsia and all educated people exasperated me, for in them I found only an incomprehensible indifference of both heart and mind for the fate of Russia. Exasperation is the source of all politics: in fact politics *are* exasperation. So I wondered how it was that our people, our armies, should be beaten and that you and those like you should not be sorry for them nor care about it.

'I can understand why no one is sorry for the people: they don't even know how to be sorry for themselves. I know something about them. Forgive me for saying so, but in my opinion there is no such thing as *a* people – they don't exist as a unity until you collect them into a heap and shout at them, frighten them, and order them about. That a people should have but one interest, one idea, is absurd – such a thing doesn't exist. They are like sand or clay. And to make them fit for the foundations of a kingdom they must be kneaded thoroughly and baked in a good fire.

'So you are not sorry for the people? Very well, I agree with you. But – are you not sorry that your own dream has been dispelled? A man just lives for his aspirations – he has nothing else to live for. Every one of us has a determined aspiration for the most beautiful things in life – and that is the power which energizes people. There is the dream of a wonderful state, which should be better than any other in the world. All nations have a dream like that – except the Jews, of course, who, having lost the country they once possessed, can only dream of their own interests. The dream of the embellishment of life in general is just as impossible for a Jew as it is for a gypsy or any other nomad race. I know you will not agree with this, for you are devoted to the Jews, a thing which is simply incomprehensible to me. Forgive me, but it seems to me a sort of kink in the soul, like a disease of some kind.

'But that is beside the point. So let us get on to the year 1905. A year of turmoil all over the world, everybody busy making revolutions, even people who do not know how to sew a button on their trousers. Everybody running about the streets like a happy bridegroom, but many of them with the presage of funerals in their souls.

'And then my dream was born; it flashed into my mind. Three hundred years ago the town of Nizhni-Novgorod saved Russia from premature destruction – is it not time to recall and repeat that noble feat? What is revolution? I used to have a clerk called Leonidka, an intelligent youth, who enlisted with the revolutionaries and used to shout communism in the streets all day long. I said to him: "Very well, Leonidka, you'll make a revolution all right – but what will you do then?" "I?" says he, "Why, as soon as all this is finished and life has entered its new stream I'll go back to my mushrooms, and rear more of 'em, and pickle them in vinegar. I've got a special way of doing it – I can make every bit of mushroom-spawn yield forty per cent more than it would normally." "You fool," I said to him, "What on earth is the good of destroying the whole order of things in a state just for the sake of mushrooms?" And it's like that everywhere today – no matter whom you ask about the aims of the revolution – in the end you find that the whole thing is paltry, like mushrooms.

'Well, we, the "black hundred,"* made a worthy stand against your – excuse me – madness and folly, and even gave some people a jolly good licking. I admit that in some cases it was undeserved, as, for instance, in the case of your friend, the apothecary Heintze. But what is one to do? One cannot count hairs in a brawl. As the proverb says, "Devils enjoy seeing a decrease among the blessed." Having got the upper hand in the revolution, we, of course, rejoiced greatly and started to consolidate the victory. Eventful dates were approaching: the years 1912, 1913, the centenaries of the greatest happenings in Russia. . . . I began to prepare for them . . .

'I tell you frankly – you don't mind me speaking plainly, do you? – I'll tell you frankly that I was delighted with the boldness of your letter in answer to mine. I said to myself: that's how our Nizhni people write! But as to agreeing with your ideas, that I couldn't do, and cannot do even now, when the foundations of the empire have crumbled to pieces and the Tsar is the captive of his own subjects. It is terrible to think to what madness we have been brought through that unhappy union with the French. Here we, too, have abolished the monarchy!

'So you see I cannot possibly agree with you. I know the people. They don't care a cent who is sitting on the throne – it might be a Tartar or a Kirgiz for all they care – so long as there's someone, something, on which to hitch their dreams. The people live by their dreams – they need to have strong imaginations to enable them to withstand the hardships of life, to resign themselves to their life; for it's the only life they are likely to know on this earth.'

I interrupted Breeff here, pointing out that we were still living in days of revolution. At this he jumped to his feet, his face darkened with excitement, and he said in a smothered voice:

'Revolution! Freedom! Are you serious? Tomorrow anyone has merely to jump up and cry: "Hush! I'm going to show you how to live!" And they will follow wherever he leads them, until they came back once more to the drudgery whence they started. Believe me, my greatly honoured fellow-countryman, the true

* The ultra-conservative party of nationalists.

freedom of the people is only the freedom of their imagination. Life is not a blessing to them and will never be a blessing, but it will be for ever and ever an expectation, a hope that it will become a blessing. The people need a hero, a saint – General Skobeleff, Feodor Kusmich, Ivan the Terrible – they are all alike to them. And the more remote, the more vague, the less accessible the hero, the more freedom for the imagination, the easier it is to live. There must be a "Once upon a time there lived" about it – something of the fairy tale. Not a God in heaven, but here, on our dismal earth. Someone of great wisdom and monstrous power; someone who should be all-powerful, who would merely have to wish it and everybody would be happy. That is the kind of man one should dream of!

'So that to try to prove to the people that the Romanoffs are Germans is useless. It is all the same to them; they might be Mordovians for all they care. I tell you I know the people! They do not need a democracy, they have no use for an English parliament, they do not care for mechanics, machinery of any kind – they want mystery. They need the power of a great entity, even though that entity be zero: they will fill the zero with their own imagination. Yes, yes!

'But I must finish about your letter. I had five copies made of it and distributed them to several of our countrymen, while I took the original to Governor Khvostoff himself. "Here," I said, "see what Gorki is writing!" Why did I do that? Why, because I thought it necessary to inform the Nizhni people of your ideas, even though those ideas be pernicious ones. No one could possibly question my patriotism, and although you have strayed away from your flock, you're one of us, all the same. As to the Governor, I took your letter to him in order to anticipate any blame for distributing the copies. I wanted nothing more than to bring you back to your native land in time for the solemn festivities in honour of the great events which took place in this wonderful country in 1812 and 1813!'

Breeff pressed the palms of his hands to his ears and rocked his head to and fro. Blinking hard, he murmured:

'This counting backwards always muddles me up: '13 – '12, then – '14; this shifting of numbers is all wrong! If the election of the Romanoffs had taken place in 1611, and the victory over the "twelve nations" in '12, as it was, then, maybe, there would have been no '14 . . .'

Unclasping his hands, which he had pressed tightly to his head, he sighed and rushed on again:

'We, who believe in the rule of autocracy, were prepared to celebrate the suppression of the revolution and the victory over Europe far and wide and with a tremendous splash, with an annihilating splendour, as a hint, so to speak, to others. "Just look at us: our great Patriotic war against all Europe with the seizure of Paris – and why? Because three hundred years ago Russia was seized by the lucky hand of the Romanoffs!" You see the idea? This little plan was born in my mind, and under the weight of it I felt like a child-bearing woman.

'The thing had to be done in such a way that the brilliancy of the celebrations should eclipse in the memory of the people the mournful failure of the Japanese war, the shameful follies started by that new Mazeppa, that priest Gaposhka, and in fact all the sinister events of the past. It was the bright sunny days of our history that were to be exhibited in all their dazzling glory.'

He jumped up in his chair as though someone had pricked him with a needle, and, placing his hands on the arms of it, bent forward. A green light glinted in his eyes; his red, perspiring face darkened and became broader, for his cheek-bones seemed to have swelled out and his nostrils dilated. His Adam's apple moved as though he were trying to swallow something. For a moment or two he was unable to control his excitement; then, wiping away the tears from his cheeks with a sweeping movement of his hand, he smiled wryly and went on, just as excitedly, but in an undertone, almost in a whisper:

'And all of a sudden I was told: "Vassili Ivanovich, our friendly union with the French does not allow us to make too much noise about the 'Patriotic' war, for fear it might offend our allies." Yes – yes, that's exactly what I was told! I remonstrated: "Allow me! If my intelligent face does not please my companion, does it mean that I must put on the mask of a fool? It seems to me we have been wearing that mask for too long and that those who laugh at it, pointing out that when an autocrat dances with a republic it will be the autocrat who will feel giddy first, are perfectly right. The autocrat is feeling giddy already: already our parliament is growing boisterous, and Mr Miliukoff is aiming at being president!"

'You know, of course, that this Franco-Russian alliance was considered by the "Union of Russian People" as an unfortunate mistake, like the friendship of a vulture and a bear – one in the skies, the other in the woods, and both of no use to each other. We thought justly that friendship with Germany would be of far greater profit to us – a stone-cut, cast-iron friendship that should be absolutely insuperable.

'Briefly, the celebration of the edifying Patriotic war did not come off. Here and there in the squares Tchaikovsky's "1812" overture was played, and the people went to sleep after that. All the more ardently did I begin to prepare for the jubilee celebration of the third centenary of the Romanoffs as Tsars! I gathered students of the Art Academy round me and said to them: "Now, boys, paint what you can in the way of pictures of life in Nizhni-Novgorod in 1613, paint and decorate Minin's monument, put all your heart into the job!" Well, I can truthfully say they did their best and they painted some beautiful pictures. I had some picture post-cards made from them later on and sold thousands of copies. I hired a barge, arranged an art exhibition on it, and sailed all down the Volga; this was by way of telling the people, "See what you were capable of once!" People followed us in thousands. But they just watched and grunted – Ah, the people, what a people ... A cast-iron brood ...'

Throwing his hands back and clasping them behind his head, Breeff tilted his face to the ceiling, and, closing his eyes, remained silent for some time.

'Those were great days in my life. I felt exalted high into the air. Everything in parade order, feastings everywhere, church bells ringing in all the Volga towns, music – it was just as though all our unsightly life had suddenly become an Imperial Opera! Great days they were ...!'

He took up a teaspoon from the table, examined it intently,

leisurely, and pensively, rolled it round his finger, then put it back on the table, sighed, and passed his tongue over his lips.

'All that time I was living in a state of complete intoxication, and it was then that a thundering blow was struck me. I was presented to Tsar Nicholas. He was very gracious to me, and even gave me this ring with the ruby in it. But – the famous circus director, Akim Nikitin, boasted to me that he too had a tsar's ring . . .

'This is what happened to me when I met the Tsar. Imagine to yourself that you believed in some inaccessible person, thought that in that person were united all the finest human qualities, all the strength, the wisdom and holiness of Russia, that he was like a kind of spiritual axle, supporting everything – the axle of the nation's life. And all of a sudden, at the bidding of an irresponsible fate, you are placed eye to eye with that person and you see – with sorrow and fear you see – that he is not what you supposed! Not what you lived for, not your ideal! The glitter around him and the splendour are all there – but it is all a sham! Thus I saw in front of me, not the Tsar of my imagination, not the sovereign of my dreams, not even a big man, but just a little fellow on very ordinary legs. And moreover, as it seems, no cleverer than Vassili Breeff himself who from his youth up has been his own teacher. Just an ordinary face. Yes, very amiable; yes, very gracious – but that is all.'

Breeff got up, bristling all over, lifted his hand as though reciting poetry, and again announced with a low, strange exasperation:

'The R-russian Tsar must be terr-r-rible and fierce! Terrible even to look at, not only by nature. Or else he must be a beautiful fairy-tale prince, or just an improbable monster: but – a R-russian Tsar must be terr-r-rible and fierce . . .'

Putting his hand to his throat, he went up to the window and spat into the street, into its incessant noise and bustle, then turned round and asked in a subdued tone:

'Do you know the picture of the Tsar Ivan the Terrible by Vassnetzoff? – Well, there you are! That's a Tsar for the Russian people! Do you remember how one of his eyes squints ever so slightly? That's a tsar's eye for you! An all-seeing eye. A tsar like that sees everything and believes in nothing. He stands alone! His personality is to be felt in every finger. One pulls oneself together in front of him and feels whether everything is in its right place, that everything is in parade order. The tsar of the tsardom, the lord of the realm . . .'

Breeff sat down again, leaned his arms on the table, and continued in a quieter strain:

'The rest of the story is wearisome. I happened to be thrown by my horse. I had lived like everybody else, worn a hat like everyone else, then one day I woke up to find that my head was missing! Then the year 1914 came, and the cursed war began. Well, I thought to myself, that will put an end to Russia – all that remains for one is to find a deep hole and hide in it to the end of one's days.

'I decided to go to Siberia, where, through Feodor Kusmich, the holy hermit, my luck began. At that time many of us thought that the Germans would be sure to bundle us out of the way, across the Urals. We knew our own people! They can endure, but they can't resist. Moreover, I was attracted to Siberia for another reason: I had met a young Siberian girl who was studying in Kazan, where I have a bookseller's shop as well as a house and family. It's well known that love never counts years . . . We loved each other, although I am past fifty and she is not quite twenty. I said to my wife and children: "I have worked for you all my life – now I'm through with it! I'm going to live for myself now! I'm taking fifty thousand roubles; all the rest, here and in Nizhni-Novgorod, is yours. You can take it all. Good-bye." And I went away.

'In Siberia I chanced to meet a man who knew all about the earth's riches – so I started to work in the mines. One has got to build up something. It's not my habit to tramp the earth idly. I had lost my dream. I saw Russia wrapped in folly – forgive me – and drowned in fermenting notions. I did not recognize my own people. I don't believe that they can be expected to go on for ever shelling sunflower seeds and gadding about . . . They'll soon be pressed down to the ground again . . .'

He spoke hesitatingly, and it was evident that he was thinking of something else. His little greenish eyes blinked and flashed, and again I could see the pointed sparks in the dark pupils. He opened his mouth like a fish and passed his tongue swiftly over his dark, parched lips. Then, all of a sudden, as though choking over some word, he flung his hands in the air, interrupting his own speech, rose, and grabbed the back of the chair with his hands. It was clear that a desperately exciting thought had suddenly flashed across his mind. He half closed his eyes; the stubbly hairs of his eyebrows bristled in their familiar way and trembled. He coughed drily and began speaking again, almost in a whisper:

'A man lives on his dream, his ideal, say I. He must have an immense imagination in order to be able to accept life as a blessing, without bitterness, without protest, simply as material to be cultivated by reason. A man – and a people – without an ideal is like a man born blind. Therefore . . .'

He coughed again and rubbed his chest. His eyes shone more and more brilliantly:

'If one knows how to avail oneself of this aspiration of a man's soul, knows how to picture to his imagination a thing of beauty, accessible to him, he will follow you on foot across the seas. And he will forgive everything, forget all errors and sins. Therefore . . .' Snatching my hand in both his, he pressed it vigorously:

'Why, you, too, you are the man of a dream! And see what a noble task lies in front of you! Your talent can set everything right in an hour . . .'

He seemed almost delirious, for he trembled all over, and I began to think that he was crazy. I was not at all surprised therefore when he began whispering into my ear, tugging my hand all the time:

'You want to know how? It's very simple. There's a legend among the people that the unknown hermit, Feodor Kusmich, is Alexander the Blessed. Gregori Rasputin is the son of the Russian Tsar by a simple peasant woman, and the Tsarevich Alexei is the son of Rasputin, the grandson of Alexander the Blessed, the Tsarevich of a people's blood! You see? Absolution! All the sins of the past, all the errors, wiped away by a true Russian, a real people's, blood. A Tsar of peasant breed!

'Yes, yes, I may be all wrong, it may be quite different, but, believe me, there is no need of truth in this matter. What is needed is the dream; you can't build an empire on the naked truth, there couldn't be such a thing. And if you with your talent would serve the great cause of the resurrection of the dream, a true Russian dream of a state . . .'

He lifted his hands as though about to ascend to the skies, and with a mad – or was it a childish? – smile cried out hoarsely, choking over his words:

'And only think what it would mean to me, Breeff Vassiutka, Vassili Ivanovich! – I began my life on the strength of the mysterious hermit Feodor – and Feodor – why, he is Philaret! The father of Michail Romanoff! And I would finish it praising his name to the skies. What a dream! Eh?'

Below in the street the Russian people were clamouring with the noise of thunder, smashing and annihilating the iron framework of the empire, which had taken so many ages to build up . . .

# *Triumph Disappointed*

THE window-panes shone blue in the darkness; the bony face of my companion disappeared in a mist – the shadows under his hollow eyes were particularly thick. The wild, vacant look in his eyes seemed to have become more concerted, concentrated, and the dreary words of complaint acquired more earnestness. His hoarse voice grew softer. Twining the colourless hairs of his scanty beard so tightly round his finger as to cause him to wince, he said:

'About ten years ago I had a dream, in which I saw a people celebrating their conquest of freedom. I was in the Orel prison at that time and the events of 1905 were still fresh in my mind. You know how cruelly the prisoners in Orel used to be beaten? Well, my dream began by a nightmare: a small crowd of people, among them Borisoff, a printer, my pupil, was poking and jabbing at a lacerated body with sticks. I asked Borisoff why they had mutilated the man's body.

' "He is an enemy!"

' "But he is a man all the same!"

' "What?" Borisoff cried, and, brandishing a stick at me, "Thrash him," he shouted to his companions.

'But the stick fell out of his hands, and he stretched out his arms and began whispering in an ecstasy, dancing about:

' "Watch for them: look! There they come! It's all over; they are coming!"

'Innumerable masses of people, phantoms, were walking along; I could see a supernatural starry light issuing from thousands of eyes. I became aware that it was in those eyes that their secret lay: the people were resurrected. You understand what I mean? Resurrected – spiritually transfigured. At the same moment that I realized this I instantly disappeared among them, as though I had flared up and been burnt to ashes.'

My guest struck his pencil against the table, listened to the dull sound and struck it again.

'Now that I am wide awake I can still see the triumphant people, but I feel that I am a stranger among them. They are still triumphant, but I no longer see in them that new element which I saw in my dream and in which their whole essence lies – I mean their transfiguration. They are triumphant – I have exhausted all my strength in trying to help them to this triumph – and I still remain a stranger to it myself. It is very queer . . .'

He looked out of the window and listened. Hesitatingly, cautiously, the bells were ringing for Mass. In the Peter and Paul Fortress a machine-gun was rattling; the soldiers and workmen were being taught the technical side of defending freedom.

'Maybe I, like many others, do not know how to triumph. All my energy went in the struggle, the expectation; the capacity for enjoying possession is stunted, killed. Perhaps it is merely weakness, lack of strength. But the point is that I see lots of ferocity and revenge about me, but never any joy – the joy that transfigures a man. And I do not see any faith in victory.'

He rose, looked round, blinking blindly, stretched out his hand, and shaking mine, said:

'I feel utterly miserable – just as Columbus would have felt if he had reached the coast of America only to find that it was repulsive to him . . .'

Then he went out.

*

Nowadays there are many people who feel like he did. It is like a watchdog must feel at the end of its life: the beast has been accustomed from its youth to growl and bark at everybody, and has had an unshatterable faith in the righteousness of its job – though its only reward has been kicks. And all of a sudden the dog realizes that there was really nothing to guard or keep watch over. Why, then, did it spend all its life in the kennel of duty, on the chain of obligations? The poor old honest beast must feel indescribably hurt . . .

Another man of the same type once said of the revolution:

'We loved her, like romantic lovers do; but then came someone who boldly and impudently committed violence on our
beloved . . .'

\*

On the subject of mating Russian popular wisdom with European
culture –

A washerwoman, disfigured by syphilis – she already had a
deep hole in the place of her nose – said one day to A. U. D., a
lady-doctor:

'I, too, comrade, know something about the benefits of curing
people. Yesterday I went to the Electric Central Station to
exorcise a hernia, and got a 25 candlepower lamp as a reward . . .'

# Seeing Clearly

THE railway carriage next to ours swayed, and its axle squeaked irritatingly:

'*Riga – iga – iga – iga . . .*'

Then the wheels struck up in unison:

'*Com – pan – ion – quick, Com – pan – ion – quick.*'

My travelling companion was an old fellow – so blanched and colourless that probably he would have been imperceptible in bright sunlight. He seemed to be composed entirely of fog and shadows; the features of his face, which bore traces of hunger, were indefinable; his eyes were closed by heavy eyelids; his wrinkled cheeks and tangled beard appeared to have been hurriedly made out of hemp. A grey, crumpled cap accentuated that impression. He exhaled an odour of naphthaline. His legs were curled up under him; he was sitting in the corner of the seat, cleaning his nails with a match, and presently he muttered in a hoarse voice:

'Truth is an opinion, saturated with a feeling of faith.'

'Every opinion?'

'Well, yes, every one.'

'*Riga – iga – iga – iga . . .*'

Outside the window in the dim light of an autumn morning, the trees were brandishing their black branches; leaves and sparks were fluttering by.

'The prophet Jeremiah has said: "The fathers ate grapes and the sourness of those grapes set their children's teeth on edge." That's quite true of our children – their teeth are on edge. We fed on the sour grapes of analysis, and they accepted both the denial and the lack of belief as true.'

He wrapped the tail of his sail-cloth overcoat round his pointed knees, and, picking his nails intently with a match, continued:

'Before entering the Red army, my son said to me: "You are

an honest man. Well, just tell me this: in theory, all the foundations of life have already been demolished by you, by the many-sided criticisms of your generation through many years; what, then, is it that you persist in defending?" My son was not clever, his thoughts were moulded clumsily, ponderously, like books, but he was an honest lad. He became a bolshevik immediately after the publication of Lenin's thesis. My son was right, because he believed in the forces of negation and destruction. As a matter of fact, my mind, too, agreed with bolshevism, but my heart would not allow me to accept it. I admitted this to the inquiring judge in the Tcheka, when I was arrested as a counter-revolutionary. The judge, quite a young fellow, a fop and, evidently, a law-student, questioned me very adroitly. He knew that my son had perished on the Judenich front and he treated me with a certain amount of affability; I felt all the time, however, that he would have better enjoyed having me shot.

'When I told him of this contradiction between my heart and my reason, he said thoughtfully, stroking the papers in front of him with his hand: "Yes, we know that from your letters to your son, but that does not improve the situation."

' "You're going to shoot me?" I asked.

'He answered, "That is more than probable, if you are unable to give us any assistance in this tiresome business." He spoke without any reticence but with a sort of apologetic smile. I think I was smiling, too – I liked his attitude towards his duty. And he disposed me still more in his favour by adding quite simply, as though it were a perfectly natural thing: "Perhaps it is better for you to die – don't you think so? For to live in such discord with one's own self as you do must be rather a torture." And he added immediately: "Forgive me for mentioning a matter which clearly has nothing to do with your case." '

*Iga – riga – riga – iga –* the axle squeaked.

Yawning and shivering, my companion looked out of the window, ripples of rain streaming down the pane.

'But he set you free all the same, didn't he?' I asked him.

'Obviously. I'm still alive, as you see.'

And turning his hemp-fringed face to me, he said with a slightly scornful smile and something of a challenge in his voice:

'I helped him to see clearly in some of the questions before the inquiry . . .'

*Com – pan – ion – quick, com – pan – ion – quick* – rumbled the wheels of the railway car. The rain grew heavier, the axle squeaked still more shrilly: *igui – igui – igui – igui* . . .

# The Fearless Dynamiter

SOMEWHERE in Eletz, Mitia Pavloff, a workman from Sormovo and a countryman of mine, has recently died of typhus.

In 1905, in the days of the Moscow insurrection, he brought from Petersburg a big box of nitroglycerine sticks and fifteen metres of Bickford fuse, which he had tied round his chest. The fuse had contracted with the man's perspiration, or perhaps had been too tightly laced round his ribs; anyhow, on entering my room Mitia sank down on the floor exhausted, his face blue and his eyes protruding wildly as though he were about to die of suffocation.

'You're mad, Mitia! Don't you realize that you might have collapsed on the way? You can guess what would have happened to you if you'd done that.'

Panting for breath, he answered a little guiltily:

'Yes, we would have lost the fuse and the nitroglycerine.'

M. M. Tikhvinsky, rubbing the man's chest very hard, also scolded him gruffly, while Mitia, half-closing his eyes, asked:

'How many bombs will it make? Shall we be beaten? Are we still holding Priesnia?'*

A little later, as he lay on the sofa, his eyes followed Tikhvinsky, who was examining the explosive, and he whispered to me:

'Does he make the bombs? Is he a professor? Once a workman? You don't say so!'

Then suddenly he said anxiously:

'He won't blow you up, will he?'

Not a word of himself, not a word of the danger which he had just escaped.

* A Moscow suburb.

# From Citizen F. Popoff's Letter

'CONSIDERING that the celebrated Darwin has firmly established the fact that the struggle for life is essential and that there is nothing to be said against the abolition of the weak, that is of those who are unable to work, and taking into consideration the fact that this was already known in ancient times many centuries before Darwin – old men were seized and thrown into a ravine to die of hunger or pushed up a tree from which they fell and broke their necks – it follows clearly that science has outstrode our hypocritical morality. However, protesting against unreasonable cruelty, I make the following suggestion: that people incapable of performing socially profitable work should be exterminated by milder measures; for instance, they should be fed with something good to the taste, ham or sweet cakes mixed with strychnine, or, as it is cheaper, arsenic. Humane measures such as these would soften the struggle for life, which now prevails everywhere.

'In the same way should one treat idiots, village cretins, cripples and people suffering from incurable diseases like consumption or cancer.

'Such legislation will not, of course, appeal to our whimpering intelligentsia; but it is decidedly time to stop considering its reactionary ideology.'

# Poetry and Shooting

A July mid-day sun is blazing fiercely in a sky of brass. The town is sweltering in heat, stricken dumb and buried in a silence, which is interrupted only now and then by vague delirious sounds. A snuffling, nasal falsetto pensively drawls a song:

> 'Over the silvery stream
> In the golden sand,
> For the footsteps I search
> Of a maiden fair . . .'

A deep, thick voice inquires gruffly:
'What were you doing, early this morning?'
'I was doing a bit of shooting.'
'How many?'
'Three.'
'Did they howl?'
'Why should they?'
'Do you mean they made no noise about it?'
'None. They don't usually make a fuss . . . they've got a discipline of their own, you know, which tells them that once they've got into trouble, the account must be settled sooner or later.'
'Gentlefolk?'
'No – at least I don't think so. They crossed themselves in front of the pit, so I gather they were common people.'

A moment of silence, then the falsetto continues plaintively:

> 'Bright moon, be my guide . . .'

'Did you shoot too?'
'Why shouldn't I?'

> 'Tell me, oh where does she hide? . . .'

The deep voice jeers:

'Here you are, singing about "maidens fair," and yet you have to mend your shirt yourself just the same . . . You fool!'

'You wait a bit; the girls will come too, in time. Everything will come . . .'

> 'Gentle breeze, confide to me
> What her idle thought might be . . .'

# Atheism, Marriage, Dancing

THE pillars of the large hall are adorned with red fustian and with the tender green of birch trees. Through the leaves gold letters flash, shaping themselves into words:

LONG LIVE . . . PROLETARIAT . . .

A fresh spring breeze comes through the window, and outside one can see the shadows of the trees and the stars above them. In the corner of the room a dark man, craning a long, thin neck, is hammering away on the keys of the piano with his long, thin fingers. Sailors and workmen are sliding and wriggling on the floor, their arms around the waists of young maidens, clad in every sort of colour, shuffling their feet and stamping loudly. It is all diabolically noisy and extravagantly festive.

'*Grang rong*, you devils!' a gigantic youth cries in despair. He is wearing white shoes and a blue shirt; a rebellious lock of hair adorns his forehead, and a scar runs across his brow and down his cheek. 'Hold on! it isn't *grang rong* I mean, it's the other thing. What the devil do you call it? Grab the hands and round you go!'

They form a shrieking, dancing circle. A whirligig of multi-coloured blotches revolves madly, the floor groans under the pressure of the heels, the crystal glass of the great chandelier tinkles anxiously.

Behind the pillar, under the folds of the crimson banner, a couple, tired of dancing, has taken shelter – a barebreasted, broad-shouldered sailor, with red hair and a pock-marked face, and at his side a curly-haired little damsel all in blue. Her small grey eyes shine with astonishment – probably it is the first time that such a great bear of a fellow has bowed down before her in submission, that a man has peered into her china-doll face with kind, round eyes. She is fanning herself with a piece of white cambric and blinking incessantly. Clearly she feels happy and at the same time a little frightened.

'Olga Stepanovna, let us discuss your religious convictions once more . . .'

'Oh, do wait a bit – it is so hot . . .'

'Bother the heat! Very well – let us take it that God does exist! But God, whatever you say, is but an imaginary object, while I'm a very real fact, of which, however, you seem not to be aware . . .'

'It isn't that at all . . .'

'Pardon me! – Can't you see that your views are uncomplimentary to me? The Thing of your imagination draws you into the void of the unknown, into a state of helplessness, while here you have in front of you a man, ready to go through fire and flames for the sake of your dear soul . . .'

'Draw up in a line facing the ladies!' the giant commands fiercely, his huge arms stretched above his head. 'Run in eights round those columns!'

'Olga Stepanovna, if you please!'

The sailor seizes the damsel round the waist, lifting her off the ground, and with her feet dangling bears her into the gaudy, boisterous whirlwind of dance.

A little later she is sitting on the window-sill, panting for breath, while her partner stands opposite her and speaks very persuasively, in an undertone:

'Of course we, the people of a new nation, we're outspoken folk, straight folk; but, whatever we are, we're neither beasts nor devils . . .'

'As though I ever said that! I never said anything of the kind! . . .'

'Allow me! If you insist on being married in church, why, of course, it's not worth making a fuss about; but the boys here might begin making fun of me . . .'

'Don't tell them anything about it . . .'

'Do it on the quiet, you mean? I'm ready to commit even that offence against atheism for your dear sake . . . Although, Olga Stepanovna, I don't mind telling you that it would be better if we began getting into the habit of atheism at once. Really it would! In life we must rely upon ourselves, Olga Stepanovna, without any fear – there's been enough of that already! Nowadays one should fear nothing and nobody except oneself... What is it, comrade? What the dickens do you want, may I ask? This perhaps?'

He raises his fist slowly, a fist as large as a twenty-pound weight.

And in the centre of the room the giant, who is the master of ceremonies, shrieks frantically:

'Retreat before the ladies, two steps back and bow – one – two! The ladies choose their partners according to their tastes. No forcing, *if* you please!...'

# A Coincidence of Thought

STRANGE coincidences of thought happen sometimes: in 1901, in Arzamas, the priest Feodor Vladimirsky ruminated: 'Every nation possesses spiritual eyesight – the eyesight of purpose. Some great thinkers call this capacity "the instinct of the nation," but to my mind instinct raises the question: "How should one live?" whereas I have in mind the vague anguish of the reason and of the spirit concerning the question: "What should one live for?" And I say that we Russians have an undeveloped eyesight for practical purposes, because we have not yet reached that height of culture which would enable us to view the road which the history of humanity ordains that we shall follow. I am of opinion, however, that we, more than others, are doomed to be tormented by the question: "What should we live for?" Meanwhile we live blindly, groping in the dark, and clamouring; but we are, all the same, already a people with some achievements, some advantages . . .'

Five years later, in Boston, William James, the pragmatist-philosopher, remarked:

'The present events in Russia have aroused a world-wide interest in her, but have made her still less comprehensible to me. When I read Russian authors I am confronted by irritatingly interesting characters, but I would not venture to assert that I am able to understand their aims. In Europe, in America, I see men who have accomplished something and, relying on what they already possess, are striving to augment the number of things that have a material as well as a spiritual designation. The people of your country, on the other hand, seem to me to be beings for whom reality is not an obligation, not a law, almost an enemy. I can see that the Russian's mind analyses with great care, with a spirit of research and revolt. But I do not see the purpose of the analysis, I do not see what they are seeking for beneath the manifestation of reality. One might think that the Russian considered as his mission to find, to discover, and to note everything unpleasant and negative. I was especially struck by two books: *Resurrection* by Tolstoy and *Karamazov* by Dostoevsky. To me the characters exhibited in them seem to come from another planet, where everything is different, and better. They have landed on earth by accident and are irritated by this, almost insulted. There is something childish, ingenuous in them, and one is reminded of the obstinacy of an honest alchemist who believes that he is capable of discovering the "Cause of all causes." A very interesting nation, but I think that you are working in vain, like an "idling motor." Or maybe you have been called to astonish the world by something unexpected . . .'

# The Veterinary Surgeon

AMONG the many peasant-worshippers whom I have met in the course of my life, the one that struck me most was the veterinary surgeon, Mili Samoilovich Petrenko.

A tall, stooping figure. A long, narrow sail-cloth coat, reaching to his heels, ludicrously increases his height. His clean-shaven face is adorned with a luxurious moustache, the ends of which fall picturesquely down his chest. A pair of light-coloured eyes gleam in a sinister, implacable way from under thick eyebrows. A protruding forehead is furrowed with a deep set of wrinkles, hard tufts of grey hair stick out wildly on his head, they are covered by a wide-brimmed, faded hat, the hat is pushed down the nape of the neck and this lends a belligerent, provocative air to the old man.

I got to know him in 1903 in Sedletz at M. Romas's house and Petrenko expressed the desire to acquaint me with 'the work of his life.' He was a bachelor, he rented a room in the dirty, wooden house of a Jewish cab-driver; the windows of this mournful room faced the red, solid, imposing walls of the Sedletz prison.

Gesticulating with his arms, long as oars, the veterinary made me sit at the table and roared in a deep bass voice, uttering each word separately:

'Sura. Beer. For-two.'

He threw his hat into the corner, on to his bed, pulled out a thick oilcloth copybook from a small yellow chest of drawers, and with a loud grunt, began:

'Here it is. It's called:

"A few observations on the question of assimilation of food-stuffs by consumers of different classes. A socio-economical essay."'

Partly narrating, partly reading, he took a good hour and a

213

half to acquaint me with his work. It was based on a chemical investigation of excrements. The conclusions maintained convincingly, in long columns of figures, that the higher a man stood on the steps of the social ladder, the worse did he digest his food, his intestines rejecting a large number of valuable stuffs unassimilated by his body. In this respect clerks and particularly members of the legal profession behaved most objectionably, the latter digested less than 50 per cent of the food they absorbed – the rest they rejected without any profit for them and obviously to the detriment of the State's economy.

'Sedentary life!' Petrenko roared victoriously. 'The abnormal activity of the gall-bladder. All clerks are bilious.'

Clapping the broad palm of his hand with little tufts of hair on the knuckles on the pages of the copybook, the vet triumphed.

'This is the calculation: four pounds a day, 120 pounds a month. 2640 a year. For each. 800 more than necessary. I take the minimal average length of life – thirty years. Ah?'

And lowering his voice to the deepest octave he yelled with wrath and horror.

'The privileged classes, what? So-called ones. Useless destruction of food. To the amount of several millions of pounds a year. Plunder, eh?'

He proved further irrefutably that the stomach of the peasant assimilated food stuff in the most ideal manner – in the peasant's intestine undigested food is almost completely absent.

'The peasant assimilates everything. 100 per cent.'

He rose from the chair and waving his hand above my head he sniffed:

'Figures! The peasant's expression: sponger, parasite – it has a deep scientific meaning. The figures side with the peasant! The figures prove it. Who can deny figures? Truth always lies in figures. At the root of all precise science are figures.'

When he uttered the word 'figures' – his luxurious whiskers spread out triumphantly. He sat down, poured a glass of beer under the whiskers, wiped his mouth with the edge of his coat and went on, knocking with his strong finger against the copybook.

'There lies the radical solution of the problem of a rational nutrition of Russia's population. Do you understand? Oh – oh! Either we can reduce 50 per cent of a peasant's labour or feed the whole world. Either that or the other. Because the peasant evacuates his bowels honestly. He digests his food honestly, oh, yes! The peasant is the original substance of every social body. He is the sacred one. Everything is his flesh and his blood, oh, yes!'

He jumped from his chair once more and knocked his fist against the wall twice. Immediately three red-haired little heads, three swarthy little snouts peered through the half-open door. One of them asked something in a thin little voice in the incomprehensible Yiddish language. The vet pulled out of somewhere a crumpled rouble note and showing four fingers to the children, ordered them:

'Four. Careful not to shake.'

A curly-haired boy of about seven ran up to him, seized the note, spat on it with relish and began to iron it out carefully on the palm of his hand.

'Sha!' the old man shouted, but this did not frighten the children at all. I asked him:

'Have you read the book about ideals and idols?'

'Don't remember. No. What is it? Marxist?'

His eyes were wide open, his nose grew red and red stains appeared above his brows.

'I don't like Marx. Hate Marxists. Enemies of the people. It's a Jewish teaching. I'm an anti-Semite. Oh, Yes! Jews are parasites. Like all non-agricultural people. Christianity is a Jewish trap. Nietzsche is right. Christ is poison. A vampire. Land is the mother of man. A man is a peasant, everything comes from him, through him. That's my faith. Tolstoy is a troublemaker. Faith is simple. Simple and clear. D'you know Yusov? Kablitz? Read him? That's an honest thinker for you. I knew him when I was young. A wise man. He loved. He knew. He believed.'

I asked him:

'Have you tried to publish your work?'

'No. No money. I sent it to periodicals. They won't have it. Of course not! The intelligenstia! A parasitic education. Deep in their minds – they hate the peasant. Consider him as a physical power. A weapon. That's all. They hope to seize power through his strength. Oh, yes! The swindlers!'

He struck the table with his fist, the glasses, indignant, began to tinkle.

'The peasant knows it. He won't follow the intelligentsia. He has his own path. His own intelligence. Everything that is not he – is superfluous. He knows it, oh, yes!'

The children arrived, running. The eldest carried two bottles – the other two – one each. The old man smiled, but grumbled:

'Didn't I say: "Don't shake"!'

And stroking the boy's red curls, pushed some coins into his little paw and when the boy shrieked, jumped with joy and ran away, the vet followed him with a broad smile.

'I love them. They digest honestly. Jewish children are nice creatures, eh?'

'I thought you were an anti-Semite?'

He smiled, shook his head.

'In theory. Of course the Jews are worth nothing. Look how they live. But if you gave them land ...'

He leant his chest against the table and looking at me with the imploring eyes of a fanatic, he begged: 'Give them land. All the land. To all. Nothing else. The land. Everything else will follow. Life begins with the peasant. Only the peasant can make it ideal. Towns are wrong. History is wrong. Everything should start from the beginning ...'

He seized the bottle with an abrupt movement and pouring the warm, foaming beer into the glass, said in a calmer tone:

'Never mind! The peasant will put it all right again.'

Then he again began to talk about the rational assimilation of food, told me long stories about the wise stomachs of horses and cows, spoke with special admiration about the sheep's stomach and ended his speech with a passionate exclamation:

'Spiritual energy is the result of the work of the stomach and the intestines! Only that. Nothing else!'

And when I left him he said to me by way of farewell:

'One must digest one's food honestly. This is the core of the problem. The peasant has proved it. And how!'

# Anna Schmidt

On the most fashionable street of Nizhni Novgorod, Anna Nikolaevna Schmidt, reporter of the Nizhni-Novgorod News, races along with the speed of a mouse, like a black rolling ball. The cab-drivers say to each other:

'The Schmidt woman is running in search of scandals.'

And obligingly offer:

'Eh, lady, we'll drive you there for ten kopecks.'

She bargains, and always, for some obscure reason, suggests seven. So they take her for seven; the cab-drivers and indeed all 'simple' people consider her 'not all there'; and are ready to oblige sometimes even contrary to their own interests.

From early morning, Anna Schmidt runs round all the local institutions gathering 'information', pesters the dignitaries with questions and they chase her away, like a bee or a wasp. This sometimes forces her to resort to measures which she claims to be 'American': one day she persuaded the janitor to lock her up in a cupboard and sitting there made a verbatim report of a conference of local government officials, – a disinterested feat because the information she gathered could not be published because of the censor.

Watching her it was hard to imagine that this meek, polite human being was capable of such comical spying activities.

She was small, soft, quiet; a pair of sapphire-blue eyes smiled luminously and gently on her face ravaged by age, her sharp, bird-like little nose quivered amusingly. Her hands were dark like a duck's feet and a small pencil always trembled nervously between her fingers – like a sixth one. She suffered from the cold and wrapped herself up in the winter in three or four woollen skirts, two or three shawls, which gave her the appearance of a round cabbage-head.

As soon as she arrived at the office, she rushed to a corner and pulled off some of the skirts, revealing her legs up to her knees in thick, coarse woollen stockings, threw off the shawls and smoothing her hair, sat down at the long table in the middle of the big room littered with torn bits of paper and old newspapers, permeated with the oily smell of printing paint.

She would write in a clear, small handwriting, for a long time, in silence and then suddenly, with a start, as though given a push, she would throw up her head in an abrupt movement, look around as though she had never been in this room before. Her eyes would grow darker, the wrinkled face undergoing a sharp change – her cheekbones standing out as though she had tightly pressed her teeth together. She would sit like that motionless for a minute or two, observing everything around with a dark glance. It seemed as though Anna Schmidt was overcoming a paroxysm of sharp disdain for everything that was creating a noisy bustle around her and one of her colleagues, A. Yarovitsny, would whisper to me:

'Aniuta is being swept over by a wave of subconsciousness.'

Anna's numerous skirts were extremely shabby, her shoes badly patched, her blouses laundered to threads and inefficiently mended. Her mother, an ailing woman of eighty, could eat nothing but chicken broth, Anna had to buy a chicken every day, which cost sixty-eight kopecks, that meant thirty-four lines and she managed to get printed an average of sixty.

When she spoke of her mother, she sounded like a teenager, who loves her mother and considers her the highest authority on all problems of life. It was strange and touching to hear the tender, soft word 'Mamma' in the mouth of this old woman. I was told that that 'mamma' was egotistic and irritable as most women of that age can be; if the chicken was hard or she had tired of it, she stamped her feet and threw bread, forks and spoons at her daughter. Anna was very friendly in her attitude to me, but I found nothing interesting about her and avoided her rather intrusive questions, – they mostly concerned the intimate sides of life. On the whole she spoke little and almost always 'shop', the town, the paper. I could discover nothing original in her colourless little speeches, not one incisive word which would forever sink into the memory and I was very keen on such words – like rays of sun they lit up the darkness of a human being's soul, suddenly showed an unexpected corner of it and created a communion of spirit.

The mediocrity of Anna's outward appearance was stressed by the mediocrity of her judgements about the politics of the town and the state and that justified the attitude adopted by her colleagues, the same as that of the cab-drivers, as to someone who is slightly 'touched', unhinged.

Therefore one can imagine my complete amazement when the priest F., a talented organizer of public discussions with the numerous Nizhni-Novgorod sectarians, said to me, with an unfriendly twitch of the nose:

'A cunning little devil of an old woman, your Schmidt! A skilful catcher of men. A noxious creature.'

Disbelieving the sincerity of my amazement, with an ironic smile, he answered my questions:

'You really know nothing about it? It is difficult to believe it, knowing your curiosity about your fellow-beings.'

He suffered from some incurable disease, his ascetic, Christ-like face was covered with a dark skin, his eyes had a feverish gleam, he often passed his tongue over his lips and nervously cracked his long fingers. In his arguments with 'heretics' he was malicious, used the art of dialectics with great skill and knew how to irritate his opponents so well that by their blunders they contributed always to his oratorical victories. I liked to watch his tricks, but it seemed to me that this man with the face of a martyr did not love either God, faith, men. He was disappointed in life and went to the discussions in the same way as he would go to a pub to play billiards. He reminded me of the actor who plays the part of the orthodox Jew in Tasgo's 'Uriel Acosta'. Cracking his fingers he questioned me:

'You don't even know that Schmidt corresponds with the philosopher Vladimir Soloniev, who is rightly accused of a tendency towards the Catholic heresy?'

I said:

'It is just as staggering to me as it would be if you, Father Alexander, would suddenly turn out to be a fireman instead of a priest.'

To my growing astonishment the priest burst out laughing and began, amidst laughter, to accuse me of being a liar:

'There, you've let the cat out of the bag! You're a pretty poor diplomat! So you know her pupil, the fireman Simakov?'

After my insistent and even angry declarations that I did not know the fireman, the priest, hardly concealing his disbelief, lazily told me that Anna Schmidt had organized a religious circle, capable of developing into a sect; members of it were car-drivers, workmen, a prison-inspector and a fireman.

'Our people like words and have a weakness for fairytales. That fireman was a sectarian of sorts, now he is an ardent disciple of the Schmidt woman. But, being a fool by nature, he is the most talkative of the proselytes of the new sect and if you wish to acquaint yourself of how the twaddle of this old woman takes roots in the brains of simpletons, try and get to know him. He comes to my meetings, yells his head off . . .'

Luka Simakov was a private of the Grenadier regiment – a large, heavy man with a black, prickly moustache and a blue, clean-shaven skull. His cheeks were also blue and the thick lower lip – the colour of raw beef. The left, dark eye was smaller than the right one and ran anxiously towards the temple, particularly so when Luka was excited and rubbed his skull very hard with his large spade-like palm, so hard that one could hear the hairs crack. His right eye, big and protruding, was almost motionless, dim and surrounded by very long eyelashes, reminding one of some insect.

In a dark pub, his chest pressed against the table, he instructed me in a hoarse voice:

'In your opinion – how should one understand Christ?'

Luka did not have to be questioned, words poured out of his mouth, like a stream from a crack in the stone. He talked with the violent impetuousness of the faithful, one who does not admit the possibility of an argument.

'Christ is lightness, easiness – you understand? Christ is easy to live with. A tie-rope – you move through Christ to true faith. Only you must understand: Christ is not a being or a substance, he is just one word . . .'

'Logos?'

Simakov gave an astounded cry:

'Ye-es!'

And he drew closer to me, asking:

'How did you know? Who told you? The old woman? What a creature she is!' he continued now in a whisper. 'To look at her – she is nothing, a beggar. We dress up and boast – and she, the holy one, is unnoticeable. Wisdom hidden in a fly . . . And as to this word, don't you repeat it to anyone,' he warned me. 'Particularly not to priests, it's poison to them. If they only hear it – you'll get into trouble . . .'

Then he announced to me the great secret: 'Christ was alive, he lived in Moscow, on the Arbat.

'It's the priests who invented that He died on the Cross and then ascended to Heaven, no, He's on earth, amongst us. You can't kill the word! Try to! You see?'

I listened for two hours to the obscure words of the fireman, as he went away, he said to me reassuringly:

'You just wait, I'll bring you together with the old lady, she'll teach you!'

Anna Schmidt learnt about my meeting the fireman before I had had time to tell her about it. Restlessly knocking the pencil against her nails she asked:

'What did this man of God tell you?'

Having learnt that Luka told me that Christ lived in Moscow, on the Arbat, she became even more restless with the pencil and said:

'He's not quite rational, he's had some hard experiences with fires, they have had a bad effect on him.'

Her eyes grew darker, something stern appeared in them, she pressed her lips together and her small face gathered into sad wrinkles.

'If you are seriously interested in these matters, – let's have a talk, I'll be free at Whitsun.'

And she asked with a smile:

'But you're only doing it out of curiosity, out of boredom, yes?'

I told her that life did not bore me and that the desire to know how people think could not be called mere curiosity.

'Of course, of course!' she cried softly, and suddenly in an undertone, but very coherently in the language of an experienced orator, turning round the pencil in her mummified fingers, she spoke of the distance that exists between people, how little desire and skill they show to penetrate the sacred soul of their fellow beings.

'We float in the dim stream of life, dumb like the fish. "Grant peace to the world" we pray but peace means harmony of souls, their fusion, and how can one fuse with something unreachable?'

She was called to the office and as she went, she asked me, meekly:

'Don't make fun of Luka. He is one of Christ's innocents – true faith is built by such men.'

*

In the evening of Whit Sunday she came to my rooms, dressed up in her best clothes: a brown skirt with a patch at the bottom, a bit of the skirt had obviously been torn out either by a nail or on a dog's teeth; a blue cotton blouse was ornamented with a blue bow on her chest and new galoshes gleamed on her feet, though the weather was dry and warm. It turned out that she had given her shoes to be mended and the shoemaker had not delivered them so that was why she was going about in galoshes.

We drank tea with cherry jam and biscuits, – I knew that was what Anna liked best. And towards midnight I learnt that the funny little old reporter of a provincial paper Anna Schmidt was an incarnation of one of the myrrh-carrying women – I believe Mary Magdalene, who in her turn was the incarnation of Sophia, Eternal Wisdom. From Mary Magdalene to Anna Schmidt, Eternal Wisdom went naturally through several incarnations, one of them was Catherine of Siena, another – Elisabeth of Thuringen, and several others, the names of whom I do not remember.

At first I was rather embarrassed listening to Anna Schmidt, all that she said seemed so incongruous with the everyday chicken, oilskin galoshes and all the rest of the external incarnation of Eternal Wisdom. I sat, my head lowered down trying not to see that incarnation break the biscuits, pick up the berries with them and suck them with her thin lips; it was funny to hear the biscuit crack on her teeth.

But it was a stranger who sat facing me, talking in a strictly professional way, ornamenting the speech with quotations from the Fathers of the Church, mentioning gnostics, Vassilidas and Enoins, the voice sounded dictatorial and powerful, the blue pupils of the eyes had widened and gleamed at me in the same new way as did the words and thoughts. Gradually everything commonplace and comical in this stranger disappeared, became invisible and I well remember the glad and proud amazement with which I observed how the flame of thoughts on the evil of life, on the contradiction between flesh and spirit were born and burst out from under the grey outward shell, with what firm assurance resounded the ancient words of the searchers of perfect wisdom, of implacable truth. All that remained of Anna Schmidt was the little pencil indefatigably, swiftly turning in her dry, mummified fingers. She seemed a little intoxicated as she drew a whimsical design in the air with her pencil, a design of the ways of thought; she jumped on her chair and said, with a smile full of glee:

'Imagine the Devil's desperate plight.'

On her chin shone a ruby-coloured drop of jam.

Lifting her right hand above her head she added:

'And Christ is alive!'

I learnt that Christ was Vladimir Soloviov, he was also Logos. Christ was eternally and constantly being reincarnated into a man and was always among people. But the reincarnations of Sophia did not submit to the destructive influences of this vain world with the same ease as the reincarnations of Logos, particularly hostile to the Devil.

'The pure spirituality of the Logos cannot stand distortion but the man who incarnates the Logos often blackens the spirit through the wisdom of Satan.'

She took out of the pocket of her skirt a leather parcel and carefully pulled out a few letters:

'Those are Soloviov's letters, – you can see how hard it is for him . . .'

Stressing some words very significantly she read out a few fragments – I could not understand any of them, but in one of them Soloviov quoted the words of Frederick the Great with which he addressed his soldiers on the battlefield, when they ran away from the enemy:

'Scoundrels! Do you wish to live for ever?'

These words reminded me of a poem of Soloviov's;

> A marsh in the wood
> A moss in the marsh
> Someone was born
> And then kicked the bucket

And then his epitaph:

> Under this stone
> Lies Vladimir Soloviov
> Once a poet
> Later a philosopher
> Passer-by! Learn from this example
> How destructive is love, how useful is faith.

I asked Anna what she thought about these jokes.

She threw herself back in her chair, her sharp little nose grew red, the pupils very blue and there was anger in her voice:

'Who told you that this was written by him? It's mere slander! His friends making fun of him!'

But very soon the grey little old woman who looked like a female sparrow began to speak about a man of glory, about a philosopher, a talented dialectician, a great poet, in the tone of a mother anxious about her son's behaviour.

'You know, even Christ was seduced by the Devil who promised him earthly glory.'

She uttered these words as though consoling someone and looked at me so inquisitively, so imploringly, that I was forced to respond:

'Oh, yes ...'

'He is drawn towards people because he is so kind. But a man can resist temptation only when he can remain himself in all surroundings. Christ was drawn to men after he had strengthened his spirit in the desert, Soloviov does it too prematurely . . .'

She called Soloviov the crystal receptacle of the Logos, the Holy Grail, the greatest scion of the century and a child that wanders in the dark grove of sin and forgets his bride, sister and mother – Sophia. Eternal Wisdom.

'You understand? Both bride and mother.'

At times it seemed to me that I distinguished in Anna's words the pain of a woman in love, even the sentimentality of a spinster, but this only flickered like pale specks in her speech and was instantly replaced by a protective attitude to Soloviov, who had to be directed on the path of life.

In a whisper she went on as if imparting a secret:

'People keep putting temptation in his way, devils do it even more obtrusively. He knows it. He wrote to me that devils peep into his windows and one of them even hid in his shoe and sat there all night, teasing, pestering him.

She talked about devils as simply as one would talk about beetles or mosquitoes.

'And glory, too. Glory makes an actor out of a man,' she said very impressively. 'If you stare at a man he begins to hide behind a pretence of sorts, he wishes to be what people want him to be. You know that, don't you?'

Unfortunately I did know that. And I could hardly believe my eyes and ears observing how true were the thoughts that burnt in the heart of this insignificant human being. She began again to talk about the desert, of the great value of self-concentration in solitude and spoke about this at such length that the thought crossed my brain: maybe she is too lonely and therefore so open with me? Like a small bird parted from her flock she flies over the seas to a distant fire in the night, to a lighthouse on an unknown and invisible shore. That lighthouse is Vladimir Soloviov and this is all that lightens and lends a meaning to her quiet, solitary life among men of reason.

'Didn't Christ experience a human fear before fate?' she suddenly asked and closing her eyes began to recite in a sing-song voice, like a psalm, somebody's poem:

> The soul descended from heaven into the flesh
> Life on the earth was dear to her
> The soul became one with the earth
> And like a tired bee
> She sucked the sweet poison of earthly evil.

The poem was long. Anna read it in a low voice, as if to herself and uttered only the two last lines loudly, like a triumphant warning, opening her tearstained eyes and brandishing her pencil in the air.

> And the bells of eternity
> Cannot wake the dead soul.

Long past midnight I accompanied her home. The wind raged in the streets, raising dust, rustling the leaves of the birches, the birches were tied up and some had fallen down. Drunken men wandered about, from a distance one could hear a woman shrieking, a black kitten rushed out of a gate. Anna kicked it away in disgust.

'Like a little devil . . .'

A drunken postman pursued us, telling in a drunken way how somebody had offended him; he beat his breast with his fist and kept asking, with a sob in his voice:

'Am I an enemy?'

'Let's hurry up,' said Anna and quickening her step, complained, too:

'Is that the way to celebrate? Don't they know it is a feast day?'

*

After that evening, when I saw Anna Schmidt in the office, I was always incredibly embarrassed, I could not behave with her as I had done before and talk about the lazy trivialities of every day. She, however, had interpreted my restraint differently and talked to me in a dry, distant way. Her sapphire-blue eyes gazed beyond me at the map of Russia stained by flies in such a way that it seemed as though a black hail had burst over the whole of Russian soil.

226

I wanted very much to meet Anna's pupils, but she told me:
'I don't think they'd interest you, they're all very simple people, very simple.'

And Luka Simakov, scratching his skull and anxiously twitching with his eye, declared to me:

'The old lady didn't take to you, she told me not to talk to you . . .'

But a few minutes later, pressing me with all the weight of his body against the cage where he lived, the fireman whispered:

'Christ hides from the priests, they want to arrest Him, they're His enemies of course! And He hides near Moscow at the station Petushki. Very soon the Tsar will know about it; they'll reveal all these lies, both of them, in no more than three days! Down the priests! Death to them!'

In Luka's absurd words one could distinguish the blind hatred of the sectarian and the fear of something which he was unable to express. Dark, desperate fear gleamed in his left eye that ran to the temple. My impressions after two or three talks with him was a weird one! He imagined Christ to be a revengeful gloomy creature, hostilely observing people's lives from a dark corner and waiting for the moment to pounce upon them.

'He wants to destroy churches,' – he whispered. 'That's how he started, remember, in Jerusalem. Yes – yes.'

He brought me together with one of Anna Schmidt's disciples – a lonely little seamstress, Palasha, aged about thirty. She had short legs, stooped, had no neck and a flat face with sharp little glassy eyes. She was hypocritically soft in her speech, but obviously had no confidence in people. She lived in a remote little street over the ravine, and large black flies constantly buzzed in her two rooms, knocking against the dim window panes. A fat cat lay motionless on the window sill, a three-coloured cat, brown, white and black. I was surprised by his attitude to the flies: they sat on his head, crawled over his body, but the cat gazed motionless through the window and never shook himself to chase them away.

In a sing-song, with purposely disturbed words, Palasha spoke, skillfully sewing buttons to her cotton blouse:

'Our life, my nice gentleman, is godless and sinful – a horror, that's what it is. And Christ walks about unseen, sad and miserable: oh, you hopeless folk! Why did I destroy my soul for your sake . . . To be insulted, debased . . .'

She read poems from the apochryphal 'Dream of the Virgin,' and at the dismal end declared to me:

'The real name of the Virgin was not Mary but Enochie, she came from the Prophet Enoch, who was not a Jew but a Greek.'

When I asked her whether she knew Anna Schmidt, Palasha, her head bent, biting at the thread, answered with a question:

'Schmidt? Not Russian, is she?'

'But you know her!'

'Who knows about it?' asked Palasha, scratching her large nose with her little finger and looking at her blouse with a certain preoccupation.

'If it was Simakov – you shouldn't believe him, he's a damaged man, an insane one.'

While Simakov told me about Palasha:

'She's a wise girl, sir, she's like a wing to the old lady; she and another man class her very high above people.'

I couldn't conceive what the seamstress could have learnt from Anna Schmidt, the more I questioned her about it the more lengthily and falsely did Palasha talk about Simakov and the traps of the devil.

'The Evil Spirit throws us like urchins throw stones from the mountains, we roll down, twist about, beat up each other and there's no salvation for us . . .'

She smoothed her red hair with the palms of her hands, though it was already almost stuck to her skull, and watched me with her glassy eyes as though saying:

'You won't get anything out of me.'

\*

I went to see her twice, she welcomed me in a warm friendly way and almost lasciviously spoke to me about the lives of martyrs. I listened and watched the cat.

'The Romans beat her white body, her silky breasts with iron rods and out poured her blood and gurgled –' she went on in her sing-song way.

The flies buzzed. The cat was indifferent, motionless, and the room was permeated with an acid smell of ointment.

Very soon, because of ill-health, I went to the Crimea and have never seen Anna Schmidt, the Nizhni incarnation of Sophia, the Eternally Wise, again.

# Bugrov

IN 1901, having released me from prison, the authorities adopted a very comical measure for 'stopping and anticipating crime' – house arrest. One policeman sat in the kitchen of my flat, another one in the hall and I could only go out if accompanied by one of them.

The one in the kitchen helped the cook to bring in wood, clean the vegetables, wash up; the guardian in the hall opened the door to visitors, helped them take off their overcoats, pulled on and off their galoshes and when there was no one with me would fill in the door into my room with his clumsy figure and ask in a falsetto voice:

'Mr Gorkov – sorry – but couldn't you tell me: is there anything in common between satin and satan?'

His face, disfigured by smallpox, was ornamented by a stub nose, flabby as a sponge, under the nose little fluffs of black wool peeped out, his left ear was torn across, he squinted with his left eye towards the left ear.

'I am fond of reading books about the lives of martyrs,' he went on in a somewhat guilty tone. 'Wonderful words you find in them.'

And he would ask again, shyly:

'And – pardon me – does untouched mean the same as unbeaten, for instance: untouched virgin?'

Briefly explaining to him the difference between the two, I begged him not to interfere with my work.

He agreed, adding generously: 'Go on, go on writing.'

Then again five or ten minutes later came the irritating falsetto:

'Eh, pardon me . . .'

One day about 7 a.m. I was woken up by his voice:

'He's still asleep, worked till daybreak.'

Another voice was asking:

'You're on guard also at night?'

'What else? It's at night they're dangerous.'

'Wake him up. Say Zarubin's come.'

A quarter of an hour later old Zarubin was sitting in front of me, coughing and wheezing, his heavy head was shaking, he wiped his beard with a chequered handkerchief and peering into my face with faded eyes spoke hoarsely:

'I've come to get acquainted with you personally. Wanted to visit you in prison – the prosecution wouldn't let me.'

'Why did you want to see me?'

He winked slyly at me.

'They must be shaken up, our lords and masters! They imagine there is no resistance to their illegitimate ways. So I show them: liars, that's what they are, there is a resistance!'

He looked round my room, with half-closed eyes, red as a rabbit's.

'A dingy room you've got here. The rumour goes that you've been given a lot of money by foreigners for the "Gordeev" book, the revelation of our merchants' disgraceful doings. Well, it's a book that deserves praise – it may be merely a story, but there's truth in it. People agree when reading it: he's describing it all correctly, that's the people we really are! Jakov Bashkizov boasts: "Majakin, – that's me! It's me he's describing, can't you see how clever I am?" Bugrov too, has read it. "A bitter book for us," he says. I've really come to see you on his behalf: to congratulate you! He doesn't believe you're from the people, a bare-footed wanderer even, he wishes to look at you in person. Get dressed, we'll go and have tea with him.'

I refused to go and see Bugrov, this angered the old man very much, he raised himself heavily from his chair, shaking his unstable head and spitting.

'You've got a silly pride! Bugrov's no more sinful than you are. And as to your not being able to get out without a policeman, Bugrov doesn't give a damn about all these laws and regulations.'

And the old man left without saying good-bye, angrily shuffling his feet. The policeman saw him out and asked:

'Came to no agreement, is that it?'
Zarubin shouted back at him: 'Shut up, you . . .!'

*

A millionaire, a flour merchant, owner of steam mills, a dozen
ships, a flotilla of barges, large forests – Bugrov was a sort of
Independent Prince in Nizhni-Novgorod and the surrounding
district.

A sectarian, of the 'no-clergy creed,' he had built at a mile's
distance from Nizhni a large cemetery, surrounded by a high
brick wall, with a church and a secluded monastery on it, while
peasants were given one year's prison according to para. 103 of
the 'Code of Law' for organizing secret 'services' in their huts.
In the village Popovka Bugrov erected a huge building, an old
men's home for sectarians, – it was widely known that sectarians
were given instruction in this old men's home. He openly sup-
ported secret sectarian homes in the woods of Kerzhenetz and
on the Irghiz and altogether represented not only an active sup-
porter of sectarians but was a firm pillar of strength for the
'heretics' of the Volga, Ural and even parts of Siberia.

The Head of the State Church, the Synod, the nihilist and
cynic Konstantin Pobedonostsev made – I believe in 1901 – a
report to the Tsar about the menacing anti-church activities of
Bugrov but this did not prevent the millionaire from going on
stubbornly with his work. He addressed the eccentric governor
Baranov with the familiar 'thou' and I saw him in 1896 slap
Witte, the Prime Minister in a friendly way on the stomach at the
All-Russian exhibition and stamp his foot impatiently, shouting
at the Minister of the Court, Worontzov.

He was a generous philanthropist: he built a fine doss-house
in Nizhni, a huge home of 300 flats for widows and orphans, a
well-organized school, a water system for the city, granted a
building for the Town Hall, presented the local government
with building material for village schools and altogether spared
no money for charity.

My grandfather told me that Bugrov's father had 'grown
rich' on counterfeit money, but then my grandfather considered
all rich merchants of the town as counterfeiters, plunderers and

murderers. This did not prevent him from handling them with respect and admiration. One could draw the following conclusion from his epic stories: if a crime has failed then it is a crime worthy of punishment, if it is cleverly concealed – it means success worthy of praise.

It is said that Molnikov Pechersky had described Bugrov's father under the name of Maxim Potapov in his book 'Forests'. I had heard so much slander about people that it was easier for me to believe Molnikov and not my grandfather. It was said about Bugrov the son that he had doubled the millions of his father during the hunger in Samara in the beginning of the eighties.

Bugrov was alone to deal with his manifold business, dragging about documents in the pocket of his overcoat. People persuaded him to get himself an office, to engage a bookkeeper, he rented an office and richly equipped it, hired a bookkeeper, but passed no papers and documents to him and at the bookkeeper's offer to make an inventory of his property said thoughtfully, scratching his head: 'It's such a large business! I have a lot of property, it would take a long time to count it!'

After having spent three months in the empty office without any work the bookkeeper declared that he did not want to be paid for doing nothing and asked to be relieved of his job.

'Sorry, friend,' said Bugrov. 'I've not got the time to spend in the office, it's a useless burden for me. All my office is here.'

And with a smile he clapped his hand on his pocket and on his forehead.

I often met that man on the busy streets of the town: tall, heavy, in a long frock-coat that looked more like a jacket, in brightly polished boots and a cloth cap he went about with a heavy gait, his hands in his pockets, passed people without noticing them and they made way for him not only with respect but almost with fear. A thin little Mordovian beard grew in disorder on his reddish cheekbones, the straight, spare hair did not conceal the ears with tightly pressed lobes, nor the wrinkles on the neck, on the cheeks, and drew out the blunt chin, lengthening it in a funny way. His face seemed unfinished, incomplete, there was not a feature in it that remained in your memory. These elusive, purposely uncharacteristic, eyeless faces can be often found in the Volga area; under their dull, indefinite mask these people cleverly conceal their sharp, cunning brain, their commonsense and a strange, inexplicable cruelty.

Every time I met Bugrov I experienced an irritating dual feeling – a tense curiosity together with an instinctive hostility. Almost always I forced myself to remember all his 'good deeds' and always the same idea cropped up in my brain:

'It's strange that in the same town, on a narrow stretch of the earth two people so alien to one another as I and this "tycoon" can meet.'

I was told that after reading my book 'Foma Gordeev' this was Bugrov's estimate of me:

'He's a pernicious writer – the book is written against our kind. Such people should be sent to Siberia, far, far away.'

But my hostility towards Bugrov was born several years before this: it came from a number of reasons like the following: he used to take the daughter born in a poor family, lived with her until he tired of her and then got her married to one of his many workmen or employees, with a dowry of three to five thousand roubles, and built them a small house with three windows, brightly painted, with an iron roof. In Seim, where Bugrov had a huge steam mill such little houses could be seen everywhere. New, cosy, with flowers and tulle curtains in the windows, with green or blue shutters, they impudently teased with their bright colours and the seemingly purposeful uniformity of their shape. Probably these houses, by stimulating imagination and greed, greatly contributed to the trade with women's bodies.

This millionaire's hobby was widely known, in the suburbs and in the villages girls and boys sang a dismal song:

> You surely are a Bugrov girl
> You've given him your heart
> But faithful you'll not be to him
> While I till death will smart.

A mechanic I knew, a widower of thirty, a catcher of birds and the author of a very good story about birds of prey, published, I think, in a periodical, 'Nature and Hunting', married one of these 'tried out' girls.

A good, honest man, he thus explained to me the motives of his marriage:

'I was sorry for the girl, she'd been abused and she was a good girl. I admit there was also the four-thousand dowry and the house. This helped to seduce me. I thought: now I'll live quietly, begin to study, to write . . .'

In a few months he took to drink and on Shrovetide got beaten in a drunken brawl and died soon after. Shortly before his death he sent me the manuscript of a story on the cunning nature of a fox in its hunt for the bird and I remember the story started like this:

'The autumnal forest is adorned in bright, festive colours, but the smell it emanates is putrid and dismal . . .'

*

A woman once came to me, driven almost insane with anxiety: a close friend of hers had fallen desperately ill in far away deportation, near the Polar Circle. She had to join him at once and needed money. I knew that the man was a distinguished character, but I did not have enough money for her journey.

I went to the eccentric and rich Mitrofan Rukavishnikov; this small hunchback lived like Des Esseintes, the hero of Huysman's novel, an artificial life, considering it to be beautiful and refined: he went to bed in the morning, rose in the evening, his friends came to see him at night; among them was the director of the high school, a teacher of the institute for noble maidens, officials from various ministries. They spent the night drinking, eating, playing cards and sometimes, having invited local beauties of easy virtue, organized small orgies.

In the semi-darkness of the study packed with furniture made from the horns of Texas bulls, the hunchback with the face of an adolescent sat in a deep armchair, his legs wrapped in a rug; looking at me with dark, frightened eyes he listened to my request in silence and handed me a twenty-five rouble note. I needed forty times more. I walked out without a word.

I raced round the town for three days searching for the money and meeting Zarubin by chance asked if he could help me.

'Why don't you ask Bugrov? He'll give it to you. Let's go and see him, he's at the Stock Exchange now.'

We went. Among the noisy crowd of merchants I immediately saw Bugrov's stately figure, he stood leaning against the wall, pressed by a crowd of excited people who shouted something at the top of their voices while he now and then dropped a lazy, calm: No! And that word in his mouth made one think of the 'Hush' with which one stops the barking of intrusive hounds.

'Here's that very Gorki in person,' said Zarubin, making his way unceremoniously among the merchants.

A pair of small, tired eyes looked at me with a suspicious and slippery glance from a face wrinkled with age. One of the eyes was paralysed and hung helplessly revealing the white of the eye variegated with red veins, a tear dropped constantly out of the corner nearer the nose. The pupils seemed to me dim, but they suddenly lit up with green sparks and for a second the Mordovian face was illuminated by a pathetic smile. Pressing my hand in his soft but strong one Bugrov said:

'Honour to our town . . . Would you have some tea with me?'

In the 'Stock Exchange Hotel' in which everything was prostrated before him and even the canaries in the windows respectfully stopped singing – Bugrov sat down firmly in a chair and asked the waiter for some tea.

A fat, red-nosed old man with a soldiery moustache stopped Zarubin and shouted at him:

'You're afraid of the police, but not afraid of your conscience!'

'Our indefatigable warrior keeps fighting with his tongue,' said Bugrov, with a sigh and wiped the tear off his face with a blue handkerchief. Then, piercing me through with the sharpness of his gaze he asked:

'I heard that you achieved your skill as a writer without any schooling, on your own? This is an honour to our town. And you've known great poverty? Lived in my doss-house?'

I said that as a boy it happened to me on Fridays to be in his doss-house; on that day, as a 'wake' for his father, he gave beggars two pounds of wheat bread and a silver coin.

'This proves nothing,' he said stirring the grey hairs of his brows. 'For a silver coin even people who weren't poor came to the doss-house out of greed. But that you actually lived in the doss-house surprises me greatly. Because I used to think that there is no way out from that slough.'

'A man is an enduring creature.'

'That's true, but one should add: when he knows what he wants.'

He spoke solemnly, as befitted a man of his position, chose his words carefully, probably that was why his speech sounded elaborate, heavy. He had small teeth, closely composed in a line of yellow bone. The lower lip was thick and twisted like a negro's.

'How is it you know the merchant class so well?' he asked and to my reply said:

'Not everything is true in your book, many things are treated too severely, but Majakin – is a remarkable character! Did you happen to know someone like that? I haven't, but I feel that such a man must exist! Russian through and through both in soul and reason. A political brain . . .'

And with a wide smile he added merrily:

'Very instructive the way you tip a merchant how he should live and think, very good!'

Zarubin came up, angrily threw himself into a chair and asked – it was not clear whether it was me or Bugrov:

'Gave the money?'

This question embarrassed me so much that I was on the point of swearing and probably blushed profusely. Noticing my embarrassment Bugrov asked quickly with a smile:

'Who – to whom?'

I explained briefly what it was about but Zarubin interrupted, saying:

'It's not for himself – he lives very modestly.'

'Who is it for, then, may I ask?' Bugrov turned to me.

I was irritated, did not feel like telling a story and told the truth, expecting a refusal.

But the millionaire, rubbing his cheek, chasing a tear from it with his finger, listened to me attentively, took out his note-case and counting out some money asked:

'Will that be enough? It's a long journey and many awkward things can happen.'

I thanked him and offered to give a receipt – he smiled politely.

'Perhaps only to have a sample of your handwriting.'

And looking at the receipt, he remarked:

'You write as if it were a Charter, like a sectarian, each letter separate. Very interesting!'

'I learned from the Psalms book.'

'One can see that. Would you like the receipt back?'

I refused and in a hurry to pass on the money, went away. Pressing my hand with exaggerated politeness Bugrov said:

'Glad we know each other. May I send my horses for you one day – you live so far. I would be happy if you visited me.'

\*

Several days later, about 8 a.m. he sent a horse to fetch me and there I was, sitting with him in a small room with a window looking out into a yard, crammed with stone buildings, anchors, ironmongery, bast, matting, bags of flour. A small samovar was boiling loudly on the table, there was a plate of hot 'kalachi'\*, a dish of caviar and a sugar bowl with little cubes of coloured, 'lent' sugar.

'I don't use the ordinary one,' Bugrov said with a smile. 'Not because it is supposed to be bathed in dog's blood and other mapulations – is that the scientific word? – done with it.'

'Manipulations?'

'That's it. No, but lent sugar is better and easier for the teeth.'

The room was empty – there were two chairs on which we sat, a small table and another table and chair in the corner by the window. The walls had cheap wallpaper on them, of a dim blue colour, by the door in a frame hung the time table of the cruises of passenger ships. A newly-painted rusty-coloured floor shone brightly, everything was impeccably, boringly clean, there was something cold in this cleanliness, something unlived in. There was a strong smell of incense, of church oil in the room, a

* A kind of round bread.

large blue fly buzzed in it. In the corner hung an ikon of the Virgin Mary, in a pearl frame, there were three red stones on the nimbus and in front of it an oil-lamp of blue glass. The blue light vacillated sadly, and it seemed as if drops of sweat – or tears – poured down the ikon. Now and then the fly would sit on the frame and crawl on it like a black stain.

Bugrov wore a frockcoat of light cloth, a long one, closed high up on the neck like a cassock. Drinking lustily the scented tea Bugrov asked me:

'So you really lived in a doss-house?'

His voice rang with compassion, as if he was speaking of some lethal disease from which I had luckily recovered.

'It's hard to believe,' he said, pensively wiping a tear from his cheek and continued – 'Our barefooted beggar is like an autumn leaf. Even more useless because the autumn leaf serves to enrich the soil.'

And echoing the buzzing fly, he went on:

'We've got a foreman here, he has a team of longshoremen. His name is Sumarokov. He comes from a noble family, in Catherine the Great's time his grandfather was a man of great importance and the grandson is an impudent fellow, lives like a gangster, drinks with his workmen and covers up their thieving. Isn't it a strange reverse of fate? You are just the opposite. It's difficult to understand on what scales fate weighs men . . . Take a little more caviar.'

He chewed leisurely his kalach, smacking his lips loudly and tried to assess me with his glance.

'I don't usually read books, but I've read yours – they were recommended to me. What odd people you have come across! For instance Majakin on one side – and on the other that "ne'er-do-well" – what's his name?'

'Promtov.'

'Yes. Some of them, unsparingly, do their best for Russia, for all the people of our country, the others make a mess of their lives, with their bad language, the filthy awls of their brains. And you tell about them both in a way I cannot express, as though they were strangers to you, not Russians at all, but at the same time of a kindred spirit, eh? I can't quite understand it.'

I asked if he had read a story 'My Companion.'

'Yes. Very interesting it is.'

He swung back on his chair, wiping the sweat from his face with a large handkerchief with a coloured rim, then flung it in the air like a flag.

'Well, that one was certainly a wild man, not a Russian one. The ne'er-do-well – was he true? You say that Majakin is not quite real?'

Shaking his head with its grey-and-yellow hair, closely sticking to his skull, he said in a low voice:

'There is danger there. Our state, so they say, is a house that needs repair, needs some rebuilding. Yes. But who is to do it? Who do you consider has the power to do it? How can there be any unity in this, if some of them graze in freedom, like cattle put to grass and want nothing better? And what about Majakin? The Master? He sacrifices all his life, his conscience, to his country, without sparing himself, and all the others spit on him – is that so?'

This very significant conversation was interrupted by the fly – it flew blindly to the faint flame of the oil-lamp, extinguished it and fell into the oil. Bugrov rose, went to the door and called out.

A pretty girl, dressed all in black as a nun, answered his call; she saluted us, pressing her hands to her stomach and laying several telegrams on the table, then went silently to the oil-lamp to put it right. Then, with the same greeting, without lifting her eyes, she disappeared, moving with her fingers the leather rosary hanging from her belt.

'Business, pardon me,' said Bugrov, his eyes slipping over the telegrams. He took a pencil from his pocket, wrinkled up his nose and made some marks on the papers, dropping them on the table.

'Let's go to the other room.'

He brought me into a big room with windows looking out on the Volga. Clean unbleached floor-cloths lay on the painted floors, chairs stood along the walls. There was a leather sofa against one wall. It was a dull, empty room and permeated with the same oily, churchy smell. And through the windows came uninterruptedly the frenzied, iron noise of a working day, ships whistled on the river.

'A fine picture, isn't it?' asked Bugrov pointing to a copy of Surikov's 'Boyarina Morosova' on the wall.

On the wall opposite – was a beautiful picture of flowers, an old one, a very distinguished and fine one. A small metal plate underneath said that it was the work of Rosa Bonheur.

'You like that one better?' the old man asked with a smile. 'I bought it in Paris. I was walking down a street, saw the picture in a window and underneath a figure – ten thousand! What could it be – thought I? It was lovely – but what a price! It meant three thousand roubles. I sent a friend of mine to find out why it was so expensive. He asked and was told it was a valuable piece. So I went to have another look. No, I said to myself, what folly! But the next morning I asked my friend to go and get it for me.'

He laughed.

'A whim, of course. But I took such a fancy for it – I couldn't let it go!'

Everything around shone with a cold unlived-in cleanliness evoking a dull, solitary life.

'You must forgive me – I must go to the Stock Exchange,' said Bugrov. 'We didn't finish our interesting conversation, unfortunately. May I ask you to come again? So long!'

He often sent a horse to fetch me and I readily went to have morning tea with him, with the 'kalachi', caviar and 'lent' sugar. I liked to listen to his cautious, groping speeches, to watch the clinging glance of his intelligent eyes, to try and guess of what consisted the life of that man beyond his business interests and what was the source of his influence beside money.

It seemed to me that he wanted to draw something out of me, find in me an answer to some question, but he obviously did not know how to do it, or was not clear about what he actually wanted to know.

He often returned to the dreary question: 'How did it happen that you, wandering along dangerous and even destructive paths, finally found yourself doing some useful work?'

This irritated me. I told him about Slepushkin, Surikov, Kulibin and other Russian autodidacts.

'Really, so many of them?' He was reluctant to believe it, scratched his cheek pensively, trying unsuccessfully to close his bad eye. And closing the good one, he insisted on knowing:

'In a life without roots, without responsibilities – there must be so many temptations, how is it you didn't succumb to them? How did you become rooted in your work?'

Finally he got hold of the thought that disturbed him.

'You see what interests me is this: here we are living a good and rich life, but beneath us there are those people of another peculiar kind whose aim is to destroy this life. Wicked people, as you describe them in your books, merciless people. Now if these people beneath us begin to push forward – our lives will crumble down in one go . . .'

He spoke with a smile, but his eyes, growing green, watched me with a dry, piercing fire.

Realizing the uselessness of my arguments I said rather abruptly that life was unjust throughout and therefore unstable and that sooner or later people would alter not only its shape but also the basis of their relationship.

'Unstable!' he repeated, as if having misheard the word. 'That's true, unstable it is. The symptoms of it are all too obvious.'

And then he fell silent. After a minute or two I began to take my leave, convinced that our relationship had come to an end and that I would no longer be coming to have tea with Bugrov with hot 'kalachis' and caviar. He shook my hand silently, drily, but in the hall suddenly began to talk again, in an undertone, very tensely peering into the corner where darkness had gathered.

'Terrible, that is what man can be! Oh, how terrible! At times, when you come to after the bustle of the day, your heart suddenly sinks and you appeal to God in silence at the thought that all people, or many of them, live in the same cloud of darkness as you do yourself! Can it be possible that the whirl-wind of life tosses them about as it does you? It gives you a shudder when you think that anyone you pass in the street, a mere stranger, can penetrate deep into your soul and that your own perplexity is akin to his . . .'

He talked in a sing-song and I was surprised by his confession.

' – A man is like a grain in a millstone and each grain would like to avoid such a fate; that is, in fact, the important problem around which everyone turns and which leads to the confusion of life.'

He fell silent again, smiling wryly and I said the first thing that came into my head:

'It must be hard to live with thoughts such as yours!'

He smacked his lips.

Soon his horse was sent again to bring me to his home and as I talked to him I realized that he wanted nothing from me, that the man was simply lonely and liked to have the chance to talk to someone with other interests, other thoughts. He was less and less uneasy with me and began even to adopt a fatherly tone. Knowing that I had been in prison he remarked one day:

'That's a mistake! Your job is to tell the story, not to untie it.'

'What do you mean by that?'

'What I say: revolution – means the untying of all knots, which are tied by legislation and serve to keep people together and working. Either you are judges – or defendants.'

When I told him of the growing imminence of a constitution, he replied with a broad smile:

'Don't you see that with a constitution, we, the merchants, we'll tighten the screws on you, restless folk, even harder than we do now?'

But he was reluctant to talk about politics, treated the matter with a certain disdain, rather in the tone of a chess-player about a game of draughts.

'Obviously every draught wishes to become a queen and all the other draughts become the losers because of that. That's a small matter. In chess – the core of the game is: Checkmate to the King!'

He had spoken several times with Tsar Nicholas.

'No fire in the coal. When he utters ten words – seven of them are useless and the other three – not his own. His father was no genius either, but he was a solid chap, pungent, a master! This one is gentle, with a woman's eyes . . .' He added an ugly word and gave a sigh, then continued:

'They don't walk on the earth, these Tsars, they don't know how the street lives. They live like starlings in boxes in their palaces, but they can't even peck beetles, and they're going out of fashion. No longer awe-inspiring they are. A Tsar is a sovereign only while he is awe-inspiring.'

He spoke in a casual way, lazily, trying vainly to catch with a tea-spoon a tea-leaf lingering in his glass.

'This is what one has to give a thought to, Mr Gorki, – what is it we'll live by when fear disappears, eh? When fear of the Tsar disappears. When Nikolai's father came to Nizhni, the townspeople had Thanksgiving Te Deums officiated in Church for having had the chance of seeing the Tsar. Yes! And when this one came to the exhibition, in 1906, my janitor, Mikhail, said: "Not much of a man, our little Tsar! Not much to say about the face and not tall enough for such a big tsardom. Foreigners must be saying to themselves as they look at him: What's there so good about Russia, if their Tsar is such a dud!" Yes, that's what he said. And he was one of the Tsar's guards on that occasion. And nobody rejoiced at that visit, as if they were all thinking the same thing: "Not much of a man, our little Tsar!"'

He glanced in the corner, at the faltering sapphire light of the oil-lamp, rose, went to the door and opening it, shouted:

'The oil-lamp needs attention!'

Noiselessly, as usual, the dark maiden came in, bowing down almost to the floor, stood upon a chair and put the lamp right. Bugrov glanced at her slender legs in their black stockings and grumbled:

'Why is it that this lamp always burns so faintly?'

The girl disappeared, swam away like the fragment of a dark cloud.

'Also about God,' continued Bugrov. 'Even in our lives, in which we treasure and love God more than you do, you Nikonians,* even with us, God is no longer as stable as He was. As

* Nikon is the orthodox symbol of the orthodox faith, in contrast to sectarians.

though His Greatness had been diminished. There is no longer any fondness for Him and forgetfulness sets in. The distance from Him is greater. Tricks everywhere, tricks screen away the miracle of life which He created. Listen to this.'

With a sense of its importance he told me this story in strong, heavy words.

A teacher had brought a gramophone to a remote little village on the Volga and on a holiday began showing it to the peasants at school. When a human voice suddenly started singing a familiar tune from the small wooden box on the table, the peasants rose, frowning heavily and one old man highly respected by everyone in the village, shouted:

'Shut it up, blast you and yours!'

The teacher stopped the gramophone and then the peasants, having examined the whole machinery, decided:

'This Satanic toy must be burnt!'

But the teacher had advertently equipped himself with two records of church songs. He persuaded the peasants to listen some more and when the box started loudly to sing 'The Cherubim' song the listeners were stunned and terrified. The old man put on his cap and went away, pushing his way through as if struck blind, the others, like a flock of sheep, followed their shepherd in silence.

'That old man,' Bugrov went on ponderously, peering with half-closed eyes into my face, 'said to his family when he got home: "Well, the end has come. Get me ready, I want to die." He put on a shroud, lay down under the ikons and died on the eighth day – of starvation. And the village from then on became inhabited by bad people. They shouted, God knows about what, about the end of the world, Antichrist, about the devil in the box. Many have become drunkards.'

Knocking on the table with his fat finger he went on, anxiously, bitterly:

'God gave man a horse to work with. Now here comes something along the street – moved by what? No one knows. I asked some scientists: "What does it mean: electricity?" "It's a power," they say, "but what power – we don't know!" Even scientists say that. And what about a peasant? He can't be told

245

that it is God who chases carriages along the street without a horse? And if it is not God – who is it? You see? And then comes the telephone, the telegraph and everything else. I have a foreman, a clever lad, who can read and write, but even today, when he goes up to the telephone, he makes the sign of the Cross and after talking into it washes his hands with soap – he does! Tricks, all of them. There is some good in them, I'm not against them, I'm only asking: how is a peasant from the plough to understand them? He knows all there is to know about beasts, fish, birds, bees, but – when a wooden box sings church songs, then what is the use of a church, of a priest and all the rest? It seems the Church is of no use at all! And where is God in all that? Was it He, maybe, who fancied to put an angel in the box? That's the question.'

Biting at a lump of fruit sugar Bugrov greedily drank up his tea, wiped his moustache and went on, in a low, persuasive tone:

'A dangerous time has come, a time of a great disruption of the soul. You talk about revolution, about the rebirth of all the powers of the world. What powers, from where do they come? The people don't understand that. You stride on and on, further and further, while the peasant lags more and more behind . . . That's what one must think about . . .'

And suddenly he turned to me, almost gaily:

'Come with me to the public house! Let's have some fun, eh?'

Like the earth, every man is wrapped in his own atmosphere, in an invisible cloak, composed of the emanations of his energy, in an invisible cloud of smoke from the fire of his soul.

Bugrov was surrounded by an atmosphere of preoccupied boredom, but sometimes this boredom turned into a slow turmoil of anxieties. He wandered and circled in his empty rooms like a caged animal, long ago tamed by exhaustion, stopped by Rosa Bonheur's picture and touching it with his blunt, yellow fingers, he said pensively:

'Here on our earth, in our gardens, these exotic flowers don't seem to grow. They're lovely. I haven't seen any like that.'

It seemed that he lived like a man whose eyes are too tired to look at the world and they go blind, but now and then every-

thing around him becomes lit up by a new light and at such
moments the man becomes indescribably stimulating.

'You say: – Majakin is an invented character. But Jashka
Bashkizov tries to prove that Majakin is him. He's lying. He's
cunning, but not so clever. I'm saying this because you can invent flowers, but you can't invent a man. He can invent himself
and that would be to his own grief. But you can't invent a man.
That means that you have seen people like Majakin. And if there
are people like that, – that's all right.'

He often returned to this subject.

'In theatres they expose merchants with scorn, as eccentrics.
That is stupid. You made of Majakin a serious man, worthy of
attention. That's very creditable.'

And from time to time he would go on asking:

'So you really lived in a doss-house? How far it seems from
the truth!'

One day he wanted to know:

'Do you see the difference between people? For instance
between me and the sailor from the barge?'

'It isn't a great difference, Nikolas Alexandrovich.'

'That's what I think, too. For you the difference is not great.
But is that true? In my opinion it is important and delicate to
differentiate between people. A man must be made to understand what in him is his own and what is not. But what you do is
like in a recruiting office: Capable, Incapable! Capable for what?
For a brawl?'

Knocking against the table with the edge of his hand, he said:

'There is one way of assessing a man – his work! If he loves
his work, knows how to go about it – he's capable. If he doesn't
know, away with him! There lies the whole wisdom: with that
you can go on without any constitution!'

'Had I the power,' he went on, closing the good eye to the
narrowness of a knife's edge, 'I'd stir up the people here to the
amazement of the Germans and the English. I'd give medals and
crosses as rewards for work to carpenters, mechanics, to all sorts
of workmen. If he's succeeded in his work – honour and glory to
him! Go on competing further! And if on the way, you've
stepped on someone's corn – never mind! We don't live in a

desert, we can't make our way without pushing! When we raise the whole of the world and get it working – then we'll have more room to live. Our people are fine, with such people one can move mountains, plough over the whole of the Caucasus. But one thing one must remember: you wouldn't take your own son to a whore just because his flesh is in need of it? In the same way you can't dip our people head first into our muddled world, they'll choke, they'll stifle, in our vile smoke! One must be careful. For a peasant – reason is like a strumpet – she knows all the tricks but has no caresses for the soul. A peasant's neighbour is a wood sprite, he has a pixie under his stove and we bang him on the head with the telephone. Consider too, that it is hard to understand where is the invention and where – the truth? When the invention comes from afar, from ancient times, well, then, it also retains the power of truth, doesn't it? So that the wood sprite, the pixie, have more truth in them than the telephone, the trick of today.'

He rose, looked out of the window and murmured: 'What fools!'

He knocked against the frame of the window with his fist and then threatened someone with his finger, reproachfully shaking his head. His hands thrust in his pockets, still standing by the window, he continued:

'If you like, I'll tell you a story – maybe you'll find some use for it. A remarkably beautiful girl lived in Murom, beautiful enough to make your heart go faint. She was an orphan, lived at her uncle's – the uncle was a steward on the pier, a thief, a miser, with many children and a widower, the niece worked round the clock as a nurse, as a cook, as a janitor. She was twenty years of age and because of her beauty many men, even wealthy ones, wanted to marry her, – but her uncle objected – he didn't want to lose a woman who worked for him for nothing. A young official fell in love with her – drank himself to death. They said the priest tried to seduce her – nothing came of it for him but grief and misery. She was pious, her greatest joy was to go to church and read religious books. She loved flowers, knew how to look after them and grew them both in the home and in the garden. Modest, gentle as a nun, with eyes of unbelievable purity. '

He paused, scratched his cheek and blinked weirdly with his good eye.

'In fairy-tales you read about such eyes. One day the uncle's master, a merchant, an old man of dissolute habits, saw her – and was stunned, became quite insane. During a whole winter he pestered her, but she did not react, did not seem to know what it was all about. No money had any effect on her. Then he arranged that the uncle should send her on business to Moscow and when she came he persuaded her to go with him to the "Yar" restaurant. When she arrived at this den of vice and looked around – she suddenly saw everybody else and herself as naked. She told the old man: "Now I see what you want and I'll agree to everything, only let me live in such splendour for a whole month." The man of course was delighted, offered her anything she wanted and "just now let us go to the baths," he added. "No," she said, "I can't go now, but tomorrow is Saturday. I'll go to Mass and after that – if you please!" Five years have gone by and she is now the most expensive whore in Moscow.'

He moved slowly from the wall, sat down and went on, in a pensive, low voice.

'Of course there are many cases like that one, if only one didn't remember what the girl had been like before. But you see the temptation of tricks, how strong it is! Compare this case with what we spoke about before and think: a soul lives in the dark captivity of boredom and suddenly this is revealed to her. Here it is, real Paradise! But it isn't Paradise – it is mere dust. And not for ever, only for an hour! But to return from these tricks to brownies, pixies and wood sprites – is impossible, unfeasible! Thus the soul is buried in earthly dust.'

He knew of many such funerals, they were all alike and he told about them in a boring way as if thinking of something else, more significant, more profound.

He watched through the windows. From the outside the window-panes were covered with dust, with the soot from the ships; through their dimness one could see the water of the Volga with its wharfs and barges. Everywhere on the shore – mountains of boxes, barrels, sacks, machines. The ships hissed and whistled, clouds of smoke floated in the air, on the stones of the quay lay an incredible accumulation of refuse, the clatter of iron, people shouting, carts jingling and rattling, – life running on uninterruptedly, great work going on.

And one of the men who, having created this ant-like life and developing year after year its tense activity, watched his work through the dirty window-pane with the indifferent eyes of a stranger and repeated pensively:

'Not at once . . . not so suddenly . . .'

*

He spoke a lot about work and that was interesting and there was always something religious, sectarian about it. It seemed to me that he had an almost religious attitude to labour, a great faith in its inner power, which with time would link people together in one invincible whole, one rational energy and its aim was to transform our filthy earth into the garden of paradise.

It coincided with my ideas about labour, for me it is a field in which my imagination has no limits. I believe that all the mysteries and tragedies of our lives can find a solution only through labour and that labour alone can achieve the seductive dream of equality of men and of a just life.

But very soon I realized that Bugrov was not a fanatic of labour, he talked it about dogmatically, like a man who has to fill the emptiness of his life with dignity, feed the insatiable greed of the boredom that reigned over his soul. He was too healthy and too prominent for drink or cards, too old for debauchery and other refuse with which the people of his kind fill up the gaping abyss of their spiritual emptiness.

One day on the train to Moscow, the conductor came to tell me that Bugrov would like me to come to his compartment. I had to see him, so I went.

He sat there, his coat unbuttoned and stared at the ventilator in the ceiling.

'Good day! Sit down. You wrote to me something about some bare-footed wanderers . . . I can't quite remember.'

Dmitri Sirotkin, shipowner, sectarian, I believe, of 'Austrian concord', later a bishop, Mayor of Nizhni, editor of a periodical, 'The Church', an intelligent, ambitious man, energetic and with wide interests, had offered me to organize a daily shelter for the unemployed – this was necessary in order to protect them from the exploitation by public-house owners. In the winter people were thrown out from doss-houses into the street at 6 a.m., when the streets were still dark, there was nothing to do and the 'bare-footed' and the unemployed went to dirty public houses and drank tea and vodka to the amount of about sixty roubles per winter. In the spring when work started on the Oka and the Volga, these pub-owners could dispose of this free labour as they wished, squeezing out the debts of the winter. We hired a building where people could sit in the warmth, were given tea for 2 kopecks, a pound of bread, a library had been organized, we got a piano and on holidays arranged concerts and literary readings. Our shelter was in a house with pillars, it was called 'The Posts', was packed from morning till night with people and the 'bare-footed' felt themselves to be its real masters, they watched after its cleanliness and general order.

Of course all this cost a large sum of money and I had to ask Bugrov to give me some.

'It's all very trivial,' he said with a sigh. 'What is the worth of such people? What are they for? Idlers, ne'er-do-wells, all of them. They can't even wind up their clock.'

I was surprised.

'What clock?' I asked.

'There's a clock in the doss-house, it's gone wrong so they don't know the time . . .'

'Well, you must have the clock mended or buy a new one.'

Bugrov flew into a rage and grumbled:

'It's always I, I who have to do something! Can't they do it themselves?'

I told him that it would be strange if people, who had no shirts and often not a kopeck for bread would, while dying of hunger, collect money to buy a clock.

This made him laugh, he opened his mouth and closed his eyes and for about two minutes practically shook with laughter, clapping his knees with his hands. Then he relaxed and began to talk in a more cheerful way.

'Yes, that was nonsense I was talking. But it happens to me

sometimes that I see myself as a poor man and become stingy. Other men of my kind pretend to be poor knowing that a poor man has an easier time; God and men are less exacting with him, he is freer. But with me it's different, I simply forget that I'm rich, that I own mills and ships and money, I forget that fate has harnessed me to a large cartload. I'm not stingy at heart, money doesn't mean much to me, I give when I'm asked.'

He wiped his wet eye with a handkerchief, and went on:

'It happens that I wish I were sitting in a poor public-house and drinking tea with rye bread, down to the last crumb. One could understand this had I ever been poor, but I was born rich. Rich – but longing to ask for my palm to be crossed, in order to understand how hard it is to be poor. I can't understand this curious whim and you, probably, can't understand it either. I've heard that pregnant women have such whims.'

Swinging back in the sofa and closing his eyes he murmured softly:

'Man is a capricious creature . . . oh, yes! Gordei Chernov threw away all his riches, his business, and became a monk, on Mount Athos, too, where they're so strict. Stiopa Kirillov lived piously and wisely, was modest and well-read; when he got to be sixty – he suddenly threw everything to the winds, started a life of debauchery, to his disgrace and became the laughing-stock of people. "Everything is false," he said, "everything a lie, an evil lie, the rich are beasts, the poor are fools, the Tsar is a villain, an honest life is mere self-denial." Yes. Then there's Zarubin, Savva Morosov, a man of great intelligence, Nikolai Meshkov from Perm, they all are in cohorts with you revolutionaries. And how many others! As if they had been walking in darkness all their lives, on strange paths and suddenly they saw: here it is, our straight path. And where will that path lead them to?'

He remained silent, after a heavy sigh.

Behind the window, in the twilight of the moon, trees ran along at a great speed. The iron clatter of the train breaking the silence of the fields was chasing the dark huts of the villages into the unknown. The moon rolled in fear and hid behind the trees, then suddenly reappeared in the field and swam slowly over it, exhausted.

Bugrov made the sign of the Cross and said sullenly:

'We have a peculiar conscience, in Russia, it is as though it were insane. It gets a fright, loses all control, rushes into forests, gullies, slums and hides there. A man will pass by going his own way, when it will suddenly jump at him like a beast and bite at his soul. And that's the end of him. His whole life goes to ashes, to froth . . . All the good and the bad in one woodpile . . .'

He crossed himself again. I bade him good night.

'Thank you for coming! Look here, come to Testov's restaurant tomorrow at one. Ask Savva to come too – will you?'

*

When Savva Morosov and I arrived at Testov's, Bugrov was already sitting in a separate room, the table laid in front of him, two waiters dressed in white like corpses in shrouds silently and respectfully bustled around, laying plates with 'zakuski'. Bugrov spoke to one of them calling him by his name and patronymic.

'You'll give me that wine from the Rhine, – what's its name?'

'I know, sir.'

'Greetings – Russia!' he exclaimed on seeing us. Morosov, shaking his hand, said:

'You're spreading, Bugrov, spreading very much lately. You won't remain much longer on this earth.'

'I'm not in a hurry.'

'What about leaving me your millions?'

'I'll think about it . . .'

'I'll find where to put them . . .'

Bugrov nodded in agreement and added:

'I know you will, you ambitious creature! Come, sit down.'

Savva was in a nervous, irritable mood. Bending his clever Tartar face over his plate he began hurriedly, with harsh, abrupt words to tell the story of an Astrakhan industrialist about the destruction of herrings in the Caspian sea, where millions of them were being buried in the sand.

'One could prepare out of it an excellent mineral fertilizer, by using the fishes' scales and making gum of them.'

'You know everything,' Bugrov said with a sigh.

'And people like you sit like idols on their millions and don't want to know anything about the needs of the soil which allows them to suck it. Our chemical industry is at a stop, there are no workers to develop it, we must have an experimental chemical institute, special courses of chemistry. Oh, you barbarians!'

'Now, now, don't swear' – Bugrov said appeasingly and gently. 'Eat something, you'll be kinder.'

'We've learnt to eat, when will we start working?'

Bugrov tried the wine, smacked his lips and said peering into his glass:

'You demand a lot from people, Savva, they, on the other hand, ask little from you. Don't interfere with their lives.'

'If one didn't interfere, they'd still be walking on all fours . . .'

'I'll never understand that!' Bugrov exclaimed angrily. 'Some silly idlers invented that man comes from an ape. And they seem happy about it!'

He asked with astonished bitterness:

'You can't believe that nonsense! Even if it were true, one should hide it from people.'

Savva looked at him with half-closed eyes and said nothing.

'In my opinion one shouldn't nag a man because he was a beast, it would be better to tell him that he was better than he is now.'

Morosov smiled and replied abruptly:

'Well, will an old woman grow younger because you'll remind her that there was a time when she was young?'

We neither ate, nor drank much, Morosov's mood acted depressingly. When coffee was brought in Bugrov asked compassionately:

'What's the matter, Savva? Something wrong? At the factory?'

Turning to him brusquely Morosov began to talk in the tone of an older man:

'Everything is going wrong with us: at factories, at mills and especially in the brains!'

And he began to speak about the destructive conservatism of agricultural resources, about the predatory behaviour of banks, that industrialists were uneducated and did not understand their importance, about the justified demands of the workmen and the inevitability of revolution.

'It'll flare up prematurely – there's not enough strength for it – and chaos will ensue!'

'I don't know what will ensue,' Bugrov said pensively. 'A Nizhni general of the gendarmes, a fool, also tried to frighten me the other day. He was saying that workmen are becoming restless, in Sormovo, on the Viksa, and in Seim, in my factory. Well, Savva Timofeich, you say yourself it's justified. Let's be truthful – the workman has a bad life with us, but he's an excellent workman.'

'Well, not all that good,' Morosov murmured in a tired voice.

'No, you're wrong there. Our people are good. They've got fire in their hearts. You can't buy him for a low price, you can't seduce him with trifles. He has, you know, a sort of maiden's dream about a good life, about truth. Don't laugh! – it is a maiden's dream! I talk to them now and then in the evenings, on holidays, at my house on the Seim. I'd ask them: "Well, boys, is life hard?" "Ye-es, a bit." "And what do you think, can it be made easier?" And I can tell you – they have an intelligent understanding of life. Perhaps it's not their own, perhaps they've learnt it from the booklets they get from Sormovo. Gorki here knows all about these matters. He takes money from me for the booklets. And I give it . . .'

'Don't boast!' said Morosov.

'I don't!' the old man said calmly. 'It all goes against me, but I give. Not much, of course. But if even small figures make a difference in this business, what would it be if we launched all our capital into it, you and I?'

'Well, what about it?'

'There's a great temptation to do so. It's mischievous, perhaps, but there's always temptation in mischief.'

He clapped his fist on Morosov's knee, bending on the chair as though ready to jump, and continued:

'Of course it's mischief when man goes against his grain, that I understand. But people do that, believing it to be righteous and true. I know people like that. And perhaps I even envy their foolishness. Gorki was telling me that a prince Kropotkin is his name, also . . . Oh, of course, it's a temptation, to throw down the yoke . . .'

'All this is nonsense, Nikolas Alexandrovich,' Savva said.

I was attentively watching Bugrov. He could drink a lot and didn't get drunk, this time he had only had one glass. But his face was strangely flushed, the marsh-coloured eyes, grown very green, glistened excitedly. And he spoke hurriedly, as though breathlessly.

'From times of yore men felt that life was unstable, from then on good men have tried to escape it. You know yourself that riches are not bliss, they're more of a burden and a prison. We're all the slaves of our work. I waste my soul to make three thousand a day, when the workman is happy with thirty kopecks. The machine thrashes us into dust, till we die. We all work. Who for? What for? This is what is incomprehensible – for whom do we work? I love work. But sometimes when you strike a match in the dark you say to yourself, – what meaning is there in this work? Well, I'm rich. Thank you very much. And what else? A repulsive feeling in my heart.' He sighed and repeated:

'Yes, repulsive.'

Morosov rose, went to the window and said with a smile:

'I've heard this talk before from you and from others.'

'Holiness is possibly a weakness, – but it's sweet for the soul . . .'

The ponderous conversation stopped, both were silent. It had given me a strange feeling as though my brain and my mouth had been filled with treacle. I had no reason to doubt Bugrov's sincerity, but I had not expected to hear from him what he had said. Yet, even before, he seemed to me a man whose life was devoid of inner meaning, progressing in a dull way along dark paths, meekly submitting to the jolts of familiar worries and relationships. But I had thought that human labour had stood high in the estimation of Nizhni's Independent Prince.

It was strange to know that this man lived on the work of many thousand people and at the same time to hear that this work was of no use to him, meaningless in his eyes.

I could not help thinking:

'Only Russian people can live and feel in that way.'

\*

One day I met him in a small village, among the forests behind the Volga. I was going to Lake Kitezh, stayed in the village for the night and heard that Bugrov 'was expected', he was going to a remote monastery.

I was sitting on the bench outside the hut, it was almost dark, the herds were home, the sweet smell of fresh milk came in waves from the yard. In the sweltering sky in the west a dark blue cloud was melting, reminding one by its shape of a tree torn out with its roots. In the opal-coloured sky two vultures swam over the village; a strong smell of pine and mushrooms came from the forest, beetles buzzed in front of me around the birch tree. Tired people were slowly packing up after a hard day in the streets and in the yards. The fairy-like life of unknown people faded, drowsing, bewitched by the silence of the woods.

When it grew dark, – a carriage rolled into the village street, it was harnessed by a pair of large, bay horses and in the carriage sprawled Bugrov, surrounded by cases and parcels.

'How come you're here?' he asked me. And offered immediately:

'Come with me! You'll see some fine girls. Near by there is an orphanage, the girls are taught to embroider.'

The coachman led the horses to the well and we rode away, followed by silent greetings from the peasants. They bent low down, like in church in front of a venerated saint's ikon. Old men and women murmured:

'Benefactor . . . master . . . Bless you . . .'

Even the mooing of the cows seemed to ring with grateful emotion.

Having trotted through the village the horses carefully turned into the wood and went on along the dark beaten track, mixing the smell of their sweat with the thick aroma of pine and flowers.

'Wonderful these forests are, so dry, no mosquitoes,' Bugrov said contentedly, waving his handkerchief over his face. 'What a curious man you are, look where you've got to! You'll have a lot to remember when you're old – even now you know more than an old man would. And we, we know only one thing: where, what and how much it costs.'

He was in a good mood, joked with the coachman, told me about the life in these forest villages.

We came out into a small clearing, two black walls of the forest met at an angle and in the angle stood a hut on the velvety background of the soft darkness, a hut with five windows and beside it a yard covered with a new roof. A greasy, yellow fire lit up the windows of the hut as though a bonfire were burning inside it. A tall, hairy peasant with a long stalk that looked like a spear stood at the gate and the whole picture seemed like a fairy-tale. The dogs barked, almost sobbing, and a woman's voice screamed in fright:

'Ivan, stop the dogs barking, may God protect us!'

'She's all astir,' grumbled Bugrov, frowning. 'She remembers the masters. There's still a lot of fear of the masters among the people.'

Trembling and bending low down, nodding her head repeatedly we found a small old woman by the gate. She was dark as the soil and, shrieking, she seized Bugrov's hand.

'Little father ... the angels have brought you ...'

The angels, snorting, hit the soft ground with their hooves and clattered with their harnesses.

A buxom woman swam onto the porch, dressed in the national costume; she bowed low down pressing her hands to her breasts and behind her, giggling and rustling with their frocks, stood a crowd of girls of different ages.

'Honour him with songs, you little fools!' the woman screamed loudly.

'No, no,' said Bugrov, 'how many times have I told you, Evfimia, that I don't want it. Greetings, girls!'

A choir of gay cries answered him and a dozen teenagers rolled in a wave down the steps of the porch to Bugrov's feet.

The woman was murmuring something, as he, stroking the girls' heads, said:

'That's enough, that's all right! Quiet, you mice! I've brought you some presents. Look here, you're squashing me. Here's a friend of mine, he'll write all about you, about your mischief.'

Pushing them lightly ahead, he was coming up the steps of the porch, while the woman screamed:

'You've been told to be quiet!'

Suddenly, with an odd movement of her arms the older woman uttered a hissing sound and the children were instantly silent and marched in good order and in silence to the hut.

The large room which we entered was lit by two wall-lamps, the third under a red paper lampshade stood on a long table among crockery, tea-cups, plates with honey, strawberries, biscuits. A tall, good-looking girl met us at the door, holding a basin with water; another one, very like her, almost as a sister, was handing a long embroidered towel.

Cracking jokes Bugrov washed his hands, wiped his face with a wet towel, dropped two golden coins into the basin, walked up to the wall, where stood about four embroidery frames, combed his hair and beard in front of a small mirror and looking into the corner at the oil lamp in front of the ikons and a large ikon-case with golden carvings, threw his head back and made three times the sign of the Cross.

'Greetings to you again!'

The children answered promptly and loudly – the old woman stood up at once at the door, shaking her snake-like head and disappeared like a shadow.

'Well, how are you, girls? Is Natalia being naughty?' Bugrov asked, sitting down at the table in the place of honour.

The children pressed against him, without constraint, with perfect ease. They all looked healthy, pink and almost all of them pretty. And the one who handed the basin was exceptionally beautiful, with her slender figure and the fine features of her sun-tanned face. Her eyes were particularly lovely, with thick eyebrows that seemed to soar up boldly on her forehead.

'This one,' pointing at her with his finger, Bugrov told me, 'is the main mischief-maker, you can't control her! I'll send her to the nunnery, a very remote one in the Irghiz where bears walk about in herds . . .'

But then, with a sigh, scratching his cheek, he went on:

'If I could get her to Moscow, she ought to have lessons, she's got a remarkable voice. But her father, a sea-pilot and a widower, won't have it: "I won't give up my progeny for entertaining the Nikonians".'

A huge, hairy peasant, with a heavy gait, puffing out his cheeks, brought in a brightly polished samovar and flung it on the table so that all the crockery began to clatter, he then opened his eyes wide in amazement, pushed his hands into a head of red hair and bent it very low, with what seemed to be an effort.

Evfimia came in, her breasts standing out like two watermelons, she had heaped up on them boxes with sweets, supporting them with her double chin; behind her three girls carried plates with nuts and gingerbread.

Bugrov, as he watched the girls, became brighter, younger, he kept whispering to me:

'That one over there, with the snub nose, blue eyes, is an interesting character. She looks cheerful enough, but is remarkably pious and a rare one for embroidering. She embroidered air with silk thread and an angel with palm leaves – wonderful! It's a touching, a moving sight. She copied it from an ikon, but the colours are her own.'

He told me stories about all his wards, finding in each a special quality. The girls were happy and excited, one could see that Bugrov's arrival was a feast for them, and that the portly Evfimia didn't overawe them. She was sitting at the end of the table, chewed gingerbread uninterruptedly and with concentration, then, with a deep sigh, poured out the tea and then again, in silence, ate strawberries with honey, squashing them on her plate into a porridge. She worked on, paying no attention to the girls and the visitors, apparently oblivious of all that was going on, wrapped in her own business. The girls became more and more rowdy, but every time when the old woman with her convulsive movements appeared in the door, the large, echoing room suddenly grew still and cold.

After tea, the beautiful Natalia took a psaltery and began to sing:

> 'Christ the Child had a garden.'

She sang out of key the dismal religious tune, obviously not knowing the score written for these words. She made them sound almost sinister, even menacing, and sang peering into the corner, her soaring eyes gleamed sternly. But her voice, deep, of great range, was beautiful indeed, strangely rich in intonations. It was amusing to watch how the high notes made her rise in her chair and the low ones – to bend down her head and hide her legs under the chair. The psaltery was not well tuned, but the singer, apparently, did not notice it, her sun-tanned hands pulled at the strings harshly and powerfully.

Bugrov listened, sitting motionless, his mouth half-open. The paralysed eyelid seemed to hang even lower and a tear poured out in a constant moist streak from his eye. He gazed at the black square of the window, it looked out into the darkness of the night: that window, like the two others, was adorned with embroidered towels, they looked like ikon-cases, into which ikons covered in dust had been stuck. If one peered long enough into this black night, one began to imagine huge faces without eyes.

It was stuffy in the room; the timbered, cleanly scrubbed walls emanated a smell of soap and tar while over the table rose the subtle aroma of honey, strawberries, a greasy smell of pastry. The girls were now silent, intoxicated from abundant eating, their friend's songs lulled them to sleep, one had fallen asleep already, snoring gently, her head resting on her neighbour's shoulder. Evfimia sat as a monument, her cheeks were shining as if smeared with butter and so was the yellow skin of her round arms, naked to the elbow.

The girl, stubbornly gaping into the corner, pulled the instrument's strings and sang in an angry voice the sad, tender words:

> 'I dropped the ring of my beloved
>   Into the deep blue sea . . .'

'Well – thank you very much!' Bugrov suddenly uttered in a strangely anxious and too loud a voice.

The old woman shook in the doorway, hissing:

'Shleep!'

'Yes, go to sleep, my girls, good night to you! Evfimia – show us their work!'

As he saw the girls out he kissed their heads and when Natalia came up he said, putting his hand on her head:

'You sing well ... Better all the time! You've got a bad temper, – but your heart ... Well, God bless you!'

She smiled, – her brows quivered and she swam lightly to the door and the old man, following her with his eyes, scratched his cheek and in a childishly pathetic, offended tone said:

'Yes, yes, that's what she's like ...'

Evfimia brought a heap of neatly folded rags and spread them out on the embroidery frames on the table under the lamp.

'Look at them,' suggested Bugrov, his eyes still fixed on the door.

I began to examine the embroideries for pillows, slippers, shirts, towels. They were done in beautiful colours, very delicately, with copies of head- and tail-pieces of ancient books and some were advertising designs for a well-known firm of soap. One of the embroideries struck me particularly by the strength and strangeness of the design: on a grey stretch of silk was embroidered a violet and a large black spider.

'The girl who did this is dead,' Evfimia said in an absurdly careless manner.

'What is it?' asked Bugrov, coming closer to us.

'Varia's work ...'

'Ah ... Yes, she died, poor child. She was a hunchback. Eaten up by consumption. She saw devils and even embroidered one in wool. We had it burnt. She was an orphan. Her father disappeared, they say he got drowned. Well, Evfimia, arrange for us to sleep.'

We went to sleep in the clearing, under the windows of the hut – Bugrov in a cart, richly filled with hay and I on a thick piece of felt spread out on the grass. As he undressed, the old man grumbled:

'Evfimia is a stupid woman, but we can't find a cleverer one. We ought to have a real teacher, a learned one, but the fathers and mothers object. They say she'll be a Nikonian, a heretic. Our piety doesn't live on good terms with reason, may God forgive us! Then there's that old woman, she just won't die. A harmful woman. She's there to inspire the children with awe. Or perhaps because of my bad reputation . . . Ugh!'

He knelt down and gazing at the stars, moving his lips began to make the sign of the Cross, broadly waving his arm, pressing his fingers close to the forehead, the breast, the shoulders. He kept sighing deeply. Then he turned heavily on his side, wrapped himself up in the blanket and grunted:

'That's nice . . . I'd like to live like a gypsy . . . And you – you don't say your prayers? This I cannot understand. And what I can't understand doesn't exist for me, therefore I think that you must have your own God. I'm sure of it! Otherwise – what is there to lean upon? Well, let's sleep.'

In the unshakable silence of the forest boomed an owl, gloomily and purposelessly. The forest stood like a firm, black wall and it seemed that it was from it that the darkness came. Through the damp mist, in the small, dark sky over us a golden crop of stars shone dimly.

'Yes,' said Bugrov, 'these girls will grow up, will begin making sour cabbage, cucumbers, salt mushrooms – what will they want with embroidery? There is a sort of insulting stupidity in it. There's a lot of stupidity in our lives, isn't there?'

'Yes, there is.'

'Yes, and that's the truth. Have you heard the rumours that I've debauched many young women?'

'I have.'

'Do you believe it?'

'I suppose so.'

'I won't conceal my sins – such things have happened. In that matter a man is more muddle-headed than an animal. And greedier, too. What do you think about it?'

I said that in my opinion, our outlook on matters of sex was an ugly one. Sex life is considered by the Church to be a sin. It is insulting for a woman that she should have a cleansing service officiated over her on the fortieth day after giving birth to a child – but women don't seem to understand that. I even gave an example: one day I heard a woman I knew, an intelligent woman and a philanthropist, reproaching her husband:

'Stepan, – you forget about God! You've just been feeling

my breasts and now, without even washing your hands, you cross yourself!'

'Oh, but this is nothing,' Bugrov said grimly. 'Women are beaten because on Wednesdays and Fridays, Lent days, they allow their husbands to touch them! It's a sin. I had a friend who whipped his wife on Thursdays and Saturdays because of that same reason – she had induced him to sin! And he's a sturdy, strong peasant and sleeps in one bed with his wife, – how is she to prevent him touching her? Yes, yes, our lives are foolish . . .'

He fell silent and the odd noises of night life began to be heard, – dry branches cracked as they broke, the pine rustled and it seemed that someone was suppressing a sigh. As if from all sides something invisible but alive was stealing up to us.

'Asleep?'

'No.'

'Life is foolish. It is strange because it is intricate and the meaning of it is dark. But it's a fine thing, all the same.'

'Yes, it is.'

'Very fine. But one has to die, you see . . .'

After a minute or two he added in a whisper:

'To die . . . soon . . .'

And then said nothing more, probably fell asleep.

In the morning I said good-bye to him. I was going to the Kitezh lake and never saw Bugrov again.

He died, I believe, in 1910, and was solemnly, as behove him, buried in his own town . . .

# Conclusion

I HAVE lived among people like these for half a century.

I hope that this book is sufficient proof that I do not avoid the truth when I do not wish to avoid it. To my mind, however, truth is not so necessary either to the extent or in the completeness which it pleases people to imagine that it is. Whenever I have felt that such and such a truth merely slashes cruelly at the soul and teaches nothing, that it degrades a man without explaining him to me, then, of course, I have thought it better to omit it.

There are, I assure you, many truths which it is best not to remember. These truths are born by lies and possess all the elements of that poisonous untruth which, having distorted the relations of man with man, has made of life a hell, at once filthy and absurd. What end does it serve to remind humanity of something which should disappear as quickly as possible? It is an ugly task to record and to expose only the ugly things of life.

I first wanted to call this book 'The Book of Russians as they have been.' Then I thought that this would sound too solemn. And am I quite certain that I want these people to become different? However foreign all nationalism, patriotism and other diseases of the spirit may be to me, my vision of the Russian people as exceptionally, fantastically gifted and uncommon, does not fail me. Even the fools in Russia are peculiarly foolish, foolish in a way of their own, just as the sluggards have a genius of their own.

I think that when this marvellous people has passed through its share of torments, and freed itself of all that tortures and confuses the mind, when it begins to work in the full consciousness of that cultural, indeed, that religious importance of labour, which joins all the world into one, then it will begin a fairylike, heroic life and in many a way will enlighten a world exhausted by strife and maddened with crime.

## MORE ABOUT PENGUINS
## AND PELICANS

*Penguinews*, which appears every month, contains details of all the new books issued by Penguins as they are published. From time to time it is supplemented by *Penguins in Print*, which is a complete list of all titles available. (There are some five thousand of these.)

A specimen copy of *Penguinews* will be sent to you free on request. For a year's issues (including the complete lists) please send 50p if you live in the British Isles, or 75p if you live elsewhere. Just write to Dept EP, Penguin Books Ltd, Harmondsworth, Middlesex, enclosing a cheque or postal order, and your name will be added to the mailing list.

*In the U.S.A.*: For a complete list of books available from Penguin in the United States write to Dept CS, Penguin Books Inc., 7110 Ambassador Road, Baltimore, Maryland 21207.

*In Canada*: For a complete list of books available from Penguin in Canada write to Penguin Books Canada Ltd, 41 Steelcase Road West, Markham, Ontario.

*The Penguin Classics*

GORKY

# MY APPRENTICESHIP

Translated by Ronald Wilks

*My Apprenticeship* begins where the first part of Gorky's
autobiography, *My Childhood*, leaves off – at the point where
the eleven-year-old Gorky is sent out into the world to fend
for himself. The world he encounters is one of almost incredible squalor, misery and barbaric violence, in the period
of Russia's belated and ruthless Industrial Revolution. But
through the book shines Gorky's resilience and strength of
character, his ultimate optimism, and the brilliant clarity
with which he recalls and relates his experiences, whether
they are of life as a dish-washer on a Volga steamboat or of a
child's enraptured discovery of the world of books.